The Matriarch

Dianis, A World In Turmoil Chronicles

Book 2

Frank Dravis

I0614249

1

Copyright

This is a work of fiction. All of the characters and events portrayed in this novel are either fictional or are used fictitiously. Any resemblance to actual events or persons, living or dead, is entirely coincidental.

The Matriarch
Dianis, A World In Turmoil Chronicles

ISBN-978-0-9996886-3-2   Paperback

Six Factors Publishing
N1358 State Highway 35
La Crosse, WI 54658

https://www.facebook.com/thefoundrybookone/
https://www.dianisworld.com
Twitter @FrankDravis

Cover: Chris McGrath
Isuelt Map: Jerry Mooney

Table of Contents

Cast of Characters

Protagonists

- IDB (Interspecies Development Branch), Avarian Federation
  - Director Clienen Hor, leader of IDB Margel Damansk
  - Achelous Forushen, cultural anthropologist and Chief Inspector of Civilization Monitoring (CivMon)
  - Baryy Maxmun, CivMon agent and sociologist
  - Outish, astrobiology intern
  - Agent Illian Meridia, Ready Reaction
  - Lieutenant Hearter, commander enforcement cutter *IDBS Shields*
  - Sergeant Mears, watch commander enforcement cutter *IDBS Shields*
  - Chief Ivan Darinarishcan, leader of Ready Reaction for Margel Damansk
  - Sergeant Horalznick, Ready Reaction
  - Jeremy, CivMon Central Station artificial intelligence (AI)

- Mother Dianis (Life Believers)
  - Christina Tara, Al suri Ascalon Defender
  - Alex, Defender

- Timberkeeps, Mearsbirch Doromen clan
  - Woodwern, clan chairman
  - Sedge the Warlord, mercenary, Wedgewood garrison commander
  - Ogden, master weaponsmith, warden of the Second Ward
  - Lettern Stouttree, archer and scout, Second Ward
  - Rachael Stouttree, sixthsense kinetic, sister to Lettern

- o Mbecca, master sixthsense healer
- o Cordelei Greenleaf, sixthsense diviner
- o Brookern, sixthsense voyant
- o Barrigal, mercenary captain

- Oridians
  - o The Oligarch, leader of Oridia
  - o Captain Lucifar, commander of Oridian Lancers
  - o Sergeant Veri, standard bearer

- Tivor
  - o Ropert, aorolmin, the Duke of Tivor
  - o Marisa Pontifract, owner of Marinda Merchants
  - o Eliot, huntsmaster for Marinda Merchants
  - o Sifle, Master at Arms, commander of the City Watch
  - o Lieutenant Rayamars, First Tivor Rifles

- The Silver Cup Couriers Guild
  - o Akallabeth, guild overseer in Tivor
  - o Prince Fire Eye, prince of the wryvern nation
  - o Trishna, sixthsense telepath
  - o Zil, bravo

The Matrincy

- The Matriarch, the leader of the Matrincy
- Counselor Margret, special envoy to Dianis
- Counselor Breia, planetary counselor to Dianis

Antagonists

- Nordarken Mining
  - o Rocl Binair, senior vice president of Resource Production
  - o Director of aquamarine-5 production, responsible for ore procurement
  - o Quorat, Intruder contractor

- o Junko, owner contract mining operation
- o Krch, contract miner geologist
- o Sysreq, contract miner pilot
- o Gof, contract miner
- o Geezer, contract miner

- Empire of Nak Drakas
  - o Uloch, Drakan decurion and commander of the Drakan expeditionary force
  - o Larech, Washentrufel agent
  - o Baldor Prairiegrass, Plains Doroman spy

- Diunesis Antiquaria (Paleowrights)
  - o Helprig, viscount of Diunesis Antiquaria
  - o Captain Irons, captain of the Scarlet Saviors
  - o Duck Peren, examiner

Map of Continent of Isuelt

Map of the Margel

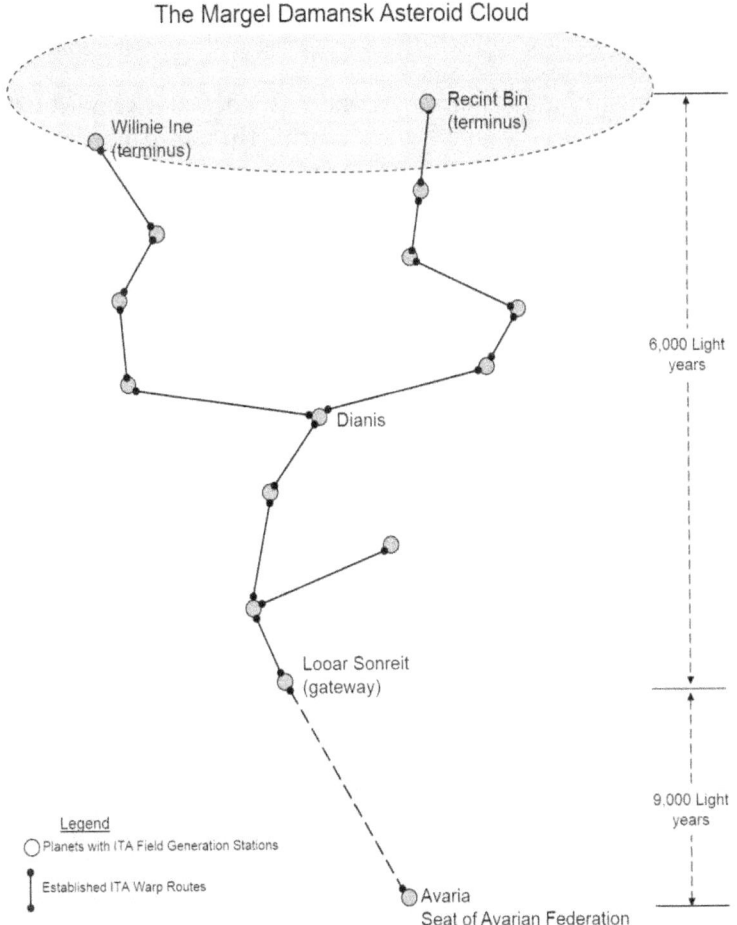

The Margel Damansk Asteroid Cloud

Recint Bin (terminus)

Wilinie Ine (terminus)

Dianis

Looar Sonreit (gateway)

6,000 Light years

9,000 Light years

Legend
○ Planets with ITA Field Generation Stations

▮ Established ITA Warp Routes

Avaria
Seat of Avarian Federation

Margel Damansk Arm of ITA Transportation Network

Norma Spiral Arm, Milky Way Galaxy

Prologue

Outish flung his arm over the rock edge and slapped his hand down, scrabbling for a grip. He pulled himself up and rolled over on the granite ledge. At that altitude, some fourteen thousand feet, he swayed from the exertion. He staggered around and faced south. "Wow," he breathed. He could see all the way to the plains below. If he leaned over the edge just a little bit, he could see the farms below Wedgewood. The town was hidden amongst the massive Ungerngerists, and from that elevation was a sea of green.

"Outy, give me a hand," Baryy called, attempting the same climb as Outish, but he wasn't as strong as the Halorite.

"Uh?"

Baryy was waving his hand.

"What?" Outish whirled around, "Did I hear— A turnbuckle ptarmigan!" He fumbled for his multi-func, swiping pages hurriedly to bring up the video recorder. He began stalking the bird.

"Outy!" Baryy called, but his grip slipped, and he fell back to land on the ledge next to Achelous.

"Where's Outish?" asked Achelous.

"He ran off! Chasing a bird."

Achelous rolled his head, Avarian style. "Fine. We'll sling the grapple and pull ourselves up."

When they found Outish, he was kneeling at a crevice in the rock, running the spectrum analyzer in his multi-func examining a flame-red lichen. "Anything interesting," asked Baryy, long accustomed to Outish's eccentricities.

"This is new. We've not cataloged this species."

"Yea, well, we've other things to investigate," said Achelous. "This way." He led the three of them across the flat top of the lower peak of Mount Mars. It had taken over a day of climbing up through the Twistynook drainage, with Outish taking soil samples along the way. They had made camp the night before, just below the snow line. It was early summer, and the snow was receding, but here, at the top of the Isuelt continent, winter held sway. A brisk wind blew, scouring the level expanse clean of snow. They approached the edge of the plateau where it dipped down into a snow-covered saddle and, on the opposite side, climbed up to the higher, knife-edge peak of Mount Mars. Achelous breathed deep, taking in the vista. "I've always wanted to come here."

"Me too," said Baryy.

"Wow, this is spectacular," said Outish. "That's the head of the glacier?" He pointed to where the mountain formed a horseshoe valley filled with an unmarked slope of pearl essence. Farther down, near the bottom, the glacier showed its age with cracks and fissures.

"Yes. That's where we are going," Achelous pointed to the saddle above the glacier. Wind, blowing up the valley, had stripped the blanket of white from the mountain, exposing grey rock and a rubble scree.

Baryy held up his multi-func, in telescope mode, and zoomed in on the image of the saddle. "There's something there," he showed Outish, "and it's not natural."

Achelous proceeded in that direction. "Affirmative. The early satellite scans showed an anomaly there. The question is, what."

"Atch," Baryy said, hurrying to keep up, "We're finally here! We're so close!"

They reached the saddle and approached what was officially known in Avarian historical records as *Loch Norim Site Five Hundred Twenty-Seven, Probable, Uninspected*. It was the last word in the description that drew the team of former IDB agents to that desolate spot.

Achelous put his hand on what, from a satellite in space, looked like a rock crag, but now, from an arm's length away, was the remains of a plasto-concrete wall.

"Is it?" asked Outish.

Achelous didn't answer; his heart, surprisingly, was pounding in excitement.

"Over here!" Baryy called.

They half ran, half stumbled in the thin air to where Baryy knelt and began scraping the snow away from an artifact. He stopped, then stood. The three of them didn't say a word until Achelous broke the silence. "That's a radiator housing." He drew his short sword, made from the finest steel that Ogden, one of Isuelt's most renowned weaponsmiths, could craft, and took a cut at the pipe that protruded from the snow. The blade came away with a divot. Baryy inspected the pipe. "Nothing, not a scratch."

"Spectrum analyzer?" Outish asked, excited.

Achelous nodded. "Yes, but we already know what it is." He looked around at the ruins of what must have been a sizable building spanning the saddle. Where the snow was blown clear, he saw foundations and other fragments of wall protruding from the top of the glacier.

"Confirmed," reported Outish. "The metal is albaminia."

Baryy and Achelous stared across the saddle to the largest extant structure. "That didn't show in the satellite survey," whispered Baryy.

Achelous was peering at the base of it. "No," he said as he started walking to the structure. "The snow must have been deeper when the satellite came over. Spring thaw uncovered it."

"So it's confirmed?" Outish asked. "Can we confirm it?" His excitement pitched his voice.

"Yes," answered Achelous. "We can confirm the site as being of Loch Norim origins. We'll flag it with a *cursory inspection.*" He already had four Loch Norim site findings accredited to his name, but for Baryy and Outish, this would be their first. The problem was in order to update the Avarian historical registry and claim the credit, they'd have to come out of hiding.

When they reached the remains of the building, Outish asked, "What happened here?"

Achelous dug his foot in the snow. Bending over, he asked Baryy for his pickaxe.

"What? What is it?" asked Outish.

Achelous started digging and scraping snow away from what appeared to be a large, flat area, potentially a floor of a building. "Baryy, look for slag marks. Any sort of melting."

"Roger."

Achelous kept digging and scraping snow away. "Outish, make sure you take whatever soil samples you can. I don't see a lot of loose dirt, but maybe what you are looking for has contaminated some of these rocks."

When he was done, Achelous waited for the two to finish their inspections. "Well?" He was looking at Baryy.

"Nope. Nothing. Just—" he waved his hand at the buried ruins, "this mechanical damage."

"Mechanical damage?" Outish looked confused.

Achelous pointed about fifty yards off to the right, half buried in the snow. "Did you see that?" he asked of no one in particular.

Baryy squinted, moved to get a better view, and studied the phenomenon. "Oh."

Achelous nodded at Outish before the intern could ask the obvious question. "Blast damage. From the cultural anthropologist's perspective, we call that mechanical damage. That is a crater, a bomb crater. Definitely not a meteor. The rest of this damage was caused by above-ground explosions. And this flat area we're standing on is made of albaminia."

Outish paled. "Really? This place was attacked?"

"Hmm," mused Achelous, walking over the area he'd cleared of snow.

"Someone attacked the Loch Norims?!" said Outish. "Who would do that? Is that why they left Dianis?"

"Sixteen hundred years ago, Atch." Baryy was standing there puzzling over what Achelous had uncovered. "We now know the Loch Norim colony here essentially ceased to function about sixteen hundred years ago. We know they left descendants behind, but we had no explanation for the colony collapse. An attack could be an explanation."

Achelous thought about all they knew, all the data they had uncovered about the Loch Norim presence on Dianis since the early Avarian transportation engineers had landed here nearly four hundred years ago. "That's a plausible explanation. But yes, all Loch Norim activity on Dianis ceased sixteen hundred years ago. We can do electron dating of the damaged albaminia molecules. They would have a different age from the other artifacts. It would support your conclusion.

"But now we know they didn't purposely try to demolish this site. Otherwise," and Baryy bent down and rapped the huge albaminia plate they were standing on with the pickaxe. It rang with a deep, hollow sound. "Otherwise, they would have blown up the structure from within, and there would be a massive crater here instead of just this surface damage."

Achelous saw Outish trying to work out the implications. He couldn't fault him for trying and failing. Outish was an astrobiologist, Achelous was a cultural anthropologist, and Baryy was a sociologist. Of the three sciences, Achelous was the best suited for unwinding this puzzle. He retrieved the pickaxe from Baryy and rapped the metal structure. The hollow sound beckoned. "Outish, your answer is down in there. See that line and those hinges?" He toed a large hinge uncovered during his excavation. "This is a huge vertical lift hatch of some sort. Whoever attacked this site does not appear to have gotten inside, at least not here." He pointed down.

"Not that we can either," grumbled Baryy.

Achelous walked to where he could see all the way down the glacier. "No. Not today. And maybe not here."

Chapter 1
The High Priestess

IDB Central Station, the Planet Dianis

Ivan, the Ready Reaction chief, sorted through his equipment and team manifests; they were entering potentially hostile territory. "Squads, weapons check," he ordered. They were going in heavy. Their high-value package dictated unusual precautions. Dianis was his former home base. Ivan had served here for eighteen years, but now, with the departure of the IDB and the war between the Troglodytes, Paleowrights, and Timberkeeps, what had been the peaceful continent of Isuelt was now consumed with strife.

His two squad leaders called out. Normally, on a rescue mission or snatch-and-go, he went in-country with a single squad of five Ready Reaction troopers. Today, however, was different.

The first squad leader called out, "Alpha, weapons check, loaded."

Then the second squad chimed in, "Beta, weapons check, loaded." All ten men of the two Ready Reaction teams were former members of the IDB Dianis Ready Reaction before they were transferred out to Dominicus Three, three months ago.

"Spec One, weapons check, loaded." That was the squad leader for Special Forces team One.

"Spec Two, Spec Three, weapons check, loaded," came from the other two Special Forces teams. Then, the same message came from the two-man personal escort teams for the two Matrincy counselors and the expedition's high-value package.

The chief looked at the Special Forces captain, who nodded back. No small amount of professional competition existed between the two. Normally, Special Forces operated independently, and as a result, their operations command had complained to the Matrincy of having their men subject to the authority of an IDB chief, but the orders from the Matrincy were clear. They were going in-country on a Class E world, a world of sudden strategic value in the Turboii war, a war waged against Humanity by the Turboii across the galaxy. Eighty billion Humans dead.

"Horalznick," Ivan called out.

"Yes, chief."

"Clear the shift zone, please."

"Roger that. Bravo team, take your positions on the shift platform."

Ivan turned to his high-value package. Like the other two Matrincy counselors, the package was dressed as an Auro Na priest in a heavy black robe with a deep hood, voluminous sleeves, and the signature burgundy embroidery. The brooch of the Auro Na pinned over the left breast. The priests wore sandals on their feet and simple belted frocks beneath their robes. As per Auro Na custom, one of the three major religions on Dianis, a silver pendant in the shape of a seven-pointed star hung about their necks.

Neither the high-value package nor the counselors were, of course, Auro Na priests. That was their in-country cover. Ivan had selected the Auro Na cover story as the similarities in philosophical beliefs and skill ranks between the Matrincy and the Auro Na were remarkable. The Matrincy governed the sixthsense practices of the Avarian Federation, and the Auro Na guided the sixthsense practices of the adepts on Dianis.

"Last chance, Madam Matriarch," as if to punctuate his offer, the pulse of the field generator vibrated the floor, and Sergeant Horalznick's team, mounted on their eenus, disappeared from the platform. "I'm sure Special Envoy Margret and Counselor Breia are fully capable of carrying out their mission. There is no need for you to take this risk."

The high-value package returned his smile with patience, as he suspected she would. "Thank you for your offer, chief, but we've already covered this."

Counselors Margret and Breia watched the interchange, their faces deep in the shadows of their cowls.

"Shift zone clear," came Sergeant Horalznick's voice over the audio implants of the teams. He was in-country now, on the surface of Dianis.

"Captain, you may send in your teams," Ivan instructed.

The Special Forces troopers, garbed in clothing and armor typical of Isuelt free mercenaries, led their mounts to the platform and began to teleport in-country. Per IDB, Interspecies Development Branch policy, all non-IDB personnel must be escorted on Class E worlds. To do that, Ivan had selected troopers who'd lived on Dianis, fought there, and knew the indigenous populations and cultures. Injection learning, the special training for just this mission, only went so far, especially when the protection of their high-value package was at stake.

"Madam Matriarch," Ivan said, "I've not been able to ask, and please forgive the intrusion; why exactly do you want to come to Dianis?" The Special Forces captain, protective of his package, moved to intervene. A quick glance by the matriarch stayed his advance.

Endowing Ivan with the same patient smile, she became wistful. "A list of reasons." Looking at the troopers cycling through the field generator bay, she gathered her thoughts. "I have heard much of this world. For prescience, it is time to visit. I've seen the vids, Ivan. Dianis is truly beautiful and unspoiled. No Turboii, no extrasolar depredations—"

"Yet," he interjected.

She nodded, but her hood stayed motionless. "As you say. If I am to see this world in my visions, to sense it, to appreciate its presence in the galaxy, I need to come here to experience Dianis, to *feel* it. I need to have a perspective of its people, the life, and the soul of the world."

That would be the demand of her prescient, distance-viewing skill, he reflected. *She can't see what is happening on the planet if she has no relation to it.* "And you have other reasons?"

Her wistfulness left with the second Special Forces squad disappearing from the shift platform. She gazed directly at him. "And I've come looking for your friend."

Ivan's weathered, craggy features went blank, "Friend—" he caught himself. "Atch?" Inexplicably, he could feel angst rising. "You think Achelous is here on Dianis?" he asked incredulously.

She studied him. Air currents swirled about the departure of the last squad as they shifted onto the surface of the planet. She motioned to the captain and her two personal guards to assume their positions on the platform. Looping an arm through Ivan's, the matriarch steered him in that direction. "Honestly, I have only a vague notion of where our good chief inspector is. I know he is not on the Farless Isles on sabbatical, as his sojourn itinerary says he should be. He has not contacted our counselors as he said he would, and we do need his help, as you know, with our investigations on this planet. He is, after all, the galaxy's foremost expert on Dianis."

As the IDB Chief of Civilization Monitoring for Dianis, before IDB operations on the planet were terminated, Chief Achelous Forushen had been responsible, for twenty-eight years, for leading the ground surveillance teams that monitored the planet for uplift readiness. As part of his own in-country cover story, Achelous had even established an extensive trading practice in gems, spices, and weapons and spent much time in-country with the provincials. During that time, Ivan had been the Chief of Ready Reaction, who would, when needed, shift in to rescue Atch or any of his teams when they were in trouble.

Ivan let the Matriarch, the most powerful person in the Avarian Federation, guide him to the platform while he considered the vast implications of why such a person would be involved in the search for his friend.

Counselors Margret and Breia, along with their guards, took their positions in the shift queue behind the matriarch and Ivan.

He was hesitant to ask but went there nonetheless, "Are there other reasons for coming to Dianis?" They were standing on the platform. Ivan watched the field generator operator ready the machine for the teleport while he waited for the matriarch's answer. That she considered Atch might still be on Dianis was a stunning revelation. He wanted to ask her why.

"I've come looking for a woman."

"A woman?"

"Yes." They stood watching the field gen operator manipulate the controls, "And I would learn more of the Mother Dianis faith. Do you know much about it?"

"You're looking for Mother Dianis?" The incredulity in his voice almost comical.

The matriarch did indeed laugh. "No, no, not that mother. But I am interested in the beliefs of Mother Dianis faithful."

"Then what woman?" Ivan asked, desperately trying to catch up to where the matriarch was headed. The field gen operator pointed to the countdown timer of their shift. Ivan nodded absently.

"The mother of Achelous's son."

Ivan was speechless. That Achelous would still be on Dianis without knowledge of the IDB was bad enough. To have fathered a child with a provincial was grounds for prosecution against the laws of ULUP, the Universal Law of Unclaimed Planets. "What?" he struggled to ask.

She gave him a benign smile. "Yes, I think we need to find her. There is a connection between her, the Mother Dianis faithful, and the need to uplift Dianis to Class D. Chief, the federation, and Humanity needs what Dianis has to offer if we are to defeat the Turboii. To end this war before it ends us. To bring Dianis into the federation, it must be uplifted to Class D. As a Class E world -- Dianis -- under ULUP, is untouchable."

He was shaking his head. The timer read twenty seconds. "Achelous has a son? Here? On Dianis?"

From the depths of the burgundy-embroidered cowl, her ebony eyes studied him. The shift clock read fifteen seconds. "Yes, Ivan. Here on Dianis. And we need to find the mother. You may care about his transgressions, but I believe that fate, that our collective Human spirits have connected Achelous to her for a purpose, and we must follow that purpose."

"Purpose?" Ivan was a chief of a team of agents that rescued and arrested people, not a master of the metaphysical.

The clock read five seconds. "A thread of fate leads here, chief, to her. We can still choose our destiny, but the actions of the Turboii are eliminating, cutting threads. I don't know how many options we have left."

Air rushed into the shift bay filling the vacuum of the teleported mass.

Counselor Margret, the Matrincy's special envoy, watched the shift and considered the matriarch's last words before she disappeared. The matriarch had been purposely oblique. Never one to share her innermost thoughts, the matriarch always kept her deliberations oblique, but Margret now had a better sense of the matriarch's visit to Dianis. Up to this point, Margret had thought it was about Wedgewood and aquamarine. Now, however, Margret realized the matriarch was after something bigger, much bigger, and it involved a woman, Achelous's lover.

Chapter 2
Shift Zone

Foothills of Mount Mars

The matriarch patted the muzzle of the eenu. It was a lovely animal, but her attention kept straying to the speckled grey bull with trimmed horns. She walked over to it. "May I?" she asked the Ready Reaction trooper holding its reins.

"You can, ma'am, but eenu geldings can be high-spirited. We usually reserve them for the best riders, and Boomsha here can be ornery."

She reached up to touch the beast's muzzle, and it flinched. She waited for it to calm, and Boomsha snuffled her hand. She patted its neck, stroking it in simple, silent gestures. "Do you mind?"

Not knowing what the matriarch meant, the trooper hesitated.

Grasping the reins, she pulled the bull's head in, put her boot in the high stirrup, and before anyone could intervene, swung expertly up in the saddle. Sitting astride the largest eenu in their expedition, the matriarch settled in comfortably. "I hope you don't mind trading?"

Ivan, setting the search patterns for the recon bots, stopped and stared. "Uh—"

"What's that, chief?" came the voice of the combat controller in his audio ear implant. The controller was onboard the Avarian cruiser *Alexis* in geosynchronous orbit above their position.

"The matriarch just saddled up on Boomsha."

A laugh came over the A-wave channel. "I see that. Shall I drop the alert threshold?"

"Yes, how much time will it take her to hit the ground?" Ivan asked.

"Half a second, give or take, depending on how far he throws her."

"Set it, please."

The combat controller on the *Alexis* issued the instructions to the AI running the field generator onboard the cruiser to shorten the trigger time, the time from when the AI calculated imminent harm to the matriarch to when it would trigger the field generator to shift the matriarch back to the ship. That meant keeping the field generator running in high-ramp, ready to pulse. The energy required for high-ramp was enormous. The only other functions the cruiser could sustain during high-ramp were command, navigation, and life support. Which is why an entire Avarian battle fleet was orbiting Dianis: to protect the defenseless cruiser.

Ivan turned away from the scene. He had other things on his mind; the Special Forces captain and troopers would just have to deal with it. The matriarch wore Synflex body armor under her robe, and her repulsor earrings would ward off projectiles aimed at her head, but they did nothing for a fall.

Working on his multi-func, Ivan established the patrol pattern of the Falcon defense drones that would accompany their ride to Wedgewood. The Falcons were the medium-weight hitters. The single-shot defense bots that swarmed about the column were the lightweights. All two hundred of them. The heavy defense that Ivan coordinated with the *Alexis* were the plasma, kinetic, and laser cannons in the fleet above their heads. Not to mention the full battalion of Assault Marines onboard the carrier *Spirit's Fury*. Of those seven hundred battle-hardened veterans, forty of them, at any given time, sat fully armored in their assault crafts in the hangar deck on the carrier, all for the protection of their high-value package. They were locked and loaded for all Dianis could offer, and yet the matriarch threatened it all by riding a cranky bull eenu.

"Sergeant Horalznick?"

Both the sergeant and Ivan recognized the matriarch's voice over the comm channel.

"Yes, ma'am." They'd been riding in a double column for twenty minutes or so. The trees, pastures, and abandoned homesteads – their wreckage littering the normally tidy farms– formed the somber scenery as they navigated their mounts.

"Can we pick up the pace? I'd like to see what Boomsha can do."

Silence on the line.

"He wants to go," she said. "I'm having to hold him back."

"Umm," came the sergeant's voice. He was leading the column. His squad had point. The matriarch and her two personal Special Forces guards were stationed safely in the middle of the expedition.

Ivan turned to his left when he heard a commotion. It resolved into a single galloping rider.

An eenu, a bull eenu, was galloping up the left flank of the column. Its head was down, nostrils flared; hooves churned the verge leaves into a cloud. The matriarch ripped an airstream past the stunned troopers. Her hood blew back. Platinum blonde hair streamed behind in a bound braid, the pale skin of her face and hands contrasting starkly with the black of her robe.

Boomsha streaked past Ivan with two Special Forces troopers in pursuit, furiously whipping their mounts. "Ready One, go!" Ivan yelled into his audio implant. "She's gonna beat you!"

Ivan knew Sergeant Horalznick, Ready One squad leader and the best eenuman in the troop, if issued a challenge, would take care of the problem.

The squad at the head of the column vaulted to a gallup.

Crouching low on the bull, the matriarch held the reins loosely, giving the beast its head. Wind flushed through the bull's trimmed horns and scruffy mane, flooding the matriarch's robe billowing it out behind her. Trees with young leaves whipped past. Birds flittered out of her way. Nano-defense bots buzzed around her like angry hornets, their tiny wings flailing in hyper-drive. Two Falcon drones soared behind just above the trees. She glanced behind; her coal-black eyes took in the charging column behind.

They raced by a burned-out farmstead. The smoke was gone, but the wet stench of burnt timbers lingered in the air.

"Matriarch, pull up. Your speed is excessive. Your mount could stumble."

Ignoring Ivan's voice in her ear, she focused on the pelting Ready Reaction riders ahead of her. They were expert riders; they rode low, angled forward, and their hands easy on the reins. When Ivan had asked her, even pressed her, as to why she came to Dianis, she'd not admitted to a desire to leave the crush of troubles and turmoils of Avaria. As a child and later, as a counselor posted to outer worlds, she had taken to riding the saddle animals of those worlds. It had become a passion of hers. Horses on Earth, diagonems on Pelatar, ugavs on Squasislor, they were all different and yet the same. If treated right, they would take care of their rider. "Ha! Go!" She jammed her heels into Boomsha's flanks.

Sergeant Horalznick led his squad more by memory than AI telemetry. He'd been here before. The trail split left and right at various divergences, but he kept them racing on the widest trail if not the shortest route.

"Left, sergeant, left," came the matriarch's call in his ear implant.

Now, how does she know where to go? he thought. Up ahead, the trail forked. He had just enough warning to veer the squad down the left branch.

The open pasture called to her, a spot about halfway across. In the distance was another farmhouse, the fields around it newly tilled. A farmer was spreading seed. There was something about the place... She had come searching, and her search led her here.

Ivan saw the matriarch slow from her pursuit of the lead squad. "Ready One, pull up."

Slowing the bull to a walk, the matriarch stopped and dismounted. She appeared to be looking for something.

Ivan came up at a trot. "That was a damn fool thing to do," he growled at her. "While we are on this planet, you are my charge, and you will follow my direction."

"She is the matriarch—" cantering up, Counselor Breia, his mount winded and snorting, sought to interject but was trumped by the Special Forces captain.

"Hold your tongue, Chief. If you have issues with the matriarch, you are to bring them to me."

The matriarch ignored them all. "Chief, would you have one of your men fetch the farmer over there for me? Please?" She looked up and gave him an apologetic smile. "I would learn what happened here."

Ivan's dark countenance softened to a scowl. All the eenus were panting, stomping, and their flanks running with sweat. He issued the request to Horalznick.

While waiting for Horalznick's team to return with the farmer, Ivan dismounted from his eenu, grudgingly curious. Aside from the trampled grass from their party, there were signs, indications of a battle. "Captain, have your men move their mounts over there—" he pointed. "We need to clear the immediate area."

The matriarch prodded at something with her sandal.

Ivan bent to retrieve it. "It's the head of a mace. Crude. Probably a Troglodyte mace."

She had her insulated gloves on, protecting her hands against aural energies. "I'll not be touching that any time soon," she joked. "I've enough nightmares."

He watched her. "My apologies, Your Matrincy, if I was abrupt with you. You are the most important person in the federation, maybe all Humanity and I cannot let you take unnecessary risks. At least not on my watch."

She moved to another object, a secret smile playing on her face. "Then don't watch."

He gave her an exasperated frown but followed her.

The next item was a small leather pouch on a severed lanyard.

"That, I would also not touch," he said. He stooped, picking up the soggy pouch by its lanyard, and gave it a sniff. He nodded. "As I thought." He carefully pulled the drawstrings apart to open the pouch. Holding it up, he said, "Take a smell, carefully—"

"Is that safe?" demanded the Special Forces captain.

It was Ivan's turn to smile. "I wouldn't know. I'm not watching."

The matriarch leaned forward, then immediately jerked back. Her eyes wide. "That's strong. What is it?"

"Yes, even wet from rain it's pungent. They call it sage rose. It's a type of ground opiate poppy. The Paleowrights buy it from the farmers in Ompo, part of the Drakan empire. They grind it to a powder and give it to the Troglodytes."

"Give?" she asked.

"Oi," he slipped into the tongue of the Timberkeeps. "It's addicting to Troglodytes. Humans can get addicted to it as well, but more so for Trogs who go wild if they run out. It's the way the Paleowrights control them. Turn them into their surrogates. The Church is the only source of sage rose outside of the empire. You can tell if the Trog is a chieftain or other dignitary by if they carry a sage pouch and what it is adorned with." He closed the bag. "Judging by this bag, the Trog that died here was probably a rampager overseer."

"Died?" she asked.

Sergeant Horalznick rode up with the farmer on his eenu.

"Yes," answered Ivan. "No Troglodyte would willingly leave their snuff bag behind. The Trog didn't just lose it; they can smell a mouse fart in a tornado." Looking around, "Judging by the bits of clothing, trampled ground, discarded weapon, and other things, there was a fight here, and the Trogs lost. Especially since the farmer is still alive," he added with a nod at the man.

"Oi, I'm still alive," the farmer said, sliding off the rump of Horalznick's eenu.

The matriarch caught the farmer's attention. "Ula," he exclaimed, "we don't get many Auro Na in these parts. And you must be important, got a whole troop of mercs with you. Kinda young to be a priestess, aren't you?"

"High-priestess," Breia interrupted.

Taken aback, the farmer worked his jaw. "I thought you were all old and craggy by the time you got to be so lofty."

The farmer, a middle-aged Human male, a Timberkeep, was the first indigenous Diesian the matriarch had met, and he fascinated her. It was true that her gene therapy made her appear decades younger than she was, which on Dianis would pose a credibility problem. "Do you know what happened here?"

"Oi! A sharp little fracas. Still is some fighting, though the wards have chased most of the loglards back east. Got the Plains and Red Elm clans helping out, too."

"Tell me about what happened right here," she said, pointing at her feet.

"Ula, that was two weeks ago. The loglards, you know, Troglodytes, were attacking my house. They'd already torn apart Blichern's and Ordartern's farms, and now they were coming for me. Had me and my family and the field hands barricaded in the house. We were keeping them back, but it was getting nasty. Poking their snouts in the windows and us hacking at them. They almost had the back door off its hinges when the mercs came riding down the same trail you did." The farmer waved an arm at the slope that led into the forest.

"Very good," she said patiently, "but what about the fight that happened right here, on this spot?"

"I was getting to that. Them mercs come riding down the trail, fast, just like you did. Though there weren't that many, maybe ten or so. A band of Trogs attacked them here. One of their riders was thrown. When they got in the scrap with the Trogs, we were watching from the loft window. Kinda good for us because the Trogs attacking us went to fight the mercs. But those mercs were real good. We learned they were all ex-soldiers when they brought the woman to the house, Oridian lancers, 'Kilden Rangers, even some Tivor Marines. Never met anyone from Tivor before."

"A woman?" the matriarch asked.

"Oi, a good looker, that one. Some special trade envoy from Tivor."

"Black hair, black eyes, olive skin?" she asked.

"Oi, that's her. You know her?"

The matriarch appeared to consider the question but asked, "Was she injured?"

"Banged up a bit from the fall. Hit hard, she did. A Trog got her with a mace cut her leg good."

"Where did she fall?" the matriarch asked, looking to where the mace head lay discarded in the turf.

"Oh... somewhere hereabouts." He looked about.

Then Horalznick called out, "Someone fell and bled here." He kneeled by a dark red, almost black, stain in the grass.

"Could be from one of the Trogs," Ivan suggested.

"Hmm, I don't think so," said the farmer. "We drug off all the Trog bodies and burned them on that bonfire over there. There weren't no dead Trogs where he is."

Walking to where the sergeant inspected the scene, the matriarch kneeled in the grass. Carefully, she pulled the glove from her left hand. With one finger, her index finger, she reached towards the stain.

"Oi, you're one of those," said the farmer.

"And what is that?" challenged Breia.

"I've been around enough of the clan sensitives. That one," he pointed at the matriarch, "she's a distance viewer, a prescient, isn't she?"

"Correct," said the matriarch, "now let us see what the blood tells us." She placed her finger into the stain and pushed hard. Her eyes became distant, unfocused. Everyone, including the eenus, was still.

After a long moment, she settled back, kneeling in the grass. Finally, she stood and wiped her finger on a proffered neckerchief and donned her glove.

For everyone, Ivan asked, "Well?"

She looked past him to the farmer. "Of the mercs that were with her, was there a man?" and she described Chief Inspector Achelous Forushen to him.

"Oi, hovered over her like a herd dog he did. Seen him before. He'd come through here every so often. A trader, friendly enough, would always wave as he rode by. Kind of funny; he'd always come down from the same trail you did. Where'd you folks come from anyhow? There's no Auro Na temple anywhere around here. Not till you get to Promontory Point, and that's seventy miles west. You came from the south."

Nodding, she ignored the farmer and looked back to Ivan. Her face somber, "I'm sorry, chief."

"Sorry?" He asked rhetorically. He didn't want her sympathy of Achelous being here just two weeks ago.

She took a deep breath. "I have found clues to the two things I came for," she paused, "the blood of one and the tears of the other."

Chapter 3
Quorat

The town of Wedgewood at Mount Mars

"Flash, flash, in-bound Dianis orbit alert."

Quorat pulled up hard on his mono-peller. He hit the power button; the antigrav impeller sled settled to the ground. "What?" he growled into his collar mic.

The voice of the Intruder's AI came over his ear implant, "Comm satellite sensors indicate a battle fleet matching the emanations of Avarian ship designs is orbiting into position over the continent of Isuelt."

"Whaaaat!" Quorat screeched. He even startled himself. He looked around. The deep forest of the mountainside was quiet, serene, and sunny, all the things he did not feel.

"Affirmative," came the AI's response. The AI's avatar was tuned to Quorat's idiosyncratic tendencies. During its tenure, the AI had continued to augment its database of Quorat's behavioral patterns to the extent that it could now reliably respond to the Human in a simple – for an AI -- verbal shorthand. "The fleet, I calculate, shifted into orbit on the far side of the planet twenty-three hours ago and has since been conducting operations."

"Operations?" he hissed.

"Affirmative. They are conducting an aural scan of the planet and, according to my probabilities, are shifting ground-mobile assets planetside."

"Bloody hell. And the comm satellite is just seeing them now?"

"Standard intrusion protocol dictated we launch the satellite on the far side of the moon, program the satellite to orbit the moon, and circle into clear view of Dianis every—"

"I know all that. What sort of aural scan?"

"Sentient and mineral analysis."

Quorat's stomach fell. "Are they, are they after me?" Ground-mobile assets from an Avarian battle fleet meant Marines.

"Aural scan-event horizon is approaching. An Avarian frigate from the fleet has separated and is following a standard planetary search pattern. It will reach your area in nine minutes. Suggest you go to full black-out protocol."

For once, Quorat didn't argue the AI's guidance. "Take the Intruder dark as well."

"Affirmative. All A-wave, neutrino, and other emanations will cease in six minutes."

Then, a more menacing thought came to him. "Are the Turboii here? Are they invading? Are they coming for the aquamarine?"

"Passive sensor capabilities of the communication satellite are limited. No other starships have been detected. Do you want it to go active with sensors?"

"No! No!" He was flustered. "If the Turboii are not invading, then why is an Avarian fleet here?"

"I continue to catalog the signal emissions, and the satellite now has visuals on the battle group. It is composed of five *Leopard*-class cruisers, three destroyers, two frigates, and a Marine assault carrier matching the build of the *Spirit's Fury*. The heavy cruiser *Alexis* is transmitting encrypted messaging in the pattern of a flagship. Task force ship-roster matches a reserve battle group normally on ready-alert at Avaria."

Quorat thought through the problem. "We're a long way from Avaria. What is a reserve battle group doing way out here? Not exactly what you would send to block a Turboii invasion."

Even though the AI didn't have additional relevant data to add, its behavioral model for Quorat indicated a response was required. "Okay."

He stepped off the sled and opened the aft cargo pod. The machine looked more like a motorcycle doing a wheelie. The impeller housing hung at the bottom, and the controls and handlebar were at the top. Quorat rode the sled by standing on the foot pegs and sitting on the narrow seat. Strictly a single-person conveyance, easily hidden, the machine was powered by a neutrino energy cell that fit in the palm of his hand. Cargo pods were strapped to both sides and the rear. He pulled out his aural-energy-absorbing poncho and checked his diffusion bracelets, anklets, and collar. Anything that could reflect an aural energy scan was covered. His own aural energy emanation would be shunted to ground by the diffusion jewelry. If they followed the aural scan with an infrared sweep, they would see a modest hot spot where heat leaked out from his poncho and the cooling antigravity sled, but that couldn't be helped. He had a more significant problem: he was over sixty miles from where he'd parked the Intruder on the bottom of a mountain lake. His geo-positioning system indicated he was five miles from Wedgewood. With the Avarian fleet moving in overhead, he dared not communicate via A-wave, energize a neutrino fuel cell, or activate the antigrav impeller. Tight beam laser only, but that was out as well due to no power.

"Three minutes to blackout," signaled the AI.

"Shiren," he cursed. He'd brought just enough food and water for a short overnight excursion from the Intruder. If the fleet sat above him for any length of time, he would have to go native. Going through the various options, he considered making a bolt back to the Intruder, but he'd never make it. A second option was to leave his sled camouflaged where it was and start hiking back.

The vision of a mansion, a gaggle of women, and all the things that a million credits could buy gnawed at him. All he had to do to earn it was scan and videograph the point source. *A million? Screw that! Whatever it is, I should just pack it out myself! Could be worth maybe fifty million credits on the aqua market?*

A third option grew larger in his mind: hike the five miles to the point source and take it.

"Intruder going dark in sixty seconds. Have you adopted aural concealment protocol?"

"Yes," answered Quorat. In less than a minute, he would be on his own, stranded in an unfamiliar land with no AI, no sled, and an Avarian fleet overhead. In the few seconds he had left, he checked the charge indicators for this plasma pistol and plasma rifle. The chemical projectile rifle, of course, didn't need a charge. It fired bullets.

Chapter 4
Wedgewood

The town of Wedgewood on Mount Mars

Ivan led the column to the checkpoint where he signaled a halt. They'd been riding most of the morning; he dismounted, glad to be off his eenu. Not having ridden in three months his butt was sore.

"State your purpose," came the challenge from a Timberkeep warder wearing a conical steel helmet, a chain mail hauberk, and a double-headed battle axe strapped to his back. At his hip was a dirk long enough to be a short sword. Behind him, a half-ward – twenty warriors – stood arrayed on either side of a newly erected gate that was closed. The gate blocked the road but not much else. To either side of the lane massive Ungerngerist pine trees marched off in the distance like the pillars of a god's cathedral. A treefort was built high up in the Ungerngerist nearest the gate. Six archers stood at the railing with strung bows at the ready.

Ivan languidly stretched his back and removed his gauntlets. The expedition's thirty-four troopers and priests made a respectable show. Subsequently, the Timberkeep warders were alert.

He approached the axeman. "Been a while since I've been to Wedgewood. There wasn't a gate here last time. Ula, we could ride right into town without so much as rousing a squirrel. What's the reason?"

"That was a while ago," agreed the warrior. "Since the Trogs and Paleowrights attacked, things have been different." The man edged to the right and peered down the double column of what appeared to be mercenaries. "We can't be letting you all into town." He narrowed his gaze and squinted at Ivan. "Not since the Drakans came dressing as free mercs. Now, we question everyone. Especially mercs."

"Oh." *This is going to be a problem,* Ivan thought. Their mission goals depended on access, unfettered, to Wedgewood. "We've come a long way and counted on resting and provisioning here in the town. I've three Auro Na priests with me, one of them a high priestess. They've come to see the town and speak with your adepts and sensitives."

"That's no mind to me. Orders are orders. I'll not be letting you mercs into town."

"Riders coming!" Called the lookout from the treefort. "I see pennants. Could be the Oridians."

"You'll be needing to move your column off the road, merc. We've word the Oligarch of Oridia is on his way, and we'll be needing to let his troop pass."

The matriarch, accompanied by her two Special Forces guards and the two counselors, rode to the head of the column, listening to the interchange.

Seeing the priests arrive, the Timberkeep warrior chose to ignore them and instead focus on the approaching double-column of lancers.

"Gonna get crowded around here," said one of the warders.

A female archer in the treefort climbed up on the fort railing, grabbed the spring line, and jumped off. The spring-loaded drum coiled out the rope as the archer dropped the thirty feet. As the line paid out, the spring tightened, slowing the drop, and the woman landed like a cat just as the pawl on the drum caught, locking the spring. She let the rope go and walked around the gate to where the three Auro Na priests sat astride their eenus. "I'm Lettern, branch warden for Second Ward. Which one of you is the pathic?"

The matriarch arched an eyebrow, and Counselor Breia responded, "We all are, of sorts."

Lettern scowled. "Then stop it."

"Stop what?" asked the matriarch.

Lettern had turned to walk away when she halted and turned back. Gazing levelly at the high priestess, she said, "We're not fools. It's best to not treat us that way."

The lead pennants of the approaching column came on the lance points of three full squadrons of Oridian Lancers. The riders were resplendent in burnished helms with white and blue plumes, the colors of the Oridian nation. Their breastplates were likewise burnished, the exposed sleeves of their tunics were dyed in the same pattern of white and blue. Their shields, secured to the saddle straps, bore a painted sigil, the white and green lily of Mother Dianis. Pointing at the sky, the long lance tips made a forest of steel.

"Ho there," called the lancer standard-bearer, "All hail the Oligarch of Oridia!"

The Timberkeep warder clumsily doffed his helmet and bowed, as did Lettern, who demonstrated a fluid grace. Ivan, savvy to the ways of Dianis and particularly Isuelt, called out, "All hail the Oligarch of Oridia!" He signaled to the matriarch and Special Forces captain to follow his lead. He removed his helm and bowed low.

A tall rider who bore no lance but whose sliver helm was filigreed with fine scrollwork and whose tunic sleeves were adorned with broad gold bands followed his herald to the gate. From shoulder to hip, a broad red sash dressed his breastplate. On the center of the red sash was a large white lily pendant. He took in the crowded gathering with a mischievous smile and a glint in his eye. "What? All this for me? Heard I was coming? I was afraid of that."

"Yes, your Excellency," Lettern answered. "We were told of your coming, and we welcome Oridia's support in these trying times. Tell us, what is the word from the Drakan frontier? Have the Drakans marched?"

"And you would be?" he asked.

"Lettern," she again bowed low, "branch warden, Second Ward."

"Rise, child. I heard tell of the Second Ward in the Battle for Wedgewood." He looked at the doughty axemen arrayed to either side of the gate. "I assume these are the Second?"

"They are your excellency," answered Lettern.

"Then we'll not be charging that gate anytime soon," he smiled. "Is Ogden here, your master weaponsmith? I've a mind to carry one of his swords."

"He is at the forge, sir," she replied, "I will relay your desire."

Appearing satisfied, the oligarch said, "Good. And no, the Drakans have not marched, yet. But they will. They've too many soldiers to feed and keep busy. No one builds an army that big and doesn't use it." Then he noticed the three black-robed figures in their distinctive Auro Na garb, sitting astride their eenus. He lengthened his inspection, glancing along the line of mercs, now dwarfed by the Oridians. "And what do we have here? The Auro Na have come to Wedgewood?"

"And we refuse them to enter, my lord," said the Timberkeep gate commander.

The oligarch considered that.

"They are telepaths, my lord," Lettern pointed to the priests. "They are concealing their identities from our sensitives. You will understand because of the treachery heaped upon us by the Paleowrights and the deception of the Drakans, we are ever more vigilant."

He smirked, turning to the black-robed figures. "Met your match, eh? I've one or two Timberkeeps telepaths with me as well. Remove your hoods; I will see to whom I speak."

Ivan sensed rather than felt the front squad of Special Forces troopers tense. He could well imagine what the captain was thinking. He stepped forward to intervene, but the matriarch said, "It's okay, Ivan, we will comply."

The oligarch's expression narrowed at the Ready Reaction chief.

The matriarch, followed by Margret and Breia, pulled back her cowl. "As you can see, my lord," to which the matriarch bowed in the saddle, "that we are neither Paleowrights nor Nakish Drakans."

Shuffling his feet, the Timberkeep gate guard looked uncertain.

"And we know they are certainly Auro Na," glared Lettern, "as Brookern and Cordelei have alerted Sedge that the priests are interfering with our aural surveillance."

The oligarch snorted. "Yes, that certainly proves they are not Paleowrights. The churchmen and their suspicions have chased every sensitive from every church and cathedral they have." He spurred his mount closer to the matriarch until he was blocked by Ivan, who, standing his ground, refused to be intimidated by the mount and rider. The ruler of one of the most powerful nations on Isuelt again narrowed his gaze at the supposed merc. "Priestess, your merc captain here should learn some manners."

"High priestess," retorted Breia.

The oligarch's eyebrow went up and, for the first time, decided to look closely at the woman whose red lips and black eyes were in stark contrast to her pale, flawless skin and blonde, nearly-white hair. "High priestess?"

"Sire," she inclined her head. "And my apologies for my guard captain, but he is sworn to protect my life with his own, and he is very good at what he does." The last she said as a subtle challenge. A gambit, if you will, between two powerful leaders, a game they would both understand if those around them didn't.

"The last I was told, there are three high priests on Isuelt, and they are all in the north at Terrabac fi Sur with their deacons electing the new Coroscone." He paused, eyeing her appreciatively. "And aren't Auro Na high priestess usually old crones, wizened from the long years? You are certainly no old crone." He responded to her gambit with a subtle challenge of his own.

"We are from the Seahorse Isles, not Isuelt," the matriarch answered. "We seldom stray into the affairs of the continent, but the stories of the adepts in Wedgewood have compelled us to cross the straights and investigate the rumors. As for the election of the Coroscone, Isuelt is indeed gathering, but those of us from the Isles have never submitted to the rule of the Coroscone and, therefore, are not inclined to the test." The cover story, like all IDB cover stories, was carefully researched and, in this case, entirely true, up to a point. The Seahorse Isles were famous for their isolation, and while they did at one time have a high priestess, the Auro Na adherents on the islands had mostly migrated to the more active Auro Na society on the continent, making it convenient that there was no one left on the islands to dispute the matriarch's claim.

"Mayhap just as well. One so young as you could scarce compete against the likes of the high priest from Neuland." He looked to Lettern. "Which is a problem for the Western Alliance. Neuland may be in the alliance, but their high priest is definitely not. He favors the Ompeans, the poppies, and the women they supply him. If he is elected Coroscone, he will certainly ally the Auro Na with the Drakans, though it may not, at first, be obvious."

Without a visual clue to Boomsha, the matriarch's dapple-grey bull moved forward until the massive steed was shoulder to shoulder with the oligarch's own large mount. "Do not underrate us of the Isles." Little could the oligarch know that the matriarch was decades older than he.

The oligarch smirked. "And what rank would the vaunted high priestess of the Seahorse Isles be? The priest of Neuland is reported to be an octogan, highest in the realm."

Using the reins, Breia urged his eenu closer. He and Margret had studied the potentially competing Auro Na clerics and compared them to the matrons of the Matrincy. "The high priestess is a decimar." In truth, the grading scale of the Auro Na did not go high enough to adequately test the matriarch, so he settled for what standards Dianis had.

Before the oligarch could utter his laugh, Margret added, "Tis true. A ten."

The oligarch's near laugh turned to a glower.

Taking a deep breath while looking the oligarch in the eye, the matriarch's face set, she raised a hand and, with her other, removed the glove. She held up the index finger on her bare hand. "Shall we find out, lord?" The crowd of two hundred was dead silent. "Hold out your hand, dear sir. I shall tell you what you are, who you are, where you are from, where you will go."

He shook his head. "Nay. I shall have none of your Auro Na whimsy."

She rolled her head, common for Avaria but very uncommon on Dianis.

Ivan grimaced.

"Fine," she said, "I shall settle for your mount." She stuck her finger on the muzzle of the oligarch's eenu and froze the animal in place. The matriarch's nostrils flared, and her cheeks flushed. Holding her finger there, she plumbed the depths of the memories the unguarded eenu willingly offered. She smiled maliciously. "You've known this beast since birth. You arranged it to be sired. You raised it. You call it Moonsmoke, though your children call it Smoky. You love it like your children, and it adores you. You train on it relentlessly, and it gives you all you want. You have fought innumerable battles from that saddle, and Moonsmoke has seen much blood, some of it yours and some its own. It prefers a saber fight instead of a lance charge. It will bite left as you strike right." The matriarch's smile crashed. "You let your wife ride it because you had complete trust in Moonsmoke to protect her. The day she died was not the animal's fault; they were surrounded, the eenu was pinned by a Drakan lance—"

The oligarch viciously sawed the reins away, breaking contact. His anger glowed hot in his chest. The emotions, feelings, and hatred of that day seared through him like a branding iron.

Dropping her head, the matriarch said, "I am sorry, my lord. I ask your forgiveness. I had not sought to cause pain. But...but...the passion of your life flows through your eenu. I only said what...what it wanted, what the mare wants you to know. The beast loves you and is forever tormented by the day Celeste died."

Studying her closely, the oligarch gradually let his anger ebb. He sat there cognizant that his squadrons, all of whom knew the story of the ambush of Celeste and her guard, watched him intently. Revenge for that day was in their hearts. Glancing about, he finally moved Moonsmoke back to the matriarch. He reached out with his gauntlet and raised her chin. There were tears on her cheeks. "You truly are a decimar. You have given me a gift this day." He reached down and stroked the neck of his eenu. Combing the mane aside, he kissed the animal on the ear. "Was not your fault. We shall ride, and the day will come when the Drakans will pay."

The eenu raised its head and piped a rallying call to all the other eenus who stirred at the sound.

He said to the matriarch, "If only you were to test for the Coroscone. I would pay a mountain of gold to see the high priest of Neuland, Ghost-I, thwarted."

"There are mysteries in this world undiscovered by modern man," she said. "Perhaps we may oblige you."

Margret harkened back to last night. After dinner, around the campfire with the stars aglow, the firelight flickering off the matriarch's black eyes when she had voiced a new plan. A bold plan, a scheme that skirted or perhaps flirted with violating several ULUP –Universal Law of Unclaimed Planets – laws. It was another clue of the goals the matriarch had for Dianis, which, in the end, would possibly solve three strategic problems for the Avarian Federation and Humanity. A key part of the plan rested in Wedgewood, but now the town was barred to them by both its psychic and physical defenders. Another facet, one of greater urgency, demanded their participation at Terrabac fi Sur. The matriarch had proposed to Ivan to turn their IDB cover story of Auro Na priests from fiction into reality by having Margret stand for the position of Isuelt Coroscone. There were many challenges to the idea: the legality, influencing indigenous peoples, Class E intervention, and timing. If they were to attempt the scheme, they would need to shift or fly immediately to the Auro Na conclave, gain entrance, submit Margret's credentials as a priestess, present her case as a suitable candidate, and then take the test.

Margret watched the matriarch, who was conversing with the oligarch. Margret's thoughts strayed: *Her plan is to uplift Dianis, which may appease ULUP. But am I the mother she seeks? The mother to lead Dianis' unification so the planet can be declared Class D and take an active role in the defense of Humanity in the Turboii War?*

"Then you will have to hurry; Terrabac is many leagues from here," the oligarch said.

"And we have business here in Wedgewood." Breia was on guard for the matriarch's prerogative to pursue what he thought were arcane tangents, but what she called strategic redirections.

"The docent is right; we have immediate business to conduct with the adepts here in Wedgewood." Then the matriarch looked to Ivan, "but I would ask my captain to consider the logistics of traveling to the Auro Na conclave."

"Good, then you shall dine with me tonight." The oligarch bent at the hip but did not remove his helmet. "I would apprise you of the intrigue in the North, in Neuland, before you meet your fellow Auro Na." He glanced at the warder blocking the gate and then to Lettern. "I will vouch for the high priestess, and," he said frowning at Ivan, "her guard. If it would keep the peace," he added.

Seeing the branch warden was unmoved, the matriarch sought to mollify her. "We have much to learn from Clan Mearsbirch, and we have much to offer you. To this point, the Seahorse Auro Na have stood aloof in the affairs of Isuelt. But the winds are changing. Forces greater than all of us are swirling. They have yet to coalesce into a storm, so we have time. If we partner together, we may yet prepare to withstand that turmoil."

Lettern, a woman who trusted to arrows more than the words of clergy, remained suspicious.

Ivan sensed that though Lettern may be irritated with the Auro Na, her, and hence the clan's chief resistance was allowing so many well-armed mercenaries of unknown loyalties into their town. "I propose, should the oligarch be willing, that a portion of our company be bivouacked with the Oridian lancers, and the remainder find suitable encampment here, outside of Wedgewood. I might suggest we hire the mill on the Twistynook." His Ready Reaction agents had stayed at the mill in other visits to Wedgewood. "One of our priests can encamp at the mill, and the other attend her excellency in Wedgewood." He had a reason for the arrangement. What the Wedgewood sensitives thought to be purposeful interference, a Black Viel cast by the matriarch, Margret, and Breia, was probably the aural dampener signets carried by the Special Forces soldiers. Ivan and his two squads of Ready Reaction troopers wore the more sophisticated IDB aural impersonator signets on chains about their necks. Those signets carried a costly aquamarine-5 gemstone imbued with the aural signature of a fictitious Isuelt mercenary. The talisman transmuted their aural energy into the signature of another persona. The Special Forces soldiers wore no such amulet and instead relied on blanket disruptors to conceal their identity from prying sensitives. The matriarch and two counselors, on the other hand, were psychically skilled to portray whatever aural impression they desired and needed no talisman.

Ivan knew the Special Forces captain, if not the admiral of the fleet, would not accept the arrangement, but if the matriarch was to gain access to the town, the Special Forces soldiers would have to stay behind, along with a priest who would pose as the person maintaining what was known as the Black Veil, the veil of aural darkness that Wedgewood sensitives assumed was being cast to obfuscate their personas. He refrained from glancing at the Special Forces captain to see his reaction.

"And who do you suggest we allow into town?" challenged Lettern.

"Myself and my squad, and Sergeant Horalznick's squad. Most of us have been here to Wedgewood," and said with feeling, "in better times. Some are former soldiers of the Western Alliance." At least those were their cover stories. It was the irony of being an in-country IDB agent. After years of serving on Dianis, portions of cover stories became a reality. He'd long since crossed the point where the real experiences as a Dianis mercenary life blended with those of an IDB Ready Reaction trooper. In a way, he was a real Isuelt merc.

Ivan decided to play his trump card. "I should remind the warden that several of us are friends of Achelous, the trader; he hired us in the past. We have fought with Sedge, your warlord, against the Trogs at Battle Park. Perhaps Sedge will vouch for me?"

Lettern squinted. She strode forward to stand in front of him, looking closely. "I was at Battle Park. I was the scout for Achelous with Ogden's escort. We were ambushed." She examined him, making sure. "Your beard is gone, and your armor is new." Then she remembered fully. "You saved Outy. At the creek, when we rallied."

He smiled. "The intern—" he caught himself. "The apprentice and that eenu of his saved themselves. We just rounded them up."

"Hmm, Tulip," she mused.

"Yes, that was its name. Smart old mare."

She turned to the gate commander. "I'll vouch for this merc captain and his two squads. You can let them pass. But," she glanced up at the matriarch, "no funny business from you. If Cordelia or Brookern complain of interference from you, out you go."

"Excellent!" said the oligarch before the high priestess could refuse. "You will ride beside me," he said to her. "You can tell me of your journey from the Isles, and I will share news of Isuelt." Then he pointed with his gaze, "I will have you put your glove back on."

Ivan looked to the matriarch, and she gave a slight nod. *I wonder how much trouble I'm in for this,* he thought. Swinging up into the saddle of his mount, he caught the glare of the Special Forces captain.

Chapter 5
Murali's

Wedgewood

"Lettern, a moment, please." The column was dissembling, and the branch warden was on her way to her ward's stables. She waited for Ivan to catch up. Inside Wedgewood, everywhere was wreckage and fire-wrought destruction. Brick chimneys stood as mute testament to buildings that once were and now ashes. Two mighty Ungerngerists immediately in front of him were fire-scarred, the lower branches burned away, and the needles on the upper branches turned brown. Further in, however, Ivan could see substantial portions of the town were still intact.

"The crowns are still alive," Lettern said, riding beside him. "Still green way up top, though for how long is anyone's guess."

"They're tough," he said, awe in his voice. He'd read the reports of the assault and seen the aerial surveys of the aftermath, but being there, in person, at ground level, brought it home.

"They are. Their bark is fire-resistant and two feet thick on the biggest trees. These two may still live."

He dismounted from his eenu, keeping an eye on the matriarch where she chatted with the oligarch. The Oridian lancers were moving to their bivouac, and Ivan had the challenge of finding lodging for his two squads and the two matronens. The imagery of the town from the *Alexis* gave him some ideas as to where he might look.

"Lettern," he prepared himself to ask the question he didn't want to.

"Yes?"

"I was wondering, have you seen Achelous?" It was a shot in the dark, but he needed to start the search. Achelous was gone completely off the grid. The frigate

Trilonair had done a complete aural scan of the planet and cataloged the aural signatures of every sentient being with a Human profile, all eighty-seven million, yet not one hit on the IDB chief. That meant he was wearing an aural disruptor.

"I saw him this morning. When I went on watch. Why," she grinned, "you need a job? Tough being a chaperone to your high and mighty priestess?" She tilted her head in the direction of where the oligarch was bidding goodbye to the two matronens.

The floor fell out beneath him, and he thought he swayed on his eenu.

"What's wrong, captain? You look disappointed."

He shook his head, "No," he said distantly, "he's a friend, and I'm just looking for him."

"Well, then you should be happy! You've found him. He's here somewhere." Looking past him, she saw the high priestess was waiting for him. "I think you should go. You don't want to keep her Auro Na-ness waiting."

He said nothing when Lettern turned her mount and trotted off.

He led his eenu to the matriarch, surrounded by his two squads. His feet were lead. The air, though it was cool, felt oppressive.

"Something wrong?" the matriarch asked.

"Yes, I need to find lodgings for you and Priestess Margret." He sent two of his troopers in search of accommodations.

The matriarch and Counselor Margret slid off their eenu's and handed off the reigns. A pair of troopers led the eenu's away in search of a likely stable, if one still stood, or at least a temporary paddock.

"That's not what's wrong," the matriarch said quietly. Margret stood close.

"No, it is not." He continued to omit her honorific.

"Shall we walk?" the matriarch asked, "I see much of the town in that direction is intact; it looks extensive. Give us a tour. I've heard so much about it. Perhaps meet some of the sensitives."

"He's here."

The matriarch continued walking, taking in her surroundings, the people, the treeforts, and the provincial dress. A wind carried in the smell of Ungern sap and pine needs, blowing away the acrid odor of wet, charred ruins.

"Achelous is here," he said again.

"Yes, I know."

"He has to be arrested, he's—"

"Where do you think they keep the aquamarine-5 pegmatite that has the federation so excited?"

"Please, ma'am, do not refer to it as dash five; the provincials have no notion of aquamarine grades."

"Yes, of course, my apologies. Where do you think it is?"

"The aural scan from the *Trilonair* pinged it here. They haven't moved it."

"Close?"

Exasperated, he felt like snapping; it was as if the matriarch didn't care that Achelous was on Dianis -- *if he had ever left!* He opened his multi-func and checked the scan coordinates. "Yes, ma'am. Somewhere near that tent." He pointed.

She brightened, offering an illuminating smile. "Shall we go look?"

The front flaps of the huge canvas tent were pinned open. Above the opening, nailed to a temporary wooden frame, was a charred but still legible sign that read *Murali's Inn, Food, and Fine Rakia.* Beside the tent, workers dug through the wreckage of a building, shoveling out ashes, debris, and charred timber frames. "What's rakia?" the matriarch whispered in his ear, not wishing to commit another galactic faux pas.

"The form of a liquid, alcohol-based intoxicant, ma'am. Fermented tree sap, to be specific."

"Is it good? I mean, is it safe to drink?"

He hesitated, wondering what was *safe.* "I've had my share. Hasn't killed me yet."

"Why am I not surprised," she said lightly. "How long was it, Ivan, your tour here?"

She knew the answer, so he suspected she was leading to a point. He answered, "Eighteen years, ma'am."

"And was all of that with Achelous?" Her black eyes, standing there at the entrance, regarded him openly.

"Yes, ma'am, you know it was."

She nodded, "Then let's not be so quick to convict."

"But—"

Before he could finish, she went through the entrance into the dim interior. Their six Ready Reaction troopers entered and fanned out to assess the risk. Nanobots buzzed, fluttered, or flapped through the opening depending on their conveyance.

The Avarians, with their gene and embed-augmented senses, could see in the gloom without waiting for their eyes to adjust. The principal lighting in the tent being the sun radiating through the canvas walls. Wooden trestles were set up. A hodge-podge collection of chairs and tables were spread out. The bar, positioned against the back of the cavernous tent, was a set of boards laid across four barrels standing on end. A barkeep and a pair of maids served the place. It being early afternoon, traffic was light. Not waiting for the troopers to signal *all clear,* the matriarch moved ahead of them and went to the bar and read the menu. Hung from the wooden tent frame was a short list of the simple fare that the inn, or rather, tent, in its current state, could muster from the kitchen out back. Her injection-learning for the Doroman language let her pick items off the sign. There were three different drinks; one of them read, "Fire-hardened Shield Rakia."

"Fire-hardened? What does that mean?" she asked of the barkeep. In her injection learning, nowhere did she remember the term used in conjunction with alcohol, so she thought it safe to ask the provincial.

"Oi, we don't get many Auro Na like you in here. Tammyrn," he said to one of the maids, "you ever seen any Auro Na here before?"

The serving woman glanced their way, taking in the distinctive black robes and the mercenary bodyguards.

"Noi. Got enough guards, don't they?" Two more troopers filed in.

Turning back to the matriarch, "Maybe you didn't know we had this wee fire," the barkeep said, "with the *festival,* we had with them Paleowrights, and Trogs, and Drakans and all."

Ivan waited restrained, wondering if he'd have to intervene with the sarcastic Timberkeep.

"But!" The barkeep smiled hugely and leaned on and across the bar's planks that bent with his weight, his face just inches from the matriarch. "You, my lady, are in luck."

Leaning back, she asked, "How so?

"Because before the fire destroyed the storeroom, we managed to rescue most of our hard spirits stock. The brewery is toasted pine nuts, but the distillery is up by the mines, and that wasn't touched. And that there rakia," he hooked a thumb over his shoulder, "is from one of the barrels that were scorched in the storeroom, not burned, mind you, and it is a rare treat. The heat on the barrel caused the charcoal in the barrel to accelerate the aging, and it is fine stuff."

"Okay..." she said, drawing it out.

"You want some?"

Taking the matriarch's subtle incline of her head as a *yes,* he offered, "One shot or two?" He tossed his head in a way that said he thought she was a lilting flower.

"Two," she answered, rising to the challenge.

The barkeep turned to Ivan, "How about you, soldier?" He looked him up and down, taking in his weapons and armor.

Ivan shook his head.

When the barkeep turned away to get the matriarch her drink, Ivan whispered, "I've no easy way to test to see if it is safe. I can't really run the spectrum analyzer on my multi-func here in the tent in front of them."

"Test?" she started, "it's not as if they are going to poison the local populace. It would be bad for business. Besides," she said with a smirk, "what happened to your real tester?"

49

"Real?"

When the barkeep handed her a short porcelain cup with a pale, amber liquid in it, she handed it to Ivan. "There you go, test that for me." She said and smiled rosily. "And another two shots for me," she said to the barkeep.

"Ah, at last, there you are!" A voice called from the tent opening.

They turned, and a Timberkeep strode up to them and stuck his hand out Doroman-fashion to Ivan. "I'm Poatif, secretary to chairman Woodwern, our elder clansman. We've just had a visit by the oligarch, expected, of course, and much welcomed. He informed us of our good fortune to be hosting a high priestess of the Auro Na. My goodness, but a rare treat that is!" He let Ivan's hand go and bowed to the matriarch. "Woodwern has offered lodgings for the high priestess and her assistant," and he turned to see Margret sitting on a tree log used as a bench. "Right. Now, mind you, we've only one lodging room in the hall to offer, but if the high priestess doesn't mind sharing with her assistant, I think it will do."

"That's very gracious of you and your chairman," the matriarch answered.

"Oi, thank you, priestess, er high—"

She rescued the secretary, "Madam will suffice. And where will my guard stay?"

"Oh," the secretary looked to Ivan.

"Don't worry, high priestess," Ivan offered, "It is customary for escorts to bunk with the house guards. I assume you have a bunk room for the Timber Hall guards?" he asked the secretary.

"We do!"

After the secretary made his excuses for not staying and departed, the matriarch said to Ivan, "Ask the barkeep where the pegmatite is."

The barkeep overheard the question, "Why? You be wanting to steal it?" He looked around at the eight troopers, "If so, you'll be needing more men than this!"

"Noi," she tried out Timberkeep slang, "but I am curious to see what compelled the Paleowrights to such great destruction." Then she added, "And their demise."

The barkeep gave her a nod of appreciation and hooked a thumb toward the end of the bar.

Margret rose from her log and went to look.

"Oh, Spirits," Marget breathed, peering around the barrel that was the end of the bar.

Sergeant Horalznick looked over her shoulder. He turned to Ivan wide-eyed. Then, the matriarch got her first look at it. The pegmatite, a full three feet high and as wide at its base as a saddle, sat on a flat slab of wood. A sign, tied by twine, hung on the monolith. It read, *Hell-prick: Next time bring a bigger army.*

The matriarch stood rooted at the sight of it. "The Source of Fates."

"Don't know what all the fuss is," the barkeep called from where he leaned on the bar. "What good is it? Just fancy jewelry for them damned churchmen."

So they would not attract more attention, Ivan drew them, including the gawking Ready Reaction troopers, away from the monolith.

Huddled in a corner, with the troopers keeping eavesdroppers away, Margret whispered, heedless of what galactic words she might use, "At current market rates, that's what, thirty million credits!"

Sergeant Horalznick snorted. "Counselor," he said sotto voce, "I don't know what market you are following, but with the collapse of Nordarken Mining's aquamarine reserves, that's worth three *hundred* million credits."

"How many ships do you think that could shift?" the matriarch asked Ivan.

He tilted his head, peering at the monolith. Finally, he said, "Hmm, I bet there is enough aqua-five there for four carrier-sized field generators."

Margret turned to the matriarch. "We have three carriers waiting in the shipyards now for their aqua-5 containments. The delivery schedules keep getting pushed out."

The matriarch, de facto leader of Humanity's most powerful nation and hence Humanity's greatest champion against the Turboii, stood there looking at what could be a massive aid to the war. Both the Turboii and Humans were hurting for aquamarine resources to power their various aural devices; often, a battle hinged on who could supply those devices in the greatest quantity. Men, women, and all manner of free sentient beings were dying in the Turboii scourge. She wanted, badly, to order the *Alexis* to just shift the monolith aboard. No one on Dianis would know what happened, but in the federation, it would be a different story. ULUP was enacted for a reason. Until the aquamarine shortage was finally deemed a critical crisis by the Strategic Resources Council, her hands were tied, almost.

She turned away, not wanting to think of it. She needed answers, thinking of the woman in her voyant vision of Achelous. Staring into her porcelain cup, the amber liquid enticed her. She felt a premonition stirring. Taking a sniff, the heady alcoholic aroma imbued with a mixture of woodland spices and flowers assaulted her senses. An augur, a vision, started to come. She took a sip, hoping the vision was about the woman. "Hmm, very smooth," she murmured.

Ivan looked startled. "Matriarch," he broke protocol, "I've not tested it."

"Too late." She raised the cup and knocked it back. The amber fluid, at once both smooth and burning, landed in her stomach with a fiery burst that sent shivers out her limbs. "Oh-wa," she said uncharacteristically. Her eyes grew wide, dilating to their extremes. Her ears flared red, and she looked to Margret. "Vision, vision, it's coming, hard, catch—"

Margret calmly, fluid in practice, caught the matriarch as she collapsed in her arms. Before Ivan could pull his handbolt and shoot the bartender, Margret said, "It's okay. This happens. Sit her down."

Troopers rushed to her side while others drew weapons and formed a perimeter. "Shall we extract?"

"No," commanded Margret, the Special Envoy to Dianis. "We may need her vision. A shift will disrupt the premonition." With a mental command, she called up, on her optic implant, the matriarch's vitals; the readout scrolled across her optic nerve. "As I thought. Andromeda, are you recording?"

"Yes, counselor," came the voice, in Margret's auditory implant, of the matriarch's personal AI.

"Hold in there, Andy," Margret brushed loose hair from the matriarch's unconscious face.

Ivan and Horalznick shared a glance. Horalznick silently mouthed, "Andy?"

"Stay with us," Margret coached her matriarch, holding her in her arms as the two sat cramped on the log end. "Stay with us and give us what we need. What do you see? Go there, go there." The matriarch's body convulsed. "Yes, that's it. Go there." Margret held on fiercely, balancing on the log, keeping the matriarch tight against her. The matriarch started mumbling something, her head tossed left and right. "Andromeda, are you getting it? She is in the throes; her pain graph is going mid-scale."

"Master barkeep," Margret called out, "that's some strong stuff you sell. What's in it?"

He smiled, unmoving. "Kicked her ass, did it? Hey, cap, you should try yours."

Suddenly suspicious, Ivan sniffed his cup. "Sergeant, anything happens to me, kill the bastard."

The bartender flinched straight, "Hey, no one said—"

Ivan downed the double shot of rakia spirits. It flamed all the way to his belly, and he shivered. The warm afterglow infused him. He looked at the cup thoughtfully, then tossed it over his shoulder and watched the matriarch and the counselor.

"Well?" asked Horalznick.

Ivan shrugged his shoulders. "It's the woodland herbs. She's probably sensitive to one of them. It's pretty good. Real good." Thinking about it, he said, "You can spare the bartender."

In their chamber in Timber Hall, Ivan paced while the matriarch, lying on the bed, recovered from her episodic vision. An autodoc, shifted down from the *Alexis,* was attached to her arm; numerous readouts had turned green, only three remained yellow.

Waking up, her gaze drifted about the room and settled on Ivan. "Ug. I'm surprised you didn't pull the cord and have me extracted."

"I told them not to," answered Margret.

The matriarch rolled her head on the pillow to look at the counselor and rested a hand on Margret's bare arm. "Thank you for helping me." The three of them were alone in the room except, of course, for the nanobots hanging on the ceiling and two plasma-armed battle drones that squatted in their black menace in the corners. Ivan and Margret were ready with their capes to throw over the non-camouflaged drones in case anyone was to enter, but they'd have to get past the two Ready Reaction troopers outside the door and the squad of four that loitered nearby.

Ivan answered, "We don't want to do that, anyway. I know we'd planned for you to spend the evenings back aboard the cruiser and not rough it down here with the rest of us, but with the aural security the Timberkeeps are running, they'd know if you two suddenly disappear. We've no intel to indicate the Timberkeeps had become that sophisticated." He shook his head. "You need to stay with us. If you were to suddenly disappear, they'd come looking for you, and that would be awkward."

"We didn't think of that," admitted Margret.

Ivan sat in a bent-wood rocker and started rocking, impatient.

Then Margret said what was on both their minds, "The town you saw, the one in the battle, that was Wedgewood, wasn't it?" She and Ivan had seen Andromeda's recording of the matriarch's vision.

The matriarch looked to Ivan. "Was it?"

His chin bobbed once.

"Was that the battle with the Paleowrights?" she asked. But they both knew it wasn't. The matriarch's visions were of the future.

"Drakans," Ivan said.

"But there were Drakans in the fight with the Paleowrights and the Trogs. The barkeep said so," noted Margret.

"Yes, Drakans dressed as mercenaries," Ivan replied, "the Drakans in the matriarch's dream were in empire armor. I saw a legion standard in the recording, and I searched for it in our Nak Drakas database." He pulled out his multi-func, brought up the relevant display, and handed it to them.

The matriarch took one glance and laid back down. "That's them."

Margret read the caption under the high-aspect picture, typical of a recon bot, "5th Legion, hoplites."

"They have that blue laurel wreath on their shields," Ivan noted. "It's an honor awarded by the emperor."

Margret let the import of the vision hang. The matriarch's visions were ninety-two percent accurate. The outcome of the last eight percent was subject to interpretation. The only real question of the matriarch's augurs was *when*.

When all readouts turned green, Ivan detached the autodoc. Then, he came to the point that refused to go away. "We have to take Achelous into custody. He's here in Wedgewood. It would be best if you and the counselor were to return to the care of Special Forces at the mill. Achelous has friends in the town. We can extract him quietly if he goes willingly."

Margret clasped her hands in her lap, preparing a response. Either she or the matriarch would have to reconcile Ivan with the multiple threads in motion. Plucking one thread, now, the wrong one would unravel others.

"It must be nice to live in a black-and-white world," said the matriarch, "mine is nothing but infinite shades of grey."

"He's gone rogue." Ivan never thought he'd ever say that about Achelous. "He needs to be brought in." Wording it was exceedingly painful for him. He'd lived and fought on Dianis for the last eighteen years, all of it under the tutelage of the chief inspector, his friend. Year after year after year, he'd witnessed all the good the man had done for the planet, the corsairs thwarted, the slavers captured, the knowledge gained. Ivan had saved Atch's life twice as the chief inspector carried out his duties, putting his life at risk, and now he was seeking his arrest.

"How so?" asked Margret.

Ivan swiveled on her. "He's off the grid, purposefully avoiding all means of detection and communication. He was supposed to leave the planet when we shut down. He said he went to the Farless Islands, but who knows where he actually went? Now we find out he's right here," Ivan stabbed a finger at the floor, "on a Class E world doing exactly what he was sworn to protect against." He said it coldly, clipping off the words.

"None of what you say is actually illegal." The matriarch replied, watching how Margret handled the Chief of Ready Reaction. He was in for a big surprise.

Ivan's mouth hung open; he struggled to form a rebuttal.

"He still has his charter for Dianis, Class E," Margret said, her hands folded in her lap. "As do you and all of the other IDB Dianis staff."

"What?"

"IDB Dianis was ramped-down, mothballed, not de-chartered."

"But I stood there with all the others at the decommissioning ceremony. The flags were lowered. We were all given our reassignments to Dominicus III."

"True," answered Margret, "I was there too. That's when I met Chief Inspector Forushen."

Seeing the frown on Ivan's face, the matriarch stepped in, "Ivan, an IDB charter on a Class E world is only revoked when it is officially canceled by the ULUP commission."

"And in this case," added Margret, "no such decision was made by the commission."

"What?" he drew out the word.

"The decision to leave Dianis was a federation IDB act, not a ULUP directive," Margret said.

"Because we were hacked, Ivan," the matriarch interjected, an edge to her voice. "Achelous was correct. His suspicions were founded. Internal Security confirmed it. We still don't know who exactly, and there is evidence there may be other moles in IDB, at headquarters, or elsewhere," she let him take the implications where he may.

"Hacked?" he asked incredulously.

"Yes. They exfiltrated the Dianis aquamarine deposits data that Clienen and Achelous so adroitly seeded with false geo coordinates. The ULUP commission left the charter in place in case we, the IDB, were to come back to Dianis. It's too difficult, too much bureaucratic work to have a world re-listed as Class E," Margret said. "However, someone successfully manipulated the government of Looar Sonriet to demand the closure of the Margel ITA transportation network and with it all IDB operations in the arm, which included Dianis. They cast a rather wide web in getting that transportation network shut down, but however they manipulated the federation congress, we believe the culprit's ultimate target was either access to Dianis or the Margel asteroid belt. Both have strategic resources. I'm here, as Special Envoy, to investigate the Dianis aspect."

"But we've all been posted to Dominicus III," came his rebuttal.

"Irrelevant," said the matriarch.

But Margret added more commentary. "That is true. The commitment to Dominicus III is made. We can't undo that. And we may not want to rescind it if we could. If the federation were to suddenly reverse itself and restart IDB operations on Dianis, whoever is responsible for this subterfuge might suspect we are on to them, and then," she paused, "we'd not be able to spring our trap."

"Trap?" he said, frowning.

The matriarch was sitting up on the bed now. "That's the most you can know, chief. Counselor Margret has been assigned responsibility for it. It's her plan."

"Does Achelous know?"

Margret shook her head. "No, of course not. How could he? He is," she paused, "out of communications."

Ivan was shaking his head. "I'm sorry, counselor," he looked at Margret and then to the matriarch, "Madam, he's broken too many IDB rules, even if he has not exactly violated any ULUP laws. He needs to be brought in. IDB headquarters will demand it when they hear of this..."

Margret waited, then, "Yes, IDB headquarters. Good point. Did you know that Clienen Hor, your former boss, has been assigned to IDB counterintelligence?"

Of guard, Ivan said, "I'd heard he was there."

"Yes, and did you also know that since the IDB charter for Dianis has not been terminated, Clienen is still the official director of IDB Margel Damansk operations?"

Ivan absorbed the news in silence, putting the pieces together.

"So," Margret continued, "if you complain to IDB headquarters -- as you should -- that an IDB officer is taking his two-year sabbatical on a Class E world, the world he is chartered for and has protected for the past twenty-eight years, that complaint will logically go to the current director of IDB Margel Damansk."

"Clienen," said the matriarch. Everyone in IDB Margel Damansk knew that Clienen's number one lieutenant in the arm was Chief Inspector Achelous Forushen. He'd even been offered Clienen's job, before Clienen, but had refused the posting.

Margret added, "I've spoken with Clienen, and while neither of us at the time was aware of the inspector's supposed transgressions, we both agreed it was critically important to find Achelous and ask him to return to Dianis. We needed him here to help with the planet-side investigations as to how someone could close the whole Margel Arm just for this planet. And now he's here!"

"I think we know why they shut down the arm," the matriarch said from the bed, sitting cross-legged, "we saw it in a canvas tent, watched over by a bartender. Spirits, Ivan, if that's what they have just sitting around, imagine what's in the ground?"

His eyes narrowed. "And how do we know Atch isn't here to gather all that aquamarine-5 for himself? He could be one of the richest men in the galaxy." He looked at her, cocking his head, "And then there is the small matter of him consorting with a provincial." He threw up his hands. "You've said yourself that he's fathered a child on the woman! There is no charter allowing him to do that! And I know Counselor Breia," he looked to Margret, "suspects Atch of all sorts of other ill deeds. Breia wants to interrogate Atch under a full memscan."

The matriarch laughed, a genuine mirthful laugh.

As the matriarch quieted, Margret reacted to Ivan's irate demonstration. "I was of a similar mind as you, or at least had some of the same thoughts until the matriarch fully explained her perceptions when she inspected the Achelous's Constellation Spark back on Avaria."

"He's a zealot, Ivan," the matriarch said, acid in her tone. "You know that; I know that. A moon will not change its orbit. Money, power, none of that means anything to him. He has a deep-seated anger against all things that would hurt this world. He would fight and die to save this world from whatever fears he has, whether real or imagined."

Ivan grudgingly admitted, "He almost did."

"He's here for a reason," the matriarch said, "and it's not for the aquamarine." She shook her head. "He's here for love, for a woman, for a son, but there is something else. I don't know what. He could have just taken them off the planet and been done with it, but he hasn't. He's after something, something else."

"And we need to know that it is," interjected Margret.

"And what of this woman?" Ivan came after the two of them like a terrier on a rat. "Think of what she might know, what he may have told her. He's consorted with her and had a baby. At the minimum, she'll need to be mind-wiped."

This time, the matriarch didn't laugh; she gave an impolite snort instead. "Ivan," she raised her hands palm up. "As if Achelous is the first Avarian galactic to get a Dianis provincial pregnant. How many ITA engineer babies are on this planet?"

"That was before ULUP was enacted. It's against the law now."

"That's if he is proven guilty of the crime," Margret interjected. "Remember, as the matriarch has said, let's not rush to the verdict without the evidence."

"But the matriarch's visions are admissible as evidence in the court of law. Her visions have proven to be ninety-two percent accurate by a strict definition."

"Yes, I know." The matriarch shifted on the bed, stretching her legs towards Margret. "But we've reviewed Andromeda's recording of my vision of Achelous and his woman. While it does show him having sex with her, it does not show where, when, or if she became pregnant. Yes, the inspector has a son, and yes, it can easily be construed that the woman is the mother. Hardly a case for mem-wipe," She sniffed.

In some ways, the matriarch respected Ivan for his tenacity, but now she found it tiring to the extreme. "There are things I can feel, sense, perceive that cannot be recorded, just like a memscan. And those things are not admissible in a court."

Knowing he was getting nowhere, he decided to take a different tact. "I take it neither of you wants to arrest Achelous. Why?"

It was Margret's turn. "Because we're not convinced he's doing wrong. Breaking consorting laws, maybe. But we need to know what he is up to. He was right about the hack when everyone else thought he was irrationally paranoid. He's the one who obfuscated the aqua-5 geo data when he knew it would attract attention. He's the one who filed and then downplayed the findings of the sensitives here in Wedgewood, and now we have reasons to suspect he knows why there are so many sensitives here. Powerful adepts. Spirits Ivan, even you think the Timberkeeps have master and grand-master sensitives monitoring our every move.

"And that was a total surprise," remarked the matriarch with irritation. "We could use them in the war."

"He's ahead of us. Way ahead of us. He knows of threats we have no clue about, and that worries me," Margret said emphatically. "Yes, I need *you* to find him, but *don't* arrest him. Don't even alert him. We don't want him running. He's already too good at hiding."

"And find me the woman." The matriarch stared at the Ready Reaction chief. "I want to meet her, to talk to her, as a high priestess of the Auro Na."

He scowled. "Why? You're not going to arrest her or mem-wipe her either!"

The matriarch took a deep breath and slid off the bed. Standing, she strode to the window and looked out through a gap in the Ungerngerists at the far distant farmland wavering on the heat rising from the lower plains. "She is something else, Ivan. I don't know what, but I know she is important." Turning, "And she is definitely not just some fling or a whore." She smiled. "She is one of the reasons Achelous is doing what he is doing. I need to, to," she hesitated to say it, "I need to meet her and touch her, to put my finger on her." She held up the same index finger she used to touch the oligarch's eenu and Achelous's Constellation Spark. The same finger that, back on Avaria, had made the aural connection and triggered the first vision that had led them all to that room in Timber Hall. She wanted to touch the woman not only to learn who she was but to spawn the next vision, to strum a chord of fate.

"Okay, but what about Margret's and Breia's mission to here, Wedgewood, the aquamarine-5, and the Timberkeep adepts? What do I do about that? You certainly can't be thinking of letting Special Forces run amok here?" He meant it figuratively. Special Forces thought themselves experts on everything and able to insert themselves into any indigenous culture. With the sixthsense adepts in Wedgewood, such hubris would end in disaster.

The matriarch looked to Margret.

Margret said, "First, we need to get to the Auro Na conclave. If I can test for the Coroscone, then we can then provide your teams with greater flexibility as to how you fulfill our mission. The aquamarine is vitally important, as are, and perhaps to a greater extent, the Timberkeep sensitives. We need them on our side; we need them in the war with the Turboii."

At least she is being honest about it, thought Ivan. *That's the first time any of the three matronens have admitted to me that they wanted to recruit Timberkeep adepts for the war, but how can they do it with ULUP laws firmly blocking the way? Engaging Class E indigenous populations beyond the charter allowed for the IDB was expressly forbidden. Not even the matriarch can bend that rule.* Which is why she came to Dianis under the auspices to assist in locating the missing IDB chief.

Margret upped the ante. "Ultimately, chief, what is the most important, even more vital than the aquamarine, is learning why there are so many adepts here in Wedgewood? Think about it. If we could unlock that secret, we could not only deploy sensitives to every combat unit facing the Turboii, but we could eventually change the face of Humanity."

Taken aback, Ivan, a non-sensitive, didn't know how he felt about that.

After leaving the meeting with the matriarch and Margret, he walked down the grand staircase in the hall and checked the Ready Reaction sentry postings. Nodding to the Timberkeep warder posted at the great doors, he pushed them open and stepped into the early evening, his head full of turbulence, his emotions a jumble of conflicts. At least he didn't have to arrest Atch, but that wasn't right. He leaned against a pillar of the Hall veranda. The one side of him demanded enforcement of the law; the other side of him, however, had an equally stubborn belief that his friend intended good, and if valid, he was hiding for good reason. That Atch had gone to ground, evading his friends in the IDB, Clienen, Gail, himself, bothered Ivan greatly. Something indeed, as the matriarch suspected, was afoot, but what? *If I assume Atch is in the good, then what*—It came to him, not so much as a sudden revelation, but as a slow dawning thought. *What if he knows the source, the cause of the higher birthrates of sensitives in Wedgewood? What if he knows something about the Matrincy I don't?*

"Oi, you've come to accept my offer?"

"Uh?" Ivan surfaced from his morose thoughts and focused on the accented voice behind him. Sedge the Warlord, commander of the Clan Mearsbirch wards and Wedgewood militia, stood there with a smirk. "I'd heard you were playing nursemaid to the Auro Na. The oligarch mentioned you." Sedge laughed. "Pissed him off, you did. I set him straight, though. Told him you were as stubborn and tough as he thought but a good merc to have on our side." Softening, Sedge stuck out a hand in Timber fashion, his long grey hair tied back in a ponytail, his finely embroidered vest immaculate.

Ivan grasped the hand and shook it. "No, I'm not looking for a new employer." He smiled back. The last time the two had seen each other was at Battle Park after a nasty encounter with Troglodytes just before the Battle of Wedgewood.

"Oi? But you're working for the high priestess now. What happened to working for the trader?"

Before Ivan could issue a suitable rejoinder, Sedge said, "I suppose the Silver Cup is a step up from your crew, eh?"

Ivan's brows creased, "Silver Cup?"

The Silver Cup was the continent's foremost courier service, employing telepaths to send messages, but additionally, they ran a security service.

Sedge nodded. "They're running security for the foundry and our special project. You're behind the times, man. Come, I'm going to the Command Loft. Gonna put my feet up, but first, I need to go by Murali's' and pick up supplies," he winked. "Join me? I should always be seen with people who annoy the aristocracy; it helps maintain my reputation."

Ivan shrugged. "If you try to recruit me, the answer will still be no, but I'll drink your rakia."

Chapter 6
Tolkroft Mine

Wedgewood

Quorat waited in the dark for the little recon bot to make its way back to his position. While the tiny device ran on a neutrino fuel cell, the discharge emanations were so miniscule he figured it was worth the risk. The last thing he wanted was to stumble into some sort of guard shack or security perimeter, but he dared not let the bot transmit its findings via A-wave. So he sent the bot out to the reported position of what seemed to be a mine, a quarter mile distant, recording all the readings and images its bot-sized AI thought were relevant and then return to him.

It was a moonless night. The stars, in the pollution-free atmosphere, shown like so many fireflies. Looking through his image-enhancing binoculars, he dialed to the highest magnification and searched the stars for gaps, for holes in the fireflies.

"There you are, you bastards." He counted one, two, three blots in the starscape: Avarian warships. Silent, stealthy, blacked-out, with no navigation lights, they hung up there like giant hawks ready to swoop. *What the hell are you doing up there?* He wondered for the thousandth time. *Just how is the customer supposed to get the aqua off this planet with you up there?* He smirked, waiting for the bot to return. *Not my problem. My problem is to get the findings information to them so they can credit my account.*

In the stillness of the night, against the ambient noise of crickets, nightjays, tree frogs, and the occasional owl, he heard the whine of the bot before it reached him. *How is that supposed to sound like a bumblebee?* This was the first time he'd used the new model, and he was disappointed. He laid his multi-func on the ground, a commercial, non-camouflaged version. Using the multi-func as a landing pad, the bot lighted on the device. It tic-tac'd across the surface to the I/O port and began to download its data feed. Somehow, on this alien world, away from the Intruder, disconnected from his AI, and with the hostile Avarian fleet overhead, the little bot was a comfort, a companion in the wilderness. The fake bee lifted off, landed on his backpack, and crawled back into the bot bin.

Checking the download, he grunted. The data looked good. There was a clear route to what was arguably a mine. Tailing piles were scattered about, shovels and picks rested on piles of rock at the ready, and vegetation was cleared away. For sampling, the little bot had chosen a rock pile ready for processing near a building. It had lighted on the pile and flashed it with an X-ray flicker, and sure enough, the bot's refractometer registered wavelengths for beryl and, more specifically, the chemical variant of aquamarine. It was a simple test adequate to detect aquamarine but not for dash-5

He stashed his multi-func. He was as ready as he would ever be. His hooded tunic, rustic pack, pants, boots, and shirt were as close as he could get to period-specific clothing for this world. Whether it matched the styles on this continent, he wasn't terribly concerned. *I'm not going to live here!* All he needed to do was walk through the town, ask a few questions, buy a few provisions, and move on. Just to be safe, he'd acquired an entry-level injection learning program for the planet; it had been hard to find, strictly black-market stuff. Dianis was Class E, and a cultural course for off-limits, Class E planets wasn't exactly a hot market item.

Moving slowly through the forest, his enhanced eyesight was sufficient without the use of artificial illumination. He needed to keep from sweating. His Nakish costume and makeup, including hair dye and fake beard, were waterproof, but he didn't want to test it. *Do they have Nakish here? I hope not. The last thing I want is inane chit-chat with some idiot indigin.* Going through the injection learning data, his AI suggested the Nakish ethnic group to masquerade as. They were the closest to his own ethnic appearance, and the Nakish homeland was far enough from Wedgewood where he was unlikely to bump into a fellow countryman he'd have to talk intelligently to.

Nearing the mine, he avoided the light wells cast by the lanterns and torches. They were another good sign of activity. Sneaking up to a large building, away from the lanterns, he skirted the wall in the starlit darkness. The pile the recon bot had found was just around the corner. Peering about, he pulled his multi-func out of his tunic. He did a passive, thorough aural scan: no Humans within three hundred feet.

He strode up to the pile as if he worked there and sat on the mound, acting like he was resting. With his multi-func, he flashed the pile with an X-ray flicker and then checked the image rebound on the multi-func display. "There you are," he breathed. Two or three good aquamarine nuggets, a coarse bluish-green, lay near his foot. He picked one up. It was aquamarine, but was it the dash-five variety? By outward appearances, they were identical, but aquamarine-5 was flux-free, a rare chemical composition that allowed penetration and flow-through of an electron beam without diffraction. If the gem were not flux-free, the electron beam would heat the crystalline structure and cause it to shatter.

But how to verify it's dash-5? He mused over the problem. It was one thing to flash an X-ray flicker that would be lost against the background radiation of the cosmos, but he'd need to ping the stones with an A-wave emanation to confirm the sample would energize. Dirty, or flux-corrupted aquamarine, when subjected to A-wave remained dead as a lump of coal. He looked to the stars again, "Damn you," he cursed the dark blots in the starscape.

Then, an idea began to take shape, an idea spawned by greed. He placed the stone deep in a tunic pocket and positioned it directly in front of the multi-func emitter. He'd go into the town, find a crowded space, and light off the A-wave emitter. He looked skyward. Let them figure out who or what discharged it, but then he had another thought: *what if they are in Wedgewood? Nah, that would be an astronomical coincidence. Then, again, there is a shortage of aquamarine. Maybe they came here to collect it?* That thought pissed him off. If the Avarian Federation was now in the business of digging aquamarine rather than going through the mining consortiums, there would be hell to pay in the markets, a massive destabilization. That would be a direct contravention of ULUP. He almost laughed. *Fools, you can't break ULUP, but I can!*

On the command deck of the sensors frigate *Trilonair,* an A-wave ping triggered a signal intelligence alert. The sensors AI sent a message to the sensors officer. "Roger. Log the event. Does the emanation match any profiles?"

"Standard A-wave ping, sir. Potentially a multi-function hand-held device or other low-intensity communicator."

"Fine. Keep your eye on it." The officer smirked at his joke. AIs didn't have eyes, not this one at least; it had a ship full of arrays and antennas. "Could be someone in the matriarch's party. Probably one of the Special Forces troopers sneaking off a love note to a girlfriend. I've seen them break protocol before. Let me know if it happens again. I'll inform their captain."

Quorat ran back to the anti-grav sled. There was a gathering at an odd little shack village with a bonfire near the town, and it had been a simple matter to just walk by, not attracting any attention. Disguise and makeup be damned, though, his little excursion excited him. The data from the mine and the A-wave ping met three conditions in his contract, plus a bonus clause. *Two hundred thousand credits!* He'd get another hundred thousand credits if he actually delivered a physical specimen, which he had, back to the contracting agent.

Stumbling in the dark, his enhanced sight failing him, he slipped on a pair of low-powered infrared goggles and finally found the mono-peller. He opened up the cargo box and withdrew the laser comm transmitter. His hands were shaking. *That whole pile must be full of it!* It was literally the find of his life. He had to get the information back to the contracting agent and demand immediate payment with deposit verification before he exfiled the planet to deliver the samples. *I am destined to be obscenely rich!*

He ran the orbital problem solver on the multi-func. The relay satellite would climb above the horizon and be in a clear line of sight in twenty-eight minutes. Lonely Soul, Dianis's moon, was rising, and the comm satellite hung in orbit above it. Casting about, he had to find a clear sight line through the damned trees. Holding the precious laser transmitter in his arms, *it's worth two hundred thousand credits,* he went downslope searching for an opening.

Finding a spot on a downed log, he set up the transmitter and connected it to his multi-func. On the holographic display, the moon climbed just coming over the horizon with the projected satellite position and tree blockage superimposed on the image. Rotating to where the laser could, according to the orbit solver, beam the comm satellite, the laser's *Ready to Upload, Seeking Target* light came on. The positioning motor on the transmitter oscillated, then the *Target Obstructed* indicator lit.

"Oh, oh." Flustered, Quorat paged through the displays on the multi-func. "Oh, oh. Damn! Damn!" He almost hurled the multi-func into the forest. The Avarian fleet was in the way. The starscape blackouts were directly between him and the emerging satellite. "No, no, no."

He slumped on the pine needles in the clearing. There was nothing else to do but wait until the relay satellite climbed clear of the fleet. The laser only needed a micron of clearance, but if he hit a ship, even with that tiny low-powered beam, the fleet would come instantly alive and know his exact position.

Squatting in front of the holograph display and munching on a synthetic carbo bar, he watched the gradual progress of the satellite. It was a virtual representation, of course, a calculation of where the satellite should be. Designed for stealth communications, the basket-size capsule could not be seen or detected.

At least one of the ships was in the way, one of the bigger ones. The tension gnawed at him. Would he get a clear shot? The image plotter was too imprecise to be definitive. Suddenly, the *Target Obstructed* text switched to *Target Acquired*. Without hesitation, Quorat hit the send button.

The micron-wide beam carrying two hundred thousand credits worth of data zipped between the two engine nacelles of the *Alexis,* crossed the armored decking of the missile destroyer *Richelous*, and hit the satellite array off-center by fifty-eight percent. With data redundancy and packet repair, fifty-eight percent was good enough.

Receiving the successful end-of-message transmit from the capsule, Quorat waited for the string of return packets indicating the progress of communicating with the relay antenna stationed at the edge of the solar system and then, ultimately, to the contract provider.

Unfortunately, operations on board the *Alexis* dictated an attitude change when the shuttle airlock was opened. The comm satellite's clear view back to Quorat with the good news was blocked.

Chapter 7
Timber Hall

Wedgewood

The matriarch awoke to the sound of steel clashing against steel. It was an unmistakable: swords against swords. Yet there was no alarm. Her escort had not come to shift her back to the ship. The battle drones, cape-covered lethality, sat quietly in their corners, the recon and defense bots hung undisturbed on the ceiling, and the *Alexis* soared aloft, mute. The clashing of the weapons came from outside the window. It had a repeated, rhythmic pattern followed by muffled grunts. Dawn, filtered by the Ungerngerists, suffused the room in a peaceful radiance. She lifted the covers and eased out of bed. Tip-toeing to the window, a floorboard creaked.

"Andy?" Margret sought with her hand underneath the covers and then opened her eyes. The matriarch, still naked, was attempting to look out the window without being seen. "Andy?" Margret asked again, this time propping herself up on an elbow.

"Shsss," the matriarch whispered, "go back to sleep."

Margret looked uncertain, so the matriarch left the window, pressed the palm lock on her in-country bag, and dragged it back to the bed. "I'm going to go for a walk. No need for you to bother. Get some sleep. You need to attend the Auro Na trials. It will not be easy."

The counselor watched the matriarch, sitting on the bed, pull on her synth-tec body armor. It looked like thick silk, but it could stop bullets, blades, and resist -- for a brief period – medium-strength lasers. The armor fit her like a second skin. Over that, she slipped on her energy-displacing plasma deflector vest but left the front open. Around her upper arms, she clipped plasma deflector bands designed to look like Auro Na signets of high office. She reached into her bag and made to pull on the larger deflector bands that went around each leg. Conscious that Margret watched, the matriarch pivoted and brought a long leg up on the bed. She held out the thigh band. "Want to put it on for me?"

Margret offered a grudging smile. Grasping the band, she reached along the matriarch's long, synth-covered leg. Lifting the matriarch's knee up to her shoulder and holding it there, Margret reached to where she could feel the warmth of the matriarch's bottom. Managing the clasp, she clipped the band around the matriarch's upper thigh.

After a moment, the two women looking at each other, the matriarch said, "You didn't have to strap it on so high." It was more of a tease than a rebuke.

"Sorry." Margret reached back and slowly pulled it down to mid-thigh.

They repeated the process with the other leg, and the matriarch rolled over onto her belly. She was staring out the window, listening to the clash of swords.

Margret laid her head back on her pillow. The matriarch's perfectly manicured feet were at her face. Their trip to Dianis was well within ULUP guidelines and laws, but the matriarch's gear and protection services were not. Ivan had balked at bringing her in-country, not so much because of who the matriarch was, but because of how she looked. He'd specifically remarked, nay demanded, that the matriarch wear boots, not sandals, fearing the stir they'd cause if someone saw painted and manicured toenails. The Auro Na cloak and in-country tunic and trousers would cover the illegal—on a Class E world—body armor, but they'd filed for an exemption for the gear, which ULUP granted for the matriarch.

"Should we have invited Breia?"

Margret shifted her focus from the matriarch's feet to the question. "Invite him to what?"

"Bed."

"Hmph, no. He's such a stiff, and not in the right way."

The matriarch pulled her legs up, set them on the floor, and stood. "Good. It's hard for me to know, sometimes, who I should keep happy." She gave a secret smile to her envoy to Dianis. "How about Ivan?" It was another tease.

"You'd never make him happy. The man is impregnable."

"Good. We need him that way."

"I love you, Andy."

The matriarch's face turned thoughtful. They were conscious of each other, their minds wrapping together. Their thoughts twisted and revolved around each other in an invisible dance of pursuit, flight, and tease. Then, abruptly, the matriarch turned and walked to the window. "Thank you for that," she said, looking out the window. "It means much to me." Leaning back, she pulled on the window frame, trying to open it. It was an alien design, at least to her, some sort of clever hinge mechanism. Puzzling over it, she said, "Andromeda, scan and resolve, please."

Her AI, connected via the optic nerve implant, scanned the mechanism and responded with instructions.

The matriarch lifted and pulled the window up, and it dutifully tilted over her head, making a creaking noise. The sound of swordplay stopped.

She ducked below the frame and leaned out. Margret, from the bed, was appreciating the rearview.

The warriors in the courtyard, two stories below, were looking up at her. "Good morning, High Priestess. Fear tell, have we awakened her graciousness?"

Not caring if her synth-tec bodice and vest were odd-looking, she offered the oligarch a good view. She wore no bra under the synth-tec, and male and female warriors alike gave her their attention. There were twenty or so Oridian lancers and Timberkeep axmen in the courtyard, which had been commandeered as a practice ground for the oligarch's personal guard. They had been taking turns training against each other, and as happenstance would have it, the oligarch himself was at center ring facing a burly Timberkeep she recognized from injection learning. "Good morning, my lord," she paused, making eye contact with all, "and ladies and gentlemen, defenders of Wedgewood. The victorious and the humble. What an auspicious gathering. Please forgive my interruption."

Bowing low, the oligarch, with a flourish, indicated his combatant. "Yes, I struggle against none other than Ogden, master weaponsmith, warden of the Second—"

"Ula," Ogden interrupted him, "if you keep wasting your breath, I might actually be able to beat you." Ogden stood a hand shorter than the oligarch, but his barrel chest and corded muscles stretched his chain mail armor. He wielded a massive double-bladed war axe and had been sparring against the oligarch's cavalry saber, the practice version with a dulled blade. Ogden's long hair was bound behind, and his dense beard cropped short lest the forge fires singe it.

"Are there none of your vaunted Life Defenders? I've been so hoping to meet them," the matriarch asked with genuine respect.

"Noi," Ogden made to advance on the oligarch, "they were here but trained early. Now, if I can just—"

"Ha!" The oligarch laughed, struck at Ogden's upraised ax, and danced away. "Shall the High Priestess deign to come down and visit with us? Perhaps I can get a stroke or two at her mercenary captain."

Dogged, Ogden stalked the oligarch around the ring.

"Perhaps," she replied, leaning back and stretching her arms to work out a morning kink.

Ogden caught the oligarch's distraction and pounced.

"Ha," the oligarch laughed. "You are a dog, mastersmith." He blocked, dodged, deflected, and otherwise fled from a flurry of ax swings.

"The good weaponsmith may be a dog, but I think he is more of a wolf, my lord," the matriarch said. Testing her injection learning, "If the poets have it right, lore says it was his ward that counter-attacked the Drakans from those gates," and she pointed at the Hall Gate.

"Yes," the oligarch answered, staring with respect at his opponent. Then he shoved his blade tip into the dirt, signaling the match was over; he ceded it. Turning to the balcony window, "Will the High Priestess break her fast with me? I meet with Woodwern and Sedge, and it would be an honor to have you seated at our table."

The matriarch considered the offer. She tilted her head and leaned back out the window. "It will have to be abbreviated, I am afraid. We've had a change of plans and need to depart this morning, but I will visit with you nonetheless."

She watched the oligarch give a flourished bow, and she stepped back and closed the window.

Margret was still watching her. "Will I have to share you with him?" She teased.

The matriarch acted surprised and waggled her head in typical Avarian fashion. "Why Margret," she sauntered to the bed and leaned down to kiss her on the forehead and whispered, "That would be consorting with a provincial." Their noses were touching.

Margret replied, "And we know how you feel about that."

Chapter 8
Christina

Wedgewood

The two Ready Reaction troopers standing guard at the door made to intercept her before she could scoot past them. "I'm sorry, High Priestess," Sergeant Horalznick said, using her in-country title with no effort. "But orders are orders. You cannot walk about without an escort. Under any conditions."

She tested his aural veil; it was in place and tight. The man was a professional.

He sensed her probing him and gave her a tired but firm smirk.

Realizing she would lose the contest if she forced it, she relented. "Very well. How about you two? Have Ivan send replacements to guard the suite. The battle drones and flock of bots--," she looked about to ensure no one was listening.

"Don't worry, ma'am," said the other trooper, "the recon bots are running a continuous search; the nearest sentient is two doors down, asleep. Their door is closed."

She nodded, "Will protect Counselor Margret." She finished her proposition, "We can bring the bots. I just want to go for a stroll without attention or interference. Somehow, I think Wedgewood is a safe place. Have you seen all the soldiers walking about?!"

Horalznick nodded, not in a happy way.

The Ready Reaction chief came double-stepping up the stairs. The matriarch gave him a bemused grin. "It appears I've been found out."

He rolled his eyes at her.

To the matriarch, his irreverence was refreshing. "Your guard captain will have a fit. He's already demanding I swap my agents out for his troopers here at the Hall. They'd cause all sorts—"

"It's alright. Andromeda?" she called to her AI.

"Yes, Matriarch," came the voice in her ear.

"Remind the battle group admiral that Ivan and his teams are not to be interfered with. "Make sure he understands the standing directive is to be enforced. That includes Special Forces."

"Yes, Matriarch."

"Ready Reaction Chief Ivan Darinarishcan is in charge down here, and I will comply with his directives."

"Yes, Matriarch."

She smiled at Ivan. "Good enough?"

He sighed but kept his scowl. "The shuttles are scheduled to pick us up at an hour before noon, local. It's an hour's ride from the mill to the landing site; we've not much time."

"Surely you can delay the shuttles? I do so much want to...." A premonition, as yet ill-defined, was beckoning, not a vision, but a presence, an event, something... She needed to go into town.

"I understand, Madam, but we've been monitoring the conclave at Terrabac, and it appears the Auro Na hierarchy has accepted all the applicants they expect and plan to open the proceedings prior to measurements and testing at midnight. As it is, it will be quite a shock when we make an appearance; they may balk. They will certainly refuse us if we arrive after the opening proceedings." He let that sink in. "I believe the oligarch is right. The Neuland high priest will not be happy to see us," he sought the right words, "there will be a considerable stir, especially from his supporters."

"Very well, then I should take my walk now." Her gaze and voice were firm. "And Ivan, why the fuss with the shuttles? Margret hates assault landers. Can't we shift there?"

"We can, ma'am; a few of us will. I plan to send Horalznick and Breia ahead as Margret's heralds to warn the conclave of our pending attendance. It should help alleviate some surprise. But, as you should know," he reminded her politely, "the personnel field generators on the *Alexis* and *Spirit* are much smaller, tiny actually, compared to their ship field generators. Normally, we can shift an entire squad at one time using the personnel shift bays, but when you add in eenus..." he let it trail off as they started walking down the stairs. Careful to watch for eavesdroppers, "All said and done, it's faster and more secure to go in with assault landers rather than shift in two by two. Generator cycle time being what it is."

The town was coming alive. Carters rolled by, their wooden, ironbound wheels muffled by the pine needles on the road. Laborers climbed scaffolding, passing tools and lumber to carpenters. At a site nearby, they heaved shake shingles up onto a new roof; it looked to be a granary.

A full ward of forty Timberkeep warriors hustled past.

"They're going to their muster points," said Ivan, noting the axemen. He walked beside the matriarch. Horalznick had point, and the other trooper walked behind. Nanobots flitted and buzzed from loiter to loiter. Some were camouflaged as bees, others as moths and even finches. The larger bots were the multi-weapon defense bots.

"For?" The matriarch asked.

"The journey to Tivor. The wards are forming up as escorts. Almost half the town is moving."

"Is that sad?" she asked, watching a teenage girl lift a dropped hammer to a worker. When the hammer left the girl's hand and levitated up, the matriarch stopped and stared.

"Sad? No, I've talked with a number of Timbers. I think they are reconciled with it. They believe Tivor will be good for them."

"Anything else?" asked the girl of the workers on the newly framed roof.

"Noi. Thanks, Rachael."

The matriarch watched the girl, in her plain homespun dress, skip -- happily skip -- away down the street. "Amazing."

"What?" Ivan asked. "That she used telekinesis to lift that hammer?"

Then the matriarch's breath caught, and her eyes grew wide.

Ivan, seeing her shock, wheeled about making to draw his weapon.

Down the street, beyond various pedestrians, Rachael came to stand in front of a tall, blonde woman. She wore a leather vest over a simple white linen blouse, a sword belt with a long sword hugged her hips. Her form-fitting leather britches were tucked into knee-high boots made to fit armored greaves. At that distance, with the matriarch's enhanced vision, she could see the sword-woman bore a simple diadem about her neck in the shape of a white flower. Her high cheekbones were proud, and her face comfortably hosted a scar above her left eye and another on her left jaw. Neither scar detracted; rather, they accentuated her handsome looks. A group of townsfolk clustered about her, some visiting and then leaving. A young mother handed her a baby, but it wasn't the Amazon warrior that attracted the matriarch's attention; it was the woman next to her.

"What?" asked Ivan, tense. His hand on the handbolt's holster. The two other Ready Reaction troopers instantly on alert.

Calming, the matriarch breathed deep. "We can leave now. I've seen what I came for."

Puzzled, Ivan looked at the warrior holding the baby. Then he called to the *Alexis,* whom he knew was monitoring the situation. "I.D. those women, please." The answer came back promptly, and he asked the matriarch, "You don't think?"

Holding the baby to her bosom, the warrior made a sign of blessing and looked directly at the matriarch.

"Think what?" the matriarch asked.

"That Christina Tara, *al Suri* Ascalon Defender, is the woman Atch is having an affair with?"

Christina Tara, the blonde warrior, passed the baby back to its mother and put a hand on her hip, studying the three mercenaries and the Auro Na priestess. Both Rachael and the woman beside the warrior caught the focus of her attention. The woman with the warrior had lustrous black hair done up in a high bun. She had black eyes, olive skin, and cheekbones as proud as the warrior's. From there, they differed, however. Where the warrior was dressed simply, the other was outfitted as a merchant princess, a Tivorian by the cut of her black riding boots, green velvet sea cape, and expensive cutlass at her waist.

The three women, each distinctive in their own hardened, elegant, and commanding ways, stared at each other.

"Auro Na," said Marisa, the woman in the sea cape, to Christina.

"Rachael," said Christina.

"Yes, Alon," answered the girl.

"Fetch Alex, will you."

"Okay," Rachael said with hesitation.

The Alon turned to Marisa and looked at her closely, studying her face as if she'd never seen her before. "You should go. Now."

Marisa's black eyes knitted into a looming glare.

"Please," Christina said forcefully. "The Achelous and the others are waiting for you. I need to speak with this Auro Na without you to distract her."

Ivan watched the woman in the green sea cape walk away. At first, he was certain it was the Ascalon Life Defender that had been the object of the matriarch's attention, for Christina was the arch-Defender of all Mother Dianis paladins. He knew this because Christina had an IDB dossier, current as of the IDB Dianis shut down. The Ready Reaction duty sergeant at Central Station read off the highlights of her file to him. "No mention of Wedgewood?" he asked the sergeant.

"No, chief, that happened after shut down."

Ivan acknowledged the input. The only reason he knew of Christina's heroics during the Battle for Wedgewood was Sedge told him last night while drinking rakia in the loft of the command treefort.

"Read the file on the other woman, "Ivan asked of the duty sergeant.

"Boss –" Horalznick was backing up, his hand on his handbolt.

"Don't," commanded the matriarch. "Do not signal an alert. I will handle this."

The Ascalon was striding purposefully toward them; she bore an intense expression. The three Ready Reaction troopers knew trouble when they saw it. The busy street gradually grew still as the Timberkeeps paused to watch their patron on a mission.

Before something could go awry, the matriarch seized Horalznick by the shoulder and pulled him back. She stepped forward.

Christina slowed her pace and came to stand a spear-length in front of them. The Ascalon put her hands on her hips, her feet set. A group of Oridian lancers, off parade, paused with the other passersby. Nanobots went into auto-alert, lifting off from their laggers. The comm channels of all three Ready Reaction troopers were buzzing with demands for a situation report. Back at Timber Hall, the other seven Ready Reaction troopers were running out the door. The plasma and laser cannons in the Avarian battle group cycled up. The field gen operator onboard the *Alexis* had his finger on the actuate button. Programmed to the micro-frame of the matriarch's body, the generator was set to extract her. The scene had activated an auto alarm at Matrincy headquarters on Avaria, where counselors now watched.

Alex came through the growing crowd. They parted when they saw the white lily on a field of green with a sky of blue painted on his shield. "Oi, visitors," he said cheerfully enough but looked askance at Christina. Rachael followed in his wake, as did someone else who said loudly, "Ula, clear me a path, or I'll fart in your face."

The matriarch smiled at the growled command.

Rachael, as impertinent as ever, squirmed her way to the fore. She raised her hand, and three lead pellets –

81

muzzleloader bullets – lifted from her palm and began to spin in a lazy circle.

"Oh," fourteen thousand light-years away on Avaria, a Matrincy counselor exclaimed, "she's a master!?" The teenage girl, by levitating three objects simultaneously and performing a continuous synchronous movement, had demonstrated she could pass a master's competency test in telekinesis.

"Is she higher?" asked another counselor. "A master in kinetics is nasty in a melee."

"Very nice," said the matriarch. "You are to be congratulated on your skill." She inclined her head at the girl.

Seeing a telekinesis master so close to the matriarch, the field generator operator almost energized the shift. However, the captain of the *Alexis* had just made it to the shift bay. He carefully moved the operator's hand away from the hologrid and placed his own finger squarely on the actuate button. He was pressing down, but not quite enough...

"Why are you here?" asked Christina. It was not a challenge, but neither was it a welcome.

Ogden finally got through the crowd. "Oi, I had to fart more than once." There was laughter, except for the Defenders and Ready Reaction.

Sensing a tense situation, he said, "Hmm, ah—"

"If you will, master weaponsmith—" the matriarch said at the same time as Margret, monitoring the situation from the Hall, said into the matriarch's ear, "It doesn't say in the Ascalon's IDB file, but she knew you were focused on the woman beside her. Somehow, the Ascalon has a clue as to your intent, which even I don't. So be careful. Whatever sixthsense skill she has, it's good. Probably a pathic, could be a voyant, maybe a medium?"

Continuing to speak, the matriarch said, "Please let me introduce myself. I am Andrianola, High Priestess of the Seahorse Isles Auro Na, and let me say that I am both honored and humbled to meet—" she bowed, "the Alon."

Unmoved, Christina asked, "And your reason for being here?"

Letting the question hang. The matriarch let her pathic sense settle over the crowd, tasting, flirting, drifting, and taking in their emotions, sensations, and aspirations. She watched the three muzzleloader bullets spin above the girl's hand, whose expression had grown thoughtful. The matriarch idly wondered when the master kinetic would tire. Finally, she said, "Peace." She held her hands out, palms up, and let her consciousness soar up and away, past the boughs of the Ungerngerists, above their crowns ever spiraling higher.

The word had been simply said, but to the average Timberkeep, it meant peace with the Paleowrights. To the warders, it meant peace with the Troglodytes. To the Oridians, it meant peace with the Drakans. To Margret, it meant peace after a long, terrible war with the Turboii. To Ivan, it meant there would be no fight this morning.

Rachael let the lead bullets drop to her palm.

Christina cocked her head. Waiting, for she somehow knew the matriarch was elsewhere. When the matriarch's arms lowered, Christina asked, "And what does peace mean to you?"

Disconcerted, the matriarch expected a challenge, a counterpoint arguing the amorphism of peace, but instead, she was asked what it meant to her. The matriarch's wandering aspect snapped back to Christina. It was a new question, one she had never confronted. Calm settled over the crowd while the high priestess pondered the question.

"Silence," was her reply.

The answer surprised Margret. It was an admission she never expected to hear. Ivan suspected he knew the meaning. The crowd certainly did not, but Christina did. She inclined her head a touch. "They are a burden?"

"Ceaseless."

"Then why are you here? You're not seeking more voices?"

The matriarch gave a slow smile. "No. No, I am not." She looked at the crowd, the stolid people, the Ungerngerists, the devastation, and the smell and sound of the pine boughs when the mountain winds cleared away the char stench. Her memory of this place would last forever. "I'm here to *see* two people: one, I have, but don't know her name; the other, I have not but know his name: Achelous the Trader."

Christina's eye twitched.

Shocked the matriarch told the truth, Ivan waited for the reaction.

"I've never trusted your motives," Christina said. "The Auro *Na* are not known for their selfless service."

The way Christina said *Na* made Ivan wonder if she doubted the charade.

"Those that are dull to sixthsense are invisible to you," Christina went on. "Yet here you stand in Wedgewood. These are my people. Mother is All. We do not worship the ether. It is but a tool to us." She gently grasped Rachael's hand and raised it up.

Rachael smiled brightly at Alon's touch.

"A powerful tool it is nonetheless," the matriarch noted.

Margrett, viewing the conversation via holograph, was discomfited. Christina had not asked why the matriarch wanted to see Achelous or what the black-haired woman meant to her, but telling the truth mollified her concerns. She doubted it was that simple.

"Perhaps we should continue our conversation where we are not such a distraction?" the matriarch offered. "I've been invited to the oligarch's table. Would you join me? I'm sure the lord would not mind if I brought a guest." She smiled at the jest. Next to the oligarch and clan chairman, Christina was the most noteworthy person in the town.

The Alon, a subtle smile of her own echoed in response. She inclined her head. "I will take you there."

As they were walking side by side, and the bulk of the crowd thinning behind them, the matriarch asked, "And your friend," looking to where Marisa had gone, then she

84

peered down, contemplating her words. "May I ask who she is?"

The captain of the *Alexis* kept his finger poised over the shift command.

Both women knew to whom the matriarch referred.

"And your interest is?" answered Christina.

"I believe we have a mutual acquaintance."

"And this is important to a high priestess of the Auro Na?"

The matriarch took a deep breath. Her proven intuition told her the arch Defender was above reproach. "Yes."

They walked a few more paces, and then Christina said, "Then I would understand why."

The matriarch slowly nodded, in rhythm with their steps. "I should, too. The more I experience of..." she wanted to say *this world,* "Wedgewood, the more I learn. The quest here, Alon, has just begun."

Chapter 9
Exodus

Wedgewood

Four full wards mustered in their uneven ranks outside the Hall Gate. Never sticklers for military decorum, the doughty, part-time warriors spent their precious drill time in the shield wall, planning woodland ambushes or practicing eenu charges, not on parade-ground maneuvers. They waited in some semblance of order as their charges mounted the wagons. Seven hundred Timberkeep settlers had volunteered to migrate to Tivor. Of the seven hundred, a quarter had symptoms of the Timber's Curse. The other half, like Ogden, had lost their homes, farms, and businesses in the battle for Wedgwood. The four wards were all Sedge could spare as guards for the colonists bound for the Ungerngerists of Mount Epratis.

Achelous swung up in his saddle and waved at Sedge, who leaned on the railing of Woodwern's balcony at Timber Hall. Outish waited with the security contingent from the Silver Cup for the party to move out. Baryy and Marisa were still absent; Baryy had gone in search of her.

Ogden came trotting up on his eenu. "Bit of a bother getting out of town just now. The Alon met the Auro Na high priestess, and I didna think things would end well."

Achelous surveyed the growing crowd looking for Baryy, then turned his attention to Ogden. "Is this the first time the Auro Na have come to Wedgewood?"

"Oi, and an odd lot they are. They don't believe in Mother." Ogden looked to where he knew Achelous kept his Auro Na bible in the vest pocket of his jacket.

The former IDB chief inspector picked up on the cue. "No, they don't." He and Ogden, his business partner, had many a forge-side conversation, one of them being what Achelous believed in, which was a tricky conversation for an incognito galactic on a Class E world. Achelous' grey eyes met those of his friend. The two men were stark contrasts: Ogden's hair and beard were long; Achelous kept his hair short and did shave, just not as much as Marisa wanted. Achelous was lean, driven, and analytical, whereas Ogden was jovial, calm, and accepting. The two men had come together with a shared vision that bound them tighter than any chain.

"It *is* strange the Auro Na would come here," said Achelous. "And I'm not surprised there would be a clash between an Auro Na high priestess and the Alon. The Auro Na look down on Timberkeep adepts. And they've come here to Wedgewood?" He shook his head. "What were they thinking? They'd get a welcoming party?"

"Oi," Ogden snorted. "I don't think it was real trouble, more a clash of wills. You know the Alon, made of steel, that one. And that high priestess...have you seen her?"

Achelous shook his head.

"A real looker, but no mountain orchid, that one." Mount Mars orchids were notoriously delicate.

Achelous frowned. "I've not seen her." When he and Baryy had heard that a high priestess of the Auro Na from the Seahorse Isles had come all the way to Wedgewood, they had searched the IDB Dianis database of provincials and came up empty. Which was both puzzling and disconcerting. How could they, in their past roles in IDB civilization monitoring, have missed psycho-graphing someone of such importance? Unless the high priestess was new to her post, very new, or she was an imposter. "Outish heard she had two other priests with her and a whole company of mercs?"

"Well, not a whole company, but Lettern counted thirty-eight. The priests disrupted our pathics by putting up that Black Veil thing, which disturbed our voyants and flustered Brookern and his cadre."

Achelous refrained from comment; something didn't sound right. Auro Na priests seldom ventured from their protected enclaves, preferring instead to have the citizenry visit them. Moreover, paying for a half-company of mercs as guards was expensive. He thought the Auro Na used their own liveried men-at-arms, not mercenaries. Then, there was the issue of launching a Black Veil to protect their aural entities. The use of a Black Veil was an aggressive sixthsense tactic bound to offend any local pathic. It was almost as if the priests had something to hide.

"Maybe they thought they'd be welcomed because that friend of yours is their captain."

"Friend?" Achelous's spider sense came wide awake.

"Ula, you didn't not know? I thought he'd come looking for you."

"Who?" Achelous didn't mean for his voice to carry.

Ogden blinked, "You know, that merc we met at Battle Park. You said he worked for you. Ivan."

Ogden saw Achelous go pale; his hands slumped on the saddle pommel. "What?"

Marisa came trotting up on her eenu. "Sorry, I'm late. I was saying farewells to the Alon when that Auro Na priestess came strolling down the street with her merc guards." Marisa bit back her words.

Wondering what he'd said to bother Achelous, Ogden responded, "The Alon will set her straight."

"When the Alon saw the priestess, she told me to leave. She didn't want me there." Marisa bore an expression that was at once irritated and confused. "At first, I thought the Alon was being rude, but when I saw her approach the Auro Na, I was thinking there would be trouble."

Achelous's shock turned to alarm. If Ivan was back on Dianis and had come to Wedgewood at the head of a force of mercs, probably Ready Reaction, who were the Auro Na priests that the Alon was encountering?

A cantering rider came through the growing throng mustering to leave for Tivor. It was Baryy, and with dread, Achelous could tell by Baryy's face something was amiss.

He rode right up to Achelous, ignoring everyone else, and said, "Atch, friend, we need to leave, now." He stood in his stirrups and searched for Outish.

Achelous wrestled himself out of his funk. Baryy had used the code word *friend,* an in-country IDB signal for *danger is near*. Ogden and Marisa exchanged bewildered glances.

"Outy!" Baryy waved to him. He circled his arm in the air for the signal to move out and indicated the direction. "We're leaving."

Baryy gave spurs to his mount and said, "Now."

Achelous waved at Ogden. "Og! We have to go, but we'll see you in Tivor just as we planned."

Seeking to soften Marisa's growing consternation, Achelous used his pet name for her as he called over his shoulder, "Lace, Baryy's in a hurry!" Then he put heels to his mount.

She hissed an unheard word, then said to Ogden, "First the Alon and now him." She aimed her mount at the passage cleared by Baryy and Achelous and gave it a hard kick. Startled, the steed leapt to a canter and made after the two men.

"Ula! What's up with them?" Outish asked Ogden as he trotted past.

Ogden just shook his head, mystified. Having no alternative, Outish forced his eenu, Tulip, to a canter, but seeing Marisa now low in the saddle throwing clods of pine needles, he gave the wise, old cow free reign and yelled, "Ha! Go!"

Looking low under his arm, Baryy saw Achelous pounding to catch up, and behind him came Marisa galloping even harder, her cape catching the wind. He hoped Outish had taken the clue. Baryy began spurring his mount.

Watching Achelous accelerate to keep pace with Baryy, Marisa hung low over the eenu's neck and let it dig, its herd instinct driving it. Something was very wrong, that was clear. Baryy was never one to be abrupt or rude, except, perhaps, when he teased Outish.

Rabbits darted out of Baryy's path. The pine needles on the road gave way to gravel as he galloped around a mountain spur. A carter and his wagon pulled to a halt to let the riders race past. Baryy saw a likely side trail and slowed the steed. Waiting to make sure Achelous saw him, he diverted up the narrow track and into an isolated dell.

Achelous came up the track, his eenu huffing and snorting. Then Marisa joined them. "Well?" Achelous asked.

Baryy refused to talk until Outish finally followed Marisa up the trail. Baryy had his multi-func out in passive aural scanning mode. "Atch, the matriarch is here. She's actually here in Wedgewood."

When Achelous failed to respond, Marisa and Outish burst out. Marisa asked, "Who is the matriarch?" And Outish guffawed, "Whaaaaat? Nooo way!"

Achelous blinked, his mind trying to comprehend the absurd notion.

Baryy, seeing his chief's consternation, implored, "She is, Atch, believe me. She's with Ivan, Horalznick, and Sendrant."

At the further evidence, Achelous' eyes grew wide, and he began shaking his head.

"Whaaaat? Nooo way! No way!" persisted Outish.

"Who is the matriarch?" Marisa asked, pulling aside a long, errant lock, her tone rising.

Achelous began to grimace. This was the worst news. *What is* she *doing here?* he asked himself over and over in a recursive loop.

"I'm serious, Atch. When I went to find Marisa, I almost bumped into Sendrant. I was walking around looking for Marisa, and I turned the corner at the Din Din, and there was Sendrant and the others. They had just walked past. I had to duck behind a carriage. He was holding the tail position of a bodyguard. I almost choked. Then I saw the back of the two other troopers. I could tell one was Ivan, and that's when I knew we were in the shits. Ivan doesn't travel light. They appeared to be guarding what I thought was one of the Auro Na priests, one of the women. When I got closer, they stopped. The woman was facing away from me, having some sort of encounter with the Alon. A crowd was gathering. The priest's hair was blonde, pure white, which threw me at first. I had to get a look, even shaking as I was. You know, who would *Ivan* be the bodyguard for? Hell Atch, he doesn't pull escort duty. He's Chief of Ready Reaction!"

Achelous began to nod; it was making sense.

"No way, no way!"

"Shush   Outish!   Shush." Marisa   gave   the astrobiologist her best impatient mother's glare, and he backed off. "Who is the matriarch?" she asked him.

"The leader of free Human space!" Outish exclaimed. "She is the grand sensitive of the Matrincy. They are sort of like the Auro Na in the federation, except bigger and waaaay more powerful. The Congress is in charge of the federation, but the Matrincy does so many things the Congress can't run the federation without it. What the matriarch says goes. What she wants, she gets. She is the biggest deal there is!"

Turning to Achelous for confirmation, Marisa saw it in his eyes.

Outish's explanation was close enough to the truth that Achelous wasn't going to quibble.

Then Marisa asked Baryy, a chill running down her spine, "Blonde hair? Dark eyes, pale skin, and is Lettern's age?"

Baryy nodded, thinking the matriarch and Marisa had the same eyes.

Achelous finally found his tongue, "She is over seventy years standard; don't let her looks fool you. Why, you saw her?"

"I saw her. She saw me. That's when the Alon told me to leave, to come to you. She wanted to talk to the Auro Na alone."

"Well, she wasn't alone," said Baryy. "Alex, Ogden, half a troop of Oridian Lancers, and even Rachael were there with her. You can imagine how sick I felt when I got a side view of the person that Ivan was protecting. The matriarch was not alone either. You can bet that troop of mercs she's with are Avarian Special Forces. Spirits Atch, if there is trouble, Special Forces will flatten Wedgewood."

Achelous shook his head. "If we had run a passive scan for energy sources, we would have gotten neutrino signals from all the bots and drones they probably deployed." His shock was wearing off, or perhaps he was just getting better at dealing with it. "It would explain the thirty-eight mercs they have escorting them."

Baryy blinked, but Outish put words to it sooner, "Smokes Atch, thirty-eight Ready Reaction! We're doomed! They're on to us! How can we run from all of them?"

The former chief inspector almost laughed and would have if the situation weren't so dire. "Outy, they don't send the matriarch looking for a couple of IDB agents on sabbatical. If they were on to us they would already have arrested us. No. She came here for something else. The escort is the price of coming to a Class E." He looked up at the sky. There were too many trees and branches in the way, but he could see it in his mind's eye. "The Avarian fleet is up there, Baryy. I don't know how many ships, but there are more than a few. Fleet would not let her come down without a substantial force in the solar system."

"What is she doing here?" asked Marisa, her frustration cooling, fascinated by the uninhibited conversation between the three. They were exposing more of their world to her in these few heated moments than she had dared hoped for.

He lowered his gaze. "The same thing Counselor Margret and Breia wanted."

Baryy swallowed. "The aquamarine. If she's here, something must have happened in the war or with the aquamarine market."

Achelous cocked his head, "Perhaps. Yes, perhaps the aquamarine too."

"You don't think—"

"The sensitives!" exclaimed Outish. "They're after the sensitives! They're after my discovery!"

Marisa expected Achelous to contradict the young apprentice; she referred to him as such because it was easier to see him as a trader's apprentice rather than an astrobiologist intern, which she was still struggled with. But Achelous let Outish's assertion go unchallenged.

Baryy took a deep breath. "It almost doesn't matter what they are after: Aquamarine-5, the sensitives, or us. We need to get away from Wedgewood. Too many of those troopers know us by sight. If they suspect we are here, they will have 'bots flying all over doing facial recognition scans."

"Atch, what about the aural scanning you told me about?" Marisa asked. "You said they can do it from the ships."

"I've been thinking about that." Achelous pulled his aural signet out from underneath his shirt. The simple aquamarine gem hung on a chain. "Outish, Baryy, and I are protected. Our signets emanate auras of provincials unknown to the IDB. But we have a different problem. If Ivan or the Matrincy learn about Marisa, they could search the IDB database for her. Her aural signature is on file. Gail used it to run searches for me." He hadn't told Marisa about Gail Manner, the former head of Dianis Solar Surveillance, or why he would ask for monitoring of Marisa. "If they find her, they find us. And we are out of signets for Marisa to use."

"We can't make more?" asked Outish.

Baryy shook his head. "They are expensive. Implanting a fake person's aura on an aquamarine-5 nugget is not a simple thing. The cost in aquamarine, by itself, is exorbitant."

Achelous added, "Real soon, they'll figure out scanning for our real signatures is fruitless. The signets we wear are from Field Outfitting. They are part of inventory." He said to Marisa, "We wear them in case extrasolars scan for IDB agents or provincial adepts try to read our auras."

Baryy snorted, "It didn't help with Cordelia Greenleaf. She saw right through it."

Achelous shook his head, "No, she saw me through her voyant vision, not by reading my aura. We need to dump these signets."

"Then what do we do?" asked Outish.

"If it's a matter of aquamarine," said Marisa, "why is that a problem? We have lots of it. We can go back and ask Woodwern to give us some."

"You're right." Achelous struggled with the notion of pilfering provincial resources, which was ludicrous. "I could ask Og to send a runner to the mine foreman and get us some from the diggings." The idea so simple he wanted to laugh.

Baryy voiced another concern, "Okay, so we can get the aquamarine," he smirked at the irony of that, "we still don't have the gear at the repair bay to imbue the aqua with someone else's aura."

Marisa looked to Achelous for the answer, and he said, "What we can do is create aural dampeners. Yes, I know they're not as good as signets, but we're no longer trying to fake our identities to extrasolars and provincials. We're hiding from the Matrincy. That means we construct the dampeners, our own Black Veils, so when they do an aural scan they get no read, nothing."

"What's wrong with that?" she asked.

"If they do both an aural scan and an infrared scan and overlay them, they'll get a signature on one and not the other. An AI will detect the anomaly. It will read the infrared image, determine it is a Human with no aura, and flag the Human as anomalous. Anomalous Humans are not supposed to exist."

"Unless you cool the infrared emissions of the body," said Outish.

"But what is the likelihood of them doing that?" asked Baryy. We never asked for it." He referred to IDB standard surveillance tactics when searching for in-country extrasolars.

Achelous nodded. "Yes, too many ways to thwart an infrared scan."

"What do we do?" Outish asked, and Marisa thought the young intern, a Halorite who'd undergone gene therapy to change his skin to look Human so he could do in-country fieldwork, his life's dream, was close to panicking. It was ironic he feared being arrested for being in-country, yet he stood in the shield wall, fighting nearly to his death against the Paleowrights without apparent complaint. That he could battle bravely against the one foe but so dread the other confounded her.

"Okay," said Achelous, "We follow the original plan, but with changes." He looked at each of them in turn. "We'll meet Ogden in Tivor to help plan the new foundry, though he is probably wondering why we left in such haste. There's nothing for that. He'll just have to wonder. From here, we detour back to Wedgewood and seek a private audience with the chairman. Marisa is right. It's time to ask a small boon of Woodwern.

"Then we go to Isumfast, but with the Avarian fleet up there, we don't dare run a field generator. They'll detect the energy pulse as a field shift. So we'll have to travel overland, and that will take time. In the meanwhile, I can ask Jeremy to scan the Fednet for news of the matriarch on Dianis. He may not find anything if it is a secret mission. We can't ask him to open any classified sources." He let them ruminate on that while he thought about other problems. "When we get to the repair bay, Outish, we can start regeneration on your hand. Sorry about the delay."

Outish's look of disappointment spoke for him. Ever since the flames and smoke-choking fight at the granary, where a Scarlet Savior had cleaved away half his hand, Outish lived with the dull throb and phantom pain made bearable by a neural clamp. He kept the hand carefully wrapped in bandages to hide the dampener. They had a FiPWiS, a Field Portable Wound Stabilizer, stashed in Baryy's cabin, but a FiPWis was less capable than a full autodoc. The nearest autodoc capable of tissue regeneration was at their destination: the old ITA repair bay near the town of Isumfast, a hundred and sixty miles away. Using a shift zone, minus the ride to it, they could be to Isumfast instantaneously. Now, with the fleet overhead, they faced six days of hard riding.

"Baryy, did you log your Wedgewood cabin into the IDB facilities manifest?" Achelous was worried about their gear and equipment should Ivan find the cabin.

"No. Was I supposed to?" he answered a bit defensively. "I'm just letting it."

The chief inspector laughed the first time that day, he felt better for it. "No. As long as all the devices are powered down, Ivan may not find it."

Marisa watched Outish fidget with his bandage. "Does it hurt?"

"It throbs, mostly. Keeps me awake at night. The dampener helps, but I don't turn it all the way up. It makes my arm feel like lead, and it's useless. They're not supposed to be worn for weeks on end."

"You're very brave, Outish," Marisa watched him. "Ogden said so."

He began to turn red. "Do you think so?"

"Yes, Outish, I do too."

Achelous sighed at the circumstances that forced him to prolong Outish's pain. "We'll get you fixed up. Then, when her Matrincy has left, and she can't stay here forever, we'll shift down to Tivor and meet up with Ogden."

Manipulating the passive sensor grid on his multi-func, Baryy said, "Let's hope she takes Ivan with her." He completed the alert notification setting for neutrino emissions. "Atch, maybe they're reopening Margel IDB. Maybe they need us to help?"

Achelous' troubled grey eyes and set of his thin lips gave clues he was thinking the same thing.

Marisa waited for his answer. He'd not shaved in days, but he kept his hair trimmed short. He had what she considered a handsome face, but right now, that countenance was clouded.

She thought back to when Achelous and Jeremy, their AI, discussed mysterious things like message alerts, IDB accounts, and access log entries. "Wouldn't Jeremy know if the IDB were trying to contact you?"

Baryy turned to peer at her, impressed.

"What?" she asked, "can't it work that way?"

"Yes, it can and normally does," answered Achelous. "The problem is IDB A-wave messaging is routed through a secure transport protocol. You can't pick up a message without the sender knowing it has been retrieved and later viewed."

"All of our devices, multi-funcs, and embeds have their federation A-wave message channels turned off," said Baryy. "On purpose, so we can't be tracked by our message receipts. We can do direct comms between each other but don't dare touch the fed communication system."

Marisa shook her head. "So? What does that mean?"

"See! I told you." Outish complained, "How are we supposed to know if they are reopening the Margel if they can't contact us?"

"Our direct channels," Achelous answered.

Outish blinked. "Uh?"

"But that still doesn't work," Baryy frowned and looked away.

"Why?" asked Marisa.

"Because the only direct channels we trust are those of us three. We can't accept messages from our friends, even through private channels, because we don't know who is behind it. We have to ghost them."

"Oh. So you are cut off from everyone…"

Achelous broke his silence, "Whatever the matriarch is doing in Wedgewood is secret. There have been no postings on the Fednet of the matriarch's visit."

"It's only been a month since Lights Out," said Baryy. Lights Out was the term they used for the day formal IDB Margel operations ceased. "People will start wondering what we are doing. We have to risk it and ping some of our friends, my family. Use the back channels. Be non-committal about location info. "

Prodding his mount towards the trailhead, Achelous said, "You're probably right. Up to now, I'd given up on the IDB. I figured Dianis was abandoned, and we were in this fight alone. But if the matriarch herself is here, with Ivan, then something has definitely changed. Or has it?" he asked himself more than anyone else. "Since the IDB is not here, officially, then the Matrincy has no one to monitor their actions."

Baryy persisted, "But Ivan is here, Atch. I saw him. He's IDB."

Chapter 10
Plasma Alarm

Wedgewood and Terrabac fi Sur

Trudging through the underbrush, Quorat found a huge tree at the edge of town and slumped down between two massive root buttresses. Exhausted, he started to nod off. Last night he'd been too keyed up to sleep waiting for the acknowledgment signal from the relay satellite. It finally came early in the morning when the Avarian fleet changed orbit. Then, when he'd made it back to the sled and tried to bunk down beside a log, the passive aural scanner on his multi-func had kept him awake with all sorts of proximity alerts. None of them Human origin. By the time he'd gotten the sensor tuned to rule out extraneous life forms it was early afternoon.

"Aach," he grumped. Reaching into his pack, he pulled out the stim shots. *One or two,* he mused. *I'm dead tired.* A stim shot would perk him up, but they made him edgy. Already prone to paranoia, stim shots didn't help.

Unpeeling the canister seal, he rolled up the sleeve of his tunic and jabbed the shot into his forearm. Laying back against the tree he let the drug cocktail course through his arteries and cook his system. Immediately feeling better but not quite his old self, he checked the chronograph: thirty minutes to dark.

Night settled in like a comforting blanket.

Quorat made his way back to Wedgewood.

Leaning against one of the curious little huts with steep roofs, he compared them to an outhouse. *What in the spirits are they for?* He wondered. Feeling both confounded and wobbly, he popped the seal on the second stim shot. He pulled down the collar on his tunic and slapped the shot right into his neck. *Probably shouldn't have done that,* he thought, *but screw it, I need to get this done.*

Eyeing the course indicator on his multi-func, he followed it to a huge tent and loitered outside, his stim-driven senses in hyperdrive. There were noises everywhere. The point-specific target lay just within. Indigins came and went. He needed to get a videograph of the object and then an A-wave ping from it to qualify for his next bonus. The Avarian fleet had moved. Not enough for him to risk A-wave comms with the Intruder, but far enough to the north and west where he was no longer worried they were about to drop on his head. Arranging the remote sensor of his multi-func into a buttonhole of his coat, he kept the body of the device in his pocket so he could trigger it when the opportunity came. Steeling himself, he strode purposefully into the tent.

The first thing he noticed, aside from the acrid pipe smoke, oil lantern fumes, the smell of alcohol spirits, and the stench of unwashed indigins -- all very ungalatic --was the tent had gone silent. He looked around. The smoke stung his eyes.

"Oi, I thought you Nakish had had enough?"

There was a smattering of laughter.

Quorat sought to identify the speaker. There was a group of people standing by what looked to be a primitive bar. The point-specific target was in here somewhere. Acting nonchalant, as much as two stims would allow, he walked up to the bar and squinted at what he took to be a list of offerings. Unable to puzzle out the scrawl, he asked, "What you got?"

"Who says we're serving you?" replied the bartender.

"Huh?" he managed.

"You're Nakish, aren't you? We sent you and your lot packing with the Parrots."

Then another voice sounded from behind him, "What you looking for?"

He turned around, and a youngish woman stood there, brown hair, brown eyes, slim, with an arrow quiver on her back and a bow in her hand. She was flanked by two male indigins holding large double-bladed axes.

"You're here looking for something; we know that much. You don't look like you're Auro Na. The high priestess has already left."

He frowned. His head buzzed with a faint tingling sensation reminiscent of being probed by a pathic. It didn't matter; his aural blocking signet canceled his aura, and the counter emanator would kick in to ward off the mental intruder. What bothered him more was a distinct impression that these three had been tailing him. *For how long?*

A man came into the tent. Gaunt, his clothing hung on him like a scarecrow. He nodded his head at the woman archer and looked at Quorat. She turned back to Quorat, "Buy you a drink?" she said in an innocent manner. The other patrons slowly turned their gazes away and took up small talk but kept their ears pinned to the conversation.

"Uh, sure," he replied.

"Two Squirrel Shits," said Lettern, the on-duty branch warden.

Two porcelain cups came, and she handed one to Quorat. She nodded towards the corner of the tent where they could speak in more privacy. "We don't get many Nakish sensitives in town. Oi, you would be our first."

"What, no drinks for your friends?" Quorat asked, trying to fit in.

"Noi. They don't drink. I, on the other hand, guzzle like an eenu." She tilted her head to the corner.

He went along. Maybe she would show him the target. He'd snap his videograph, take the aural scan, and then scoot.

They walked past the end of the bar, and that's when he saw it. He stopped and dropped his cup; rather, it slipped right through his fingers. The axeman trolling behind bumped into him, but Quorat barely noticed.

Lettern turned. "That what you're looking for? Pretty, isn't it?" She slammed back her shot of spiced rakia and set the cup on a barrel.

He was fumbling with something in his pocket. The two Timberkeep warders, Bratchert and Mattar, backed up. "You got a knife in your pocket?" she asked.

Absently, Quorat shook his head, shooting the vid and triggering the aural ping.

"Oi, what are you doing?" Mattar, one of the warders, asked and grabbed Quorat by the shoulder.

Quorat wheeled around, done fidgeting in his pocket. The cloak covering his tunic pulled open with the grip of the warder. Lettern's eyes flashed to the holster at his hip; she, too, backed up.

Quorat looked down to see what grabbed her attention. "Oh, don't mind that. It's just my ticket out of here. But then I don't suppose you know what this is," and he pulled the plasma pistol from the holster and leveled it at her.

"Hey!" Came the sharp rebuke from Mattar, holding his other arm. He shoved Quorat and made to grab the object in his hand.

Too late. The corsair's stim-sharpened reflexes brought the weapon about, snapped the safety off, and pulled the trigger. A high-pitched whine followed an ionic crack that blasted a fist-sized hole in the Timberkeep's chest.

The plasma-pulse alarm went off on board the sensors frigate *Trilonair*. "What is it?" asked the officer of the deck."

"Weapons discharge planetside." The sensor officer scanned the readouts posted by the AI.

"Where?" The officer of the deck asked, hurrying to the sensor's hologrid.

"Dead center in Wedgewood, almost exactly where the matriarch was this morning."

"Any of our people there?"

"No, sir. I've initiated an active aural ping of the area. Wait. Sensor logs show a ground target initiated an aural ping just prior to the weapon discharge. It's right on top of the Item of Interest." The two men looked at each other. 'Item of Interest' was code for the top-secret artifact classified as such by the Matrincy.

"Shiren," cursed the officer. "Notify the flag. We'll be going to Alert Two. Suggest they dispatch a ready assault shuttle. Let them know—"

The plasma pulse-alarm blared again.

Lettern spun. Flaming heat scorched her side, and the whole right side of her body spasmed. She fell hard to the turf inside the tent.

Quorat, for good measure, searched for another target. The whine of the cycle charger stopped, and the *ready-to-discharge* indicator lit. He didn't need to see the green color; he knew by the sound the weapon was ready. Aiming at the barkeep, frozen in shock, he fired, and the man's head disappeared. *There, that should keep them!* He bolted out the tent.

Pausing in mid-argument, the matriarch composed her thoughts; they were being psychically probed, and she was managing the defense. The den of Auro Na zealots was a viper's nest of intrigue. Margret, as the acting high priestess, let Breia make his point that the Seahorse Isles, while not visibly attached to the continent of Isuelt by land, was, nonetheless, part of the continent. The conclave of deacons, Ghost-I from Neuland chief among them, was having none of it. Ivan was staring off into space, which annoyed the matriarch; he should be focused on the task at hand. Then she noticed his hand signal: circled fingers, he was receiving an incoming message via the recombinant embed chip in his thigh. Alerted, she noticed the supervisors in their defense team were flashing the same hand signal.

Countdown to incoming message, eight, seven, six, five... Ivan was highly annoyed. At least the fleet didn't just send the message directly to his audio and optical implants. It was a severe break in safety protocol to send a message to an in-country operative's implants. If they were distracted while galloping an eenu, debating a provincial, or even fighting an assailant, the results could be disastrous. Class E protocol dictated all messages to in-country operatives be read on multi-funcs except under extreme conditions.

Countdown, two, one--. He read the message through his optic nerve implant. "Shiren," he cursed. He immediately made eye contact with the Special Forces captain. They passed a silent agreement.

"Eh hem," he said to the matriarch, who'd turned her attention back to the heated debate. He didn't know how else to do what he was about to do, so he defaulted to his normal style, direct and blunt. "Excuse me, priestess, a word, please."

She waved her hand and made to brush him away like an annoying fly.

"My apologies, priestess, but we must talk in private. *Now.*"

Again, she tried to wave him away.

Exasperated, he glanced at the captain, who shrugged, seeming to say, *your problem. You're in charge.*

Ivan grabbed the matriarch under her arm and yanked her to him. She gave a very un-matriarch, "Ouuuuch!"

Not caring whose attention he attracted, he hauled her away, hustling toward a hallway.

"Ivan!" She made to slug him in the chest, but he caught her fist in his other hand.

The matriarch looked to her guard captain with imperious anger, "Captain!"

The captain gave her an apologetic shrug, which drove her indignity to a new height. She looked at Ivan, furious, "Whaaat are you doing! I need to help Marg—"

They reached the corridor. Ivan pulled her around a corner and literally spun the matriarch away lest his arm get caught in the pending field shift. If it did, he'd lose it.

Stumbling and then righting herself, she whipped around like a cat and leveled a gloved hand, palm up, at him.

He knew what was coming both from the matriarch and the *Alexis;* he only hoped the *Alexis* was faster.

About to unleash her fury in a telepathic blast, the matriarch's curiosity stayed her hand for an instant. *Why is he waving bye-bye?*

The whoosh of air in the hallway signaled that Margret and Breia were alone in their trial against Ghost-I and his supporters.

Lettern rolled on the ground, desperately gulping for air. Her bare arm touched the rent in her chainmail hauberk, and she screeched. Thrashing about, she threw the chainmail off. The heavy leather undervest was smoking. Catching her breath, the spasm had knocked the wind out of her; she shrugged out of the undervest. The tent was in an uproar.

A face appeared over her. "Ula, Lettern, you're hurt."

Lettern closed her eyes as the man tried peeling her thin blouse away from her skin. Her scream came uncontrolled.

Another voice intruded, a woman's. She said, "It looks like a burn. Her side here." Lettern could feel a gentle hand delicately lifting her blouse under her left arm, exposing her ribcage. "Ouch, look at this," said the other voice, "whatever hit her melted the links in her chainmail and charred the padded vest."

"Poor Bratchert took the full blast of whatever it was. I saw it!" Exclaimed another voice. "Went through him and hit her."

Laying on the ground, Lettern rolled her head to the side and opened her eyes only to recognize the lifeless face of Mattar lying beside her. Something probed her side, "Ah!" she wailed and made to get up, but a hand pushed her down. "No, you don't, sweetheart," said a woman's voice she now recognized, "we need to get a bandage on that before you be going anywhere."

Lettern reached up and grabbed the woman, Murali, "Where is he?"

"Who?"

"The Nakish!"

"He run off," answered a lad crouching beside Murali.

"Where?"

The lad shrugged.

"Is anyone going after him?"

The lad shook his head quickly, "No, you and Mattar and Bratchert are the only warders here."

"Get Alex and Pottern," she hissed to him. "Hurry. And tell Pottern to bring his dog."

"How many?" asked the matriarch.

"Two provincials dead, two wounded, one critical by their life readings."

"Anyone we know?"

The task force admiral flipped through the holograph display, "Yes."

"Shiren," cursed the matriarch. The aural signatures of the four provincial casualties were matched against the IDB database for Dianis. "I know her. Damn." Thinking of the stir this would cause in the town, "I met Lettern just yesterday. Get Ivan on the hologrid. We need to know what is going on down there."

While they waited for the *Alexis* to make contact with the Ready Reaction chief, the matriarch and admiral watched the dots on the holograph display that represented the aural signatures of the Humans in Wedgewood. The display was zoomed onto a section of the town to the west of Murali's tent. "Do we have visuals?" she asked.

He shook his head, "Too much cloud cover, and there are a lot of trees. In this display, we've overlaid radar imaging with the aural scan resonance."

"No drones or bots?" she queried.

"No, we pulled them when you went to Terrabac."

"Can you send another package?"

The admiral nodded. He called up the tactical operations center. "Tactical, deploy a recon package to the surface. Target the town of Wedgewood. Full sensor suite, drones, and bots."

"Aye, sir."

"We've got the Ready Reaction chief on the line, sir." The image of Ivan Darinarishcan appeared on the hologrid.

"My apologies, ma'am. I didn't mean to be so rough."

She gave him a smirk. "I'm going to have a bruise on my arm, chief."

"Sorry, ma'am."

She nodded. "You can make it up to me. I need you and your squad to get to Wedgewood right now. And I mean right now."

Ivan appeared to look off-camera. The Special Forces captain was in the background, hand-gesturing that it was okay to talk. "That's going to be a bit of a problem. We'd be shorthanded here, but more importantly, I think the counselors could use your help. Ghost-I is demanding some sort of skills test before admitting our delegation to the conclave. I think what he really wants is some sort of face-off. A competition where he can embarrass us and make it a lesson to the others."

The matriarch girded herself at the news and then informed Ivan of what had transpired in Wedgewood. Up till then, he'd been apprised there was an emergency, but for all he knew, it might have been a Turboii incursion somewhere in the galaxy. "Are they after the Item of Interest?"

The matriarch shared a glance with the admiral. "That's what I think, but the admiral is concerned they, whoever they are, may have been after me."

Ivan pursed his lips. "Possible."

"So I need you to get to Wedgewood immediately." She turned to the admiral, "And admiral, I need to get shifted back down to Terrabac."

"I'm sorry, your Matrincy, but I can't do that," answered the admiral

Taken aback, she asked, "Why?"

"There are two dead, two wounded from plasma weapons fire. I cannot put you back on that planet, in harm's way, until we have neutralized the threat.

Remember, Fleet, IDB, and Special Forces all thought letting you go planet-side was high risk."

"And if I order you?"

The admiral gave the matriarch a grimace. "I'm sorry, Madam Matriarch, but Fleet does not report to the Matrincy. You know that. We are beholden to the Federation Senate. If you can get the Fleet Admiral to override me, fine, but otherwise, I would refuse your order. You are more important to the federation than you give credit for, and I will not accept the increased risk of losing you."

She stood there staring the admiral down. Finally, she relented. Turning back to the holograph, she saw Ivan was running, his squad behind him. "Ivan, you've made arrangements to get to Wedgewood?"

"Yes, ma'am. *Alexis* will shift me and one of my troopers directly into a secure area in the town, and *Spirit's Fury* will shift in the rest of the squad with our eenus and gear."

"Then hurry. If I'm to help Margret and Breia, you need to unravel what is happening in Wedgewood."

"Is there another counselor that we can shift into Terrabac in your place?" asked the admiral.

The matriarch peered blankly at the holograph. "Perhaps, but maybe I have another idea."

Noodles yapped and scampered through the undergrowth.

"Pots, don't let her get too far ahead. That bastard may kill her."

Pottern, Lettern's younger brother, said to Mitchern, their telepath: "Call her back!"

"I'm trying," Mitchern said as they ran past a massive Ungerngerist, "but she's a tree dog, you know that! They mind like chipmunks."

"Call to her Pots. She'll mind you." Lettern was loath to make yet more noise, but their foe was probably wise to them. In an odd twist, Pottern's dog was telepathic, but Pottern was not. Whereas Mitchern, the Third Ward's pathic, had a dog that was as dumb to sixthsense as a leaf blowing in the wind. So Mitchern was recruited into the search party to catch the images that Noodles emanated as it scampered through the forest, tracking their prey.

They caught up with Noodles, a compact white and black spotted treedog, as it circled a patch of undergrowth, then stuck its nose in the air, sniffing. Thankful of the reprieve, Lettern held her side and then immediately regretted it. The bandages were soaking through with pus; her ribs flamed with pain.

Alex narrowed his gaze at her, but her own glare kept him silent. They'd had a fierce argument as to who would lead the search party, her, Alex, or Sedge, but then Lettern had settled it by taking off with Pottern and Mitchern and not waiting for Sedge to assemble the wards.

"If there's fighting to do, you let me handle it," Alex had said to her on the way. "You and Mitchern can pin him with arrows, and I'll go in close." Mitchern was just a teenager, but he'd seen hard fighting at the Battle of Wedgewood.

Lettern, catching her breath as the pain in her side eased, peered at the Defender's shield, painted with the white lily of Mother Dianis. "That won't stop what that bastard is carrying; it went right through—" her breath caught, and tears started to well.

Alex politely ignored her emotion. "Don't worry; I won't make myself a target."

Noodles had climbed a tree and hung on the side of it, its retractable claws latching onto the bark. Its ears were up, gaze steady, and nose twitching. The dog's long, thin tail stood rigid in pointer mode.

Mitchern nodded. "Noodles has the man's scent."

"Ready?" Alex asked Lettern.

She nodded, breathed deep, and the party took off running.

Ivan walked into Murali's tent. Surveying the scene, he kept a tight rein on his expression, but his thoughts were hot. *This is the disaster that corsairs wreak. And they've only killed two. How could we let this happen?*

"Oi, I thought you were off with your priestess," Sedge said, standing amidst the turmoil.

"Need some help?" Ivan asked without preamble.

Sedge gave a quick disgusted shake. "I've got two dead, one about to die, Lettern wounded, and who knows what is lurking out there."

Not looking at the warlord, Ivan said, "Show me the victims."

Sedge stopped, paused, and regarded the merc captain. They traded subtle hints, neither willing to show more. "Follow me."

Ivan signaled to his trooper to follow. "I brought my squad back from the camp at the mill. Terris here is a healer, a good one."

"We'll see about that," replied Sedge. "Convenient, you should be so close. I thought you and the Auro Na had broken camp and were headed north?"

"Coincidences have worked out well."

In a saddlery near Murali's, Ivan saw the two dead. He didn't need to give them a second look. The crew of the *Alexis,* along with the matriarch, were watching and listening through his optic and audio implants.

When Sedge saw the merc pay scant attention to the two dead and instead go directly for the wounded Timberkeep, he asked, "You don't want to know how they died?"

Ivan paused, then said, "I've been a lot of places on this world. I've seen a lot of dead and dying. I already know what killed those two. I need to see if we can save the other."

"What killed them?" It wasn't asked so much a question as it was a test.

"Sedge, if the Paleowrights or Drakans have gotten hold of Ancient weapons, there will be more dead. Lots more."

"What Ancient weapon?" Now, the two played a game of deception and misdirection, yet they needed to be just truthful enough to solve their problem.

Ivan turned away and saw a pair of Timberkeeps, one a sixthsense healer, trying to administer to the dying Bratchert lying on a bench. The blast had hit the warder just above the right hip, taken out a portion of his side and, with it, his right kidney and the bottom half of his liver.

"Terris, you know what to do," Ivan said. "Sedge, may I have a word with you and your healers?" When they all looked at him, he said, "Outside."

They started to balk.

"Let's talk outside, and I promise you that Terris will save Bratchert, but we must get out now." By force of will, he compelled the two Timberkeeps to surrender their patient to the Ready Reaction medic.

Stepping outside the shop, Ivan pulled the door closed behind him. There were no windows beside the door, so he decided to stand guard there. Sedge was watching him closely. The two healers started bombarding him with questions, but then two more members of Ivan's Ready Reaction squad arrived on eenus; the animals were steaming in the cool air.

A trooper slid off his saddle and pulled a large pack off the eenu. He made straight for the door behind Ivan. "Got all the stuff we need," the trooper said.

Ivan let the man squeeze past with the large pack and quickly closed the door again.

The Timberkeeps immediately bombarded him, "Why can't we be in there? Why can't we help? Why can't we watch? He's one of ours! What are you up to?"

"You have my promise. We can save him. We've encountered this type of wound before."

"But," exclaimed one of the healers, "but, a chunk of his side is missing!"

Ivan stood aside to let another newly arrived trooper take his place at the door. "Believe it or not, if you are good enough at sixthsense, that wound can be healed." It was a blatant lie, but if they pulled this off, it wouldn't matter.

"Ivan," the matriarch's voice came over his audio implant, "it looks like the search party is closing in on something. You'd better get out there before more provincials are killed. This could escalate into a ULUP incident.

It already has, he thought. "Sedge, I need you to manage this. I'm taking one of my mercs to help your search party disarm whoever has that weapon." He hooked a thumb over his shoulder in the direction of the door, "Terris will come out and tell you—"

As if on cue, the door opened, and Terris came out. "We've applied the bandages, steroids, and hemostarsis. We just need to let him rest now." He left the door open, and the two healers rushed him, asking more questions. "What are steroids and a hemostarsis?" Terris wouldn't let them past, but they could see into the room where Bratchert lay covered by a blanket from the chin down. His color appeared to be good, better than the ashen grey when they left him.

The matriarch watched as Bratchert, with a full autodoc strapped to his chest, was wheeled past her to the heavy cruiser's expansive sickbay. A full surgical team was in place, ready to begin regenerative reconstruction on the intestines, kidney, and liver.

"I assume this is legal per ULUP?" asked the admiral. While Ivan had blocked the door, Terris had taken a full three-sixty videograph of Bratchert lying on the bench. He set up the holovid projector carried in the pack and turned on the dynamic projection of the image of Bratchert lying there while the *Alexis* had shifted the gravely wounded warder up to the ship.

She nodded absently. "Ivan says it is, and he would know. ULUP allows for the off-planet medical treatment of provincials wounded by an extrasolar incursion." Turning to him, she added, "Ivan's use of the holofield projector is how I can help Margret at Terrabac."

"How?"

"I'll need a quiet room. A holograph recorder. And please confirm with Captain Haarkolet at Terrabac that he has a holofield projector. We'll do the same thing with the Auro Na that Ivan is doing with the Timberkeeps. We'll fake it. I can provide psychic support to Margret and Breia from here, but I need clear recon bot-sensor feed, complete isolation, and no interruptions once I start."

Chapter 11
Avarian Marines

Wedgewood

Out of sight of Wedgewood, Ivan slipped on a pair of infrared goggles and spurred his eenu into a canter. The night was moonless. Trooper Sendrant, following, was the only man he could spare to join him.

"Chief," the combat controller aboard the *Alexis* sounded in his ear. "The admiral says the matriarch is worried about your lack of backup. She's gone into seclusion to help the counselors at Terrabac. The admiral said he'd arrange for backup."

Ivan ducked a branch and hoped Sendrant was alert enough to do the same. "Well, we'll just have to manage. Everyone else is engaged in the conclave." The thought of facing an unknown plasma-armed threat vexed him, but the lasers in the forearm stock of their handbolts were no toys. They killed just as dead as plasmas, but their pencil-thin holes demanded better shot placement.

"The admiral has a better idea."

Ivan swerved around a tree, and his eenu suddenly jumped a log he missed that blended in the infrared background. *Damn, I'm going to have to slow down.* "What's his idea?"

"Uh, command checked with the Judge Advocate's office, and they say we are cleared with ULUP."

"Cleared? Cleared for what?"

Senior Corporal Meridia strapped in. He snapped his Mk 4 heavy-assault plasma rifle into its seat bracket.

"Hey, Lewy, I thought we were standing down. The matriarch is aboard the *Alexis,* isn't she?" asked a Marine.

Normally, it was Meridia's job, as acting platoon sergeant, to keep order in the platoon, but he let the idle chatter on the platoon comm net go because he wanted to hear their lieutenant's answer.

"Yea, we got a mission, dirtside," the lieutenant replied. They had no time for a briefing. When the scramble call came, they had just enough time to grab helmets, check weapon charges, and buckle in the assault lander. "Mission briefing is in your suit AIs now."

Meridia scrolled through the heads-up display in his powered-suit helmet. He called out over the platoon net, "Check in once you've read it." The landing deck antigrav boosters jolted them into place. *They're not messing around, must be hot.* The voice of the launch-control officer for *Spirit's Fury* sounded in all the armor suits on the assault craft. "Warning, warning, expedited launch sequence commencing now."

"Shiren," someone cursed on the net.

Before Meridia could see the name of the offender on the roster, the assault lander hit eight G's. The inertial dampers in the craft's crew bay, combined with the adaptive environment of their albaminia armor, kept the platoon from being squashed like so many bugs inside their suits. Still, Meridia was sure he left his guts back in the launch tube. The Marine assault lander was out and away from *Spirit's Fury* in a blur. As soon as they cleared the hangar vapor-barrier, the pilot smacked the twin neutrino drives and kept up the eight G's, screaming past the bridge of the cruiser *Alexis,* through the battle group's escort screen, and aimed directly for the planet down below.

"How many drops, Corp?" It was the voice of the platoon's newest member.

"This makes thirty-three." Meridia struggled against the inertial forces of the flight. "Those were all against Turboii. This is my first against corsairs on a Class E."

"Wow, thirty-three."

Meridia would have nodded could he move his head. Twenty drops were the average before you were either posthumously recognized for service or transferred out of Assault Brigade. In recognition of drops-in-service, they'd given him a choice. He opted for assignment on board the *Spirit's Fury*; it was supposed to be cake duty. The only reason the old Marine carrier was still in service was Fleet needed a reserve battle group stationed to defend the planet Avaria, and it had a Marine battalion detachment, a last-ditch defense against an invading Turboii fleet. The *Fury's* patches and repairs had patches and repairs.

Ivan pulled up his eenu and looked to the night sky.

Sendrant stopped beside him, peering up. "That'll attract attention."

Ivan sniffed. "Yeah, how are we going to explain that?"

In the dark morning, the fireball eclipsed all the stars. The blaze from the Marine lander's energy heatshield went from orange to white. The vapor trail began to steepen. Anyone in Wedgewood looking to the night sky would have a growing sense that the heavenly object was heading for them.

"Where do you want them, chief?" asked the combat controller. "I have two full sticks of Avaria's finest. Locked and loaded."

Ivan considered the controller's question. Assault Marines were indeed some of Avaria's finest. They were *first in, when, for worse is certain,* or so the saying went. The pointy end of a galactic spear. He expected the Marines would be vast overkill for what he and Sendrant faced. "You got a vector for the search party?"

"Affirmative. Two-hundred seventy-two degrees to your relative. Moving south on a course of one-hundred eighty-two degrees. Dead straight, no deviations. No data on what they are following, nothing on aural or infrared. We've pinged the ground with radar, but the background scatter on that mountain with those big trees is too cluttered. Whoever the search party is tracking is blacked out."

"Right," he acknowledged. "Calculate their rate of travel, assume their target is non-motorized, and put the Marines down a thousand meters beyond the farthest possible point of travel for the target. Have them disperse in a skirmish line and advance in this direction until they make contact."

"Roger that," answered the controller.

"Where's my recon package? I could use some drones and bots for eyes and motion sensing. Whoever the search party is tracking has to be moving."

"Recon package on your location in thirty seconds."

"How is it the search party can track the corsairs and we can't?" Sendrant asked.

Ivan answered, "Dogs."

"Let's wait for dawn here." Alex stared up at the night sky. "We get much closer, and they could ambush us. No telling how far back help is."

Lettern was too tired to argue. Her whole side hurt, not just her ribs.

"What do you think that is?" asked Pottern, staring at the blazing object in the night sky. At first, it looked like it was coming straight at them, then it changed direction. The white flare streaked away, disappearing beyond the trees.

Alex shook his head. "I don't know. It's been a strange night."

"They're noisy," said Mitchern.

"What do you mean?" asked Lettern.

Mitchern gazed in the direction of where the glowing object disappeared. Like all telepaths, he could sense Human aural energy, particularly unshielded emotionally-driven thoughts. "It's confusing, but I think, I think they, whatever that is in the sky, is coming to help."

"You mean there are people on that?" Pottern exclaimed.

"Yes." Mitchern looked blank.

"Mother's sweet breath," Pottern said.

Alex shifted his shield on his shoulder. "What is Noodles sending?"

Mitchern pointed. "She's standing guard in a tree. Waiting for us."

The Defender nodded. The dog would have to keep waiting; Lettern was nearly played out. They would rest until dawn. "Keep Noodles close. Don't let her wander."

Night surrendered to a deep shade of grey. Slowly, the grey resolved to lighter and darker shades. When the first greens appeared in the landscape, the combat controller called to Ivan, "Search party has resumed movement, same direction."

"Confirmed," he said. Both he and Sendrant, running on no sleep for the past twenty-four hours, had taken stim shots. He let his multi-func project the holograph image of the tactical situation, so Sendrant could see it as well. Two recon drones were doing figure-eights over the four-mile distance between them and the probable location of the supposed extrasolars. A string of twenty recon bots hovered along the plotted route of the search party. The bots would, unbeknownst to the searchers, monitor their progress. The platoon of Marines was arrayed in skirmish order across the track a half mile further out.

"Weapons fire. Plasma weapon fire," the combat controller reported laconically. "Shots directed at the search party. No hits."

Ivan cursed. "Mount up."

"Got anything corporal?" asked the Marine lieutenant.

"Negative on visuals. Energy pulse came directly to my front, three hundred meters."

"Noodles!" Pottern yelled. "Come here, girl! Come!"

"He's got us pinned," Alex whispered to Lettern. "Probably waiting for us the whole night."

Lettern nodded. "As soon as Noodles crested that rise, he shot." She recalled the image of the Nakish standing next to her in Murali's tent just as he pulled his weapon. A cooled hatred began to boil again.

"Trying to kill our dog," surmised Mitchern.

"What is that thing he's shooting?" Pottern gasped, holding Noodles, who had jumped into his arms. The dog was a white and black bundle of squirming energy.

Alex shook his head. "I don't know."

"I'm going to kill him," said Lettern.

The Defender peered at her. She stared back, her brown eyes in a black mood.

He grudged, "How do you want to do this?"

She outlined the decoy plan. When they had agreed to their roles, she said, "Just don't get yourselves shot."

"Search party on the move," signaled the controller.

Ivan and Sendrant had been forced to dismount because the ground had become steep and rocky. "Unhitch their reins," Ivan instructed, "they'll follow. Let's run."

Moving forward in skirmish order, the Marine to Meridia's left called, "Contact."

"Contact," reported two more Marines.

"Search party is enveloping a point that matches the projected firing location." The combat controller gave a running monologue of the evolving situation. "Recon bots have motion of a single probable target. Heading due west. Directing bots to gain visual."

Alex peered around the tree. He saw a clump of ferns move and called out, "Hey you! Stop!"

"Plasma fire," reported the controller.

The white blast tore the bark off the Ungerngerist Alex hid behind. "Ula, maybe I should find a bigger tree," he said to no one in particular.

"Hey!" Mitchern had enough nerve for one short word. He was promptly rewarded with a plasma burst that spanked -- in a glaring flash -- the granite boulder he was hugging.

"Five targets closing," reported Meridia. "I have four classified as provincials and one with a visual as a confirmed extrasolar. *Fury* is running an ID search."

"Chief," the lieutenant called from the lander. "Rules of engagement?"

Ivan stopped running for a moment. "Do not fire unless fired upon. Attempt to apprehend the extrasolar. Do not shoot the provincials!" He knew it was a strange set of orders to give Marines accustomed to fearsome firefights with Turboii. He hoped they could manage it.

"Target closing, classified female provincial," the Marine immediately to Meridia's left called out. The entire platoon, along with the staff in the Combat Information

Center on board the *Spirit's Fury,* could see, via their displays, the evolving action. "Fifty meters."

Then, vivid in the Marine's telescopic sights, a woman edged around a tree and carefully climbed a log beside it. She was slim, her long brown hair in a tangled bun; she was wearing buckskin britches, knee-high boots, and a torn blouse exposing her midriff. She carried a curved length of wood strung with string. One of the Marines identified it as a primitive weapon, a bow. The woman's ribcage was bandaged, the dressing discolored with blood and ooze.

"That's a plasma shot," the Marine said of her wound. "She's taken a plasma hit." There was silent respect up and down the line.

"Hey, you there!" A man's voice called out from in front of Meridia. He saw the understory move. A cloaked figure rose and aimed a plasma pistol at the challenge. Then the woman atop the log, concealed behind the adjacent tree, stepped clear. She pulled her bow to full draw and let fly, seemingly without aiming.

The arrow hit Quorat just as he fired. The pistol, in auto-aim, sent the plasma bolt a hand's width above Alex's head as he ducked behind his tree.

Knocked down by the force of the arrow, Quorat rolled in the grass. Things were not going as he wanted. Now he had an arrow, an arrow of all things, stuck in the synth-flex armor webbing of his cloak. It had hit hard but not penetrated. He struggled to dislodge it. Whoever shot him was behind and to his left. He checked his multi-func. The device displayed her aural ID, the same from last night. *Yes, there she is. I thought I killed her?* What it did not show, because the Marines were shielded from aural emanations, was the full platoon just to his front.

Quorat was tired of this game. It was time to end it. *Got to kill them and get to the sled and back to the Intruder.* He needed to upload the videograph of the pegmatite, but the laser comm relay was at the sled.

Meridia spoke into his suit mic, "Advancing to apprehend." He perceived the woman to his left, but he focused on the extrasolar immediately to his front.

Lettern saw her enemy rise from the underbrush and turn to face her. She drew back.

Meridia saw the extrasolar raise his weapon. "He's going to smoke her. Permission to fire."

Ivan stopped.

A Marine to Lettern's right had a perfect view. He saw the sweat on her flanks, the wrecked bandage, how she balanced on the log, the tangle of her hair, and the set of her jaw.

She stopped her draw. There was something to her enemy's left. A shape, more of a reflection or a shadow. She chose to ignore it.

The Marine watched the woman come to full draw, aim, and loose.

Auto-aim flashed green, and Quorat fired.

Meridia responded to Ivan's call to fire and triggered a magna pulse.

Quorat's shot went high, auto-aim unable to compensate for the wild jerk.

Lettern jumped down from the log, adrenaline pounding her heart. The flash of white had gone over her head, but close enough to feel its heat. She notched an arrow and approached where the stranger lay in the ferns. Then she stopped. The image she'd seen shimmered and solidified into a green-camouflaged Humanoid shape. She stared, her eyes wide as saucers.

Meridia unsnapped his helmet and pulled it off. He smiled to reassure her. Trusting his suit's AI to get the language translation correct, he spoke to her through the suit's external speaker. "Nice shot. You hit him first. Almost made me miss."

She stared at him. Holding her bow at the ready, she stood rooted as he approached. Looking him up and down, she realized he had red eyes. His hair was buzz-cut short, and his face clean-shaven. Taking in the shape and construction of his armored suit, she turned and pointed at Quorat, who was dead with her arrow through his neck and the top half of his head missing. His blood poured along the arrow shaft into the pine needles. "That one of yours?"

"Nope. Definitely not."

"Who are you?"

"Me?" He gave a smile. Two more apparitions resolved themselves into other Humans who removed their helmets and stood nearby. "I'm Senior Corporal Illian Meridia, Second Battalion, Fourth Regiment, Avarian Assault Marines. And you are Lettern Stouttree, branch warden, for the Wedgewood militia, Second Ward."

"And a hell of a shot," said one of the other Marines, a woman.

"Tough, too," grunted the other Marine, pointing at her bandage.

"Knows how to hunt Humans," said the female Marine. "Tough gig for extrasolars." She pointed her weapon at Quorat's body.

"Who are? What is that?" Lettern pointed at his armor. "What are you doing here?" Her questions spilled out.

"We're here to help," answered Meridia.

Lettern gave him a scowl. "You could have come sooner."

He shrugged inside his suit.

"What is that?" She indicated his weapon with a tilt of her chin.

"A Mk 4. A heavy-assault Rifle," he said as if she'd understand.

"How do you know who I am?" she asked, frowning.

"The ship pinged us your ID. Looks like the IDB has been here awhile," he smiled.

"Ship?" Her confusion was complete.

Meridia skipped the question. "You should let us take care of that," he was looking at her bandage. "Down here, dirtside, those can get infected, easy."

Ignoring his offer, she stepped closer and looked him in his red eyes. "How old are you?"

"Twenty-one standard. On this planet? That would be twenty-two."

Lettern appeared concerned. "That's how old I am, but you look older. Way older."

This time, the corporal's smile faded, but not completely. "It's a hard life. We do our time."

"Well, I'm going to get me one of those." She indicated his rifle and then turned her back on them and waded through the tall grass to where Quorat lay.

A Marine edged closer to the female Marine and, looking at Lettern's backside, said, "Nice ass."

If Lettern heard the comment, she chose to ignore it. As she reached down, a familiar voice called to her: "You can't have that." Quorat's plasma pistol lay just within reach.

Ivan trudged up the slope. He took in the scene and shook his head.

"These friends of yours?" she asked, still bending over, hand outstretched to the weapon.

"Yes. They are."

She straightened and looked at Meridia. "Him too?"

"Yep, him too."

Alex, Pottern, and Mitchern came into the clearing, as did more Marines. Pottern dropped Noodles, who promptly ran to Quorat's body and started sniffing, circling around to the open head wound.

Alex surveyed the group of Marines as they watched him. They took in his dented shield, his scarred armor, the worn handle of his sword, the age lines on his face, and the grit in his eyes. Everyone knew who the veterans were.

Alex asked Ivan, "So, you're Ancients?"

Grudgingly, Ivan said, "I suppose you could say that. In a way, we are, and in a way, we are not."

Alex growled, "You've come back?" The turmoil, particularly to Life Believers, that the legacy of the Ancients had caused to Dianis reflective in his tone.

"Yes, well, not for long. They," Ivan pointed at the Marines, "are going back to where they came from, like right now. Corporal, take this body back to the 'Fury. Have fleet Intel run a full biograph on him and forensics on everything he's got."

Meridia motioned to the two Marines beside him to get the body. "How about his transport? It's got to be around here somewhere. A dude like him isn't walking far. Want us to sweep for it?"

"Yes, good idea."

"What was he doing here?" Alex asked as a Marine easily hefted Quorat's body with his powered armor.

Meridia de-coupled his gloves and approached Lettern; he gently reached out for her hand and lifted her arm.

Ivan watched and then answered, "He was after your aquamarine. Starting with the huge pegmatite you have sitting in, of all places, a party tent."

Meridia was talking to their corpsman. "I can do that for you," said the corpsman.

"I can manage," replied the corporal. "Hand me the free spray."

Alex ignored what the corporal was doing to Lettern. He decided that if there were to be more fighting, it would already have started. "Why aquamarine? What's it to him?"

Holding up her arm, Lettern watched the corporal spray the bandage with some sort of oily penetrant. "This may sting," he said and, without waiting, snapped the bandage off her skin. It came away clean, no skin attached, but pus-saturated. Lettern gasped. Meridia held her arm high to keep her from swaying.

Ivan answered, "It's everything to us, unfortunately. That part the Paleowrights have right. Aquamarine-5 is important all across the galaxy. But here on Dianis, it is just a pretty blue stone."

Meridia took another aerosol can from the medic, "This will hurt like hell, but it will kill the pain afterward and start accelerated healing. It will vaporize the pathogens crawling in the wound. It's usually proceeded by surface anesthesia, but we Marines take it straight."

"Pathogen?" she mumbled, watching him.

"Yes," and he began spraying the wound. She immediately *yowled,* her knees going soft.

He saw a convenient rock and sat, propping her on his armored knee before she could collapse. He kept spraying, her body twitching at each pass.

Alex paused, the tableau, the strangeness engulfing him. Finally, he resolved himself. "The Paleowrights. They are going to be a problem. When they hear about this. About you, about the Marines, the weapons, they'll come back to Wedgewood. It will be another battle. A war."

"And I want that gun," Lettern drawled, wobbling on Meridia's knee. She managed to regain a measure of clarity to glare at Ivan. Meridia motioned to the medic for the next treatment.

"Sorry, Lettern, you can't have it. None of this should have happened," Ivan reasoned.

"But it did, damn you! It did!" She was close to tears. "Bratchert, Mattar, they're all dead!"

"Not Bratchert. He's on board their ship." Ivan nodded to Meridia. "He's being operated on as we speak. They'll be able to save him."

The pain, exhaustion, and adrenalin collapse all conspired to overwhelm her. She looked away in embarrassment.

"We've all been there." Meridia put an armored arm around her waist. "It's good to see you are still Human. Some of us...some of us don't feel no more. When a friend goes—" he breathed. "Sometimes I think I should feel more, but it doesn't come. I guess it's better that way."

Ivan dreaded it would come to this, so he played the only card he had. "Lettern, I'll make you a deal. We'll save Bratchert and return him to Wedgewood. He'll be able to heal up and rejoin your ward. In return, you and Alex and the others promise me that you will never say a word about this." The alternative, an impractical alternative, was to mind-wipe them.

Lettern nodded, but Alex just studied him.

"Alex, as a docent of your faith, as a leader of the Mother's Faithful, you must understand that the Paleowrights cannot learn what has happened here, and that means keeping it a secret from even your own people."

"Not from Christina," he said bluntly.

Ivan waggled his head. "I suspect she already knows Ancients are here. Has known."

"Who else knows?" Lettern asked. Then, alarm began to register as Meridia aimed the final aerosol treatment for the plasma wound.

"No worries," Meridia said gently. "The pain should be done. This will seal the wound and start the skin regeneration."

When Ivan didn't respond, Lettern looked at him as Meridia sprayed the sealant on her wound. "Does Achelous know?" she challenged. "Is he an Ancient, too? You worked for him enough. How about the high priestess?"

Giving ground where he needed, Ivan offered up Achelous but refused to concede any of the matronens.

"How about Baryy?" she pressed. "Does he know?"

Ivan stammered, "Baryy? He's here?"

Meridia laughed. "Hand me the alcutrol," and the medic handed him a medication injector.

"What's so funny?" Sitting on his lap, Lettern looked down on Meridia's face, fascinated by his red eyes.

"There's no fooling you. Our mission brief cited Agent Baryy Maxmun." The corporal returned the Ready Reaction chief's glare. "Sorry, chief, I'm just a grunt Marine." He squeezed her arm. "We normally do the alcutrol in a thigh or butt cheek, but you've lots of muscle in these arms," he said appreciatively. To which the female Marine said, "I bet that's not all you want to squeeze Meridia."

Meridia punched the injector into Lettern's bare arm. "It's the final treatment and will put your system into overdrive. You'll need to stuff your face for the next three days. You'll be hungry."

"Ouch!" she complained. "You're not very gentle."

A Marine chimed, "Sweetheart, for the job we do, you don't want gentle."

"Now, that's going to make you feel woozy at first," Meridia said. "It's gonna creep up on you, so be ready for it." He looked back to Ivan. "Chief, can I get one of those fancy in-country camo bandages from you? Ours are all high-tech. Can't really have her running around with a blinky-light thing attached to her ribs."

When Sendrant offered up one of his, Lettern's head began to droop, her eyes unfocused.

"Lewy," Meridia called into his suit mic, "how 'bout we give the provincials and IDB a ride back to the town. This one I got here is whacked out. She isn't walking or riding nowhere."

"Affirmative," came the reply.

"How 'bout it chief? Wanna lift?"

Ivan idly wondered if the Marine corporal didn't just want to keep his hands on Lettern, but he acquiesced. Yesterday and today were total disasters in maintaining ULUP protocol. So what if he gave four provincials and their dog a ride in a galactic assault lander. "Can you do it by waking only *half* the town?"

Meridia smiled. "Chief, we may be big, bad, and ugly, but we can be whispers on the wind if you need."

Alex sat in the crew bay of the lander. Lettern sat across from him on the far bulkhead next to the corporal. Her head rested on his shoulder; she was in and out of consciousness. Noodles scampered around the crew bay, sniffing each of the Marines, its tail wagging fiercely. Ivan and Sendrant led their eenus up the ramp and tethered them to the drop handles hanging from the ceiling. Alex stared at the animals, amazed they were at ease. "They've done this before?" He said to Ivan.

"Oi." Ivan turned to offer a rare smile at the Defender. He checked the animal and then slumped into the jump seat next to Alex. "I need a different job. This one's getting old."

"You can always join us."

Slouching, Ivan looked over. "How so?"

Alex jerked as the lander rose in the air. "You're a Life Believer. One of us. I don't care where you come from. Ancient or not."

The two men, grizzled soldiers, shared a communal silence.

"That man that Lettern killed," Alex said, "he won't be the last."

Ivan looked to where Lettern snuggled against the armored chest of Meridia, who peered back at him. A deep sadness settled upon him. "No, I suppose not."

Alex felt the heave and yaw of the craft. "Help us fight them."

Chapter 12
Isumfast

The town of Isumfast

Marisa stared out the window of the room she and Achelous shared at the inn. She had an irrational urge to pinch herself, but she knew it to be true: she was in Isumfast of all places, a bustling town a day and a half ride north of Falda at the foot of the steep Gracopherous Mountains. *Isumfast, what am I doing here?* It was all so bewildering and yet exhilarating. As a Tivorian trader, a merchant princess, she seldom ventured further inland than the market or bazaar of her port-of-call, and while a fast eenu trek from Wedgewood was slower than the planned field shift, it was still exciting to experience the strangeness of the interior, and Isumfast was no exception.

Then, the wave of exhilaration passed, and she sat on the edge of the bed, overwhelmed by the prospect of what she wanted to accomplish. The dread of what might happen to Achelous should the IDB arrest him was almost too much to bear. She picked at her fingernails and then forced herself to stop. Scarred and chipped, they were in need of polish after the hard ride from Mount Mars. What would they, the IDB or Matrincy, do once they learn of her and Boyd? Baryy, not that he meant to torment her, had speculated the IDB might want to mind-wipe her and extract Boyd from the planet to remove his hybrid Avarian-Dianis genes from further mingling with the provincial gene pool. Achelous had scoffed at Baryy, calling him Mr. Gloom, and Baryy had responded by labeling Achelous ignorant of the true risks. She didn't know who to believe except that all three of them, Outish included, had taken extraordinary risks staying behind on Dianis.

She shook herself free of the doldrums. It was in those moments she bolstered herself with a saying her father had often said to her: *Are you a woman, or are you a mouse?*

Standing, she took a deep breath and rededicated herself to learning all there was. Everything about Achelous, and Baryy, and Outish, and the IDB, and the Avarian Federation. Achelous, out of sight of Baryy and Outish, had encouraged her to unravel the new mysteries that surrounded her, and yet he steadfastly refused to volunteer any information unless she asked a specific, pointed question, which she dared not. She was becoming adept at prodding for a simple response to an oblique query that slowly pulled back the veil of secrecy, inch by inch. In that way, according to IDB doctrine, she, as a provincial, had learned the information on her own as part of interacting in Dianis society and was therefore entitled to the information. A mind-wipe could not be administered to purge those memories.

Leaving their chambers, Marisa tread the polished wood floors that were swept and mopped every morning. The Isumfast inn, having stood on the banks of the Gracopherous River for generations, was built of river stone, with a shake-roof and numerous fireplaces. The innkeeper's family were an adorable lot, always asking after her, cheery in their Faldan accents. Judging by the ancient -- as in very old -- photographs sealed in a clear material they called *plastic,* the inn had been here since before *Epis Exodi,* over three hundred years ago. The pictures festooned the dining room walls and portrayed scenes of Ancients – as in galactic Humans -- in their alien garb, sitting in the very same dining room, with the same copper-topped hornbeam bar, albeit with different tables and chairs. The finish on the hornbeam wood was lighter back then, not darkened by centuries of lacquer, pipe smoke, and hand oil. The pictures showed all manner of Ancients eating and drinking, smiling for whoever or whatever was capturing the images. Some of them, judging by their poses, Marisa assumed were important dignitaries. One Ancient, whom Achelous identified as a *mechanic* distinguished by his overalls and equipment belt, raised his mug of what was purported to be Falda Dark Mash, a centuries-old brew crafted at the inn. The mechanic was toasting someone called the *planetary supervisor*, so said the inscription cut into the plastic. Marisa had studied each of the images in detail, knowing now they were of real people – not mythological super beings -- living real lives no different from hers. She spent hours in the dining room whiling away the time while Baryy, Achelous, and Outish performed their *work* in the mountains.

Baryy had groaned when Achelous had let a room at the inn, complaining with questionable logic, "But she'll see the pictures on the walls!"

Achelous had retorted, "Did you ever think that might be the point? The Isumfast Inn is in the index of, er," she smiled at the memory of how he tried to translate a *galactic* term into something benign and provincial, "uh sites of documented Ancient artifacts. Anyone, any provincial, can go there and look at them. They're part of Faldan history and therefore grandfathered under *U-lup*."

"I know that," Baryy whined. "It's just that she might be able to understand them."

"And why is that a bad thing?" he rejoined. "If Marisa grasps the meanings of the images, it will be through her own deduction. Which is sanctioned."

That was the second time he'd let 'U-lup' slip, she mused. He'd warned her about keeping any written notes, but she ignored those warnings. She could read and write in Tivor Coaster, in addition to Tivorian proper and Warkenvaal, and she had asked him if Coaster was well known, their catchphrase for *known to you-know-who*. He'd mumbled that no one had bothered to catalog it, and she sensed it was somehow his own oversight. *Now, how could that be?* So she kept notes in her tiny, cryptic, Coaster script, piecing together the parts of what she depressingly began to realize was an immense picture. Something so huge and awesome she might never comprehend it all, but she was determined to at least understand the world around the man she loved and the world she suddenly found herself in. One day, Boyd would ask, "Momma, what does daddy do?" and when that day came, she didn't want to say, "I don't know." From her notes, she assumed *U-lup* was some form of edict not to be broken, yet Baryy, Achelous, and Outish were breaking it. It made her both nervous and depressed that Achelous might be considered a criminal for loving and consorting with her. It also made her angry as Mother's Fire. *Who dare say what woman a man could love?* Beyond the obvious morality of infidelity, a man and woman should be able to love freely. But she grimly accepted that Tivorian custom might not be the norm, even across Isuelt, let alone, she took a breath, the stars. Yet the idea that Achelous should be persecuted for loving her was infuriating. She wanted to stomp the floor at the injustice of it. She could hear her mother now, "You should have married Graf Wester, the aorolmin's brother, instead of bedding that wayward trader."

Well, Mother, she thought, *it appears Achelous is not some wayward trader.* Retrieving the water pitcher the innkeeper left in the hall for her, she returned to their chambers. On the dresser lay a picture Marisa had borrowed, for a small fee, from the inn's proprietor. He kept all the best pictures in the family's living quarters, and he had invited her in to see them when she showed such an intense interest. "I'm surprised the Paleowrights haven't tried to confiscate them?" she had asked, to which the proprietor replied, "Aach, the Taldamir archive has more pictures than they know what to do with!"

"They do?"

"Aach, the Ancients loved to take pictures of themselves. Souvenirs of their travels and exploits."

"But I've never seen Ancient pictures before, and I travel extensively. From Taldamir to Tivor, to Eastport, to South Cape, Bareen, and even Toll Haven. I have never seen anything like these."

To which the innkeeper smiled in a benign sort of way. "Perhaps there were no Ancients in those places?"

Which had prompted a question from her when she borrowed the picture she now held in her hand, "Are there many Paleowright archives?"

An obvious devout of Diunesis Antiquaria, the proprietor beamed knowledgeably, "Wherever there is a cathedral, there is an archive. Hebert, Tomis, Zursh, Taldamir, Stith Drakas, Ompo," he had waved his hand as there were too many for him to name.

"And is it, well, easy to gain access?" At which point, the proprietor's smile faded, and he had looked closely at her, "Na-na. You must be three things to enter an archive."

She smiled sweetly at him, turning on her best charm. "And those are?" The man held up three fingers, "A devout of the faith, which you are not. Hold a favor from the bishop of the cathedral, which you don't," and then he rubbed two fingers together, "and have much silver, which you do."

She thought about that. Gaining access to a cathedral archive might put her well ahead in the knowledge quest. She could certainly be appellated as Paleowright, should it come to that; silver, or even gold, was the answer to that problem. Currying a favor from a bishop was something else. She'd have to meet a bishop first and didn't really want to.

Lifting the picture to the sunlight streaming through the window, she studied it anew. It was the one from the innkeeper's study that had drawn her attention, and she had tripped over a jungle of potted plants trying to get a better look at it. In the image, a crew of Ancients was standing around an incredible machine five times their height. It had a maw large enough to swallow a cabin and was ringed with rows of steel teeth set in front of what she would later learn to be dissipation arrays. The machine was covered with dirt, but the crew was beaming, prideful, at a gaping hole in a mountain face beside which a river dropped into a narrow gorge. At the bottom of the picture, crudely carved into the plastic, were the words *ITA Graco River*.

She committed to memory the image of the gorge, rock face, and road leading to the opening. She was convinced that was the location from which Achelous had led her, blindfolded, to the inn, and it was where the three traders were now. *Or should I call them IDB agents? Are they still?* It was confounding. While blindfolded, she remembered hearing the river rushing through rapids and the sharp smell of pine sap and needles. The air had been cold and thin, as if up in the mountains. If she found the place on her own, it would be her own discovery, not a shared secret. Hers to keep.

Chapter 13
Departure

Onboard the Heavy Cruiser Alexis, in Dianis Orbit

The matriarch watched the planet below turn to night. *So few lights,* she thought. By galactic standards, Dianis was a desert if measured by radiated night light. The few large cities in northern Isuelt could barely be picked out by their dim yellow lantern glows: Stith Drakas, Neuland, Zursh, Mineforest, Toll Haven, and Rhinehart. *I've not been to those. And now I won't, at least not for—*

"All hands to shift stations. Shift to commence in five minutes." The announcement came over the all-hands circuit.

"We're waiting for *Spirit's Fury*," Breia said from his crash couch to the right of hers. "Their field generator is ancient. Takes time to ramp it up."

"Well, we *are* Ancients, after all," the matriarch quipped.

Breia was immersed in his multi-func, but Margret laughed, "Speak for yourself. I'm not three hundred and fifty years old."

The matriarch hated feeling sentimental; it was a weakness. The world below, seen through the wall-size holovid, had made an indelible impression on her. Even if she had been there for only three days.

Breia, in his typical, myopic manner, said, while he scrolled through his display and punched in numbers, "It's been three-hundred and thirty-two years, to be exact, since the last ITA engineers left Dianis. The provincials call it *Epis Exodi*."

The matriarch wondered why this world had become so important to her. There were, after all, eighty-three planets in the federation, and, technically, Dianis was not one of them. She'd reviewed the helmet videos and communications log of the assault team from the encounter with Quorat, the corsair. Lettern had made a lasting impression on the Assault Marines judging from their helmet camera angles. The matriarch had watched the interaction between Corporal Meridia and Lettern. *Those two were made for each other.* The video feed from the lander crew bay during the ride back to Wedgewood was equally instructive. Lettern instinctively trusted Meridia. He would protect her, and she would protect him. *I need some way to get those two together. I need them in this fight together.* She could feel a premonition stirring. *Is it a stray imagining or a perception?* That was always the problem of being a sensitive: deciphering the early wanderings of a muse.

Margret interrupted the matriarch's gaze at the night side of Dianis as she took her station on the crash couch beside. "At least we didn't let Ghost-I win Coroscone. That would have been a disaster."

"Are you sure," the matriarch asked. "Maybe the planet would be ready for uplift sooner if the Drakans and Paleowrights conquered Isuelt, and then with a little help on the other continents, we could achieve a governmental quorum sooner. With the Auro Na helping the Drakans, they would be hard to stop."

Margret looked askance at her, pausing in the process of buckling her safety harness. "Good thing I know you're joking because, after all I've just been through with Ghost-I, I can tell you his goal is not peace and tranquility. I've been up close and personal with that man's mind, and he wants one thing: World domination. The man has grandiose visions, and he knows that I know. That's why I think they shifted tactics in the end and sought a one-year delay in the election of the Coroscone."

"Madam Matriarch, your call with Chief Darinarishcan is going through," said Andromeda in her audio implant. "He will be online momentarily."

The matriarch acknowledged the update and said to Margret, "I think they opted for the year delay because they knew we were finally besting them."

"It took a while," said Breia from his crash couch.

Ivan's image replaced the holovid of Dianis. At wall size, his face was daunting. Every crease, scar, and care line magnified five-fold.

The matriarch reduced the image size to something more tolerable. "Evening, chief. We're shifting out in a few minutes, and I didn't want to miss you before we left." The entire task force, including the battalion of Marines and the Special Forces company, was leaving to be replaced by one lone IDB interdiction cutter with a five-man crew.

"Thank you, ma'am. I hope you appreciate the delicacy of the situation here in Wedgewood." Ivan could, via his own holovid, see Breia's glare. "The situation is too..." he sought the right word "...variable to allow you and the counselors back into Wedgewood. There has already been rampant speculation that you were responsible for the appearance of the Nakish killer in Murali's tent. You and the assailant were both fascinated by the pegmatite. Some believe you sent him. I know it was an unfortunate coincidence, but try explaining that to the locals. We did well by having Bratchert healed to the extent where he can recover here in town, but even that has generated speculation and suspicions. Mbecca and Sedge have tried calming the nerves of the populace, telling them that my men and I are on their side. Alex has helped reinforce that, as has Lettern, but the fight with Quorat has not gone down well. The townsfolk, rightly so, are angry about the killings and want Quorat's body delivered to them with the weapon he used. The general environment here is potentially hostile. Because of that, we're also leaving, soon, within the hour.

"I understand that Counselor Breia has his investigations to pursue, but there is also the simple math that you cannot *physically* travel from Terrabac fi Sur to Wedgewood in less than twenty-three days. No one here in Wedgewood may do the time calculation of you getting from here to Terrabac in less than a day unless you came back to Wedgewood and drew their attention, especially Sedge. Word will reach Wedgewood of your exploits up there. The contest of sixthsense skills, and that the vaunted Ghost-I of Neuland was successfully challenged by the high priestess of the Sea Horse Isles." Here, Ivan exhibited a touch of a rare smile, "Then, maybe you might become a bit of a celebrity, as the powerful priestess who came to Wedgewood before doing battle with the Ghost." Turning serious, he said, "The oligarch, when he heard through his Timber Keep pathic of Ghost-I's failure, he became vocally supportive of you, dismissing any speculation—"

An announcement came over the all-hands comm circuit, "Two minutes to out-system shift; all hands remain at their shift stations."

"Go on," the matriarch said.

"Right. And if he is curious as to how you got there so quickly, he's not talking." Ivan looked at the matriarch. "Did you...Have you talked to him? About--"

"No."

"Hmm. Maybe Christina? I've seen them talk confidentially. By the way..."

"Yes?" asked the matriarch.

"I think he's a fan of yours. The oligarch knows what you did up there. He said he asked you to act in the interests of the Western Alliance and is pleased you did so."

Margret and she exchanged glances. Acting on behalf of one provincial social group over that of another was strictly against ULUP, and if word reached the ULUP Board of Governance, there would be trouble. At the minimum, with the intervention by the Avarian Marines on a Class E world, her actions on the planet would come under board review. In her defense, if it ever came to that, she could cite Ultimate Cause if the board accepted the convoluted logic that the Neuland Auro Na, allied with Nak Drakas, in control of all Auro Na on Isuelt, presented a strategic threat against the Avarian Federation by restricting access to Dianis' aquamarine-5. In any case, a federation strategic emergency regarding aquamarine-5 had not been declared, but if it was, it would suspend ULUP.

"Chief," she asked, "how long are you expecting to stay planet-side? There are some things I need you to do."

His holographic image thought about it. In the background, she could see the waterwheel gears turning the huge millstone inside of the mill on the Twistynook River. "As you know, the only reason my teams are here is to protect you. Now that you are leaving, we will be shifting back to Dominicus III. That's our duty post. IDB Dianis is shut down. No budget no resources, and Dominicus needs all the help the IDB can give it. There are CivMon teams there that need Ready Reaction support."

She stared at his image.

Finally, she said, "I will have a formal request submitted to the director of IDB Dominicus to keep you here. The Matrincy will also submit a proposal to Donovan, the IDB Executive Director, and enlist the aid of the ULUP commission to reopen IDB Dianis."

Ivan's jaw went slack. He blinked into the holograph. "Seriously?"

"Yes, chief. Seriously."

He started shaking his head. "That's fine, ma'am, but even if you restore funding to IDB Dianis, where are you going to get the staff? The field teams? Even the orbital surveillance platforms? Money is only half the problem. Dominicus III is a wreck. With the war—"

"I know, chief, I know." She watched the mill gears behind him turn. "Chief, do you agree that with the amount of aquamarine-5 just lying around on the surface and the inordinate number of sensitives in the Timberkeep population that Dianis may be strategically important to the Turboii War?"

His shoulders slumped. He hesitated and then said, "Yes."

"Then we need to act. To protect our assets on Dianis, do you agree?"

The matriarch's reference to *our assets* bothered him. Dianis, a Class E, was not part of the Avarian Federation, and that was strictly enforced by ULUP. "Act? How?"

"I have some things I want you to do."

The sound of the millstone came through the audio of the hologram. Ivan let the millstone roll out of earshot. He knew he had limited leeway in avoiding the matriarch's demands. Executive Director Donovan would acquiesce to her demands, to a point. "And they are?" he asked.

"First, I want you to find Chief Inspector Forushen and tell him he and I are to talk. Failure to contact me directly will result in his arrest and extrication straight to my office on Avaria. "

Ivan responded, "Yes." It was a reasonable request and appealed to his sense of justice.

"You have thirty days, chief, or the Matrincy will intervene."

He didn't know what that meant; the IDB never liked it when the Matrincy stepped into their turf. "Yes, ma'am."

"Second, Counselor Breia will be returning to Dianis in the near future. His ULUP charter as Dianis planetary counselor allows that. You will escort the counselor and assist in his efforts to assess aquamarine-5 deposits on the planet.

Ivan wagged his head. They would see how that would go. He said, "Finding Atch should take precedence."

"Third, with the assistance of Chief Inspector Forushen and whatever other IDB staff are still loitering on the planet, assist Counselor Breia in identifying potential candidates for recruitment into the Turboii War effort."

At that, Ivan winced, though the matriarch could not tell what part of the demand bothered him the most: working closely with Breia, the implication that Agent Baryy Maxmun was also still on the planet, or the notion that the Matrincy was going to start actively recruiting Dianis adepts to fight in the war. A clear violation of ULUP.

He took a breath. "Are we done, ma'am?"

"Not quite. One other thing. Stay in touch with the Alon. Let me know if she needs help rescuing their six abducted adepts. It is in the interest of the Avarian Federation that an eventual alliance be formed between Clan Mearsbirch and us. Yes, I know that is in the far future, but now is the time to—" she let the sentence trail off.

Ivan couldn't help shake his head. All three matronens saw it.

"Thirty seconds to shift," came the call over the all-hands circuit.

Since they were firmly out of bounds, he asked, "And what do you think I should do about Corporal Meridia and Lettern?"

The matriarch's brows furrowed.

"Lettern wants to see him again. She at least asked if she would. Lettern is important. The clan thinks she is a hero, and she probably is. I think there are hormones involved. Senior Corporal Meridia, within hours of getting back aboard the *Fury,* messaged me and asked if he could transfer to the IDB, which, according to his Marine enlistment contract, is allowed because he has over twenty combat drops and three years continuous in-theater combat duty. Meridia asked if he could get a posting in Ready Reaction and would I accept him in my crew for Dianis. He assumed we were here permanently."

"Can you do that?" she asked.

"Yes, but...Lettern's a provincial. Strictly off-limits—"

Aged, tested by many battles, *Spirit's Fury* finally shifted out.

Chapter 14
Repair Bay

West of Isumfast

"Move the pinky."

Outish twitched the finger on his left hand. "Feels stiff."

"It will," said Baryy. "You need to exercise it and work the neural pathways. But we're done with the regen unit."

Outish held the hand up. It was whole, instead of a mangled mess where only the index finger and thumb remained, all five fingers wiggled in the antiseptic light of the repair bay. Halorite fingers. The regen unit was programmed to use Outish's Halorite genes, and so the regenerated area of the hand was covered in his natural, sandy brown fur in odd contrast to his thumb and wrist, which were distinctly Human. Fortunately, the fur on his hands was thinner than other body parts, but fur it was, nonetheless. Outish sat up. After three days of lying next to the regen unit, drifting in and out of consciousness as the regen drugs and builder cells coursed through his system, he felt woozy, almost sick. He stood up and then bent double and vomited. Having not eaten anything solid for three days, only water came up. Baryy stood back, trying to stay clear of the spume. An autobot the size of a toolbox sprang out of a wall compartment and scuttled over to the offending goo. It bleeped when it reached Outish. When the intern, either too numb or too ill to notice, failed to move out of the way, the bot said in a scratchy voice reminiscent of an Avarian accent three centuries past, "Move please, you are obstructing. Service to perform. Service to perform."

"Huh, oh." Outish stepped gingerly out of the way.

"Sorry about that, Outy. You feeling okay?" asked Baryy. "I'm not a med tech, but the injection learning course did say the patient might feel ill after the operation."

The astrobiologist wiped dribble from his mouth with a towel Baryy handed him. "Yeah, well, they were right about that." He shook the restored hand. "Wow, it tingles, sort of like it's asleep."

Baryy nodded nervously. The experience was as new to him as it was to Outish. "That's the sensory nerves coming alive as the drugs wear off. Supposedly, it may throb or hurt for a while, but you have a nano-antigen solution that will guard against any rejection symptoms, which there shouldn't be since the builder cells were bonded with your natural Halorite DNA, but with the gene therapy treatment that morphed your outward appearance to Human it's hard to tell, at least for me."

Outish looked pale as he staggered to a bed and lay down. "Oi, the room is spinning."

Concerned, Baryy grabbed the autodoc and wheeled it over. He hit the *scan/treat* button. The autodoc immediately went to work, and a robotic arm extended from the frame and deftly clasped a band connected with tubes to the intern's wrist. A pneumatic hiss came from the band as it sunk hypodermics into the wrist. Liquids began to flow through the clear tubes.

"Great," mumbled Outish, "more drugs," and then he was asleep.

"Everything okay," Achelous asked when he came in.

"Kernetic repulsoid shock," Baryy read the diagnosis off the autodoc display.

Achelous blinked. "What's that?" he asked, concerned.

Baryy shook his head, reading the changing display. "Don't know; it wasn't covered in the regen injection learning course." He hit the *further info* cell on the hologrid. "It's all medical gobbledygook to me. I'm a sociologist. But it says recovery time is four to six hours. So I say we let him sleep."

Achelous bent over the bed and looked at the regenerated hand. "Fur?"

Baryy's face split into a smile. Then he shrugged at Achelous's consternation. "Hey, at least it's a hand and not a claw!"

"He'll have to work in-country with a furry hand?" Achelous exclaimed. Baryy kept his mischievous smile even in the face of the chief inspector's vexation.

Achelous paused. "Did you do that on purpose?"

Baryy laughed. "No!"

"Spirits, his Timberkeep friends will never give him peace over that, first his big ears and now his furry hand."

"He can wear gloves."

Achelous shook his head slowly, the corner of his mouth quirked. The look of fatherly patience plain. "He'll have to shave it. Regularly."

Baryy looked down on his friend. They'd not always been friends. Outish had been as green as new grass when he'd first come in-country with Baryy and the chief. In many ways, the astrobiologist intern was still green, but during the Battle for Wedgewood, the kid had shown guts, dumb or otherwise. He was credited for standing in the shield wall in the retreat from the Main gate, where he was first wounded and knocked unconscious, and then in his solo attack on the Scarlet Saviors burning the granary. It was in that desperate combat that he had earned renown in Clan Mearsbirch. If his Timberkeep friends mocked him for a fury hand, and Baryy was sure they would, he was equally sure it would be out of respect for the terrible wound Outish received in that lonely, smoke-choked, flame-scorching melee.

Baryy rechecked the autodoc settings and then asked, "Were you able to get Marisa back to Tivor without any problems?" Secretly, Baryy was relieved to have Marisa away from Isumfast and the repair bay. She was learning too much, too fast, and it unsettled him. There were too many new variables emerging. He had Jeremy, their AI, plug the parameters into the sociology risk models for mission success, and in several areas, they were into yellow and, in one case, red, as with the appearance of the Matrincy in Wedgewood.

"Yes," Achelous replied, though he refrained from alarming Baryy with Marisa's latest exploit. He had received a stark surprise when, earlier that day, he had left the repair bay to meet Marisa in Isumfast and take her to the shift zone.

He'd led Echo, his eenu, out of the repair bay through the narrow, hidden opening to the outer cavern. They had managed to clear the cavern with an excavator Baryy had somehow got running and recommissioned.

Riding into the daylight and trotting down the barely discernable road, obfuscated with tall pines, ferns, and errant boulders, Achelous had been brought up short at the sight of Marisa sitting on a huge granite slab. She was -- of all things -- sketching a picture of the river gorge, wearing tight-fitting riding breeches, a dark blouse with the upper buttons undone, and her black hair unbound. His breath caught. Against the wild and pristine background, she was the most beautiful woman he'd ever seen.

"How did you find, er how—" he stuttered, searching for the right word.

"Find?" she asked innocently. "I haven't found anything. And how are you doing? It's been a whole day since we saw each other. Aren't you happy to see me?"

"Well, of course I am, it's just a—"

"Surprise?" she finished for him, smiling. "I love the mountains. I've often thought of building a new hall on Mount Epratis, but now the Timberkeeps are doing it for me. I can't wait to visit them. It will be so much better."

"Mmm, I see. And how did you conveniently and coincidently come to be sitting here, sketching? Not that I am complaining, mind you." He rode close, his gaze taking in her drawing and other things. "It's just -- you know how I am with surprises."

"You were coming back to the inn, so I thought I'd meet you halfway."

Achelous sniffed, "Halfway? How about all the way."

"I have something to show you." She stood, placing her parchment and quills in a pack, and jumped nimbly to a lesser boulder, then another, and then to the ground. She opened a saddlebag on her tethered eenu and withdrew a package wrapped in a brown sheepskin bound with twine. Achelous dismounted. "What is it?"

"Something I borrowed."

The package was the size and shape of a folder, similar to the one she carried to hold her loose sheaves of sketches. Undoing the twine and unfolding the skin, he held up the plastic-coated picture she'd acquired from the innkeeper.

His face became solemn, and he turned to look back up the mountain. In the picture, a wide, gravel road ran along the left bank of the Gracopherous, now concealed. A broad opening showed in the mountain where now a boulder scree lay with hundred-year-old trees growing amongst the verges. He turned back to her. "You found it," he hesitated, "by this?"

She pointed at a distinctive basalt chimney peak to the right of the river gorge and then back to the same edifice in the picture. "The innkeeper says Beehive is a well-known landmark. He said he came up here once with this picture, just like I did, but was unable to find an opening. Lucky for you," she said, dropping her voice.

"Lairliear Gamerhau gave you this?"

"Yes," she echoed his tone. "I thought it odd they have so many Ancient artifacts at the inn, and yet he and his family aren't molested by the Paleowrights. I know Lairliear is devout, but I didn't know that was a license to create your own Ancient archive."

He shook his head. "It's not. Lairliear is an Inquirer for the Church," he smiled at her, a wry twist to his grin. "All the Examiners from here to Tomis and south to Faldamar report to him. They display the pictures at the inn on purpose. It's a honey trap, if you will. Anyone seeing the pictures and boasting they've seen similar or bragging they have an Ancient artifact like it is marked by the inn's staff, who are all Paleowrights. The place serves as an acquisition house; those in the trade know to go there to barter their goods. Baryy wasn't pleased with me putting you up at the inn, but as you may have surmised, it is the only decent place within leagues of..." and he hooked a thumb over his shoulder, indicating the old avalanche scree.

"Why was Baryy worried about what I might learn?"

Achelous shrugged, "Perhaps. This presents a problem," he said, holding the picture. He looked around, peering into the woods, suppressing an urge to open his multi-func and scan for life signs. "We can't risk the cavern being found. Return this to Lairliear and complain to him the canyon has changed so much, with avalanches and all, that you couldn't make sense of it." He began carefully to wrap it when Marisa asked, "Dearen—"

He looked up at the gravity in her tone.

"What is mind-wipe?"

He mentally grimaced. The thought of explaining it a pain in itself. He looked around, sensing this wasn't to be a short conversation. He handed her the picture and found a smallish boulder covered in orange and rust-colored lichen. Sitting on it, he asked, "You're afraid of what they might do if they should catch us?"

She nodded silently, her dark eyes keen with worry. "I don't want to forget you and Boyd—" she turned away so he couldn't see her face.

He put his hands around her waist and pulled her to him, resting her warm back comfortably against his chest. She sat on his leg. Rather than try to console her, tell her it would never happen, he decided to tell her the truth. She could decide in her own mind as to the real or imagined risks. "We or I should say the IDB, can only do a mind-wipe if you are found guilty of an offense." He smelled her hair, admiring the deep, black luster. "And you are not guilty of anything."

"But why are you and Baryy worried about mind-wipe?"

"Well, because we, him and I, might be guilty of something."

She understood some, not all, of the possible transgressions he might be culpable of, like consorting with her and fathering Boyd, which angered her immeasurably if she dwelt on it. "But why does Baryy not want me to learn anything?"

Achelous swallowed. "That is a point of contention between him and me. I agree that strictly enforced ULUP doctrine could dictate that all provincials that we have associated with and have learned information through us could be subject to mind-wipe in an attempt to unwind the impacts of what ULUP would call extrasolar influence." He waited, then, "But it's not practical in implementation, particularly if the provincials plausibly learned the information on their own. What Baryy keeps forgetting is that ITA, the old Interstellar Transportation Authority, already polluted the Dianis culture! Over three hundred years ago! The ITA engineers, who dug that cavern behind us, had roamed around on Dianis, unhindered, for seventy-five years before ULUP was established. True, it was only in the last five years of that time that they were here in any significant numbers. I suppose that at their peak, they may have had two hundred engineers on the planet, but you can see from Lairliear's inn they made their mark. Their influence had an outsized impact because they were like gods to the provincials, with all of the technology and machinery, and in some well-documented cases of abuse, they purposely acted like gods."

"So it's true."

"What is?" he asked, worried.

"What the Paleowrights believe."

He snorted. "Lace, those Ancients, those ITA engineers, are long dead. They won't be answering any prayers for enlightenment or strength or wealth."

"But they were here. They walked our world and did those things that the priests preach."

He let out a long sigh. "Yes. Much of that is correct, to a point, particularly the stuff that they use from the books the engineers left behind, but I guarantee you the Diunesis Antiquaria clergy is not beyond substantial embellishment and context perversion."

"So why do you think I won't be mind-wiped?" She kept her back to him, sitting on his leg.

He didn't know if she was crying, and he was afraid to know. "Because you are learning the information on your own, mostly." He thought, *except for now, where I am telling her way too much.* But they were practicing a rudimentary form of memory disassociation with her looking at the forest and not at him. He hoped it would be enough. "And because so much of what you are learning, even from Baryy and me, can plausibly be intuited from the artifacts, like the books engineers left behind. And because a case can be made that everything you are learning is in defense of Dianis against extrasolars. I believe," and he felt this fervently, "that if it should ever come to it, the ULUP board of control would accept that all Dianis provincials have the right to defend their planet from outside incursions and to establish those protections in whatever way they can. Including researching and bartering for information from Avarian galactics."

She turned, looking over her shoulder, a damp but teasing shadow in her eye, "Barter? I didn't know I was bartering with you? And what am I bartering with?"

He grinned. "Okay, poor choice of words. How about *spy*?"

"I don't like that word either. Will they mind-wipe you?" She stood up and turned to hold his face in her hands. "I will never let them mind-wipe you. We will fight them. If they come for you, we will fight. We may just be provincials, but we have power. They want something from us, and they will never get it if they hurt you. That's my promise."

Standing there in the repair bay, he remembered the passion in her eyes and the soft strength in her hands. He had no idea how she would make good on such a promise, but he had no doubt as to her conviction.

Chapter 15
Nordarken Mining

Conglomerate Headquarters on The planet Avaria

The director of aquamarine production heard the door of the bunker open and then close. According to security protocols, the director waited for the visitor to sit in the chair on the opposite side of the blackout divider. The walls in the comfy rooms, as their occupants called them, were painted matte black. A single strip-light fixture ran the length of the ceiling, washing the room in a dim antiseptic glow. The chairs faced the opposing walls, not the divider. Everything was unremarkable, intentionally. There were few visual clues for investigators to search for when conducting a memory scan. Because the Human mind converted sounds into ethereal data, the only reliable way for interrogators to find and retrieve memories from a Human mind was through visual frames, not auditory frequencies.

"My AI flagged a news item for me this morning," said the voice from the other side of the curtain, the voice of his boss, Rocl Binair.

The director waited; he'd read the thread as well.

"Something about the matriarch made a surprise visit to a Class E world, a planet called Dianis. Her Marine escort engaged and terminated a mining prospector. Is that true?"

The question was purely rhetorical but still required a response. The senior vice president of Resource Production was just warming up.

"Yes," the director managed to say without croaking.

"And was that *our* contracted Intruder?"

"Yes."

"By the damned spirits of all your dead ancestors, how the hell did that happen!?"

The director wondered if the guards outside the foot-thick vault door could hear the Binair's screech. Gathering his nerve, the director launched into the explanation.

"Bad luck!" Binair hammered the explanation. He was known to be icy calm in public, particularly with shareholders. He was also known to be vile when faced with failure. "How could both the contractor and the matriarch -- of all people -- be on that planet, in exactly that same place, at exactly the same time?! How?!"

The director outlined the sequence of events and then went to the survey findings sent back from the contractor, most notably the scan of a three-hundred and twenty-nine million-credit pegmatite.

Binair was silent.

"I, we," the director corrected, "believe it was no coincidence. We believe that the matriarch and her escort were after the same thing as our contractor: the point-specific source and it was only because the Marines killed the contractor that she had to leave it there. Otherwise, she would have taken it with her. If she had taken it, industry analysts would have connected the sudden appearance of the pegmatite in Federation stores with her visit to Dianis and the death of the contractor, and to them, it would have been obvious that the matriarch went there to raid a Class E world of aquamarine. The *AVS Infinite Continuum,* a *Starlight*-class carrier, and her space wing of three hundred interceptors are sitting in the shipyards waiting for their field generator crystal cores."

The director waited for Binair to fill the dead space, and he did, "Fleet needs the aquamarine."

"Yes."

"And you think she went there... that the federation is now in the resource extraction business?"

"Well—"

"Bloody hell no!"

The director heard the smack of a hand on a chair arm.

"We can violate ULUP, but they can't. It's their law!"

The director shrugged his shoulders, which Binair could not see. He didn't want to disagree with his boss, at least not express it.

"There is no way we can let the federation start mining aquamarine and cutting us out. Resource extraction is our business."

The director waited for Binair to finish.

"I will have our general counsel work this with the ULUP board of governance. I will make sure we expose that bitch for what she is: a meddling, twisted, pathic prima donna."

Taken aback, the director had no idea that his boss held so much animosity for the matriarch. He wondered where that came from and how much pull Nordarken Mining had with the ULUP board of governance, but none of those questions did he feel safe to ask. Rumors persisted that the director's predecessor's sudden disappearance was tied to the questions he asked.

Binair growled, "What are your plans now?"

The director was ready for the question. He knew the dire situation in which Nordarken Mining currently found itself. Share prices were down sixty-three percent in six months due to speculation their aquamarine reserves were wiped out. The truth wasn't as bad as the rumor, but it was bad enough. "I don't see that we have any other choice. With your permission, we should move ahead with an extraction contract. The bidding contractors, through our double-blind intermediaries, will complain about the risk, of course, so we'll have to pay higher performance bonuses on minimal amounts of returned material, but we need to get the Dianis shipment cycle running."

There was a slight pause, and Binair asked, "And?"

"And?" the director was unnerved.

"And what will you set as a production target? I need to make a commitment to the executive committee."

The director swallowed.

Binair snorted. "Since you don't have a target, I'll give you one. You need two tons of aquamarine-5 sitting at the receiving dock of our Cranium II production facility in three months."

The director felt his chest constrict. *Two tons?* His chest hurt; he rubbed a hand hard against his sternum. He wanted to say *two hundred pounds* could be possible, but his mouth wouldn't work.

Silence ensued, and the director heard footsteps moving to the door. "Two tons. Nothing less."

Chapter 16
The Plains of Hebert

The Foothills and Plains East of Wedgewood

Christina rode at the head of the column. A screen of Barrigal's Zursh mercenaries scouted and flanked their march. All three hundred troopers, men and women, were mounted on eenus. More forces were arriving at Wedgewood every day, but Christina needed to be on her way.

The mountain ridgelines and massive Ungerngerists gave way to rolling hills and thinning groves of Twitter olems, their trembling, fan-shaped leaves a stark contrast to the foot-long needles of the Ungerngerists. Lycealia, the Loch Norim amphitheater, lay behind them, the Paleowright priest and guards having fled as soon as Barrigal's scouts arrived with drawn blades.

Slowly, after the trauma of the invading churchmen and Troglodytes abated, the land returned to normal. The morning sun shined brightly. Wildlife could be seen creeping back to dens, nests, and grasslands. Christina surveyed the column behind her. Sunlight glinted off the forty spear points of the Oridian lancers, their white and green pennants streaming from the raised lances. The mere color of those pennants attested to their beliefs. They were her people, and they were on a mission. Behind them came a ward of Timberkeeps: Red Elm clan swordsmen with the red tree painted on their shields. Angling down the slope, Christina was impressed by the sight of the double line following her. She'd asked for volunteers to accompany her but was humbled when the clan leaders, and even the oligarch, had instead assigned whole wards and troops to her expedition.

A squadron of Mestrich Rovers -- mounted archers -- followed behind Red Elm, and behind them came the Fifth Ward of Clan Mearsbirch with their double-bladed axes and square shields. In their silver and black tabards rode the half-company of Zursh mercenaries, many of whom were serving as outriders and scouts. Comprising the rear guard came the dragoons of Clan Cedar Floral. She'd never ridden with them before. Their eenus bore bright red saddle blankets with gold tassels, and the dragoons themselves had burnished pauldrons and thick fur hats with a long jaunty feather fluttering with their motion. She was told the thick fur of the hats was more for armor than warmth.

Ahead, a wide downward-sloping park spread out below. They were past much of the destruction wreaked upon the Timberkeep farms by the roving bands of Troglodytes and marauding churchmen. Now, they were entering the western boundary of the Central Plains, and the destruction took on a different feel. Here, farms and hamlets were ravished, but not as part of a methodical plan to wreak ruination on the Timberkeeps, but as the brief acts of savagery caused by a desperate, defeated enemy, retreating, looking for food and water, and then moving on.

They came to a burned-out barn, still smoldering, but the granary was still standing. A lone Troglodyte, in the distance, squatted on a rise. It disappeared behind the hill when a trio of scouts trotted up the grassy slope.

Mitchern, her command telepath, all of seventeen years old, asked, "The Trogs did this?"

"No," answered Barrigal, the mercenary captain, "Trogs hate fire," he said it more to his scout's boss than as an answer to Mitchern.

"Parrots," the scout's boss agreed simply, using the derogatory word for Paleowright pikemen. "Looks like they came through here two days ago, about a hundred or more. Headed due east, straight to Quarden. Another group, Trogs, have been skirting the Parrots. Looks like they're veering south, southeast."

Barrigal nodded once. "They're heading for the Great Latitudes."

"And good riddance," the scout's boss spat a gob of leaf-chew.

Christina took a deep breath and straightened in the saddle, stretching her back. It would be a long ride to the frontier. "We need to make sure the Trogs are moving on, all the way, and not intending to regroup. They'll gather by tribes, but if they are done with the *Kurchka*, their ancestor's revenge, the tribes will avoid each other. There's too much competition for food, and the chieftains will keep them separate." She pointed her eenu, called Lilith, south. Lilith, in the Northwren language, meant lily. "Let's find a Trog tribe and see if they are mixing or running separate." Looking over her shoulder to the east, she said, "We'll come back for the churchmen. They're broken, but the Trogs could still cause trouble."

"What about the Drakans?" asked the boss.

Barrigal smiled grimly. "If we find any of them, it will be a fight." He exchanged a long look with Christina. He'd been one of her captains when they fought the two Drakan centuries at the Hall gates during the Battle for Wedgewood. Their three hundred clansmen and mercs had beaten the Drakans, but just barely, and only then by Christina luring them into a trap. At a crucial moment in the ambush, the hoplites could have broken, but the Drakan decurion had rallied his troops and led them in a disciplined retreat, saving his men and keeping the force intact.

The expedition rode south much of the morning, catching glimpses of straggler Troglodyte bands making their way back to the Great Latitude swamp from which the Paleowright clergy had enticed their chieftains with pouches of sage rose. Addicted and high on the opiate, the Troglodyte leaders were easily manipulated into joining the Paleowrights in a *Kurchka* against their old neighbors and now enemies: the Timberkeeps of Clan Mearsbirch. Having suffered a crushing defeat at the foot of Wedgewood's treeforts, the Troglodytes had scattered into the countryside to loot and pillage. But the Angraris swampland reptiles were not adapted for living off the land in the high alpine country and had quickly soured on the adventure. The Timberkeeps were not the easy conquest the Hebert archbishop had predicted.

The further south they went, Barrigal's scouts reported larger and larger bands of reptiles until finally they sighted a whole tribe, or what remained of it.

Christina eased Lilith up and out of a ravine onto a knoll where a Zursh scouting trio waited. A long bowshot away, sixty to eighty Troglodytes lingered along a sluggish creek. Until the moment the blonde female warrior appeared, the reptiles were content to ignore the scouts. When Christina, with her Defender's shield strapped to the eenu, rode to the fore, the Troglodytes rose and started gesticulating amongst themselves and at her.

"It seems they know you," one of the scouts said to her.

Another scout snorted. "They should. She held the center of the shield wall with us."

Christina studied the array. They all bore shell armlets on their upper biceps on their right arms, and their leaders carried man-made maces. She guessed the mass of Troglodytes was what was left of the Tong-Gong tribe.

"Tell Barrigal to arrange the squadrons in a double row across this rise," she said to a scout. "Tell him he is not to attack until I order it. I want to talk to the reptiles first."

"You can speak to loglards?" a scout asked, surprised.

She wagged her head. "We are all Mother's Creatures."

Easing her mount down the slope towards the creek, Christina took her time. Lilith wanted to shy, but she reassured the eenu with strokes along her mane. Holding up, she let the eenu sense her calm.

The tribe was now arrayed in its own double line across her front. She need not look behind her. Judging by the tribe's reaction, she could tell Barrigal was forming up the squadrons.

Sensing Lilith was ready for a closer look, she eased her into a slow walk.

The Troglodytes were braced. Their chieftain knew it was pointless to run. Troglodytes, while bigger and faster than Humans, could not out-run eenus.

Christina came within a javelin throw of the Trog line, and one of the reptiles made to raise its javelin, but a coarse grunt from a massive buck in the center of the line stayed the throw.

Christina made the sign for parlay: two fists smacked twice, then a pause and a clap of hands.

At first, the Trog chieftain was confused, not comprehending a Human had just used the sign language of all Isuelt reptiles, a method of communication the three reptile species used between each other.

She made the sign again, and this time, the chieftain got the message. His tribe started prattling and growling amongst themselves, and then he silenced them with a howl.

Lilith wanted to bolt, but Christina rubbed her mane and sat calmly, waiting for the chieftain's reply.

The chieftain handed off his mace, then made the same sign and strode purposefully forward. He stopped halfway and waited, feet planted, legs spread, his tail pointed straight back, still.

Now came the tricky part. Christina would have to dismount and walk to her opponent, leaving her eenu where it was. If Lilith should bolt while Christina was negotiating, she would lose face in the eyes of the Trogs, and the tribe would demand they attack. The question was, could Barrigal reach her in time.

Dismounting, Christina jammed the point of her bastard sword into the turf. She unbuckled her long sword and hung it on the pommel of the saddle. She removed the bridle from Lilith's head and stuffed it in a saddlebag. Whispering into the animal's ear, she petted it, then shooed it back to the waiting squadrons, but in a turnabout, the animal refused to leave. Instead, it dipped its head and began to crop grass.

Christina shrugged to the chieftain, expecting him to understand the whimsical nature of animals, and then approached him.

Barrigal, waiting beside Lucifar -- the Oridian lancer captain -- said, "When I give the word, you will charge straight down the hill, and through them, no stopping. See if you can rescue the Alon along the way. My mercs will be right behind. The Rovers will provide archery support. Red Elm and Mearsbirch will be on our flanks, and the dragoons will sweep around the right flank, blocking any retreat."

The scowl on Lucifar's face told Barrigal what he thought the chances were of Alon surviving until they reached her. Lucifar's lancers and their specially bred eenu's were the fastest of all the squadrons, but would they be fast enough?

The chieftain shook his head in response to a sign gesture from Christina. Up close, Christina could smell the dry reptilian musk. His body was covered with thick, green scales the size of a thumbnail, and two horns grew from either side of his head, each the length of a hand. The chieftain's vertically-slitted eyes were pale green, a difference from their Lizard Men cousins who had no horns, and their eyes were yellow. He stood a head taller than Christina, but in a twist of evolutionary fate, her Human genes gave her quicker reactions.

Christina made the sign for another question.

He uttered a grunt and growled his answer.

She thought she understood.

Making hand gestures for another question, the chief immediately answered in the affirmative. He then grunted his own question and made sign to back it up.

"No," she answered, smacking a closed fist against her palm.

He nodded once, then asked via sign, "Why?"

She replied -- hoping to get it right -- that the Timberkeeps war was against the Great Holy Man of Hebert, the man who had misled the Groglodane Nation into assailing their Old Enemy, the Stump Men, who were an enemy no more. That it was not the Stump Men who had come to the Great Latitudes, but the Groglodanes to the mountains.

And so it went, hand gestures, claw waving, grunting, and growling, to the best that Christina could manage.

Finally, nearing an agreement, Christina stated her demand, and the chieftain nodded once.

She reached out with both hands, palm out, and the chieftain did likewise. They clasped hands, and when the Troglodyte sought to test her strength, she summoned all her energy and locked his arms where they were. His pupils widened. Then she let her arms drop, nodded once, and strode away. Walking purposefully, never looking back, she pulled her bastard sword from the turf and slung it into her shoulder sheath.

"And?" asked Barrigal when Christina rode her eenu back to their ranks.

Only then did she turn Lilith about to see the tribe loping, in mass, to the south. "I think we are all tired of killing and dying, including them. They've given their ancestor's word that they'll not cross the Deelo River unless we do first."

"So that's it? We're done?" asked a merc.

"With them," she answered. "Their chieftain gave his word that he would meet with the other tribes, seek their agreement, and if they refuse the peace, he will send an emissary to Lycealia to warn us."

Lucifar, who had been watching her closely, said, "This is wise, Alon. The oligarch will be pleased. As you said, our war is not with the Troglodytes but the Paleowrights."

"And the Drakans," added Barrigal.

"But what's to stop the churchmen from just getting the chieftains high on sage rose again and then stirring them up with more lies and promises of glory?" a merc asked.

"I've been thinking about that," answered Christina. "Much of the ground sage rose comes overland through Darnkilden and Sea Haven. Up to now, they've let it go through. They consider it a nuisance but not worth bothering over. The attack on Wedgewood has changed all that. Lucifar, speak with the oligarch. Ask him to convince Darnkilden to block the sage rose trade."

Lucifar answered, "Yes, Alon. The Troglodytes are best served staying out of the issues of Humankind. They are safer in their swamps."

Barrigal snorted. "Oi. While we kill each other."

At that, Christina looked resigned. "Let us hope it does not come to that. We are all Mother's Creatures."

Barrigal gruffed, "No disrespect, Alon, you know I love you and would fight to the death for you, but you need to be telling Mother's Word to the Paleowrights and Drakans."

The column traveled north, leaving the straggling bands of Troglodytes behind. They were in the realm of Darined now, a vassal to the archbishop of Hebert. They rode with their pennants and standards plain for all to see. Never had a composite force of Mestrich, Oridia, and Timberkeeps been marshaled, and never had one paraded in strength through Heberian territory. Here and there, farmers would come out of their homes to gawk at the passing squadrons. Eventually, the forward scouts came upon a dejected pair of Church pikemen who were held captive until Christina and the lancers arrived.

The Oridian lancers eyed the two Paleowrights with disdain. The men had lost or thrown away their pikes and shields. Their colorful uniforms, blue, yellow, and green, the reason they were called Parrots, were dirty and torn. One soldier was missing a boot. Both men glanced at the long Oridian lances with apprehension.

Christina dismounted. She approached them, and the Zursh mercenary scouts held them tight for fear they would attempt something upon her person.

"Let them go," she said.

When the scouts hesitated, she said, "There will be no killing here today."

She looked at the pikemen and asked, "When was the last time you ate?"

One soldier, with dried blood caking on an ear, answered, "Two days ago."

"Captain," she called.

"Yes, Alon," Barrigal answered.

At the mention of *Alon,* the gaze of the two soldiers sharpened on Christina. One of the soldiers spotted her white lily necklace.

"See to it these men are fed."

"Yes, Alon."

"Where are you bound?" she asked of the pikemen.

"Don't know, er, ma'am. We're trying to get back to Hebert."

She pointed off to the southeast. "That's that way. What of your officers? Your unit? When did you see them last?"

"A week ago," the man with the bloody ear answered.

"Why did you leave them?" asked Lucifar from his mount. "We've seen naught but Troglodytes this far south."

When the two pikemen failed to answer, one of the scouts grabbed an arm and said, "I'll not be gentle. I killed your ilk in Wedgewood. Answer the questions."

"The major was forcing us," and then the whole sordid tale came out. Beatings, reprisals, and sacking of villages, all at the direction of Scarlet Savior squads acting as *moral* enforcers.

"They're deserters," surmised Barrigal.

Christina studied them. "Why are the battalions not returning to Hebert?"

"The major said we could not return in disgrace. We were to gather at Oled."

"And then what?" asked Lucifar.

The soldiers shrugged.

"What happened to your unit?" she asked.

"We, we," one soldier attempted to say, but then the other finished, "We broke when you captured our major. Outside the walls. On the second day."

"Ah," grunted Barrigal. "You were in *that* battalion."

Lucifar looked to him for an explanation.

Barrigal nodded to the Alon. "She set an ambush for them. A bloody, glorious fight, that was. We cut through them like a knife through parrot feathers." The other mercenaries laughed.

Christina reached up and placed a thumb first to the one soldier's forehead and then to the other. "We are all Mother's Children. I know not what Ancient to you pray to," and she looked them in the eyes, "but I have met the Ancients. They are men and women like us. Not gods." She turned and placed a foot in her eenu's stirrup and swung up. "Mother forgives you. Can you say that of your Ancients, Paleowrights?" She let the question sink in. "Go south. Find your farms and families. Think hard on what matters in life. Think hard on who you would serve, and do they serve you?"

An hour later, Mitchern rode up beside Christina as the column moved through a land of thickening woods and isolated farmsteads. "Alon, Brookern says Sedge is asking about our progress."

"Tell Brookern of our encounter with the Trogs and of our agreement. You can tell him that we are seeking contact with either the Paleowright battalions or the Drakan centuries, and we have word the pikemen are gathering at Oled."

"And our missing adepts?"

Christina had been mulling over the same question. Finding and rescuing the six adepts that had been abducted by the Drakans was her main quest. Scouting for the retreating enemy was a wise thing to do along the way. She despaired that the six were no longer in Western Alliance territory. By now, she assumed, they were in Nak Drakas. "Tell Brookern, we've no word on the adepts, but I am prepared to travel to Toll Haven and meet with the Congregation." Her eenu skirted a fallen tree on the road. It gave her time to think. Then she said, "I will seek the Congregation's guidance." Unlike Diunesis Antiquaria, the

Mother Dianis faithful had no established seat like Hebert. They instead congregated, and this year's Congregation was being held, conveniently for Christina, in Toll Haven, the capital of the Sea Haven League.

Christina fidgeted in the saddle, clenching her heels, and Lilith picked up on her agitation. Christina eased up and tried to relax. It bothered her, as it did the adepts of the clan, that the three telepaths amongst the abducted six had not attempted to contact any of their family or friends. The clan sensitives were in agreement that the six were still alive. The psychic bonds with their fellow adepts had not been sundered through expatriation. Death. The question, therefore, was how the Drakans were keeping the missing six from touching home.

By late afternoon of the next day, riding through intermittent storms, the troops were sore and stiff, their mounts lagging, and all they had to show for their efforts were thirty or so dejected pikemen straggling in small groups. Each time the expedition encountered a group they disarmed them, asked the same questions, and each time Christina absolved them, giving Mother's Forgiveness and sending them to their homes, admonishing them that rallying at Oled with the Scarlet Saviors was a fool's errand to end in more hardship. Most accepted her wisdom, but a few flinched from her blessing and glared at her patience. For those malcontents, the Zursh mercenaries advocated for imprisonment or even execution. The mercenaries would not dare make demands of the Alon, but they were loath to let an enemy go free. One such pikeman made to spit at Christina, but her hand caught his jaw just as spittle bubbled from his mouth. The mercenaries fell about him and would have killed him had Christina not intervened.

Laying there beaten, wiping blood from his mouth, Christina had looked down on him and said, "You can forsake Mother's Forgiveness. You can disrespect me, but beware the wrath of the Faithful. I can only counsel temperance to those who still have tolerance. These are the hardened of Mother's Faithful. They come forth with sword and shield and resolution." She watched him try to crawl away. "Take heed, churchman. Spit is a poor offense to die for. What is your Ancient's reward for *that?*"

A scout came riding up fast. "Alon, we can see Oled to the east, on the horizon, but there is a hamlet beyond the hill here. There are Paleowrights there." The scout paused, preparing for what he would say next. "They are pillaging, raping."

Christina's eyes narrowed. "How many Paleowrights?"

"Hard to tell. At least a forty. Could be more."

She looked at the churchman, "Whose land is this? Are those villagers Paleowrights?"

When the man failed to respond, a scout kicked him hard in the ribs and leveled his sword at the man's throat.

"Yes," croaked the pikeman, but they're of Oled, not Hebert."

Christina snarled, "You would forsake, you would rape and murder your own simply because they not of Hebert?!"

The churchman tried to crawl away from her, but the scout jammed the sword tip into his neck. Fear, nay, terror blossomed in the man's eyes.

Christina whirled. "Barrigal! Lucifar!" and then to Mitchern, "Signal the squadrons. They are to form up on the Oridians. Hurry. Order of battle."

"Yes, Alon?" answered Barrigal as he urged his mount through the gathered eenus.

"We attack the village. Spare the townsfolk."

Barrigal glanced about, found his scout's boss, and the two galloped off. Lucifar and his two troop leaders pelted after them.

On the track near the hamlet, the squadrons formed up in their attack order. Christina eased Lilith in beside Barrigal. They were immediately behind the six scouts who would lead the attack. Off in the distance, they heard a scream. Peering through the trees, there was a narrow valley to their right, and on the other side of the valley, a girl or young woman ran up the wooded hill chased by two men. One of the men tried to tackle her. She screamed, and they both fell. The second man pounced on the girl, but she rolled away clutching her dress, and darted back down the hill.

Tense, waiting for the messengers ordering the column to return, Christina looked away from the valley. Lucifar was in line behind her. Beside him, she saw Sergeant Veri, a woman and the standard-bearer for the lancers. Standard-bearer was a position of honor and awarded to a person who would fight to the death to defend it. Christina noted the woman's intense focus on the girl. Her right gauntlet held the standard like a vice. Astride her charger, with her plumed and polished helm, gleaming breastplate, and greaves, Veri was the epitome of a warrior. The sergeant noticed Alon's attention, and they locked eyes. They were ready to ride, ready to fight. Christina thought of the other hundred or so women in their column. Lilith pawed the ground and snorted, and Christina realized she was clenching her mount. "Barrigal," she hissed, "we need to go."

He looked to her and understood. The last outrider returned. "We're ready," the messenger reported.

"At last," Barrigal said. "Sergeant, signal the advance."

Swirling her pennant twice in the air, Sergeant Veri pumped it up and down; the column started to move.

Starting at a trot, the senior scout, a former cavalryman himself, eased the force into motion. Today, there would be no bugle calls or signal horns, just a swift strike into the heart of the enemy.

The scout prodded his mount to a canter, and the entire expedition surged, and the acceleration pulsed along the column.

The lead scout gave his animal a solid kick and leaned forward. They went to a gallop, and Christina felt her anxiety blow away. Glancing to her right, Veri held the lance aloft, and the banner – a white eenu on a green field -- streamed from the gleaming spear point.

Turning to face the emerging field, Christina drew her longsword free and held it aloft for all to see.

The wind blew. Dirt clods flew from hooves; the eenus snorted and huffed.

Christina saw the lead scout lean lower in the saddle and then whip his mount as they broke into the clearing.

And away they went.

Christina let Lilith go flat out.

Three hundred riders came blasting from the forest in one long, sinuous battering ram.

Heading for the village center, the column split into three.

A twitch on the reigns and Lilith broke right. Christina spurred the charger hard, pelting to the valley.

The Oridian Lancers drove through the center of the hamlet, Cedar Floral went left, and the Zursh mercenaries went right.

A pikeman stood stupidly in Christina's path, and she let Lilith run him down.

Galloping past huts, hovels, and an occasional stone building, she came to the edge of the valley.

The girl fell again. She tried to rise and stumble across the creek, but the churchman knocked her down and grabbed her hair, cursing her for running and being difficult. The other pikeman shoved him away. "Leave her. She's mine. See my face? She clawed me!" Grabbing her by the arm, the pikeman tried to drag her across the creek when the other churchman slugged him. "The hell you say! We both get her."

While the pikemen fought each other, the girl gained her feet, hoisted her skirts, and waded to the other side. When the pikemen saw their prize escaping, they paused their dispute and waded after her.

Exhausted and limping, the girl tried running to the village but stumbled. She gained her feet again but saw the men were only paces away. About to give up, she turned to face the village and prayed to Thomas the Ancient for mercy when she saw an apparition. The figure held a pale sword that caught the sunlight. It rode a charging eenu whose mane and tail streamed with the wind. A golden braid flowed behind a strange curlicue helmet, and the rider's cape blew with the wind. The girl realized the rider was a woman and was heartened.

The image came on. All four hooves dug at once and barely touched the turf as they rose again. Eenu and rider were one, an Ancient-spawned savior hurtling to her in a hypnotizing undulation.

The sword moved. In a gleaming arc, the girl saw it coming, a phantom glitter. She heard the swoosh as it went over her head and ended in a hollow cracking sound. The power of its passing took her breath.

Twisting on the ground, the girl saw one pikeman sprawled a foot away and the second running. He raised his hands, attempting to fend off a blow. Pivoting on its haunches, the charger cut him off, and the sword flashed. The man fell.

Rider and mount turned to face the girl. The bloody sword dripping. The warrior prodded her mount. Trotting closer, the eenu halted. A white lily on a field of green against a sky of blue adorned the shield. The girl had been taught by her priest what that was: the sign of the Heretic. The great blasphemer who defiled all things Ancient. The heretic's hand reached down to her. It was one of the despised Defenders whom the great Scarlet Saviors were said to have purged from the world.

She grasped the hand and arm, and it easily swung her up onto the eenu. She could smell the rose water in the rider's golden braid, and they were off. They galloped to her village, and the girl hugged the waist of the warrior as if her very survival depended on it.

A group of archers and axemen were guarding other villagers, and even some of her family were there.

The warrior said to the girl, "I'll leave you here. You'll be safe. I've more work to do."

As the girl slid off the eenu, her father, bleeding from a gash on his head, came to hug her, and an axeman rode up, "Alon, Barrigal wants to mount another charge. There is another village on the other side of that wooded saddle. It's bigger. If we hurry, we may surprise them."

The one they called *Alon* looked down on her as her father hugged her and cried, and the villagers clustered around. To the end of her life, the girl would never forget the warrior's leaf-green eyes and what she said next. "Mother loves you; we are all her children."

"Hurry, Lucifar. We need to form up."

Christina arrived as Barrigal was urging the scattered Oridian lancers into order. The eenus were huffing and snorting, their flanks glossy from the sweat of the assault.

She spurred to the rise and peered down the long valley beyond. The track coming up from the village widened considerably, with the forest sparse on both verges. The road topped the ridge where the force was now assembling and followed the center of the valley where, about a mile distant, was another much larger village. Upon a promontory in the far haze was a city: Oled.

Already, the village at the end of the road was abuzz with commotion. There would be no surprise. Pikemen, armed and armored, were running from the buildings, and the distinctive yellow and red armor of Scarlet Saviors could be seen rousting and doing their own version of Barrigal's assembling. Christina wheeled Lilith about and took her place in the center of the front rank of lancers. She pulled her sword free and held it aloft, a silent command to all those around her that they were about to charge.

Barrigal drew in beside her. "At the village, Lucifar will order the column to spread. We'll assault their line with two lines of our own."

She nodded, never taking her eyes from where the Scarlet Saviors were ordering the defense. "How many?"

"Four hundred, maybe more," said Lucifar on her left. "Our prisoners from the village said those are what's left of two of their battalions and four squads of Saviors."

"Bloody Scarlet Britches," Barrigal cursed.

Calmly, Christina peered at him. "You should ride with your Lamarans. I will lead this charge."

The unspoken command was if she were to fall in the leading rank, he would take command.

In the few short months that she had come to Wedgewood, she and Barrigal had fought side by side in many a desperate struggle. Today would be different.

He gave her the salute of the old Lamaran Federate cavalry and headed for the rear.

Now, to her right, Sergeant Veri sidestepped her mount in close.

"When you are ready, captain. And make it quick," Christina said.

Lucifar checked his lancers. They'd aligned in a column of four. "Bugler, sound the advance."

They started out, and the captain immediately took them to a canter.

"Sound the gallop."

The bugle blared a treble note, and the squadron accelerated.

Lances were held pointed at the sky. Christina rested her drawn sword across the pommel as the squadron charged at a controlled rate, closing the distance to the village. On ahead, the Scarlet Saviors had managed to form the pikemen into two lines, about two hundred men each, and getting wider as stragglers were added to the ends. They covered the central avenue into the village, but the lanes to the right and left were still open.

Cedar Floral was at a full-out race, the dragoons riding low and hard to close the gap. Behind them, Christina caught sight of the silver and black tabards of the Zursh mercenaries. Barrigal was coming fast.

At the village, the Paleowright pikemen lowered their spears, leveling them at the oncoming charge.

A cavalry assault was a matter of physics, discipline, and trust in the rider beside you.

"Form the line!"

Answering Lucifar's command, the bugler sounded four quick, sharp notes.

The front quad column slowed and spread into a line while the rear squadrons followed suit, lengthening the first line and adding a second. The lancers, stirrup to stirrup, resumed the gallop. They were riding so close Christina's leg repeatedly touched Sergeant Veri as the force thundered forward.

Already, the pikemen were fidgeting. Their pikes were wavering. Some were looking left and right. A Scarlet Savior, in his yellow and red enameled armor, ran back and forth in the center, clubbing any churchman who looked to the rear.

"Charge!"

All forty Oridians lowered their lances, spear points gleaming, pennants streaming. They drove home the charge at twenty yards.

A great crash sounded as the cavalry met the pikemen; spears shattered, lances shivered, eenus smashed into men, riders were thrown, and churchmen were trampled.

For those pikemen who stood their ground, a lance found a shield, chest, or helm. Properly held by a well-trained and disciplined force of pikemen, a double line such as what the Scarlet Saviors attempted would cause an eenu to balk at the leveled spears and swerve at the last moment.

Not this day.

This day, physics, discipline, and bravery carried it.

Christina reached forward with her shield in one hand, sword in the other, and reins across the pommel. She took a spear meant for Lilith on her shield and caved a helmet with her sword. Her blade swung at a churchman between her and Veri, and then they were into the second line of pikemen. An upraised spear came at her, and she bent her head. The point deflected off her helm, and the shaft rubbed on her pauldron. Kicking Lilith hard, the eenu vaulted forward while Christina undercut her sword across the face of a churchman. Then they were through and galloping into the village. A fountain loomed in the center, and a Scarlet Savior came running out of a building with his rachier swinging.

Christina caught it with her sword; the two blades clashed together. She held her arm and sword, twisting the Savior around so that he never saw Veri's shivered lance.

"Rally! Rally!" ordered Lucifar, and the bugle trumpeted the command. They were milling about the village fountain, fending off pikemen and Saviors; villagers were running and screaming; livestock broke from their pens; all was chaos.

Pivoting her mount, Christina sought a quarry, but then the dragoons of Cedar Floral burst through the shattered gap in the Paleowright lines, and any remaining order of the churchmen vanished. Christina watched as the dragoons did what a saber cavalry did best: slaughter broken infantry.

The Paleowrights battling the lancers in the square were first forced back by Cedar Floral and then completely swept away by the Zursh mercenaries. Red Elm swordsmen galloped by, and when Christina saw the warden of Clan Mearsbirch, she called to him, "Hold at the edge of the village. Do not go to Oled. Hold and reform all our units there."

He acknowledged her with a wave.

"Now what?" asked Barrigal as he circled back from pursuing fleeing pikemen.

"Sweep them from the village. Break any formations, but do not go beyond the village."

As the squadrons and wards smashed any remaining resistance, Christina led a group of dismounted lancers from house to house, clearing pikemen from near the village square.

After she'd seen the last of the churchmen either captured or running to the woods, Christina went to the fountain. There, slaking her thirst, she waited for Lucifar to join.

He rode up, blood and mud-spattered, his eenu huffing. He let it drink from the fountain.

Christina said, "We need to tend to our wounded and tally our dead." She fervently hoped the count of both was low. "We've dealt the Paleowrights a cruel blow today. They'll not be ready to threaten Wedgewood for some time."

"Months, if then," remarked Lucifar.

"Oled can stay with the Paleowrights today," she said. "There will be refugees aplenty. It's not our mission to carry war into the archbishop's homeland." Though she knew that was exactly what Barrigal wanted, and she sympathized with him. "We need to find the Drakans. We need to know if they have been reinforced." She and Barrigal exchanged a glance. How and when two centuries of Drakan Empire hoplites had moved beyond the Drakan frontier and were able to attack Wedgewood undetected was a grave concern of the clan and the leaders of the Western Alliance. "And I need to search for the missing adepts. If they are in Nak Drakas, that will be hard to do with three hundred troopers in tow."

Finally, Barrigal gave a hint of a smile. "Oi," he mimicked his Timberkeep friends, "but we're good at persuasion."

Lucifar sniffed. "So that's what you call breaking a line of pikemen: persuasion."

Chapter 17
Baldor Prairiegrass

Along the Darnkilden Border

Grumbling to himself, Baldor pulled up and spied the trailhead suspiciously. The track through the gloomy forest ended at a stable with a cramped paddock and a lowly stablehand's hut. A group of men, four or five, maybe more, loitered near the paddock rail. The paddock was full, and another ten or so eenus were saddled and tied to hitching posts spread around the confined opening in the forest. Baldor had been riding east toward the Drakan frontier for two weeks, searching for Drakans. His butt was sore, and his purse hurt from buying supplies.

A stable hand came up and offered to take his mount; Baldor shooed him away. "Money grubbers," he grumbled, "I can tie my own eenu." Roping the reins around a hitching post, he eyed the men hanging about the paddock. *Nakish,* he surmised from their dark skin and coiled hair. *I'm in the right place.* It was odd, though not wholly uncommon, to find so many Nakish together in one place this far west, but then he was looking for two centuries of them, Drakan hoplites specifically, the survivors of the Battle for Wedgewood. These men were definitely soldiers, dressed as they were in their mish-mash of armor and clothing. When they had attacked Wedgewood, they came dressed and equipped as free mercenaries, not as imperial Drakan troops. The subversion was an attempt to lull Western Alliance attention.

A series of cracked and moss-covered flagstones wound up the hill beyond the paddock. The stones were slick from the recent rain, and Baldor's mood matched their condition as he was soaked through. Making to climb the steps, one of the soldiers intercepted him. The soldier's short sword, a Drakan gladius, poked him in the chest. "State your business, Doroman," said the soldier.

Baldor swallowed. The soldier made no attempt to be subtle or oblique; the hand holding the blade was scarred, and the vambrace behind it was worn and scarred as well. "I was told I can find Larech here. I have information for him," which was a calculated lie.

The sword lowered, and the soldier waved to another Drakan.

Baldor followed the second soldier up the stone stairway and came to the foggy courtyard of an inn. A sign hung above the main door, and in gold lettering, it read *Hatchet Sisters*. Leading Baldor into the dim interior, the Nakish grunted, "He's in the corner."

A fire burned in the hearth, and Baldor made his way past the cramped tables and warmed his hands at the fire. Slowly, the cheery radiance penetrating his soggy rain slicker and leggings, he became aware of the quiet in the nearly full taproom. He sneaked a glance at the table nearest him; the three Nakish men sitting there were silent. One had his hand on a mug but made no move to lift it.

A man, approaching from the left, caught Baldor unaware. "You've got some cheek coming in here, Timmy. What do you want?"

"I'm not a Timmy," he shot back. "I'm Plains. And I have something for Larech."

The challenger glanced back to the corner, got a nod, and told Baldor to come with him.

There were three men at the table. Baldor took the empty chair.

"Baldor Prairiegrass," said Agent Larech of the Drakan Empire's secret service, the Washentroufel. "You are a long way from Wedgewood."

"Oi, and a hard time it was finding you too. I'd thought you'd run all the way to Stith Drakas."

The man sitting next to him pulled a dagger and slammed it point-first down into the table between two of Baldor's fingers.

Waiting for the blade to stop vibrating, the third man, the one sitting beside Larech, said, "That's a hello greeting."

After almost shitting his drawers, Baldor wanted to say they were being sore losers but bit his tongue.

"Whatever it is you've come to say, it had better be important. I'd hate to see you leave empty-handed, or maybe no-handed," Larech said.

"What I've got to say is worth gold."

A snort came from the dagger-man, and he grasped the weapon and began working it back and forth until he could pull it free.

"I need to see the gold first," insisted Baldor.

The dagger angled for Baldor's jaw, and its owner said, "And why should we pay one silver sliver when I could just take your left eye and leave you with your right. That would be a good deal for you."

Larech gave a bare shake of his head. "Not yet. You'll spill our drinks. We'll take this outside."

When the dagger wielder made to rise and follow, Larech said, "Centurion, you should stay here. You're likely to kill my *virolmir*. I can let you do that later." Then, to the other man, Larech asked, "Care to bear witness, decurion? In case I *miss* an important detail." His smirk anointed his sarcasm.

Outside, across the cobblestone courtyard, Larech said, "Okay, Baldor, what is so important that you would risk your life? Even for gold?"

Baldor unfolded a piece of parchment and explained what the drawing was, to the extent he could, how it had been used during the battle, and where the Timmies were making more.

"A rifle?" the decurion asked.

"Hmm, yes," said Larech. "He told Captain Irons the same story when we were in Wedgewood, but it appears he has more evidence. Larech handed Baldor a gold coin.

While Larech had not introduced the decurion, Baldor had seen him in the Paleowright command tent during the Battle for Wedgewood. It was widely accepted that Decurion Uloch and his two Drakan hoplite centuries were the only things that had saved the Paleowright army from destruction.

Then Baldor demanded more gold for his next piece of information.

Larech and Uloch listened.

"Captain Irons, you say?" asked Uloch. He'd met the Scarlet Savior captain and admitted the man was ruthless and suited for the mission that Baldor outlined.

"When is this supposed kidnapping to happen?" asked Larech.

"In a month, give or take. My source didn't know exactly. He wasn't going on the mission."

"Did you know any of this?" Uloch asked Larech.

He shook his head. "Bloody Parrots are tight as a vice with information about Ancient technology. But I'm not surprised. Helprig has had a hard-on for this Achelous ever since his woman, Marisa of House Pontifract, spurned Helprig in Tivor."

Baldor held out his hand, and Larech, with distaste, tossed him another heavy coin.

"And I have more information, and this one will take five gold." Before either of the Drakans could react, perhaps violently, he pulled out the proof from inside his rain slicker. He dangled it in front of them.

Larech made to grab it, but Baldor pulled it back. "Uh, uh. Five gold first. Then you can have it. Even use it. I'll show you how."

After the agent had forked over the gold, Baldor led them over to what he assumed was a storage shed. They went inside, and before they closed the door, Baldor showed Larech how to use the device. Then he closed the door.

"Well?" asked Baldor. "Have the Paleowrights given you anything like that?"

"No," answered Larech, fiddling with the controls. Then he gave the telescopic night-vision goggles to Uloch to try.

"You found that where the Ancient was killed?" Larech asked after hearing the story of Quorat.

"Yes. It was kicked under a log."

Uloch wanted to be skeptical. He didn't want to believe, but if the Ancients had come back to Dianis and were fighting amongst themselves, squabbling over aquamarine, then all the stories he learned in the church of Diunesis Antiquaria were true. Almost true. The Paleowright priests had always portrayed the Ancients as benevolent and wise, not the cold-blooded murderers that Baldor, the *virolmir* – Northwren for wisdom thief -- said them to be. As he scanned the dark storage shed with the goggles, he could see as if it were day. Moreover, there were strange numbers along the inside edges of the goggles that changed depending on what he looked at. If only he knew what they meant.

Turning, Uloch moved silently to the left, watching Larech and the spy look to where they thought him to be, but they couldn't see in the dark. He could. Going to the door, he pushed it open, and the device automatically compensated for the daylight. Fumbling for what Baldor called the 'make-big' button, he pushed it. Sure enough, everything far away suddenly leapt much closer, giving him vertigo. Scanning his surroundings, he practiced *zooming* in and out. The experience was amazing. The knowledge of what the device offered was exhilarating. He could see the smallest bird over a mile away.

Pulling the goggles off, he studied them. Somehow, knowing the Ancients truly existed and were *not* the saintly benefactors the priests preached them to be made him feel better. The Ancients were potentially just as weak and flawed as everyone else, and that made him believe even more. They were Human.

Chapter 18
Junko

In Orbit Above Dianis

"Junko!" The hatch hung open, and Krch stood in the opening.

"What, twik."

"I told you not to call me that. Geezer said we're gonna keep hanging out here until you find that cutter. There ain't no freaking cutter out here, Junko. We're wasting time. You said our bonus clause called for four tons in sixty days standard. We've already burned five days. What the stars, Junko. This is bullshit. We ain't finding no cutter. Ain't no IDB here. You—"

Junko pulled his plasma pistol and leveled it at the Tweeunar. Her mouth hung open. Tweeunars did not have teeth but a mouth of abrasive sucking tubes which were stone-still in the face of the blaster.

Lounging in the pilot's chair, the mining foreman looked up from his tablet. He was on his fourth erotic romance novel in the five days they'd been hanging out on the edge of the Dianis solar system. "Don't shoot Krch, Junk. We'll need her dirtside."

Junko emitted a belly-deep growl, "You sure?"

Krch's gaze flicked to the mining foreman.

"Yea. Let her live. I know she's a real piece of work, but we'll just waste more time finding a replacement."

Junko, the contract owner and proprietor of all the gear—some said junk--around them, lowered his blaster, but when the Tweeunar started to speak, the gun rose.

"Don't, Junk, we'll all regret it," said the mining foreman, trying to find his place where the imprisoned princess was about to lose her clothes.

The standoff between Junko and Krch persisted.

"Aaach." The foreman tossed the tablet on the console and climbed out of the chair. He wondered what bothered

Junko more, Krch's constant haranguing or the way her mouth tubes slurred her speech. Stomping over to the cracked holo-table, he zoomed out the grid to display the whole solar system. "Where do you think the IDB are?"

"The moon," Junko said, not taking his eyes off the Tweeunar.

"Which one? Which moon?"

"Dianis'," came Junko's growl.

The foreman zoomed in on Lonely Soul and studied it for a moment. "You think they are on the dark side, waiting for us to make our move?"

"Yep."

"A honey pot," mused the foreman.

"Yep," said Junko, holding his gun steady on the Tweeunar.

"They can't watch the whole planet. Of all those sites we got in the scan data from the Intruder, there's got to be some of them we can sneak into when the site rotates away from the moon. Contract intel has been right so far. All the IDB gear has been pulled. If there is an IDB enforcement cutter," and his eyes shifted to Junko's gun, "and I'm sure there is," he said hurriedly, "then it is definitely hiding. Sneaky bastards. But that means it can only check the planet when it comes out unless it has stealth drones orbiting the planet."

Junko holstered his gun but kept his eyes on Krch. "There's no counter-shift barrier up, so we can shift in,"

"Their surveillance drones have to be in passive mode," said the foreman. "Tomorrow at 11:30 AM, Dianis local, the sun will be at Noon relative to the site. There's a big electrical storm moving over the site."

Nodding, Junko added, "But we can't shift the excavator down. It's too big for a shift gen, so we won't take it." He turned his attention to the battered holo-table and slid the display to hover over an active mining site on the southern continent, a site identified by Quorat's orbital scan.

Unable to contain herself, Krch came to the table. "Then how are we gonna do the dig? Why go down there? This is—"

Junko reached for his holster.

"No excavator." The foreman thought about it. "I see. The existing mine. We take it over. We'll still need the ultraviolet sifters, but it will get us started. No way we can do four tons in sixty days, though."

Krch watched the image of Dianis rotate in the holograph; the hits from Quorat's aural scan showed on the image. The quality of the aquamarine-5 findings indicated by the shade of red and the amount of aqua-5 by the size of the dispersion circle.

"Don't know if I want the four-ton sixty-day bonus," grumped Junko. "The contract supplier listed other bonus clauses. None of them with prereqs. There's a startup bonus for five hundred pounds, no time limit."

The mining foreman looked up. "For how much?"

"Fifty." Junko didn't like exposing specific contract terms to his crew, but there were times when it served as motivation. He didn't like lying about the terms either. Doing that just got him into trouble with the crew later, but he didn't have any problems with dribbling out the terms as he saw fit.

Krch snorted, more like slobbered, her sucking tubes writhing. "Fifty ain't buying squat. Fifty won't buy—"

"Thousand," said Junko. "Bonus only. Doesn't include the going tonnage rate. That's five hundred credits per ounce."

Krch's maw hung open, her sucking tubes limp.

"Smokes, Junk," breathed the foreman, "that's a lot. Are they desperate?"

"But how are we going to dig it?" Krch screeched. "No excavator!"

The foreman watched Junko eye the Tweeunar geologist in that coldly calculating way of his. He knew his boss was figuring the ramifications of smoking her right there and then. Unfortunately for Krch, she and Geezer were both new to the crew. She'd never seen Junko in action or knew what buttons *not* to push. Outside of Junko's core crew, the mortality rate was high.

The foreman interjected, not wanting to go back to the freelance market on Contractor's Haven and recruit another geologist. Junko was getting a reputation. "We use shovels. The *old* way. We hire indigins to help dig. We shift in the gas-powered bore drillers. Nothing that needs anything more than small neutrino power cells, and those will need to be shielded." He looked down at the site map and scrolled it around. "How we getting the ore off planet? Can't count on an electrical storm every day of the week." Thunderstorms generated so much ionic noise the transmit pulse of a shift generator blended into the background

"Boost it," was Junko's answer.

While Junko explained his plan for using one of their shuttles to lift the cargo off planet and how to avoid surveillance drone detection, Krch watched the image of Dianis rotate; it exposed a dark red point-specific source whose area of dispersion was a pin-hole. Another red circle, bigger but of a lighter shade, was nearby, probably a mine. She wanted to zoom in on it but dared not. The intense red dot was on the side of a mountain and in the middle of a town whose name on the display was too small to read. "What's that?" she blurted, pointing at the dot.

Junko's gaze narrowed, but he glanced at the map. "Quarantine zone. Set by the contract issuer."

Before Krch could ask more questions, the foreman said, "They don't want us to go there. If we do, the contract is terminated. The Intruder who went in ahead of us got smoked there." And to answer her next question, he said, "Avarian Marines got him. Touchy stuff. We're not going anywhere near there."

But Krch was enthralled by the tiny dot and its dark burgundy color. Like a diamond ring to a betrothed, the thought of holding it consumed her. As a geologist, she knew something that small, yet with that reading intensity, was probably easily accessible. It had likely been extracted from a mine and was in a refined state. *Why hand-dig a mine,* she whined to herself, *when we should take that?*

Chapter 19
The Sting

The city of Contractor Haven

Clienen sat the cone-of-silence transmitter on the bar table and activated it.

"A Fuzzy Wop?" Counselor Margret asked.

"What?" replied Clienen, "They're all the rage, everyone has them." The device looked exactly like a Fuzzy Wop, a fuzzy little mammal from the planet Gefor that some smart marketer had copied and turned into an aural energy emanator that diffused aural energy waves at a calm ninety-two revabations: the field orientation that a Human mind found soothing. The little, battery-operated gizmo was expensive; it had a sliver of aquamarine-5 in it. Internal Security had modified a batch of the wops to also emit a complex, rotating band of audio diffractions, making eavesdropping on a conversation impossible as long as you were sitting within the five-foot cone of silence.

"What's your poison?"

Clienen looked at the server. She was an Artival: genetically compatible with Humans if you could get past her purple skin, mono-hair, and reptilian eyes. "Purified water, please."

She gave him a pout and looked to Margret.

"I'll take purified water as well and an Octian Sensen. I saw it on your menu. Do you actually have it?"

The waitress waggled her breasts in her tight-fitting halter top, trolling for a reaction from either of the two Human Avarians and said, "We do, just in."

Margret smiled past the overture and asked, "Is it in bottles?"

"It is," the server said.

"Then bring me the whole bottle, unopened."

The Artival wiggled her breasts again, this time at Margret, and left.

Clienen watched Margret, unfazed by the attentions of the server, tab through her multi-func. Balding, trimly fit, with an open yet serious gaze, the director could have been Margret's father. "Between the two of us," he said, "we probably have ten security personnel in and around this bar. You don't need to worry about your multi-func scan results. Someone on our team would start shooting first."

She grinned sheepishly. "I don't normally do undercover."

He sniffed with a smile. "We're hardly undercover. Any commercial AI could run a facial recognition scan and find your image in the Matrincy news reports." The implication being Margret's stunning looks would be hard to miss. Undercover agents were bland in appearance for a purpose. "It'll be a surprise to no one that the Matrincy has an interest in the Margel." The bar they were in was in the center of Contractor Haven, an independent, privately held asteroid in the Margel Damansk asteroid cloud. The hollowed-out planetoid of iron and nickel that Contractor Haven occupied was a requisition and resupply base for the many contract-mining outfits that plumbed the depths of the vast Margel Damansk belt.

"We can thank Quorat for that. Do you think Jovar makes any money off this rock?" she asked, looking around the seedy lounge, the most respectable establishment in the asteroid. Jovar was the titleholder of the rock.

"He's probably the only person making any reliable profits," Clienen answered. "All these miners are living from boom to bust. And a lot of them are bust to bust."

She slouched in her chair, trying to relax. "Who pays for the bust?"

Clienen glanced at the Fuzzy Wop. "Nordarken Mining, for some of them."

"Isn't that expensive?" This was Margret's first counter-intelligence operation, and she was new to the contract side of the mining industry. Prior to Dianis, all her Matrincy assignments had been with the Avarian military in the war against the Turboii.

He shrugged, "Depends on the payoff. At any given time, Nordarken probably has half a dozen contracts out. Maybe one of those will hit. Maybe not. But these contract miners run pretty cheap."

"So we're sure Junko got his contract from here?"

Clienen nodded. "Yes. Don't look, but the broker who issued the contract is sitting two tables over. The one getting the lap dance from the Halorite."

Margret didn't need to turn to look; there was a mirror on the facing wall. "You think the Dianis aquamarine will come through here?"

"Not this rock, but one close enough for Mr. Lap-Dance to do a day-shuttle. No shifting. They don't want the potential of a field disturbance to attract attention."

Margret used her optical implant to zoom in on the mirror, scrutinizing the person who had awarded the Dianis mining gig to Junko. "He's butt-ugly."

Clienen chuckled, and when he saw the counselor's laughing eyes, he continued chuckling. Finally, "Ah, yes, fortunately for them, they don't get paid for their looks."

"So we have to connect the broker to Nordarken Mining, *and,*" she emphasized the word, "we have to follow the Dianis aquamarine all the way to a Nordarken processing plant?"

"Basically," said Clienen.

The waitress delivered their order and finally left when neither of the Avarians gave her attention. Margret looked around the bar at the stained couches, scuffed floor, and idle lap dancers, wondering how long she'd have to be here. Her cover, as a wealthy backer for a platinum and moriaia mining operation, would work even if she *was* recognized as a matronen: the federation needed both metals, but she was not enthused about being on the fringe of Federation space in a back-water asteroid belt. It was generally acknowledged the Matrincy was aiding the Federation in the search for more moriaia sources. A search for moriaia contractors drew less attention than an investigation into who would raid a Class E for aquamarine.

"How many layers, or intermediaries," she asked, "do you think there are between Mr. Lap-Dance and Nordarken?"

Clienen couldn't help but smile at Margret's gloomy attitude about how long this part of her mission would last. "I don't know. Certainly more than two." For his part, Clienen was only on Contractor's Haven to brief Margret on the plans of Internal Security and how his scant IDB Dianis resources could help. He'd only shifted into the asteroid out of curiosity. As director of IDB Margel Damansk, the cloud was in his jurisdiction, but the sting operation was sponsored by the Matrincy and run by Internal Security, that is, until they ventured foot on Class E Dianis; there, Clienen had full authority.

"So we can follow the credits and contacts from Junko through the broker, and through the broker's broker, and yet again through their broker."

Clienen nodded.

"Which will take time, but we can do it?" Her tone held an edge of hope, not for her own situation but for the success of the operation.

Clienen nodded again. "It will depend on how well they've obscured the data trail, and credit payments can be confusing, but aquamarine is a physical asset. Eventually, it has to land in a Nordarken plant."

"But how will we track the Dianis aquamarine to the plant? What happens if they mix it with a legal shipment?"

He shrugged. "It's not as if there are a lot of legal shipments to mix with. But in case they should try, and we expect them to, we plan to stain the Dianis aquamarine with an aural signature that we can trace. We'll know where the aqua came from." He waited for her to ask how they would do that. His answer exposed the hole in their plan: they needed physical access to the aquamarine before it left the planet, and that meant finding the mining site, sneaking in, and running an irradiation protocol, ala Special Forces.

She drank from her glass of Octian Sensen.

Clienen watched her expression. "Real? Or counterfeit?"

Margret tilted the glass to the light. "Oh, it's real. Did you see the price?"

He turned to read the holographic menu projected in the air above the bar. The prices of some of the items, the more exotic drugs, allogens, and alcohols, changed while he watched. They fluctuated in real-time with demand and supply. One of them was the sensen. "Seven hundred and twenty credits a glass?" he said out loud, wondering if he read it right. It had to be a mistake.

She gave him the Avarian head-waggle. "The Matrincy can afford it. Especially if I'm going to be stuck on this rock."

He shook his head at the price, then tried to soothe her with a sympathetic grin.

She tapped his leg with her foot. "How long are you staying?"

He almost laughed but felt for her. She'd not been on Contractor's Haven a day, and already she was feeling isolated. In her past Matrincy assignments, Margret had been under marriage contracts with her mission partners. There would be no cohabitation arrangements in this sting assignment. "Just the night," he answered. "I catch a shuttle to a thorium mine in the morning. From there, a Fed corvette will pick me up and shift out."

She leaned forward and turned the bottle of Octian Sensen so that the filigreed label faced him. "No way can I drink this whole bottle by myself. Want to help?"

Chapter 20
The Dig

Corsair Mining Site, Dianis

"Junk, here comes that priest again."

Junko looked to where the mining foreman gazed. He growled something unintelligible. "Keep them working. I'll deal with the priest."

The miners, mostly villagers they'd coerced into working for slivers of silver, resumed shoveling the rocks from the ore trolley into the sluice works while others were rolling another wooden-wheeled trolley down the steep slope into the black maw of the mine entrance. Sweat rolled down the foreman's back. The heat at the southern latitude was unforgiving. To make matters worse, the gorge was steep and tight, sheltered from the wind. The sun baked the rocks into brimstone.

"Skipper, Junko is going to talk with the Paleowright priest."

A minute later, Lieutenant Hearter came through the hatch onto the command deck of the *IDB Shields*. Sergeant Mears, one of his five-man crew, had the watch. Mears had a feed from a surveillance drone up on the hologrid.

"What's wrong?" the lieutenant asked.

"Watch." Mears pointed to the energy read-outs listed along the side of the hologrid. "Notice the emanations. The contractors *were* following their standard no-emissions protocol."

"I see that," noted Hearter.

"AI, rewind the vid," instructed Mears. "Start when Junko enters the tent. Now watch. The priest and his two acolytes are waiting over there by the eenu paddock."

"Oh," said Hearter, "that neutrino emission, is that--"

"Yes, fits the profile for either a laser or plasma pistol ammo clip. It's a bit high for a laser. See that bulge in

Junko's back when he comes out of the tent?" The AI automatically zoomed the display to focus tightly on Junko as he approached the Paleowrights.

"Is there any reason for the contractors to expect trouble?"

"You mean other than the random beatings of the villagers and the fact that Junko hasn't paid the Paleowrights their cut?"

"Where are they now?"

"AI," called Mears, "resume live feed, find Junko."

The hologrid snapped to a different video feed, and the lieutenant could tell, without looking at the source identifier, that the image was coming from a recon nanobot, one of a dozen they had surveilling the mining camp along with the two stealth surveillance drones.

"Junko is leading them up into the jungle." The lieutenant watched the four people climb to the escarpment and walk away from the chasm. The distance and camera angle changed as the AI shifted views to other bots as it rotated them and a drone into position.

"Where are we going?" one of the Paleowrights asked, his voice coming through hologrid speakers with a tinny quality typical of a nanobot's audio pickup. "We could have ridden our eenus here." The man stopped at the edge of the forest.

Holding up the hem of his white robe so as not to drag in the dirt, the priest asked, "What do you want to show us, Joral? You keep your silver up here?" All three Paleowrights stopped.

Junko turned. "Show you? What do I have to show you?" He pulled the weapon from its holster at the small of his back. "This is what I have to show you." He leveled it at one of the other men.

Flashing red, the plasma-pulse alarm sounded on the *Shields* even before the man's head disintegrated on the hologrid display.

The priest jerked in shock and then raised his hands as if to ward off a blow. The discharge alarm flared red again, and the priest died without his head as well. The third Paleowright turned and started running for the escarpment. Joral, aka Junko, calmly aimed, watching the acolyte run, and then blasted a fist-sized hole through his back.

The remaining *Shields* crew came running into the command deck. "Plasma alarm?" one asked.

Hearter and Mears just nodded, numb.

The crewmen saw the dead at the jungle verge and Junko disabling his plasma pistol. The neutrino energy signal went to zero. "Shiren, skipper. Junko just slaughtered them?"

"Yeah." Lieutenant Hearter walked to the hatch in a daze; he had to fumble at the hatch open button twice before he made it work. "I have a call to make," he said to his crew before he stepped through, and the hatch slid shut.

In the tiny captain's cabin, he sat at a desk barely big enough for his multi-func. "Mears," he said into the comm channel, "get me a channel to Director Hor. Tell him it's urgent. Wake him up if you have to."

While Hearter waited for Mears to track down the IDB director, he thought of all the hours and days he and his crew had sat out here on the dark side of Lonely Soul, watching those thugs run rampant on the planet. It had been one thing to watch them break ULUP laws, but it was another to watch them murder people.

The mine foreman met Junko as he entered his sleeping quarters, a fancy term for a tent, but it came with a solar-powered air conditioner. There were only four of them in the camp, and they were hidden under infrared-reducing camouflage nets.

Junko tossed his plasma pistol on the table.

"Tell me you didn't use that," said the foreman.

"And what if I did," Junko snarled, "the bastard had it coming."

The foreman's jaw fell. He tried to formulate....

Junko said, "What? So what! There ain't no IDB around. They would have busted us by now. The ship has been running passive sensor sweeps for three weeks. Nothing, nada, no IDB."

Finally, the foreman managed a drawl, "You shot them? All of them?"

When Junko gave him the of-course-I-did look, the foreman struggled between the impulse to run and start the portable field generator -- used only in case of an emergency evac -- and the fear that Junko may use the plasma pistol on him. "Uh, then you don't mind if I power up our ground sensors, just in case—"

"In case what? In case I'm wrong?"

"No," said the foreman quickly, "in case the ship missed something. A plasma discharge can send ionic waves—"

"I know that." Junko mumbled something incoherent and then said more clearly, "Go ahead and do what you want. Just don't broadcast radar signals all over the solar system."

You mean like you just did, the foreman thought as he pulled out his multi-func. His hands were shaking. If they were caught planet-side, on a Class E, after Junko smoked three indigins, they were all headed for a lifetime mind-wipe. All their identities gone. *Poof.*

"Shiren!" cursed Mears. "AI, shut down all bots, drones, and devices in sensor range of the mine site. Hurry. Anything using a neutrino energy cell or generating an electromagnetic wave. Only shielded surveillance bots are allowed to move. Everything else goes to roost."

"Acknowledged," replied the AI. "Roosting and powering down requested assets."

The foreman waited for the multi-func to power up and then thumbed through the screens to the sensor grid controls. He found the *enable* command and pressed it.

"Junko!" Krch slapped the tent flap aside and strode into the tent. She was immediately struck by two things: how cool the air was and the sight of the plasma pistol sitting on Junko's bed. She looked at the foreman and then at Junko. "Junko, the indigins want to know where's their priest and the village elder? Are they still up on top?"

Again, her eyes strayed to the weapon, her mouth tubes writhing.

Junko stared at her blankly. "Uh, they've left."

Krch started, her sucking tubes stilled. "Left? Left where? Their eenu's are still here."

His blank look persisted. "Yeah, they said they'd walk back."

She blinked. "Walk? It's an hour back to the village! And it's hot." To emphasize, she flapped a hand at her sucking tubes to cool them.

"Thirty seconds to shut down all non-shielded bots and devices," reported the AI. "Drone three is within ninety seconds of landing."

"Blast," growled Mears. "Get it down now. Glide it down, do whatever." He hated giving that order. They had only three Dianis-environment surveillance drones, and they were hard to get. Expensive and designed to look like a Dianis avian, and with the high demand for drones in the war, it would take months, if not longer, to get a replacement.

"There is a fifty-eight percent probability of a catastrophic landing if the drone attempts a no-power glide."

Mears expected as much. He nodded. "Understood."

"Yeah," said Junko. "They said they didn't need their eenus."

Krch threw up her arms. "They didn't need them?"

"Yeah."

"And you expect me to tell that to the indigins?"

"Yeah."

"Aieeee!" Krch wailed. She pivoted and stomped out of the tent, but the flap refused to give way, so she bulled into it until it surrendered to her frenzied thrashing.

With Krch gone, the foreman turned his attention to the multi-func. He flipped to the sensor's display, and at first, he saw a red bar at the right side of the graph in the neutrino-motor-drive spectrum, but then it settled to zero. Across the energy spectrum, there was no activity. Nothing. Dead as only a primitive Class E world could be.

He thought about the transient red bar he'd seen; it was for electric motors, but looking at Junko and the gun still lying on the bed, he decided not to mention it.

As Krch stormed across the mining site, a child belonging to one of the women miners who'd been conscripted from the village came up to Krch. The boy, wandering around loose while his mother shoveled rock into the sluice track, nearly caught hell. Krch was about to blast him with a verbal fusillade of her writhing-sucking tubes when the heat, exhaustion, and idiocy of their situation hit her. She scooped him up and deposited him beside his mother, and stalked off to her shack.

A crude sign hung above the door of the shack; scrawled on it in Avarian script was *The Ghetto*. She entered the shack and slammed the door shut, if *door* was what it could be called.

Geezer lay on his bunk. "Now what?"

Krch sat heavily on her rack, one of five they'd contrived. A mouse, startled by Krch's sudden appearance, dropped a morsel of dried Avarian tofu and scurried for a large hole in the floor.

"Junko killed the priest and village elder."

A double beep sounded on the floor beside Geezer's bunk. He reached down and retrieved his multi-func. "Network's up," he said.

"Really?" Her pain and anguish forgotten, she crawled over to Geezer's bunk and yanked the multi-func from his hands. She paged through the displays hungrily.

"You're welcome," he said.

"Yess's!" She tossed the tablet back at him and sprawled, rather lay, on the rough wood planks of the shed floor. "I can call Bleep Nuts, and we can get the spirits out of here'ss. We can connect to the Interconn!"

Geezer eyed her critically. "Is Bleeper Nuts the dude with the ship and the—"

"Yess's!"

Geezer thought about it. He looked at the fifth bunk, now unassigned. All five of the newest crewmembers, all of them hired out of Contractor Haven into Junko's crew just for this contract, were bunked in the shed, the dump of the camp. One of the five was dead. Turk had fallen down the mineshaft when the indigin rope he'd been using snapped. "You're sure about this?"

"Yess's!" she slurred and sat up, her mouth sucking tubes waving like tall grass in a gale. "The first cargo is almost ready for the shuttle. You, me, Gof, and Sysreq grab the shuttle, fly to that other continent, land in that town, Wedgewood, whatever it is called, grab the goods, and then boost to where Bleep Nuts will be waiting for us." She crawled over to his bunk, "Geeze, Eight hundred million credits!"

Geezer wasn't as prone to stargazing as Krch, but he had to admit, after his own near-death mishap in the mine, working without an excavator was bullshit. As it was, if he cleared a hundred thousand credits he'd be happy. "Yeah, but why bother with Wedgewood? I have the codes for the weapons locker. I'm supposed to help with indigin suppression in case they get wacky, which they may, now that Junko has toasted their chief. We just grab the plasmas, steal the shuttle, and go. Like you said, we probably have five hundred million in raw ore."

"I'm the geologist. Geeze. I validated the survey findings from the Intruder. That point-specific source is so smalls in dispersions and so intense's it must be pure crystal. A big one. One that we can latch an anti-grav grappler on and haul to the shuttle. No pre-processing needed, Geeze. We can have a gem cutter slice and facetize it for us. What looks like three hundred million credits on the site survey could be ten times that cut up and sold to the device shops!"

Geezer, though he'd been in the contract mining business a long time, was having a hard time finding a flaw in Krch's plan. If she hadn't been the geologist, he would've scoffed.

Sergeant Mears' watch replacement entered the command deck. "What?" the corporal asked, "No bot coverage?" He was looking at the hologrid display that only showed a high-res camera view from an orbiting stealth satellite, the only one they had.

"No. The corsairs went live with their sensor grid, so we had to go dark."

"You running a shielded-bot relay?" his replacement asked.

"Yes. I have a relay of six orange birds going. You'll get the feed from the first two birds in twenty minutes. Each will have a twenty-minute video feed."

Mears's replacement nodded. They all knew the drill. One specially shielded and camouflaged bot would take a video of the camp, then fly back to the laser transponder and upload its video, while the next bot flew into camp and started filming. That way they could have continuous coverage of two different areas of the camp, albeit with a twenty-minute delay. "Who do you have the bots pinned on?"

"Junko and the foreman," Mears answered.

"Aw. What about Krch? She's a stitch. You never know what crap she'll get into."

Mears looked at him. "We're here to monitor the contractors for prosecutable offenses, not get physiological stimulation from watching Krch use her double-compression dildo."

"Whaaat?" his replacement said. "She has one? I was talking about when she steals Junko's carva mug and pees in it, then he complains that his carva tastes salty."

Mears looked away, trying not to smile. "Yeah, that too."

Chapter 21
Clienen Hor

IDB Headquarters, Avaria

Clienen Hor's hologrid image showed him wearing sweaty workout clothing. He was holding a cold bottle of some sort of electrolyte fluid.

"Sorry, sir, for dragging you out of the centrifuge, but we've had an escalation of events at the mining site." Lieutenant Hearter hunched over his tiny cabin desk. His face inches from the holocamera.

"It's alright, Lieutenant. Dianis is still my planet."

"Junko has just killed three provincials. Unprovoked. They were defenseless." Hearter went on to recount the story, starting when the Paleowright priest had begun demanding silver for his cooperation, for his support of having the villagers work the mine.

The director of IDB, Margel Damansk, set his electrolyte bottle on the table beside him. He took a deep breath.

"Clienen, I need you to order me to intervene. It was one thing to watch Junko conscript the provincials into forced labor. It's another to watch him shoot them. Junko has started killing people. This is the extreme end of what we are here to stop. This is our duty."

The director stared at the holocamera and then slowly began to shake his head. "This is exactly what Atch was afraid of. Some of us here at headquarters thought he was just paranoid. But everything he predicted is coming true."

"You mean Chief Inspector Achelous Forushen?"

"Yes."

"He predicted extrasolars would come to Dianis and start killing people?"

"And worse." The director didn't elaborate. "We haven't proved it's Nordarken Mining behind the contracts on Dianis. That's your mission profile."

"I understand that, but that was before Junko started randomly shooting people."

Clienen's lips compressed to a tight line. "That means he doesn't suspect our presence. He will get sloppy; he'll lead us to the ultimate contract issuer."

Hearter shook his head. "To do that, we have to seed the cargo before it leaves Dianis, track it off planet, follow it to the drop-off, stakeout the drop-off, and from there, who knows where? In the meantime, the provincials will still be working the mine, and more of them—" he let his voice trail off. "I know the Matrincy is running the sting, but you have jurisdiction. ULUP charters the IDB on Dianis, not the Matrincy. You can call it off."

Clienen's pale blue eyes reflected his pain. Fresh sweat beaded out across his clean-shaven head.

Hearter waited for the director to make a decision. He recognized the background where Clienen sat: the gym in IDB headquarters on Avaria.

"If we act too soon, we'll have to start the operation all over." Clienen wasn't talking to Hearter. He stared off the screen. "We'd have to wait for another contractor to pick up the bid and hope they are as dumb as Junko. Some operators are smoother." He kept looking off the screen to a place in the direction where Hearter knew the new-feed hologrid displays to be. "Nordarken Mining, if it is Nordarken, will not stop. Not as long as there are contractors willing to take their bid." At that, he looked at Hearter.

The lieutenant nodded. There were plenty of contractors roaming free space willing to take risks for big payoffs.

"But," Clienen added, "Dianis is my planet. I was stationed there for five years before— well, before we were ordered to leave. I'll contact Counselor Margret and have a talk with her. She needs to know the stakes have gone up. We have three dead now. I'll make it clear to her that my threshold of more killings is low."

It was Hearter's turn to look off-camera. "You said things Chief Forushen predicted are coming true?"

"Yes?"

"What else did he predict that we should be prepared for?"

"Well," Clienen appeared about to hedge but then said, "Do you have a drone over Wedgewood?"

"Hmm, not now."

Clienen nodded. "I have a recommendation."

"Yes?"

"Put one there." Clienen sought to choose his next words carefully, "I am interested if Counselor Breia shows up and engages any of the Wedgewood adepts. Outish, Wedgewood, the adepts, and the Matrincy, they are all tied together in a way that Achelous understood, and we don't."

Chapter 22
The Aorolmin

The city of Tivor on the planet Dianis

Ropert sighted down the long steel tube and aligned the iron fin at the front of the tube with the iron v-wedge at the rear, just as Troop Commander Rayamars had shown him. The gun felt heavy and awkward in his arms, but he held it firmly and braced his elbows against the rail of the tree stand.

Eliot stood quietly behind him. The magnificent stag took two more steps into the clearing, a full ten-pointer at least, with beams extending well out beyond the ears. For him, it was an impossible shot with a hunting bow, but with a rifle, at a hundred paces, it would be possible. The stag dipped its head to graze; the aorolmin aimed just behind the front shoulder and began to squeeze the trigger. Rayamars had cautioned him: "Squeeze, don't pull or yank. The gun's discharge should come as a surprise."

Bang!

The aorolmin lurched back, shocked by the blast even after shooting it in practice. He waved at the smoke, sneezing. Looking downfield, he said, "Well, where did it go?"

"Darted back into the trees, lord. Let's go have a look." Anxious, Eliot clambered down from the hunting stand and waited for his lordship to negotiate the ladder. A retainer came with their eenus, and the lord of Tivor mounted up.

The aorolmin spurred his eenu, cantering to where his prey had disappeared. Their scout was already there. The lord felt his blood pumping. It was a magnificent animal, and the aorolmin himself had directed the hunt while Eliot, his guide, nodded sagely at his lordship's instructions. In truth, the aorolmin had learned all he knew of hunting and woodland craft from the huntsmaster. Eliot took pride in his star pupil's skills.

The tension was almost too much for him to bear; reining in, the aorolmin asked peremptorily, "Well, did I hit it?" The scout, a girl, an impertinent little Timberkeep from Wedgewood, rose from her crouch and smiled, pointing at the ground, "Minnie, even you can see that," she chided him impishly.

"Rachael!" Eliot rebuked her, but the aorolmin merely shook his head and dismounted. "Don't mind the lass, Eliot. The little wildcat hasn't a lick of manners, but she can track a mouse over bare rock." He stopped and dismounted, aghast at the great splash of blood, a deep red stark against the vivid green of the grass. "I did that?" He asked, amazed, "That's mine?"

Rachael nodded emphatically, "Oi." She bent and wiped a finger through the puddle and held it up, the crimson bright and glistening on her fingertip, "Weren't here a minute ago, Minnie." She glanced mischievously at Eliot, knowing he groaned every time she used her nickname for the lord.

Ropert could hardly believe it; he'd actually hit the animal, and it was a spectacular beast, easily the equal of any of Tivor Castle's many trophies, none of which were his. He bent low; there was fur in the splash. Surely, the wound must be fatal? He'd long since admitted to himself and his associates that he was a willing but mediocre hunter. Coming from a long line of avid outdoorsmen, Ropert practiced hunting mainly to sustain the family tradition in the hopes that one day he would be able to add to the collection. It galled him that none of the aging, dusty trophies in the great hall were his but rather the accomplishments of his forebears, men he feared, greater than he. As a shy, childless widower, suspicious of any woman who showed outward affection for him, he didn't have any progeny to pass his realm on to. He was sure it was another source of derision for his subjects, in addition to dining in a hall under trophies not his.

Trembling, he looked at the girl, daring to ask, "Do you, do you—"

Since the Timberkeeps had arrived on Mt Epratis, Rachael had taken to scouting with Elliot and had proven a skilled tracker on the aorolmin's outings. Pointing, she said, "Plenty of blood. Do you want to track it, or shall I?"

He turned to Eliot, "How can that be? The bullet is so small, it doesn't compare to an arrow?" He held his arms out, showing the length of a yard-long shaft.

Eliot bunched his shoulders, "I don't know, milord. Both Achelous and Ogden say the bullet hits with a tremendous punch."

"It must," Rachael said, levitating a stone and spinning it in the air above her hand, "even *I* can't fling a stone *that* hard," and she sent the rock zinging off into the forest.

"How you do that, child, I shall never know," the aorolmin exclaimed, momentarily distracted from the worry of yet another escaped trophy.

She proffered him a bright smile and launched herself along the blood trail, "Come on, Minnie, let's find your stag so we can celebrate!"

"No, no child, do not say that, for surely the animal is miles from here and safe in some bog."

"Ha!" she rebutted. "Not with that much blood. There," she pointed, "and there, and there." Her arms waved as she skipped through the woods, pointing out splotches of red, oblivious to the gory nature of her work. Her singsong voice called out like a sprite counting violets, getting farther away. "And there, and there," and the aorolmin, having put on some weight in the past years, had to hustle to keep up. "And there, and there," came her twittering melody, and then she stopped abruptly and whirled around. The aorolmin came puffing up, Eliot close behind him. Rachael could hear the other members of the party riding their eenus through the forest towards them. She stooped to smell a rare blue trillium.

"What is it, child? What have you found?"

She plucked the flower. "This, your lordship." She held it out to him.

"Oh, my. A blue trillium," his fleshy, bearded face red from the exertion. He accepted the gift. "Thank you," he said as a father to daughter, patiently appreciating the gesture even amidst the gravity of the situation. "And what about—" he asked gently, not wanting to demean her present.

She giggled and pointed behind her. "And there!"

The aorolmin blinked and looked past her shoulder, but all he saw was brush and forest understory. He moved past her and found a dollop of red, then painstakingly searched for another. Then he drew up sharply. His heart fairly pounded in his chest. *Could it be?* he wondered. The brown hide blended perfectly in the understory amongst the leaf litter, but the yellow horns, the *massive* yellow horns, stood out from the bracken, catching sunlight like ship masts in the harbor. "Oh my," he breathed. "Oh my."

Trudging through the undergrowth, ignoring the clawing of the blackthorns, he stood over his quarry, hardly believing his eyes. He settled to his knees and rested his hand on the soft, warm fur. Rachael kneeled next to him and counted the points on the rack, one by one, like counting toes on her feet, though she didn't have so many. "Twelve," she said matter-of-factly.

"Twelve!" he said, awed.

"Yep," and she dutifully recounted them, the lord not daring to interrupt. "Twelve."

"Tis a truly magnificent creature, milord," Eliot said. "Worthy of the greatest hunter's hall." The last a not-so-subtle hint that the aorolmin no longer need look on his forebears' trophies with embarrassment.

Not realizing an audience had gathered behind him, the lord of Tivor just kneeled there, reveling in his accomplishment. All his life, he struggled to match the lore of his elders. Ropert loved the hunt, but not for the thrill of the kill, but for the comradery and the grand excuse to leave the castle, courtiers, and troubles behind. It was one reason he'd grown fond of Rachael. She didn't care who he was and treated him like any person, and he found that distinctly refreshing. She didn't care if he fumbled an arrow or sent a bow shot wide. She just reveled at frolicking in the forest.

"Congratulations, lord."

The aorolmin stirred himself at the voice. Standing, he greeted the rest of the hunting party.

"Oi, we heard the shot, lord, and came straight away." Ogden stood with his own rifle slung across his back, looking for all the world as if he'd been born with it.

Achelous rode up beside Ogden. These past weeks, since their arrival from Isumfast, had been a blur. They'd taken a calculated risk shifting from the repair bay to Mt Epratis, but Jeremy had worked every energy emissions sensor available and confirmed the fleet had left the system, matching the news on the Fednet that the Matriarch was back on Avaria. If any ships or recon drones remained behind to monitor the planet, Jeremy had not detected any response to the field perturbations.

"Yes, congratulations, sire," said Achelous, "I believe you have bragging rights."

"Bragging rights?" the aorolmin asked, his throat thick and dry.

Ogden, Achelous, and Troop Commander Rayamars solemnly looked at each other and nodded, knowing they'd been bested.

"Yes," said Eliot. "They were taking bets as to who would get the first shot, and you beat them all."

"And I am certain," Achelous added, "that you are the first person on D—" he almost said on Dianis, which would imply the weapon was used elsewhere in the galaxy, and how would he know that? So he said, "—in the world, that has shot a stag or any animal with a rifle."

"Truly?" the aorolmin asked, his eyes wide.

Ogden nodded gravely, "Truly."

"Shall I clean and dress it for you, milord?" Eliot asked.

"Oh, shouldn't I do it?" Ropert replied, genuinely curious.

The others laughed. Ogden offered, "Lord, if someone offers to do the dirty deed, accept it unless, of course, you have a bent for that sort of thing."

They made room for Eliot to get to work.

With a nudge from Achelous, Ogden hesitantly reached down and retrieved the aorolmin's rifle where Eliot had set it by the carcass. As he made to sling it across his back, the aorolmin asked in alarm, "What are you doing?"

"I need to take it back to the armory, sir. Have it cleaned and locked away."

"Uh," Ropert said, "I've come to rather like it."

Ogden gave a blank look, then turned to Achelous, who asked, "Yes, sire?"

"You're a trader; sell it to me. Ogden can have it cleaned and do whatever he needs, but I want to use it when the mood strikes. Moreover, I want more practice with it. I'll be your first customer."

Achelous asked Ogden for the weapon, who handed it to him. Achelous then presented it to the aorolmin. "Sire, it is yours as a gift from Ogden and me in recognition of your feat today. Ogden can etch your name on the barrel."

The aorolmin gravely accepted the weapon. "It is the third gift given me today."

"Your third?" asked Rachael as she fixed her concentration on a buttermilk butterfly. It hovered an inch over her hand, fluttering vainly to fly away. Satisfied, she smiled brightly at Ropert, and the moth fled from her attention, no worse for the trial.

He grinned, "First, Mother has provided me with this grand stag. Second, you with a blue trillium. And now, Achelous and Ogden with this," he held the rifle out with both hands.

Rayamars cleared his throat. "Lord, do you think one will be enough?"

Consternation crossed the aorolmin's ruddy features. "Why? Do they break?"

Ogden quickly shook his head. "Noi. They will foul with soot from repeated firing, but we build them well, lord."

"Then why do I need more than one?"

"For our men, milord," Rayamars replied gravely. "To defend Tivor."

"Oi," Ogden said. "If we had a full ward of rifles at the Battle for Wedgewood, the Scarlet Saviors would not have burned a single building. The Scarlet Bastards would not have gotten close enough to the Tannery to set it afire. Our arrows were stuck in their heavy shields like pincushions. None would penetrate. We needed to use ballistae mounts, but with forty rifles, not a single Savior would have survived to light a torch."

Ropert swallowed hard. He'd heard the stories and could not bear the thought of any part of Tivor burning. Not even the brothels and grog dens along the wharf. "Are you sure of that? I am mightily impressed by what it has done to reap me a great stag, but what is fur compared to armor? I understand Scarlet Saviors wear the best?"

Achelous turned to Rayamars, "Commander, I believe a demonstration is in order. Rachael, fetch a cooking pan from the field kit on the pack eenu and hang it in a tree fifty paces from here." He pointed in the general direction of several suitable targets. "Commander, if you will, ready three rounds. On my command, load, and fire at the pan as quickly and accurately as you can. Ogden will count the time." Watching Rachael fetch the pan, he added, "And, commander, it would be best if you were to hit the target." They all laughed except for the aorolmin. Everyone, except for Ropert, had seen Rayamars practice. He was Ogden's chief tester of new prototypes and had become a noted marksman.

Rachael ran to a tree, excited to see the demonstration. She stopped at one about fifty paces away, turned, and looked at the group. She gave an impish grin and ran a further fifteen paces. Snapping off a branch about head high, she hung the pan by its handle using a loop of twine. Then she gave the pan a good push and started it swinging on the branch. Eliot and Ogden laughed.

Rayamars glanced at Achelous, then bent to one knee, readied his primer horn, and set three of the new paper-wrapped powder cartridges on his hunting cap that lay on the ground beside him. With a scraping noise, he pulled out the ramrod and set it on the ground beside the hat.

"Interesting target, milord," Achelous said to Ropert, "must be sixty-five paces and swinging on a rope. How many archers could hit that?"

Ropert grunted his own skepticism.

With Rachael safely back, Rayamars said, "Ready."

Achelous replied, "Commence fire."

Rayamars bit open a cartridge, poured its contents down the barrel, seated a bullet and wadding, and rammed it home. With a practiced motion, he primed the pan with his powder horn, dropped it on its lanyard, and brought the rifle to his shoulder. He pulled the doghead of the flintlock back, steadied himself, aimed at the swinging pan, and fired. The pan bucked at the impact and swung on the branch. "Well done!" exclaimed Eliot.

Ignoring the accolade, Rayamars poured a second powder charge down the barrel. Though the pan was both swinging and twisting, Ropert could swear he saw a hole in it.

Pulling the ramrod out of the barrel, Rayamars rested it against his side, primed the pan, dropped the horn to dangle on its lanyard, and again shouldered the rifle. With the barest hesitation, he fired. Smoke and flame burst from the barrel, and a loud clang came from the iron skillet.

Rayamars rammed down the third bullet as he shuffled to the right to clear the growing gunsmoke.

Bang!

The pan jumped on the impact of the third bullet and fell to the ground.

"I'll get it!" Rachael squealed and darted off.

"Three shots in the count of forty-five sire," Ogden noted with pride.

"Forty-five?" asked Achelous. "With a full ward, that's a hundred twenty shots per minute." He let that thought sit with the aorolmin.

Rachael ran back to them and held the pan up to her face, peaking through one of three holes blasted through the metal.

Ropert held out his hand, and she gave him the target. He fingered one of the holes punched clean through.

"It's not hardened steel, sire," Eliot said, "but it is thicker than armor forged to turn a blade."

Achelous, in his in-country role as a trader of gems, spices, and weapons, never really thought of himself as an arms dealer, but if there was ever a scene of a weapons manufacturer lobbying a government official, this was it.

"Not a weapon of war, sire?" Rayamars asked. "I grant you a good archer can shoot faster, and distant is the day where Tivor will unstring its last bow, but no Tivor arrow can pierce the heavy armor of Warkenvaal lancers. And what of their bands of eenu archers that roam our plains and plague us with their hit-and-run tactics. We could counter with our own eenu riflemen." The lieutenant had clearly been thinking about the idea.

Ropert hummed. They'd had some success countering the Warkenvaal with their own mounted archers, but the Vaal were experts at the strategy. He looked at Rayamars with a keen eye. As aorolmin, he'd ruled Tivor for the past seventeen years and had seen much strife with its larger southern neighbor. "Ronny, your father served me with honor and died in the defense of Tivor at Wichin Wash. Now, you stand in my service and have added distinction to your family's name. In both your father's honor and yours, you would hold to this?"

"Sir!" He came to attention. "I look to the day when I find a Warkenvaal cataphract in my sights. With this weapon, they will learn that Mother's Wheel of Life is truly round."

Ropert seemed to deflate, the hard glint to his gaze gone. Achelous held the man in sympathy. To have lost so many for a man who considered himself a father to them all was a grave burden to bear. "How many did you say we would want?"

"Lord, I would recommend eighty to start. Enough for a full company."

Ogden saw the uncertainty in the lord's eyes at what eighty rifles might cost the Tivor treasury, so at the risk of speaking out of turn and drawing the ire of his principal investor, Achelous, Ogden blurted, "And we will supply them at cost, lord. There will be no profiting from Tivor. Oi, you have been most gracious, grand, and generous in your offer for us to settle here. It would be against our principles to treat you otherwise."

A kindly smile spread across the aorolmin's ruddy features. He reached out and placed an arm on Ogden's shoulders. "We are together in this, good smith. I know your clan has suffered much at the hands of the Paleowrights, but understand as well that your steading here on the shoulders of Mt. Epratis puts you squarely athwart the next Vaal incursion. Build not only rifles for me but for you and yours as well. The Vaal will come, surely as autumn follows summer."

"Aw, let the deep souther's come," Rachael tossed a bullet she'd taken from Rayamars, "I'll stick this in their ear like I did with the loglards and Parrots." She spun the bullet like a top on her finger and then sent it humming in a circle around the outside of the group like an angry hornet.

Ropert brushed a stray lock from the child's forehead. "Put your bee away, little wildflower. There will be time enough for that, I promise you."

She pouted, but the bullet ceased its buzzing and returned to her hand.

"Lord, on our return to the castle, may we presume on your time with a short detour?" Achelous asked.

"A detour?" asked Ropert.

"Yes, sire, Marisa is keen on a new invention of Ogden's, and it may catch your interest."

"Marisa? By all means. For once, I would like to know something of what she does before reading it in the *Littoral*."

Chapter 23
New Ungern

The village of New Ungern, on Mt. Epratis, near Tivor

The debate over what to call the new community had been rancorous at times. Competing interests and philosophies all had to have their say. They knew they'd be living with the name for the rest of their lives. In the end, *New Ungern* prevailed in honor and respect for the massive, virgin grove of Ungerngerists that stretched across the western slopes of Mt. Epratis. Ropert wanted to call the village Tree Town, but the Timberkeeps laughed at the idea, at least politely.

Everywhere there was activity. The pounding of hammers constant through the forest. The sound eerily reminiscent of the hammering of the large Lolkeen Woodpecker and Human woodpeckers the Timberkeeps certainly were. Care was taken to disrupt the forest life as little as possible, but migrating seven hundred people was certain to cause disruption. Large tracts within the boundaries of the Ungerngerist forest were set aside as inviolate in hopes that reclusive woodland species, such as the Two-Toed Mouse, Leon Chickadooder, and Angle Breath Fox, would relocate nearby rather than flee the local environs altogether. Wherever possible, current woodland inhabitants were encouraged to stay, and construction went on around them, like diverting the cesspit trail around a Stumpy Marmot's den. Hence, the trail became known as Stumpy Marmot.

"What are those?" Ropert asked, gawking at a cordoned area wherein the random placement of tiny, clapboard huts with tall, peaked roofs, bent chimney pipes, and a single tiny window with a flower box made the area resemble a mushroom patch. The shanties were decked out in different colors, some painted like a flower, others a budding bush or even a boulder. One shack was painted to resemble the hind end of a squirrel feeding on a nut, and the window was the -- well, Ropert laughed. "Those are bivvies," chimed Rachael, and Eliot gave her an exasperated roll of the eyes when she omitted "sire."

"We built them just like they are in Wedgy; it makes it feel like home already."

"But what are they for?" he asked quizzically.

"For living in!" The way she said it immediately embarrassed the aorolmin. How could he have thought otherwise?

Ogden came to his rescue, "Oi, they're for young bachelors, hermits, and some spinsters, people who have moved out of their family lodges."

"Most intriguing, and they actually dwell in them?" Ropert cast a wary glance at Rachael.

"Oi," Ogden went on, "with work to be done, the tenants are seldom in the bivvies, except on the days when snow be flying or the rain coming down in buckets, then you'll find someone at home. We Timbers are not town's folk," he cast a sideways glance at his guest, "most of our days we spend out and about. Even more so now with building New Ungern."

They passed near a new treefort under construction: a three-tiered affair with Timberkeeps clambering on scaffolding and hanging on ropes like so many bees working a honeycomb. "So that is a treefort?" Ropert asked Ogden. "That's how you beat the Paleowrights?"

Ogden grimaced. "Perhaps, lord, but that says nothing of the valor of our shield warriors. We mounted fierce counterattacks, but the treeforts were indeed a cornerstone of our strategy."

"Of course, of course," the aorolmin amended, "I meant no offense. What are the treeforts without the warriors to man them? But still, they are a novel idea employed most dramatically."

"Novel to the Paleowrights," Achelous replied, riding behind, "but natural to the Timberkeeps. It is a lesson to us all, sire: when you take the fight to your enemy, understand how your enemy fights. The churchmen deigned to think the Timberkeeps would fight like pikemen. Not so."

Ogden snorted, "Against our treeforts, the Church pikemen were like waves crashing against cliffs, imposing and impressive but impudent. But the Troglodytes, those were unnerving."

"Will the tree forts work against the Warkenvaal?" Ropert asked. "I fear the Vaal are smart where the Paleowrights are arrogant."

Rayamars and Ogden exchanged looks from astride their eenus. Then Ogden replied, "Lieutenant Rayamars has been most helpful on the tactics of the Vaal. They are different from what we've seen before, but the tree forts are mounted with rifles. We have other plans as well."

"And sire," Rayamars interjected, "New Ungern is not Wedgewood. In the story told of the battle, the Red Elm clan was days away and was not prepared to send immediate aid. That is not true of New Ungern. Tivor will be ready. It's three hours fast riding from Tivor to here. And the Timberkeeps have offered to build a forward post near the border. With their pathics, we'll know when Warkenvaal comes."

It was cold comfort to Ropert: knowing when war came, and it would, they would be better prepared to fight. He was becoming fond of his Timberkeep liegemen; it bothered him they were his new front-line defense.

"Here we are, sire," Achelous swung off his mount and handed the reins to a Silver Cup bravo.

Akallabeth, an overseer for the Silver Cup messenger's guild, came out of a two-story lodge being erected across the street from the new foundry. He greeted them. "Hello, I see the hunt went well," he nodded at the stag draped across a pack eenu. "And who had the honor of bagging that fine beast?" Already, the trophy was attracting a crowd of workers and children.

"Minnie did!" piped Rachael. "Shot it clean, first time, and it was a long way," she said with no small amount of awe, "no way you could have done that with a—"

"Uh, em," coughed Ogden, "remember what I said?"

Chastened, Rachael said, "Sorry." The secret of the clan's special project was soon to get out, but it needed to be kept low-key for as long as possible. The clan and Tivor needed as much of a head start on their enemies as possible.

"And who is Minnie?" Akallabeth asked.

The aorolmin raised a gloved hand sheepishly, an embarrassed smile on his face.

Akallabeth felt his jaw dropping but clamped it shut. "Why, many congratulations, sire," he said. "Tis a fine animal indeed."

A small boy came up to Rachael, still mounted on her eenu, and tugged on her pant leg, "Who got the stag?" he asked in a hoarse whisper. She smiled down proudly from her mount, "The lord of Tivor did."

"He did?!" the lad piped and ran to his friends gathered around the trophy, peering in the mouth, counting the horns, and bragging when they would bag their own trophy. Yelling at the top of his lungs, he said, "Ropert got it! It's the aorolmin's!" Then another chimed, "Rachael said he shot it clean through! Dropped it on the spot!"

"How far?" one of the boys asked. "A country mile," another boy said.

As the story began to grow, the aorolmin turned a deeper shade of red. Ogden steered the discomfited lord towards the half-built foundry, "You must forgive my clansmen, sire, especially the children. They know not of royalty or even class. Having grown up in the forest with birds as friends, respecting royalty is strange to them."

"Oh no, no, let them have their fun," Ropert flapped a hand at him, "though if you send them to court, make sure they know enough to doff their hats."

The mastersmith smiled at the lord's jest and ushered him into the only finished room in the foundry. Outside the room, two of the ten planned forges were glowing, and the ring of hammers on anvils competed with the sawing of timber structures. By the size and shape of the building, it would dwarf the old foundry in Wedgewood.

Ogden closed the door behind him, more to block out the noise than to retain any form of secrecy. Akallabeth's bravos stood guard, their role to thwart spies who would surely attempt to learn the formulas for the gunpowder and the process for manufacturing the rifles.

The whole village knew of Ogden's work in the foundry, if not the crucial details. They were also aware of their tenuous situation and the importance of Ogden's *special project* to the success of New Ungern. Through Ogden and his project, they had brought something of great value with them, something to endear them to the Tivor lord. As a clan, they kept news of the work close to their vests and dutifully reported any snoopers to the head of foundry security. Both Achelous and Akallabeth agreed that in order for the Timberkeeps to build a force of trained riflemen, enough to defend New Ungern and potentially Tivor, too, they had to bring more people into the secret. Eventually, it would no longer be a secret, and by then, hopefully, the endeavor could withstand the inevitable forces that would come to capture it. In the meantime, the secret was not to be spoken of and could only be referred to as the *project*. When the soldiers and warders went up Mount Epratis to the cavern to train, they were said to be going *on the project*.

In the room, Ropert, Rayamars, Ogden, and Achelous gathered around a drafting table.

"So you wanted to show me what Marisa has been up to?" Ropert asked Achelous. "As if the rifles and the Timberkeeps coming to live with us aren't enough!" He laughed.

"Og," Achelous nodded to the weaponsmith. Ogden lifted the top parchment on a stack of drawings.

Ropert blinked. The top drawing depicted nothing he'd ever seen before. He puzzled over it, looking at it from every perspective. Drawn to scale, standing next to the bulky contraption, was a man. "What is it?" he asked with consternation.

"It was Marisa's idea," Achelous offered. "You see these little wheels?"

The aorolmin nodded.

"They're so the gun can be rolled across a deck."

"Oh, so it is a gun?"

"Oi, a bloody big gun, your honor-ship, and it fires one of these," Ogden went to a corner of the room, moving building materials and carpenter tools aside. "Pottern poured it. A three-pound cannon ball." The smith held up a matt-black iron ball pitted with imperfections from a casual casting.

"Oh my, Mother," Ropert whispered when he hefted the mass of iron.

Achelous withdrew from his pocket a forty-five-caliber bullet like the one Ropert used today. "Imagine, lord, the damage *that* would do," indicating the cannonball, "you saw what this did to an iron pan," and he held the bullet between two fingers.

Ropert turned back to the drawing. The cannon was nearly twice as long as a man was tall and half as high. A large menacing hole punctured the end of the massive barrel. "But, a rifle is heavy. How much would this weigh?"

Ogden grunted, "Six man-weights. We've made one."

Ropert's frown deepened. "This was Marisa's idea? Surely, it is overkill. It would make a great hole in a man! And how would you aim it? Men could run away as soon as they saw you pointing it at them. And the wheels, where would you put it?"

Before Achelous could answer, Rayamars replied, "It would sit nicely on a stone tower, and you wouldn't have to aim it precisely. Image the havoc it would cause in the ranks of Warkenvaal pike regiment."

"But that is not what Marisa had in mind, lord," Achelous tapped the image of the man on the paper, "that's a sailor."

"A sailor?"

"Pirates, lord. Marisa wants to go pirate hunting."

The aorolmin's jaw visibly worked. He stared hard at the drawing, trying to divine Marisa's intent. Then Achelous flipped over the next page, and the sketch depicted a ship, a two-masted schooner, rigged fore and aft, only it was wider and sat lower than any in the aorolmin's current fleet. Protruding from the starboard side gunwales were seven ominous gun barrels.

"A ship," Ropert breathed.

Ogden chuckled, "That answers your aiming and running away problem, aorolmin, sir. The guns will fire where the ship points, and no pirate can out sail a three-pound cannon ball."

Achelous leaned on the table. "Marisa engaged her shipwright, under the strictest secrecy, to design a new ship. The shipwright didn't think any of her current ships would be safe to mount seven guns to a side, so he proposed building from scratch what will be called a corvette or an armed sloop."

Ropert barely heard Achelous, his mind far away. From the earliest days when the King of Taldamir had awarded the earldom of Tivor, the inhabitants of the seaside hamlet, now a city, had been at odds with their more prosperous and established southern neighbors of Warkenvaal. The King of Taldamir long needed a bulwark against the aggressive and expansionist pirates, and Tivor was the buffer. For eight generations of aorolmins, the pirates had been a constant irritant and, at times, an open antagonist. Three short, bitter wars had been fought with the Vaal, and each time, the King of Taldamir rode to the rescue of his vassal. But now the line of kings was dead, a weak Paleowright-sympathizing steward sat on the throne, and Taldamir slipped further into decay. He wondered if the Timberkeeps of New Ungern realized just how precarious their position was. He'd explained to them that they were now his bulwark against the Warkenvaal, but apparently, the allure of the Ungerngerist forest was enough to overcome the fear of invasion.

Nevertheless, the Timberkeeps may have brought with them their own salvation and his. Long had Ropert dwelt in his hall beneath the victories of his ancestors. But now, with a fleet armed with cannons, he and Tivor could be something more.

"Sire?"

"Uh, yes?" Ropert asked, thinking of a ship.

Achelous was waiting for a response, so he repeated the question. "Marisa has commissioned Ogden to build another cannon, a larger version, to be tested on the forecastle of the *Far Shore*, but if you want him to manufacture eighty rifles, Ogden will have to tell the lady to wait."

"Wait? Wait?! What on Mother's Fair Breasts for!" he turned a steely-eyed glare at Ogden. "Do not wait, my good smith. I beseech you to do it all. Whatever it takes. We need them both." Looking past Ogden to Achelous, he said, "If you've not the resources at your foundry here to do both, then I can be convinced to apply considerable labor and money to assist you. Better still, I ask that I be allowed to partner in this endeavor." He held up a hand when the trader appeared ready to balk, "A silent partner, to be sure, but a partner nonetheless. Understand me in this, Achelous; it has struck me that the future of Tivor rests in these works. It has also come to me that the Warkenvaal must *not* obtain these same weapons. Do you understand me?"

A faint smile crossed the trader's lips, "I understand, sire."

"Good, then we shall enter into an agreement where I will make it worth your efforts to provide me these weapons and to also abstain from supplying them to Tivor's enemies."

"A list of enemies to be named?" Achelous raised a brow.

"Of course, of course." The aorolmin looked again at the cannon-mounted corvette. "We will build this, and it will be the flag of my fleet. And I shall christen her," he sought for a suitable word, and then an inspiration came. "*Ascension*. I will name her *Ascension*."

Chapter 24
Krch

Corsair Mining Site, Dianis

"What?" The agent on duty nearly missed it. He'd been casually viewing the delayed video feed from the orange birds surveilling the mining site, and it was getting near the end of his watch. The AI hadn't flagged anything of note. "Scroll back," he told the AI. "Stop when Krch comes into the frame."

The orange bird tagged to watching Junko sat on a beam in the rafters of the awning the miners were using as a sun shade. Tables and benches were laid out, and breakfast for the contractors sat half-eaten. There'd been some sort of minor calamity with the sluice works, and Junko and the rest of the contractors had gone to effect repairs. Rather than risk having the constant shadowing of the orange bird be noticed, the bot had been instructed to stay in the rafters while the crew fixed the sluice works. The works were old, of provincial construction, and always breaking under the demands of Junko.

"What is she doing?" he whispered to himself.

Krch walked up to the breakfast table, glanced casually around, drank some water from a glass on the table, and meandered casually over to the other side of the table and sat down. Again, she looked around.

"I thought I told you to keep the orange bird pinned to Junko," said Mears, leaning over the agent's shoulder. It was his turn to relieve the watch.

"You did, and I did," said the agent. "This is the feed from Junko's bird. He's off fixing the sluice works with the rest of the crew."

Krch pulled a vial from her pocket, popped the top, sprinkled, or rather counted something into her hand, and put the vial away. Then, without looking, she swept the hand over a bowl of the freeze-dried gruel the crew was eating for breakfast. She casually picked up a spoon, stirred the gruel, sat the spoon down exactly where she'd picked it up, stood up, and left the frame.

The agent looked at Mears. Then, back to the video feed. "AI, go back to where Krch sprinkles what is in her hand into the bowl. Zoom in, please."

"She's dropping something in the bowl?" asked Mears.

The agent nodded absently. "AI, what is in that vial?"

The frame shifted a number of times, zooming in and out, and finally settled on three black specks sitting on top of the gruel before Krch stirred them in. "Foreign organic matter," came the AI's response.

Mears sniffed. "Well, that's helpful. What type of foreign organic matter?"

"Eighty-two percent probability the matter is rodentia feces."

"What?" said the agent.

"Sixty-three percent probability they are from *peromyscus melanotis*."

Shaking his head, the agent said, "Plain language, please."

"There is a sixty-three percent probability that Krch has deposited mouse manure in Junko's cereal. The mouse feces, when stirred in, will resemble the dried perk berries the contractors have added to their breakfast to enhance the flavor."

The agent turned to Mears. "See! I told you! She's way more entertaining to watch than the foreman! Who knows what other shit she's been doing? And I mean *shit*."

Mears rolled his eyes but couldn't help smiling.

"This is hysterical. I can't wait to watch Junko come back and eat his breakfast. Can we have both orange birds filming? I want one to watch Krch's face when Junko eats his food."

But Mears wasn't laughing.

"What? It's funny!"

"AI," said Mears, "what will happen if Junko ingests mouse poop?"

After a pause, the AI answered, "Checking for known pathogens in Dianis rodentia feces." Mears sat down in the vacant command chair. The AI came back, "Early ITA engineers were reported to come in contact with various forms of rodentia feces when their food supplies were compromised. A sometimes-fatal version of the carnotoro virus was contracted by the ITA engineers until a proper diagnosis was established and treatment provided. IDB Dianis medical records have noted that, properly vaccinated, IDB field staff are sufficiently immune from the virus. Indigenous Human populations on Dianis appear to be naturally immune to the virus."

Mears arched an eyebrow at the agent. "Krch may be wacko, but she's smart too. Is this some practical joke of hers about to go awry, or does she know what she is doing?"

The agent said, "With your permission, I'm shifting the mining foreman's orange bird to Krch. She's devious. Who knows what else she is doing?"

Chapter 25
Illian

Wedgewood

The stranger walked into the foundry. Workers were raising rafters up to carpenters on the emerging roof structure. At times, the hammering was deafening. There were so many people coming to and fro that the merc, for that's what he appeared to be, went unnoticed. Eventually, a warder from the Second nudged Lettern.

"What?"

The warder pointed at the stranger.

She squinted. The sun slanted in, and she had to raise a hand to shield her eyes. She moved to get a better look and froze. Her gaze pinned him. Others took notice, and the hammering paused. She took a tentative step forward, and when the merc smiled, she walked quickly to him and looked him up and down, then studied his face. "What happened to your red eyes?"

His smile turned to a smirk. "We had to fix them. Red eyes are not natural on Dianis."

She reached out and grasped both hands, holding them, examining them as if they were made from delicate porcelain. Slowly, the hammering resumed. She looked at the handbolt hanging from his hip. "Where's your big gun? That big plasma thingy? And your fancy armor?"

His smile flickered, but to Lettern, it was as bright as the mountain sun. "I don't do that anymore."

"Ooooh?"

He laughed and shook his head.

Again, she looked at the handbolt. "Are you?" She frowned. "Are you working for Ivan!?"

He nodded.

"Mother!" She threw her arms around his neck, and the hammering stopped. All eyes were on Lettern's unusual display of affection. "Ivan did it?"

"He said you were a pest. He said he had to leave Wedgewood, so you couldn't bother him about me."

She half pouted, and again, the hammering resumed, but at a lower tempo. "Well, he would never give me a real answer."

Illian Meridia, former senior corporal in the Assault Marine Brigade, said, "That would be chief."

He stood there, and she made no move to drop her arms from around his neck. He said, "I have something I need to ask you. It's work-related. Is there somewhere we can talk?"

"Work-related?" she asked, drawing back but keeping her hands on his neck. "So formal."

He nodded.

Dropping her arms, she said, "Okay. Follow me." She led the way out onto the lane. She pointed out all the new construction, what was going up and where, how things were being improved, and how even with a large number of Mearsbirch clan folk moving to New Ungern, there were even more Timberkeeps in Wedgewood because the other Timber clans were rallying to the needs of their Mount Mars kindred. She stopped and whirled on him, "Illy, even Cedar Floral is here! Do you know how far away that is!"

He grasped her outstretched hands, her unbridled enthusiasm intoxicating, even to a cynical, numbed, assault Marine.

Embarrassed, she pulled her hands free and wheeled about, waving to him. "Follow me."

Making their way through the town where new foundations were being dug through ash and black charcoal, she came to an area unscathed by the Troglodyte pillaging and Paleowright fires. The Ungerngerists rose in all their glorious heights, their massive limbs curving upwards to carry the royal blue sky. Snow-capped Mount Mars climbed steeply behind them. Meridia thought about it. The crisp mountain air was probably the purest natural oxygen he'd ever breathed. No machine oxygen generators and scrubbers here. He stopped and watched. High in the sky, an early-summer snow plume streamed off the peak.

It drifted away, and he stood there transfixed. A cirrus cloud scudded beyond. More snow ripped off the peak, and he felt his soul filling. The air suffused his lungs. The wind stroked the Ungerngerists, and the whispering sound drowned all his jaded pains; it washed away his faithless attitude of the universe and life writ large. An energy, a force, an essence coruscated through his soul. Something was calling to him, beckoning. *Wedgewood?* He dropped out of the reverie, his combat sense alerting him.

Lettern was close. She stood holding his right hand in both of hers. "Mother," she said it as a simple explanation. "If you open your soul, Illy, Mother will fill it. Mother created the mountain. She is here with all of us."

He stared at her. Neither of them talking. The mountain sun blessed them. The wind stroked the Ungerns. Songbirds called. Summer scents wafted.

"Mother called you to me, Illy." Lettern's gaze poured into him. "You belong here."

She dropped his hand and sauntered over to an Ungerngerist. A rope ladder hung from a massive branch way up.

He watched her climb nimbly up. Halfway, she stopped and looked down. "What are you waiting for? And what are you looking at?"

He gulped. "Uh, I'm looking at you, and..."

"And?" she teased.

"And, well, I've never climbed a tree before. A very big tree."

She resumed climbing and called, "Then this will be your first time."

Meridia stood at the railing of Lettern's tree house. His heart pounding. With a sickening stir, he realized he might be afraid of heights. *How weird is that? I've dropped from orbit more times than I can count, and I am in a treehouse, and my knees are shaking.* He triggered his embed to stifle the adrenalin, something as an assault Marine he never did. Adrenalin was oxygen to a Marine. He gripped the railing, waiting for his pulse to calm.

Lettern placed her hand beside his on the railing. "If the height bothers you, I understand. Not all of us care to live up here. During the battle for the town, those of us who couldn't stand heights manned the hardpoints."

He measured his breathing and looked across to where a nearby rope-bridge spanned the wide gap to a treefort. "So this is a house," he asked unsteadily, "and that is a fort?"

"Yep. That's Perrty. That's our Second Ward muster point when we tree-up."

"Tree-up?"

"Yes. When the Trogs and churchmen attacked, Sedge ordered tree-up. We all climbed up into our treeforts, about forty of them, and from here, we feathered the Trogs like we were on the practice range."

Meridia forgot his fear of heights and concentrated on the woman beside him. "I wish I had been here. With you."

Lettern lifted her pained gaze from the ground below. "You were with me, with that corsair. That's good enough."

"Quorat." Meridia looked down at a Timberkeep walking the pine needle path below.

"What?"

"His name was Quorat. There will be more of them. As long as you Wedgewooders keep a billion-credit aqua-5 pegmatite in a party tent instead of a vault on Avaria, you are going to have problems."

"A billion credits? Is that a lot?"

Meridia shook his head. "It's not a billion, but it is a lot. I'm not an expert, but I'm pretty sure we could use it in the war." He thought about Ivan's edict of not sharing secrets with Dianis provincials, but with Lettern, he just didn't care.

"The war?"

He turned and faced her full-on. "Yes, the war." He let it sink in. "Lettern, whatever you have gone through here, with the fire, the Trogs, the Paleowrights, the death, the pain, magnify it a thousand, a million-fold. If the

Turboii and their sizars ever come to Dianis, this world will end as you know it."

She saw the deep torment in his eyes, torment undimmed by the mountain sun, the whispering boughs, and songbirds. She hugged him. "You fought them?"

"I have."

"If they come here, will you help us fight them?"

"I will."

She raised her chin off his chest, looking into his eyes that had once been red. "Why did you pick brown?"

"Uh?"

She stood on her toes, put a finger on his eyelid, opened it wide, and placed her forehead against his. "Why brown?" They were eye-to-eye.

He smiled. His gloom gone. "Because I liked yours."

She giggled the happy sound of twittering birds, and settled back on her feet. Pulling him by the hand, she gave him the short tour of her tree house. She stopped at the foot of her broad bed, which was easily the largest piece of furniture in the house. "You said you had a work-related question?"

"Ah yes," he said, looking at the neatly laid out bed with its thick homespun blankets and feather pillows. "It must get cold up here?" he asked.

"It does," she said.

He nodded. "So my question is, have you seen Achelous? Do you know where he is?"

"Yes. Ivan asked me the same question."

She was snuggling in close, and Meridia realized that he could battle the worst enemies the galaxy could muster, but against this woman, he was defenseless.

"And?" he smiled, trying to get an inch between them.

"And what does it matter," she replied, persistent.

"Because as soon as you answer my question, I'm done working, and I'm all yours."

She returned his smile and used her archer's muscles – honed to iron from years of drawing a longbow -- to shove Meridia onto her bed. She straddled him, pressing her hands down on his chest. "Achelous is in New Ungern. He went there with Og."

"New Ungern?"

"Yea. It's by Tivor. Mount Epratis. He went there with Marisa, and Baryy, and Outish. But Outy is back here in Wedgewood. Outy must not have gone the whole way because he came back too fast."

Meridia went distant, and Lettern picked up on it. "Why? Achelous is one of you? Right? An Ancient or Avarian or whatever you call yourselves."

"Yes, but I guess we didn't know, at least for sure, that Baryy and Outish were here." Meridia didn't care if he confirmed to Lettern that Baryy and Outish were IDB agents; she was as good as they came. To Assault Marines, the most important thing that mattered was good people, people you could trust in a firefight. That trust eclipsed any oath given to the IDB or the federation.

"Why? You're not going to arrest them? Are you? I heard Ivan on that assault-lander boat. He's pissed at Achelous."

Meridia nodded, "I know. I've gotten that lecture."

"Outy and Baryy are my friends, Illy."

Meridia read her clearly. "I'm not going to arrest them. They're Ivan's problem if it comes to that. Officially, Ivan has tasked me to find Achelous. Outish, the astrobiologist, is no concern of mine. If Ivan asks about him, I'll let you know."

Her brows furrowed. "What's an astro-whatever? Is that Human?"

He chuckled, his hands on her hips. "Yes. It's what he does, not who he is." He skipped, for the moment, that Outish was not a Human but a transmuted Halorite, courtesy of Field Outfitting.

She nodded her head once. "You done working now?"

He feigned thinking about it and reached around to grasp the cheeks of her ass. "Hmm, I can't think of any more—"

Her mouth closed on his.

Meridia's embed buzzed. Again and again.

"What?" he growled and threw off the blankets. Expecting to see the haze-grey overhead of his rack on the *Spirit's Fury,* he was brought to the stark realization that he was not onboard ship. Blinking, the faint light of early dawn crept into the room. "Where the hell—" The ceiling was made of wood, the air had strange smells in it, and the bed was actually comfortable. *Dirtside?* Was his next thought. *What the hell planet am I on? What's the mission?* He asked himself in a panic. *Am I supposed to be on watch? Who has the watch? Where's my weapon?* His pulse instantly pounding, he sat up and frantically searched for his rifle. Instead, he found a warm body, a bare hip and ass. He breathed deep, again and again. In the wan light, he focused on the curve of the hip and the butt, obviously female. It would have been mesmerizing if he weren't in a panic. *Where am I? I must still be dreaming?* He tried to shake off the dream. *Wow, I really need a mem-killing. I'm losing it.* His thigh embed kept buzzing. *What the hell is that?* He asked himself. He rubbed his face, but he didn't have his helmet, so he couldn't load the heads-up display. Spirits only knew where his helmet was and who this woman was sleeping next to him. *Was that Private Epo? Spirits, no, I hate Epo.* Trying to shake that off as well, he leaned over the side of the bed, a very wide and soft bed. He saw the multi-func laying there: the vembrace for his right forearm.

Reality constricted his chest, and he rolled over. He pulled the blankets away, and there was Lettern.

Sliding in close, he slid an arm under her waist and hugged her, trying to focus on the woman in his arms and not the Turboii sizars that came at him. It was always the same, though lately they came less. Brigade medical said he needed the apparitions mind-wiped, but then he'd lose the memories of his friends, and it was a Marine creed to never forget a comrade. So he held on as they came. His body twitched. It would be over in a moment. The sizar ran by gripping the unarmored body of a fellow Marine in its maw. He gripped hard. More sizars came, and then, as the sizars overran the base, he'd rolled out of his rack, grabbed his pulse rifle, and fired over and over again.

His thigh embed kept buzzing, but he just held on, waiting for the nightmare to end.

Two cool hands cupped his face, and lips pressed against his forehead. "Illy?"

He buried his face in her neck, the tremors subsiding.

"Illy? It's all right. I'm here."

Eventually, his eyes opened.

She stroked his short, crew-cut hair. He looked like an Auro Na apostate with that haircut, but he was an Ancient. "I have nightmares, too. When they, when they..." To this day, she still couldn't talk about when the Scarlet Saviors had killed Mergund. When she lay sprawled on the deck of Murali's.

Meridia stirred. "The chief is pinging me."

Retrieving the vembrace, he lay back next to her and activated the screen on the curved steel plate of the arm guard. He smiled at her awe as an image flickered across the surface.

Lettern cuddled close and watched as the display shimmered into text. Her brown eyes were enthralled when she glanced up. He gave a secret smile and shrugged.

Ivan Darinarishcan's face formed on the display, small though it was. "Meridia?"

"Yes, chief?"

"Where have you been?"

"Sleeping." If having nightmares included sleeping.

"With who?"

Lettern could see the display and hear the audio, though she was out of the camera angle.

"With *who?*" Meridia drew out the word. "I'm sleeping. *Was* sleeping, that is. What's up?" He looked up from the multi-func, "Shiren, chief, it's dark here."

"Are you with Lettern?"

"Lettern?" Meridia looked dumbfounded. He'd been subjected to the interrogations of the most grizzled gunnery sergeants in the Brigade and knew how to play the game.

"Don't give me that shit, Meridia. Did you have sex with Lettern Stouttree?"

Meridia felt Lettern squirm next to him. He suspected she wanted to giggle, giggle in triumph. "Sex? With Lettern? Chief! What's the problem? You ping me at O'dark thirty. Out with it! Otherwise, this damn multi-gadget is going out the window."

Ivan's visage on the display narrowed. "Corporal, I was Fleet Forward Recon before I joined Ready, so don't think I'm not wise to your Marine bullshit ways."

Meridia rolled his eyes. "Then, mister Fleet Forward Recon, you know I'm going to take this damn thing and smash it against the wall because I'm just some dumb, dull-witted A-Marine who only cares how fast he can reload a plasma on full auto."

Ivan's image stewed for a bit. "Did you get anything out of her?"

"Yea, Achelous is in New Ungern. With that Marisa chick."

Ivan's image was steady. "For sure?"

"For sure."

For once, the chief's face softened. "What about Baryy or Outish? Did she mention them?"

He felt Lettern tense. "Yes. Baryy is in New Ungern with Achelous, but Outish is here in Wedgewood."

"Did she say what either of them are doing?"

"Negative. I don't think she knows."

Ivan stared at him through the display. Judging from the background, Ivan was not in-country but potentially at Central Station. The location identifier simply said *unknown*. "Okay. Go talk to Outish. Don't spook him. The last thing we need is for him to start running from us."

Meridia snorted, "As if they aren't already."

"Right. Tell him the IDB is coming back to Dianis, but it's gonna be a while. Funding, authorizations, staffing, all of that, the usual bureaucracy. Find out what he is doing. Breia wants to know in the worst way. Breia is on my case for us to start lining up adepts to interview, which—" Ivan took a breath, "I don't know if I'm good with. Dianis is a

Class E, regardless of what the matriarch wants. I need to reconnect with Clienen, Director Hor. Outish will know him. He's still the official director of IDB Dianis."

"And then what?" The answer to the question was critical to him *and* Lettern.

"And then I need you to get your insubordinate ass down to Tivor. We're going to pay my old friend Atch a visit. He has a shuttle-load of questions to answer."

Meridia thought about it, then pointedly looked off-camera. His face came back into view. "When do you need me down there?"

"Day after tomorrow. If it will take any longer, ping me."

Meridia nodded.

"And one last thing. If I catch you having sex with a provincial, I'll boot your ass out of Ready on the spot. You'll be happy to fight sizars."

"Is he always that grumpy?" Lettern asked after Merida signed off.

Meridia shook off the blankets and walked to the window, watching the dawn widen. "He's got problems." Searching for his pants, Meridia said, "Before I leave for Tivor, I have something to show you."

Chapter 26
Outish

Wedgewood

Three Timberkeep men were waiting for Lettern and Meridia as they navigated the rope ladder down from her treehouse. Meridia, coming down last -- and slowly – wondered what was up.

One of the Timberkeeps, a tall, skinny man, wore his clothes like a scarecrow: loose and baggy, his white hair long and wispy. The other two were axemen from the Fourth Ward, judging by their shield heraldry. As part of his injection learning course for Dianis, Meridia had focused on the various military formations on the planet, and in particular, Isuelt. If he was going to pretend to be a mercenary from Neuland, he needed to be convincing.

"Is he an Ancient?" one of them asked Lettern.

Meridia turned, stepping unsteadily away from the swaying ladder.

"Yea," she said. "He works for Ivan. But he's one of us. Mother calls to him. He was there when I killed the Ancient Quorat, who killed Booney and Mattar."

The four of them were looking at him. *So much for maintaining cover,* he thought. He came to stand before them.

"Brookern says that talisman is hiding your true identity," Lettern pointed at the necklace around Meridia's neck.

"Oh? How does he know that?"

"You took it off last night," said Brookern, the scarecrow man.

"Ah." He looked at Lettern, and she blushed, digging a boot toe in the pine needles. "Yeah, well, I'm new to this stuff, just like you. What you need to know is, like Lettern said, I'm one of you. I'm here to protect Dianis from the other Ancients. The bad ones. The ones that want your aquamarine and will kill every one of you to get it." He wagged his head, Avarian fashion. "I can't fight them all, but I can sure kill the ones that come in reach of this," he patted the handbolt in its holster.

"What about the heat blaster Quorat used on us? Do you have one of those?" a warder asked.

Meridia gave him a flat look. "If it comes to that, I can get one real fast."

"That was odd," Meridia said, walking with Lettern as she led the way to the cabin that Baryy and Outish shared.

"Quorat came to our town and killed our people. We have to defend ourselves," she said simply.

"That's not what I meant. All this cloak and dagger stuff, subterfuge, and being found out immediately. Either you Wedgewooders are very good, or I am real lousy."

She reached out and gripped his hand, pulling him close as they walked. "Or you're real honest. And to me, that's what matters."

Meridia exhaled. "Yea, well, I don't think the chief is gonna like me being honest."

She pressed into him as they walked on the trail. "I listened to him. As long as he doesn't have you arrest Outish, Ivan is okay."

"Yeah, and what about booting me out of Ready Reaction?"

She looked up at him and smiled. "We won't get caught."

His eyebrow went up. "You mean we can't get caught. Period. I just found you."

She smiled brightly, then looked to a cabin up ahead. "That's Baryy's place."

The log cabin was pushed into the slope. Mount Mars loomed behind, just visible through the boughs of the surrounding Ungerngerists. White lattice windows flanked a gaudy red door. A neat little porch with a knee-high railing greeted visitors. White cornerstones marked the boundaries of the tiny property. "What is that?" he asked.

"What?" asked Lettern, not seeing anything remarkable.

"That? The thing on the roof? Is it eating the roof? Is the roof made of—"

"Grass?" she answered. "Well, yeah, why not?"

"Okay," he drawled, "but—"

She laughed, and to him, it was akin to the gentle tinkling of the wind chimes. "It's a cone goat. They can be ornery if you try to shoo them away. Looks like that one has taken a liking to Baryy's roof."

Meridia made a face that said he could go with it. As they approached the cabin, the goat stopped munching roof grass and lay down, its hooves hanging over the eave. It watched them. They stepped on the tiny porch, and Lettern knocked. "Outy? Outy, you in there?"

She peered in one of the windows and then tried the door, expecting it to be unlocked, and it was. She invited Meridia in, but he was fixated on the goat, whose head was hanging over the edge, eyeing him. "Well?"

"Why is it staring at me?"

"People say cone goats are sensitive, you know, have sixthsense. If it starts following you around, just let it be." She led the way into the cabin. There was a small living room with a large fireplace. The hearth cold. Immediately to the rear was a tiny kitchen barely big enough for the table and two stools. "These are new," she said, walking about examining the various pots and containers. "Look at all of them. What is he doing?"

"Who? Baryy or Outish?"

"Outy. This is definitely Outy's work. Baryy doesn't care about dirt and animals. He's all about people and clans and religions. Outy likes plants and animals."

Meridia watched Lettern peer into a ceramic jar. Everything was neatly labeled with pieces of parchment glued to the vessels with some sort of sticky...

"Wax," she said. Nodding at the candles. One shallow tin pan was labeled *Twistynook drainage, grid 3,0.* "What's he doing?" she asked again, sotto voce.

Meridia sat in the bentwood rocker and gave it a tentative push. He knew exactly what Outish, the astrobiologist, was doing. The question was, did he find it. "Where do you think he is?" There were only two other rooms in the cabin, bedrooms, and the doors stood open. They were alone.

She shook her head. "I guess he's out gathering more of this stuff," and she waved at all the pots and jars with all their neat labels. Nearly every available shelf and floor space was occupied.

Meridia spied a piece of chain mail hanging out of a chest with the lid closed. He opened the chest. In it was a helm, mail coif, hauberk, and other gear. On the wall above the chest hung a double-bladed axe and a shield emblazoned with the anvil of the Second Ward. "They're in your ward?"

"Outish is."

He nodded once and fingered a notch in the axe that had been ground out. "Chief logged the Battle for Wedgewood in our IDB files. He recorded Sedge's description of the engagement. Ivan is nothing if not meticulous. I read the account of what Outish did. I didn't know he was in your ward, though." He turned to Lettern. "Did you know, before Wedgewood, that kid had never been in a battle?"

She shook her head.

He turned back to the axe and then lowered the lid of the chest. "Well, let's go find him. People, the Matrincy, want to know what he's up to."

"There you are. What are you doing up here, Outy? We've been all over this mountain!"

Holding a plant, examining the root ball he'd just carefully dug up, Outish looked up surprised. "Lettern! I didn't hear—" and then he saw Meridia, a stranger. At a loss for what to do with the plant, he slowly lowered it, almost as if he wanted to hide it.

"What ya doing?" she asked as they made their way through the waist-high fiddleheads and kdel thorns.

"Uh, looking," he said lamely.

Lettern stood in front of him, confused. "That's a kdel plant."

Meridia saw Outish's fur-covered left hand. Other than that, he'd never know that Outish was a Halorite. Field Outfitting had done a good job of transmuting his skin, hair, and other features so he appeared to be Human. It helped that somewhere in their dim past Halorites had been Human, but something had caused their gene pool to take a divergent branch. His bushy, unkempt hair, sparse beard, boyish cheeks, and innocent eyes tempted Meridia to discount him as a threat, but he remembered the axe.

The cone goat burst its way through the brambles, munching green berries at random. It saw what Outish was holding and made to eat it.

"No, Knot Head, no!" Outish held his precious plant high and fended off the goat that was trying to climb on him.

"Knot Head?" asked Meridia. "That fits." He plucked a handful of weeds and waved them in the goat's face. Distracted from Outish, the goat studied Meridia, then began munching the offering.

"Why did you bring him?" asked Outish.

Lettern laughed. "As if we had a choice. He's been following Illy all day."

"Illy?"

Meridia nodded. "That's what Lettern calls me. My real name is Illian Meridia, Ready Reaction Agent, IDB Dianis. Formerly of the federation Marines, Assault Brigade."

Outish went pale. He bent over and vomited.

Meridia carefully retrieved the kdel plant before Outish dropped it. "Let me hold that for you. Your work could be, depending on what you find, incredibly important to the federation." Meridia watched Lettern fuss over her friend, who vomited again when she apologized for bringing Ready Reaction to his cabin and explained that Ivan didn't want to arrest him and that everything would be okay.

Meridia carefully set the plant down on a burlap sack that he assumed Outish was using for specimen collection. Sitting down on a rock outcropping, Meridia waited while the astrobiologist wiped his face with his hands and then his hands on his pants and tried to compose himself. The former Marine watched a bird of prey circle downslope from them. Wedgewood lay downhill below the curve of the mountain. They had been climbing most of the afternoon, Lettern tracking Outish the entire way. He'd considered deploying recon bots to locate the intern, but when Lettern had just marched off reading inscrutable signs in the understory, he was amazed.

This world is beautiful, he thought. They were just above the tree line. He could see the farms, tiny little square plots down on the plains. After a while, he realized Outish and Lettern were waiting for him to do something. He said, "You know, Outish, I was on Fer IV. It was a nasty fight. The sizars were countless. Seas of them. They came at us and kept coming. We were manning a fort, more like a series of ramparts guarding a mountain pass. On the other side of the pass was the city of Seerien Aire. Ever hear of it?" He looked at the astrobiologist.

Outish nodded, "The federation saved the city. Seven million people."

Lettern's eyes went wide. She didn't think there were seven million people in the entire world.

"You were there?" she exclaimed.

Meridia turned back to the view, a view all the way down to Wayland's farm. "I was." He watched the falcon, or he thought it was a falcon, ride the air currents. "Did you hear how we won that battle? After we lost three entire regiments in that pass? After we just kept feeding them in, battalion after battalion, until the ground heaped ten-feet deep in dead sizars and Marines."

"The AI in my Sizar biology class told us you killed the Turboii controller."

Meridia shook his head. "I didn't kill the controller; I was just a grunt private scared shitless, scrounging for plasma energy packs and shooting someone else's rifle after I fried mine, which happened at least twice. Fortunately, there were plenty of dead Marines around for me to borrow theirs." He took a deep breath and focused on a distant point. "There was a Matrincy pathic that shifted into orbit the third day of the battle when things were going really bad. She was the one who located the Turboii control bunker with the aural transmitters. A single strike from one of our cruisers and all those sizars turned mindless and ran off. There aren't many Matrincy combat pathics." He looked at Outish.

Outish shook his head. "They're rare. You were lucky to get one."

Meridia snorted. "Yeah, tell that to the seventy-five hundred Marines who died defending that pass." He shook his head, looking at the ground. "Shit, Outish. Here on Dianis, there are so many adepts, the goats are even sensitive."

"Not on Dianis, just here on Mount Mars," said Outish. "Once you move the sample horizon out beyond this mountain range, the population density of sensitives drops down to near galactic-Human-normal. One in two hundred Humans has a measurable talent, one in a thousand being a possible adept."

Meridia looked at him. "And what is it here in Wedgewood?"

"One in fifty is a measurable talent. One in two hundred is a possible adept. There is a curve in the talent population. One in three hundred of the adepts is measurable to a master's grade. In the galaxy, only one in ten million talents are measurable to a master's grade."

Meridia stared at him. "You can prove that?"

Outish gave a single, embarrassed nod.

"And do you know why?" asked Meridia.

"Why what?" asked Lettern.

"Why there are so many adepts, masters grade, in Wedgewood," replied Outish.

Meridia looked at the plant on the burlap sack. He thought about all the specimens in the cabin. He recalled things he'd read in the Field Operations journal the team had filed before IDB Dianis operations were shut down. "You know, don't you?"

Outish gave a noncommittal shrug.

It was good enough for him. Meridia stood. "Well, the sun will be going down behind this mountain, and it's probably two or three hours back to town. Or were you planning on staying up here all night?"

Outish asked, "You're not going to arrest me?" The hope in his eyes and the fear in his voice made Meridia wonder how the world had come to this.

"No, Outy, I'm not." He looked at Lettern. "I gave her my word that I would not. I'm Ready Reaction in-country support. That means I'm here to protect geeks like you. Besides, I've lost too many friends, so many I can't remember their names. That's really bad, Outish, when you can't remember the name of a friend who died beside you. I owe it to them; if you can save just one life, then whatever it is, we need to do it. Seerien Aire, Outish, Seerien Aire."

Chapter 27
Duck Peren

City of Tivor

"You know the man we speak of?"

Duck shifted his bulk in the chair. Captain Irons, tall and confident, intimidated him. The captain was a hard man to get a sense of; he offered few insights into his motives or interests, which bothered Duck, whose own stock in trade – information -- relied on knowing his customer.

"I don't actually know him. I know who he is," Duck offered.

"You would recognize him?" asked the Scarlet Savior captain.

"Yes."

"Do you know where he is?" The other man with the hooked nose and bushy eyebrows asked. The captain had not introduced this person but clearly deferred to him.

Duck, a Paleowright Examiner, didn't need any introductions. He'd seen the viscount from the street, outside the aorolmin's castle, when the Scarlet Saviors had escorted the viscount's coach to meet with the aorolmin a year ago. Everyone knew how that meeting had turned out, which is why Viscount Helprig and his escorts were back but incognito. Duck squirmed; the chair creaked ominously. The pipe smoke in the seedy wharf-side grog house bothered his eyes. It wasn't his choice for a meeting place. For the devout, such as he, who sought to emulate the Ancients, the rank establishment was an affront to his dignity. But the captain had insisted on a location near their ship. They didn't want to be seen walking around town until they were ready. Whatever that meant. "I can find him," Duck offered. "I hear he's been seen riding to the new Timmy village."

The prelate, while dressed in civilian clothes, could not conceal his arrogance. He leaned back; his chair didn't creak. "Yes, the Timmies are here, aren't they? And he's a Timmy lover, a collaborator. All the more reason to—"

Irons interrupted the prelate with a polite gesture. "We need to know where he is. We need to speak with him," he said smoothly.

"Well, I can arrange a meeting," Duck said. Sweat beaded on his forehead. It was one thing to send in his reports and curry attention. It was quite another to get it from the viscount in person.

"No, that won't be necessary," said Irons. "We just need you to identify him to one of my men. Tell us where he will be and when. We will," he paused, "make our own introductions."

Duck looked over to the table at the front window where two of the captain's men sat stiff on the benches, their tankards of wharf ale untouched. A dock whore walked past their table and flashed them. Rather than laugh or ogle, they waved her away angrily. There were two more men at a table along the back wall. All four wore nondescript traveling cloaks, tunics, and britches, but hanging below the hem of one cloak was the distinctive curved tip of what Duck was sure was a rachier. A chill shivered him. Until he saw that he'd assumed the captain was from the Taldamir cathedral guard or one of the pikemen regiments.

Irons was watching him closely. His expression flat, like a python sizing up a mouse. "We're on official Church business," he answered Duck's unspoken question.

Duck swallowed. "I, I can do that. Tell you where he will be, that is."

"When?"

Working his jaw, Duck said, "I'll have to find him first. He moves around. Sometimes, he's gone for weeks."

"Well, let's hope he's here." Irons attempted a sweet smile. "I'll send one of my men with you. He'll stay with you until you find our man. Understand?"

Duck wanted to complain that he operated alone; his contacts would be unsettled if he approached them with a strange man in tow. They would clam up, rightfully so.

Leaving the tavern in a hurry, Duck wanted this business over with. At least Captain Irons agreed to have the Scarlet Savior trail him at a discrete distance and not hold his hand. Irons had called him *sergeant,* and he was just as scary as the captain, which put the Whispering Willies into him. If the Tivor guard knew there was a Savior in the city, they would sound the alarm, bar the gates, and mount a full search. News of the Battle for Wedgewood had spread far and wide and polarized the people into two camps: for or against the Paleowrights. Here in Tivor, the needle swung heavily against Diunesis Antiquaria, exacerbated by Timmies walking the streets of Tivor, trading for goods, and sharing their stories of the churchmen-Troglodyte attack. Duck silently cursed in the name of Phileas the Ancient the stupidity of such an unholy alliance. His duty as Paleowright examiner in Tivor was already a sensitive business. Now, many of his confidants, the ardent Mother Dianis believers, wouldn't even look at him, crediting the rumors that he was a Paleowright. If they did speak to him, their required bribes were double or triple. *Did Hebert consider how the Western peoples would react when they heard Troglodytes had attacked a Human town in league with churchmen?* He shook his head. To the Church cause, it was a disaster.

Standing at B Wharf, Duck waited for a crew of a Point Maris barque to finish securing a line to a bollard, and then he walked around them. The wind, warm and brisk, had shifted and came straight into the harbor on top of the late afternoon tide. Sunlight glinted off the harbor riffles like a thousand shards of glass. The outer quays were filling up as more ships came in. The vessels were marked with flags and foreign-sounding transom names from all around Isuelt: Drakan, Sea Haven, Eastport, Taldamir, even the odd Ompean. The town watch was out in force, not just because of the sheer number of merchant seamen roaming the docks swilling ale, and chasing whores but because many of those nations were not fond of each other. Tivor was an open port.

Duck made his way to the pier owned by Marinda Merchants. They were the biggest trading house in Tivor. They were so large and influential they owned their own pier, the longest one in the harbor. Walking past the stevedores loading bales of hemp, flax, and other grains into the warehouse at the foot of the pier, he stopped to see if his shadow was still with him. The sergeant saw him halt and found a pretense to do the same. Duck sat down on a mooring bollard outside the warehouse and waited. Carters came and went, hauling goods to the stores and emporiums in the city. He was looking for one carter in particular: a House Marinda driver who shuttled goods to Marinda Hall. For two silver pennies, the man would inquire at the stables for whatever Duck needed, in this case, the whereabouts of the patron's lover. A sensitive subject as Marinda Merchants was protective of their owner: Marisa Pontifract.

Killing time while he waited for the carter, Duck wondered what official business the archbishop of Isuelt had with the wayward trader? Whatever it was, it bode ill for his own welfare.

Chapter 28
The Package

Wedgewood

"In here." Meridia led Outish and Lettern through a back door of the Twistynook grain mill and across a footbridge that spanned the creek. On the other side was a storehouse. He took out a shiny new skeleton key and inserted it into the lock.

"Og made that lock?" Lettern asked.

Meridia paused, "I don't know. Ivan arranged this when the matriarch was here. When Special Forces," he gave them a frustrated look, "used the mill as a bivouac."

"You don't like Special Forces?" Lettern asked as they made their way into the storeroom that had been converted to a bunk room.

"They're overrated," he quipped over his shoulder. "Outy, close the door and lock it." He grabbed a corner of a rug that covered the wood floor and pulled it back. Tapping his forearm vembrace, he brought up the multi-func display and swiped through the panels.

"Oh, what ya doing?" Lettern cooed, leaning in close.

"Whoa, hey! What you got?" Outish hustled over when he saw the glow of a hologrid.

"Just my multi-func," Meridia said as he tapped the *authorize* command and then the *unlock* command.

"Your camo multi-func is your forearm guard?" Outish exclaimed. "That's totally cosmos! Did you see what they gave me for a camo multi-func? A water horn." Outish shook his head and showed Meridia how the leather cover of the horn pulled aside, exposing the horn, and how he had to double swipe it to actuate it and then pull away the other flap to expose the nano-configured instrument orifices.

"Yeah, that is pretty lame," Meridia said.

"Seriously! A water bottle, what the—"

"What are you complaining about?" Lettern interjected, I don't have a multi-whatever." She squeezed Meridia's arm. Giving him her best baby-girl gaze. "How do I get one of those fancy multi-things that look like forearm guards and not a water bottle?" She sneered, then smiled at Outish. "Illy is tall tree, isn't he?"

When Outish colored, embarrassed, Meridia peered at him. "Dude. I read the account of the battle." He gave him a nod. "I have got something just for you," and then he looked into Lettern's brown eyes, "and you. Way better than just a multi-whatever-thingy."

"Really?"

"Really." He swiped the *actuate* command, and a seam appeared in the middle of the floor, spread wider, and then the two halves of a hatch lifted, exposing a buried ferroconcrete chamber. Inside the chamber were three large boxes, sitting side by side, the size and shape of coffins.

Lettern's eyes grew, and Outish guffawed, "Sweetness. Who put that here?"

"Not important." Special Forces had, and he didn't want to give them credit. "It's what's inside that matters." He reached down and put his hand on the palm lock. There was a *snick,* and the lid of the container lifted like a treasure chest.

Lettern peered down into the open box. "Oh my," she breathed. She settled to her knees and was about to reach down when Meridia touched her shoulder. "Not yet. Some instructions first."

She sat back, patient, attentive, and totally focused on one thing.

"In order to use that gear, I, and only I, can authorize access. You can only open the chamber if I am here, and—"

Lettern tried to listen to the rules, but all she could think of was the day she met Illian. The day she had killed Quorat.

Meridia reached down into the cask and retrieved the object of her desire. Her sweet desire. He handed it to her.

She cradled it her arms like a baby and brushed a hand gently along the electro-optical sight.

"Uh, can you really give that to her? She's a provincial, Meridia. That's strictly—"

"Shut up, Outy," Lettern snipped. She stood, raised it to her shoulder like she'd seen the Marines do, and got the feel of her first plasma rifle. "When do I get to use it?" she asked, looking over the scope at Meridia.

He smiled and pushed the muzzle so that it pointed at something other than him. Then he put a finger to the control node, "Enable, Illian Meridia, instructor mode."

The weapon came alive in her arms, and the scope sensor indicators blinked.

Meridia walked to a window and pulled the interior shutters aside. "Look through the scope out there," he nodded at the window. "Sight through the scope just like it was an arrow. Same principle."

Lettern nestled the unfamiliar weapon against her cheek and sought the thing that Meridia called the *scope*. Then she said, "Huh? What is all that stuff? Outy! I can see way up the valley! From here!"

Meridia began to explain. "All that stuff you see are the target sights, image overlay, threat indicator, etc. And you'll get to use it when we get into trouble. And Outish, you asked if I can give that weapon to Lettern? No. I can't. But there are only six IDB agents on this entire planet; one of them is you, and only three of us are Ready Reaction. And of those three, only one is in Wedgewood: me. If shit goes down, Outy, I'm going to need you to help me defend you. Which is my new prime directive, straight from the matriarch."

"Okay," Outish nervously watched Lettern play with, or rather experiment with the weapon's unknown controls. "But you gave a plasma rifle to a provincial. No way is that—"

"Outy! Illy can do whatever he wants. He's tall tree."

"That's true." Meridia gently grasped Lettern's rifle, and when she refused to let go, he said, "If you let me have it, I'll tell you how it works."

She looked at him suspiciously. "You'll give it back?"

"Promise." When he had the rifle, he said, "Outish, Lettern will only get to use this rifle when we are in dire trouble. Until then," and he looked at her sternly, "It's bow and arrows only."

Her suspicion turned to a scowl, but she kept quiet.

"Outish," he went on, "I am alone here on Isuelt. Ivan and Sendrant are shepherding Breia around the planet, inventorying the aquamarine sites and looking for more sensitives, or at least greater concentrations. They are six hours away, minimum, without a shift, and the interdiction cutter we have up on Lonely Soul does not have a field generator."

"They won't find any."

Meridia paused. "They won't find any?"

"Greater concentrations of sixthsense adepts on Dianis. This is it. Wedgewood is the hot spot for the entire planet."

Meridia stared at the astrobiologist intern. "You know for certain?"

"Yes. I know what Atch filed. I know what is in all the social surveys that Baryy and the others conducted over the past three years, ever since we came to Wedgewood. The Dianis sixthsense phenomenon is centered here, this town, and nowhere else."

Meridia, now an IDB agent, tried to reconcile what he'd been briefed on against the revelation that Outish just exposed. "But," he sought to assuage his cognitive dissonance, "what about the Auro Na? Breia says the Auro Na on Dianis are almost as potent as the Matrincy, and the Matrincy is built on adepts gathered from across all of federation space. There aren't any Auro Na in Wedgewood. They come from everywhere but here."

"Not true," he replied. "Yes, the Auro Na may be found all over the planet, but they all originate from Isuelt." Outish's sure response offered no argument. "And the reason the Auro Na recruit adepts from all around Isuelt, except Wedgewood, is Loch Norim genetics."

When Meridia didn't appear to understand the import of the Loch Norim, Outish spelled it out for him. "Dianis was originally a Loch Norim colony. A pure gene pool not diluted with cross-breeding and mutations like me, a Halorite. The colony here had maybe ten million Loch Norim Humans. The majority, we think, lived on this continent, Isuelt. We know the Loch Norims had a genetic propensity towards sixthsense, but we've never been able to determine if that was natural or due to overt manipulation, but we do know that the genes that enable sixthsense degenerate over time and become recessive. However, and this is my own theory, I think something on this planet, something unique to Dianis, perhaps to Isuelt, and certainly prevalent here in Wedgewood, keeps those genes from going dormant, hence the higher percentage of sixthsense adepts compared to the galactic average. The reason we see it in the Auro Na is because that's the religion that scours the planet for adepts and recruits them as acolytes. Except," he added, "for Wedgewood. Timberkeeps are Life Believers. Their beliefs are in opposition to the Auro Na; hence, the Auro Na have little appeal or traction here."

"Wow, Outy." Lettern looked at him, and he blushed. He looked down and scuffed a boot-toe on the planks. "It's what I do," he mumbled.

Meridia studied him. He thought about Ivan's instructions and his comments about the matriarch when she had learned they had located Outish and all those little sample pots in the cabin. "And you haven't reported any of this?"

"Well, Atch logged what he knew in the IDB field journals." Outish looked up sheepishly. "But chief said no one ever read the field journals. They were a good place to comply with reporting regulations and not attract attention."

"And he did that because?"

Outish wondered how to answer Meridia's question. He decided to state it the only way he knew how. "Atch loves Dianis." He looked at Lettern. "So do I. He'd do whatever to protect it. He didn't want any of his findings to attract anyone, including the Matrincy, to Dianis until Dianis was ready to defend itself." He looked straight at the Ready Reaction agent. "Dianis is worth fighting for. It's worth protecting."

Meridia and Outish shared an unvoiced moment, conscious that a provincial, a proven defender of Dianis, stood in the room with them. Meridia said, "And you wonder why I'm willing to give Lettern a plasma rifle."

Outish said, "Oi."

Meridia flipped the rifle over. "Illian Meridia, instructor, enable weapon for Lettern Stouttree." The weapon emitted a double beep. "Here," he said, "grip the stock there so that the rifle will identify you as its owner."

She placed her hand on the pistol grip. A triple beep sounded.

He smiled and pulled the rifle back, a tease to his grin. "Okay, let me explain some things. Those three suits of armor you see in the caskets are for us. One each. They're not Marine-heavy armor, so they can't take as much damage, lift as much weight, and they don't have anti-sizar features, but we aren't fighting sizars, at least not today. What we expect to be the real threat are corsairs, probably contract miners coming to raid your mine." He looked meaningfully at Lettern. He hadn't told either her or Outish that corsairs were already on the planet; Junko and his nefarious crew were a continent away, and Sargent Mears had committed to alert him if they made any threatening moves towards Isuelt.

"Against corsairs, these IDB intervention suits should be adequate. They're fast, stealthy, and have better sensors than my Marine armor. The IDB armor is best against energy weapons. That's what they are designed for because that's what extrasolars usually pack. Chemical projectile weapons and their ammo are heavy; miners don't like weight unless it is ore. So if someone starts shooting bullets or flechettes, instead of laser beams, go for cover." He looked at Outish, who nodded quickly, but Lettern hesitated. "Right," Meridia said, "Let me explain bullets. Those muzzleloaders that Ogden is manufacturing?"

Lettern nodded affirmatively.

"Those kill," Meridia said, "and they kill good. That forty-five-caliber bullet, that lead pellet that Og is pushing through his muzzleloaders, have a muzzle velocity of twenty-two hundred feet per second, give or take, and that generates fifteen hundred foot-pounds of energy. Meridia looked at his two pupils, who just stared at him. He smiled slowly. "Right. Well, the reason why that matters is fifteen hundred foot-pounds behind a half-inch lead ball will punch right through that IDB armor laying down there." He pointed down into the crypt. "So if anyone is shooting at you with something that goes *bang* real loud, duck. Get behind something. If the weapon goes *fzzzzt-pock,* you're probably safe."

He held Lettern's rifle up for them to see. "This is not a Marine heavy plasma, so it doesn't pack the same punch as the rifle I carried in the Brigade, nor does it have the energy cell capacity or the cycle time. However, it has a couple useful additions." He looked at the rifle, "That is if you are an IDB agent, which I guess I am. The first is this emitter here," he pointed to a shorter, smaller tube beneath the main plasma tube-chamber. "This is the shock-stunner, good for subduing unruly provincials." He looked at Lettern and then to Outish, hooking a thumb in her direction. Outish smiled.

"Hey!" Lettern squawked.

"And this here," he pointed to the second tube under the plasma barrel, "is the chemical projectile, i.e., bullet rifle. It has a ten-round magazine and comes with a silencer." He dropped the clip out of the bottom of the rifle, showed the encased cartridges, and pointed to the silencer. "Unlike the stunner, the bullet rifle is actually useful. You use it when you don't want to advertise your presence or location to the entire solar system, like when you blast a plasma."

Lettern's narrowed brows said he should explain.

"An energy discharge, particularly in the form of a collapsing plasma field, emits a radio wave that can be measured with sensitive equipment at long distances. It's like waving a torch around in a dark room. With the right equipment, you can actually see it. You can shroud or shield energy emissions, but doing that for plasma rifles is tough because the required flux shielding grid is heavy, and plasmas emit K-band radiation that requires yet more shielding. So, plasma rifles carry no shielding. Plasma cannons on tanks have them, but not rifles."

When she nodded her timid understanding, he carried on, "The bullet," he pointed to a cartridge in the ten-round magazine, "will punch through most energy shields and is silent, but you only get ten shots unless you reload, which is a manual process." He hefted the weapon to eye level, examining it like a man whose life had depended on it many times. Then he handed it to Lettern.

She promptly recounted everything he had said, pointing to where he pointed, ejecting, and reinserting the clip. Then said, "I want to shoot it."

Chapter 29
Marinda Hall

The city of Tivor

"How did the meeting with the aorolmin go?" Marisa asked as Achelous doffed his rain-soaked slicker. He handed the cloak to Sela, one of the hall maids. "In a minute," he said, stepping back out onto the veranda. The night was dark and stormy. Marisa could hear him call, "Trishna, when you and Zil and the prince have the mounts put away, come in the Hall and get yourselves hot cider and brandy. It's a cold night!"

Baryy followed Achelous back into the Hall. "Hot cider and brandy?" He hefted the saddlebags off his shoulder while Sela waited to grab his coat. Opening a pouch, he pulled out a brown jug with a cork stopper. "Look what Og gave me."

Marisa cocked her head. "Is that?"

Achelous eyed the jug as he closed the heavy door and threw the bolt. "Rakia? From Wedgewood?"

"Nope. Rakia from New Ungern."

Marisa came to see the precious jug. "They're making it in New Ungern?"

"Yes. That's the first batch."

Marisa took the jug towards the kitchen, "Can't wait to try it, but tell me how the meeting with aorolmin went. You apologized for my absence?"

"We did, and he had Troop Commander Rayamars with him. They are both happy with the first forty rifles. Rayamars' troop has been training with Ogden at the test range up behind New Ungern, which is working out well. There are fewer prying eyes and gossips up there."

Baryy settled into one of the wicker chairs in the foyer, stripping off his muddy boots. "The aorolmin saw your new cannon. I think he was jealous."

"Oh?" Marisa said from the cubby just off the dining hall. "Which one?"

Baryy looked at Achelous. "She has more?"

"The one Ropert saw was the three-pounder. Ogden just finished forging the barrel of the ten-pounder. He's fussy about his work and doesn't like to show prototypes until he knows they work."

Baryy's eyebrows shot up. "A ten-pounder is three times bigger."

Achelous dropped his own boots on the steel grate in the foyer. "Well, the tests with the three-pounder have worked out well. Her shipwright said the *Far Shore* and her sister, the *Wind March,* could carry the weight easily up forward on the bow if they shifted the ballast aft to compensate. So the plan is to put the lighter cannon, the three-pounder, on the *Wind March*; test that one there, and then put the ten-pounder on the *Far Shore.*"

"Eh?" asked Zil, the Coaster mercenary.

Prince Fire Eye was staring at the stable doors, partially ajar. The tip of his tail upturned. His forked tongue flickered, sampling the air.

"Did you hear something?" Trishna asked as she hoisted her saddle onto the rack.

"No," replied Zil, "this eenu is clomping around too much."

"Something's got Fire Eye's attention."

Fire Eye trotted towards the doors and stopped.

Trishna, a Silver Cup pathic, watched him over the back of her eenu. Then she sensed *them,* people. They were outside the door and on the street. Too many to sort out.

Fire Eye drew both of his scimitars and launched himself at the doors.

"Ula!" Trishna yelled. "Zil!" She yanked her bow off the peg and grabbed her quiver from the saddle. Running to the door, she strung the bow on the way.

Though confused, Zil didn't ask for an explanation. He drew his sword, grabbed his shield, and went after Fire Eye.

Fire Eye leaned back on his tail and kicked the left stable door out. He charged into the night.

With dread, Trishna heard the clash of a sword on shield and the ring of blade against blade. Notching an arrow, she ran left to the open door and saw three men in the stable light surrounding the prince. Having no time to care, she drew back, aimed for a body, and loosed.

Duck watched from the porch of the inn next door. The Lizard Man had surprised the squad of Scarlet Saviors moving into position at the stables. Somehow, the reptile had sensed their presence and came through the double doors swinging, but there were five Scarlet Saviors there to deal with him. It should be short work.

Zil entered the fray on Fire Eye's left. In the swirling confusion, Trishna worried for a clear target. Then she sensed someone to her left at the inn. He stood there concentrating on the fight and was not an innocent bystander. She drew back and let fly.

There was a pounding on the hall doors.

Marisa called out, "Sela, can you get the door, please. It's Atch's bravos from the Silver Cup."

Achelous frowned.

"What?" Marisa asked as Sela went to the door.

"They come in through the kitchen from the stables. It's closer," he said matter-of-factly. "Why go all the way around in the rain?" Achelous stood up and went to where Sela hung his cloak; his multi-func was in the upper inside pocket.

The maid drew the heavy bolt and began to pull open the door when two large bodies slammed into it, flinging her backward. She fell hard on the floor. Armed men flooded the hall, lamplight glistening on their drawn, rain-wet blades. They threw back the cowls of their hoods, exposing chainmail hauberks.

Marisa, anger flaring in her black eyes, said, "What is the meaning of this!" Her voice carried like a drill sergeant's across a parade ground. Achelous reached for his cape and fumbled for his multi-func. A man, slimmer and shorter in stature than the goons around him, strode through their midst and stood in front of Sela as she attempted to scuttle out of the way.

"I am the prelate for his honor, the Viscount Helprig, in the service and honor of the archbishop of Hebert," the man responded to Marisa's challenge. In an arrogant tone dripping contempt, "We come under lawful order of the archbishop, by charter of Diunesis Antiquaria, to arrest Achelous, trader and malcontent. Harborer of Ancient technology. Conspirer against Antiquaria doctrine and blasphemer. Is the man here?" he demanded.

Multi-func in hand, Achelous pulled up the nano-bot control page.

Marisa's eyes flared in shock, and she looked to Achelous.

"There!" The prelate pointed at Achelous without waiting for an answer, "Seize him!"

Achelous glanced up from his multi-func and yelled to Marisa, "Call the guard!"

She ran to the kitchen, "Eliot! Summon the watch! Hurry!"

Four of the men rushed past the prelate and came for Achelous. He flipped to the alert page, hit the *Launch* button, and tossed the multi-func on the divan.

Baryy was out of his chair, but his handbolt hung in its holster in the foyer beyond the mass of strangers, so he retreated to the hall's weapon closet.

A recon nanobot rose from its roost in the hall rafters and, in microseconds scanned the room below. By aural signature, it tallied nine Humans – eight males, one female, and three infrared entities with aural dampers, one of which it was programmed to recognize as its command avatar. Processing the alert, it identified all hostile threats and prioritized their elimination. It passed

255

targeting instructions to the four defense bots now aloft from their laagers in the rafters.

Achelous ran for the study door and crashed through just steps ahead of his pursuers.

In the kitchen, Eliot came in from the attached servant's quarters.

"Did you send for help?" Marisa asked breathlessly as she pulled a shield and sword from the kitchen armory.

"Yes, my lady. The City Watch has been called, and the guards are coming."

She eyed his empty hip, "Quick, get a weapon. They're after Atch. Bastard Paleowrights! They burst in the door of the hall!" Without waiting for him, she ran back the way she'd come.

Eliot, alarmed at his mistress's state, grabbed the first weapon in view, a halberd, and yanked it from its rack.

Achelous spied his handbolt in its holster resting on the chair beside the window. A rough grip seized him by the elbow, but he threw it off. Taking two steps, he dove across the bed and snagged the holster as he landed on the floor. Rolling onto his back, and in a move he'd done a hundred times, he pulled the handbolt free, queued the laser, and fired. The red beam caught the lunging attacker low on the right cheek and swept up and to the left. Achelous hadn't meant to hold the trigger of the laser, but adrenalin locked his finger.

Trying to aim at the second assailant, Achelous raised his arm to block the body of the dead attacker as it fell on him.

Pouncing, the second assailant jumped on the bodies. He pulled back his mailed fist and short-jabbed once, twice, thrice.

Fire Eye swung, parried, parried, and parried yet again. He was beset by a pair of well-schooled foes wielding rachiers, and he marked the assailants as Scarlet Saviors. A yowl sounded from one, and the man spun around with an arrow in his shoulder.

Zil body-slammed an attacker rushing Trishna as she nocked and loosed another arrow. The shaft hit a helmet and deflected into the darkness, but its target jerked back from the blow, lost his footing, and fell in the mud.

Whirling about, Fire Eye whipped his four-foot-long tail around and swept his attackers off their feet. He charged the three other Saviors as they assaulted Zil. One bore a broken arrow in his hip, and Fire Eye kicked it. The man screeched and collapsed in agony.

Marisa bashed her shield into the kitchen door and burst into the hall. Her chest heaving, she went *en garde* just as a rachier slammed into the boss of her shield and drove it down. Caught by surprise, she dropped the shield and staggered back. The attacker reached for her, and she swung her sword. The man calmly stepped back and then lunged the axe-sword at her exposed side. The point missed her hip as she danced back through the door. Pursuing, the attacker led with his rachier thrust out. Eliot, running forward, slammed the heavy halberd down. The rachier clattered to the tile floor, and suddenly bereft of a weapon, the assailant grabbed the door and slammed it shut.

Baryy recognized the man who stood in front of Helprig: Captain Irons, the same man who had escorted Helprig into Timberkeep Hall in Wedgewood, the person who had fought Christina on the steps of Murali's, the commander who rallied the churchmen when Christina captured the catapults at the Battle of Wedgewood. Already three Scarlet Saviors were down, targets of the defense bots, but it didn't help Baryy. He had a sword; what he wanted was his handbolt. He darted to the right. In the chaos, he thought he could make it to the foyer. A body, the prelate's, lay in front of him, and he jumped it. Helprig himself stood in the center of the hall, sneering and yelling orders. Baryy careened in the viscount's direction on the way to the front of the hall.

Helprig said, "You dare!"

Baryy slashed at the viscount, the blade meeting solid resistance as he ran past.

Trishna heard one of the attackers yell, "Get Makim's squad!" Then Zil was slammed into her, and they both fell.

Sprawling in the mud, dirty straw, and eenu dung. Trishna struggled to get free but was pinned by Zil, who had a dirk sticking from his back. To her horror, she saw the man on top of Zil pull the dagger out and, with a practiced killing stroke, plunge the dagger into Zil's spine just above his chainmail. Then, a silver blur slashed through the killer's neck, spraying Trishna with blood and blinding her. She felt a weight slump on Zil.

"Damn!" Marisa cursed. "He's blocked the door with something. Quick, chop through it."

Eliot roughly shouldered his patron aside, took aim with the massive blade, and gouged a huge chunk of wood from the doorframe, aiming for the hinges. Another strike, and the soft metal was chopped in half.

"Captain!" A Scarlet Savior, whose black cape was open, exposing his distinctive red and yellow armor, burst into the hall. "There's too many town watch. More are coming. We need to go!"

Captain Irons, leaning over the bloodied Helprig, called to the two Saviors standing in the portal, "Get him!" Indicating Baryy, who had just slid around the corner in the foyer.

The two paladins landed on Baryy.

Fire Eye faced three Scarlet Saviors of Makim's squad. They spread out to take him on a wide front. He could see in the lamplight from the porches on the Korvastallen that a mounted squad of Saviors was charging a disorganized group of city watchmen. Slurping the air, he tasted blood, eenu dung, and Human pheromones of anger and fear. The pheromones were tainted with the scent of Heberians. He wheeled to his left, spun three-sixty, and his tail swept the paladin clean off his feet. Completing the circle, his right scimitar connected with a shoulder pauldron, glanced up, hit a helmet, and went over. That attacker stumbled away, surprised. Leaping forward, Fire Eye met the third Savior, parried his rachier, and body-slammed into his shield.

Having scattered, for the moment, the City Watch, the mounted Paleowrights decided to end the fight with the Lizard Man and ride him down.

"Prince!" Trishna called from the stable doors. "Here! Hurry!" She shot an arrow at a Savior rushing Fire Eye from behind. The attacker ducked behind his shield, and the arrow punched a third of the way through. Unfazed, the attacker rushed Fire Eye, who again suddenly spun and swept the man from his feet for a second time. Fire Eye ran for the stable doors, and Trishna heaved them closed as he ran in. She slammed her body against the doors, and Fire Eye skidded in the straw, grabbed the crossbar, and dropped it in place just as a mass crashed into the doors.

She looked at him while the doors heaved back and forth, her face streaked with blood. "Kitchen."

The forked tongue slurped twice, and they ran for the back door to the hall.

"Now!" Marisa stood back, and the three house guards rammed the dismembered table against the kitchen door, and the entire mass crashed into the hall. Eliot leaped past the men as they sprawled and righted themselves. He swept the halberd first right and then left, expecting an ambush. Marisa waited just long enough for the guards to gain their feet and charged.

Rayamars came running with a platoon of riflemen. A disheveled City Watchman ran up to him. "They're at Marinda Hall! Hundreds of them. Cavalry too! They attacked us! My men are dead!"

Rayamars squinted in the darkness. Two wagons and their eenus were galloping away from Marinda Hall, and a gaggle of eenumen remained near the veranda. "Right. Platoon at the double. Hold fire until I give the order. Keep your powder dry."

Running line abreast, keeping good order, Rayamars picked up the pace lest the riders get away.

When the riders saw the approaching line of men, they formed up for a charge, all five of them. The Tivorian riflemen, hand-picked to carry the new weapon, came on.

Abruptly, the riders slowed their charge in the face of this new, determined enemy. Hesitant, they wheeled their mounts around.

Rayamars called a halt. In front of him were dead and wounded City Watchmen. "Platoon! Shoulder arms!" The eenumen began to spur away, and the riflemen pulled free the leather patches protecting the pre-charged powder pans from the rain. "Aim! Fire!"

Marisa, rocking the dead body of Sela in her arms, sitting on the floor in the hall, heard the booming crash of the platoon volley, the first ever fired in anger on Dianis. She thought it was thunder, but Trishna, peering out the window, said, "Mother's Soul. Rayamars is here, and they've shot dead those Scarlet Saviors."

"Reload!" came a command from the street.

To Marisa, rocking Sela, it was cold comfort.

Fire Eye, with Trishna in tow, flung open the Hall doors and darted out. He saw a lone rider pelting away and took off in pursuit.

Rayamars, with three of his men, ran in through the open doors. He saw the lady on the floor holding her maid. "Mother's Forgiveness, my lady, we came as soon as we got word."

She nodded, holding Sela's head to her cheek, tears streaming down.

"Who else?" the Rayamars asked of Eliot.

"Baryy."

"Baryy's dead?"

Eliot nodded. "In the foyer. Hacked to death."

The simple, brutal fact caused Marisa to clench hard to Sela's body, her eyes tight. She waited for what was coming.

The silence went on, and she waited for Eliot to say it.

"Achelous is missing. They've taken him," then Eliot hurried to say, "but Boyd is safe. He was with his nanny in the servant's quarters."

"They've taken Achelous?" asked Rayamars.

And to that, Marisa let out a strangled sob.

Eliot drew Rayamars aside. "You must alert Master at Arms Sifle and the aorolmin. Bar all gates. A search must be mounted. These vermin, these fiends, must be found."

Chapter 30
Prince Fire Eye

North of Tivor

Dawn came slate grey. The rain continued unabated. Fire Eye stood at the crossroads. Water ran down his flanks, naked save for a loincloth. One track went left to the shore. The middle road, a better gravel road, traveled due north, eventually intersecting a larger way to Taldamir over fifty leagues distant. The fork to the right wound its way east, across the Plains of Tivor, over the Northern Coldpeaks, down into the central Isuelt plains, and into Hebert, the seat of the Paleowright archbishop. That rout covered eighty leagues and three weeks of hard riding.

Fire Eye's tail splashed in a puddle, beating a steady, agitated rhythm. He'd caught up with the wounded Scarlet Savior. The Human had fallen from his eenu and lay beside the road. When Fire Eye had waken him and attempted to carry the man to his mount, grazing nearby, the man had cursed him and spit in his face. Fire Eye had licked the man's face and tasted his fear and the fake bravado. While the prince's tail might demonstrate agitation, Fire Eye's face never did. He was a Lizard Man. He'd dropped the wounded man then and there on the side of the road and continued on. It was irrelevant what the Human might say or offer. The Skrim, spirits of the Hallowed Reed, would provide what Fire Eye needed. Whether the man would live without aid was irrelevant.

Standing at the crossroads, Fire Eye took a moment to savor the nourishing rain as it soaked his coarse, leathery hide. If he thought like a Human, he would have weighed the prospects of his quarry going north to friendly Taldamir or taking the longer road and striking directly for Hebert. Instead, the prince was a child of the Hallowed Reed, that mythical place that hovered in the swamp mist at dawn, disappeared with the noon sun, and rose again with the bright stars, willow wisps in a cold fog.

He tasted the air with his forked tongue. The rain had long washed airborne scents to the ground, and on the ground, those scents were diluted -- even for his senses -- with the rain offered by the Skrim of the Hallowed Reed. The Skrim never gave anything freely, and he would be disappointed if they did, but leave clues they always would.

Bending low, his snout just above the mud, he went along the middle road and sampled, slurped the water from the eenu tracks. Satisfied, he jogged to the eastern road. Again, he moved along, slurping water from eenu tracks. The rain, a gift from the Skrim, had done its job of smearing the eenu tracks into vague depressions.

Lastly, on the left, the western track to the sea, he slurped the eenu tracks and rose. He'd found what he wanted. If he was Human, he would have smiled, but Lizard Men were not equipped for that expression. He struck off to the west in an easy, loping run.

Ropert listened to Rayamars and Eliot recount the melee at Marinda Hall the past night. Ogden paced to and fro. Ropert watched Marisa, who stood at the front window of the Hall, not seeing the mid-morning traffic on the Korvastallen. He heard the tally of dead and wounded City Watch, of Zil, who died at the stables, and Sela and Baryy, who had been butchered in the hall, Marinda Hall. After a fight in the study, Achelous had been taken prisoner; no blood was found. Thirteen Paleowrights were dead. Most of them, judging by armor concealed by full-length cloaks, were Scarlet Saviors. One of the dead included the viscount's prelate.

"Mother's Dire Deeds," hissed Ogden. "How many Paleowrights came here?"

"And how did they get in here, Marinda Hall, inside our gates?" demanded Ropert.

Master-at-Arms Sifle answered, "I have clues to that. One of them, a Duck Peren, sought refuge and treatment at an apothecary. When the healer saw the black and white-fletched arrow protruding from the man's chest, he immediately called the Watch." Sifle unrolled a suede skin on the dining room table. In it was a bloody arrow. "I believe that is a Silver Cup arrow," he noted, looking at Trishna.

The telepath leaned across the table; holding it up, the two silver bands, painted just below the fletchings, were clear to see. "Yes. It's one of mine."

"Then you can add another Paleowright to your dead list," said Sifle.

"Duck Peren was a Paleowright examiner. So Atch and Baryy said." Marisa had turned and was facing them from the window. She looked into the foyer where Baryy died. Her jaw set. While staring at the tile floor where the hall maids had cleaned his blood, she asked, "Did he, did the examiner say anything before he died?"

"He did. I spoke to him myself. He met Helprig and Irons at a wharf alehouse three days ago. The Paleowrights and the Scarlet Saviors came on board a ship from Taldamir."

"The devil, you say?" exclaimed Ropert.

"Aye. Peren said they, Irons and Helprig, just wanted to talk to Achelous. He didn't know there was to be trouble until a second ship sailed into the harbor before dark yesterday and unloaded fifteen men and their eenus."

Ropert stood. "Did you alert the harbor master?"

"I have. Both ships sailed on the midnight tide. The harbormaster thought that odd, given the rain and poor visibility."

"They have a half-day on us," said Ropert.

"Nay," responded Sifle. "The admiral dispatched the *Sea Bright*. She was able to get underway at dawn, but it may be a futile chase. There were two ships. They could split up and go anywhere." Sifle waited for Marisa, the master sailor in the room, to comment, but she just kept staring at where Baryy had died. So, Sifle said, "Sire. We need to take immediate steps to inspect *all* ships and cargoes as soon as they arrive and secure the piers for customs permits."

The aorolmin nodded. They had a policy to do just that but had been lax in enforcing it. "They knew what they were after."

"Aye," agreed Sifle, "they scouted us well."

"He didn't say *why* they wanted to talk to Atch?" Marisa's tone dripped acid.

"No, lady."

She looked to aorolmin, recalling the day on the docks after she and the aorolmin had refused Helprig's demand to embargo Ancient artifacts and aquamarine from Linkoralis. Helprig had come to Tivor then, but in the open, not as a sneak in the night. She remembered Achelous warning her while they had strolled on those docks that the Paleowrights were vindictive and their avarice knew no bounds. Little could she imagine then that *he* would be the victim of his own foretelling.

"Lady," Rayamars addressed Marisa. "I have a question about the fight here in the hall. Sifle and I inspected the dead, looking for clues as to what happened to Achelous. Ogden told us the weapons that Achelous and Baryy carried. We found Achelous's handbolt on the floor in the study. We think he killed the attacker in the study, but it was the manner of the man's death. Half of his head was sheared clean off and lay beside the body with barely any blood spilled."

Marisa had turned to face out the window.

He asked as delicately as possible, "How did he — what did he use to shear the man's head in half?"

She looked over her shoulder, then walked to the table and sat in a chair. Hate, frustration, and fear competed for expression. "Achelous is a..." she paused, thinking about who he really was. "He could... he had many tools at his disposal. It was why I never really feared for us here in Marinda Hall." She swallowed, "It appears I was wrong. Our harbor defenses were not the only things well scouted." She and the aorolmin shared a meaningful glance.

"And the other four Paleowrights? The prelate? They all died without a mark on them," said Sifle.

Marisa turned a baleful gaze on him, "That would be Atch's work as well."

Ogden sought to change the subject. He and Achelous had grown close, and it pained him to see Marisa suffer. "Trishna, will you send a message to Wedgewood? Outish needs to know. Lettern, too, she has command of the Second. Sedge should be warned that the churchmen have not stopped their foul deeds. They are unrepentant after the defeat we heaped on them. To strike so far from Hebert and so boldly attests their hubris knows no limits."

The doors to the hall were thrown open, and one of the aorolmin's own Tivorian personal guard stepped in. "My lord, lady, a message has arrived, by carrier bird, from the Coasters."

Marisa sat up, and Eliot went to retrieve the message from the Guardsman. He unrolled the tiny scroll, barely bigger than a fingertip. He squinted, trying to read the tiny script. Moving to the table, he placed it in the best light possible. They all gathered around.

"It's from Breggor, the chieftain at our saltpeter plantation," Marisa breathed, her excitement growing as she read ahead.

"What does it say!" demanded Ropert, who couldn't read all the words.

"Fire Eye is there, at the coast," answered Eliot.

"Yes! Fire Eye!" Marisa whirled away from the hunched crowd and started barking orders to her maids.

"What? What!" demanded the aorolmin.

Elliot read the missive aloud. "Breggor says the reptile appeared at his door and said the attackers have taken to long boats on the beach and are making for a ship off the reef. He doesn't know what attackers and wouldn't have believed it was important, but the lizard has a Silver Cup heraldric. Breggor asks if he should lend assistance."

"By Mother's Own Breath, man, yes!" answered the aorolmin. "Send word!"

"A map. Eliot, get me a map," demanded Sifle.

A map was thrown on the table.

Sifle ran his finger along the roads. He was shaking his head. "I doubt any of our patrols would have headed to the coast. They would have gone north and east. How did Fire Eye know to go to the coast?"

Marisa stopped at the table wearing her green sea cape as she buckled on her sword.

"Where are you bound, mistress?" asked Eliot.

Marisa looked at Ogden. "I'll wait just long enough for my cannon, Og. Get it to me now. I'll be readying the *Far Shore*. They've a cargo to unload; it was bound for Sea Haven, but the *'Shore* will be faster without it."

"What are you thinking?" asked Ropert.

She parted the crowd around the map. Pointing to the shoals off the Coaster village some two leagues north of Tivor. "The wind will tell me that, lord. But if it blows south as it was last night, then their captain would be a fool to sail north because I will catch him. The *Far Shore* is a weatherly ship. If the Paleowright sails south, then he will set a course far out before turning south. I intercept him off of Tivor."

"And if the wind has shifted to the north or west?" asked Sifle.

"Then I will pray to Mother that his bottom is so fouled that a barge could catch him." She traced her finger north, up the coast to Taldamir. "Otherwise, he will beat me to that nest of Ancient lovers." She held her finger on Taldamir.

Ogden shook his head. "Noi. He'll not be sailing north."

Marisa blinked and looked at the map anew, searching for what she was missing.

Ogden pointed at the Red Elm, Floral Cedar, and the Rock Doroman holdings to the east of Tomis. "If he lands in Taldamir, Helprig and Irons will have to escort Achelous through half of our Doroman clans. Since the Battle for Wedgewood, Chief Ordern of Red Elm has been marshalling the western clans, and they're hostile to Taldamir. It's not open war yet, but Taldamir caravans no longer travel farther east than Tomis. The prince of Tomis is trying not to take sides."

"Ordern is a good man," said Marisa. When Wedgewood was under siege by the Paleowrights and Drakans, it was Chief Ordern of Red Elm who had marched to break the siege.

Ogden said, "We'll get word to him. He'll block the roads, but I fear the churchmen have thought of that. They may have sailed from Taldamir, but I don't think they'll be going back there."

Marisa stepped back from the table, settled her cutlass low on her hip, and strode to the front doors. She heaved them open. "Three hours, Og. Three hours. I want my cannon."

After she'd left, Sifle said to the aorolmin. "We should send help. Her crew will fight, as will the crews of all her other ships, but we should send..." and he looked at Rayamars.

Pursing his lips, the aorolmin said, "Go, commander. Muster a platoon of Marines as well. And tell the admiral, with my respects, that he has my permission to release the *Intrepid* to the chase."

Chapter 31
Requiem

Shift Zone, Mount Epratis, Dianis

The entire ground contingent of Ready Reaction, IDB Margel Damansk, cleared the Mount Epratis shift zone in good order. Before the IDB had withdrawn from the Margel, of which Dianis was the principal planet, there had been over two thousand Ready Reaction agents to cover the thirteen solar systems that spanned six thousand light years. Now, there were four, not counting the crew of six, on board the *IDB Shields*.

"Bots up and orbiting," called Sendrant over the team net.

Meridia, drawing tail-gunner position in their eenu-mounted team, liked the feel of the compact, forty-shot plasma pistol in its shoulder holster and the spare forty-shot energy packs in his vest, but he questioned Ivan's designation of the intervention to Tivor as potentially hostile. Just because Achelous had gone off the grid was no reason to label Tivor potentially hostile to the IDB. Yes, Quorat had shot up Murali's, the Marines had landed, and Ivan's face was no longer welcomed in Wedgewood, but that was again no reason to assume that New Ungern would be hostile to them. But it was Ivan's call, and because of it, the chief had invoked the ULUP exclusion, allowing them to pack plasma weaponry and don projectile-resistant armor beneath their period-specific in-country clothing. *Chief must be feeling lonely with just the bots, drones, and Shields up there for cover*, he thought. *I suppose he's right, but in the A-Brigade, we were always alone, out on the edge.* He'd gotten used to the feeling.

"Have you checked on your job?" Ivan asked.

All the team members knew what the chief meant. Only one of the team had a specific duty assigned to them by the Matrincy. Meridia tapped his vambrace and brought up the preconfigured aural tracker for Outish. "Yes, chief, he and Lettern are still at the Crevice." It had been a simple thing for Outish to connect to his aural-signature nullifier through his multi-func and disable it. Causing his aural signature to, again, be visible to aural scanning. Ivan had gone one step further and ordered Outish to expel it. The intern had, with some complaining, done so. The expel command caused the device, with an embedded aquamarine crystal, to detach itself from the lining of Outish's stomach and evacuate through his bowels. It was Meridia's responsibility to retrieve the evacuated device and return it to the chief.

"Have we assessed the origins of the Crevice yet?" asked Sergeant Horalznick.

"Good question," said Meridia. He brought up the holo projector on his multi-func.

Horalznick pulled up. "Chief, have you seen this?" The team maneuvered their mounts around Meridia's as he manipulated the display. All the while, the recon and defense bots circled above the team a hundred yards out, and one of the *Shields'* three surveillance drones hovered on station five thousand feet overhead.

Horalznick pointed at the holograph. "Outish reported to Meridia that while he had been digging samples and exploring in that area, he heard from the locals about the Crevice, a natural opening deep into Mount Mars. So I had Jeremy dig through all the geographical records for Mount Mars and Wedgewood." The team, except for Meridia, were all familiar with Jeremy, the AI for Achelous' Civilization Monitoring teams. Ivan had gained funding to reinstall the archived AI on a Central Station server. It was a friendly face, albeit an avatar. It was good to have their old friend back. What they didn't know, but Jeremy did, is just before Lights Out, Clienen had authorized Achelous to clone an instantiation or separate version of the AI. That copy now ran on a server in the repair bay. In a quirk of computer programming and what some feared as artificial intelligence attaining self-awareness, the two AIs communicated with each other but had not surrendered the existence of the other to their masters.

"Jeremy," Horalznick called over the IDB Dianis CivMon net, the first time that comm net had been used since Lights Out.

"Yes, sergeant," came Jeremy's immediate response.

Ivan and Sendrant couldn't help but smile. The team might have the only four Ready Reaction ground assets in six thousand light years, but the world wasn't so lonely with Jeremy back in Central Station.

"Report your analysis of the geographical feature known as the Crevice on Mount Mars, north by northwest of the Tolkroft Mine."

"Yes, sergeant. Given the recently uploaded scans by intern Outish, there is an eighty-eight percent probability that the Crevice is a sentient-made artifact. The first three hundred meters of the Crevice were excavated to appear as a natural fissure in the granite substrate of Mount Mars. Two specifics allude to the fissure as not natural. First, granite does not fracture in the manner of the Crevice. Second, the slope and direction of the Crevice violate the natural stress lines of the mountain's magnetic field."

"Hello, Jeremy."

"Hello, chief."

"It's good to hear you again, Jeremy."

"Thank you, chief. It's good to be back."

For Ivan, the trying days shifting back and forth between Dominicus and Dianis were almost worth hearing the AI's familiar voice. Jeremy spoke with a Calinextra III accent. He acquired it from the original IDB CivMon team that had first transferred in from Calinextra eighty years ago to bootstrap the first Dianis contingent. "Explain the slope and direction of the Crevice."

"Yes, chief. Given the information provided by intern Outish, principally his filing yesterday, of a Loch Norim Historical Registry claim on behalf of Chief Forushen, the axis of the Crevice, if projected beyond the terminus of the Crevice, precisely intersects with the center of the destroyed Loch Norim facility on the top of Mount Mars.

Moreover, the Crevice tunnel rises in elevation an average of seven degrees over its thousand-meter distance. An easy incline for bipedal sentients."

Ivan translated *bipedal sentients,* "Humans." He looked at Meridia. "Did you know Outish was going to file a Loch Norim Historical registry claim?"

Meridia shook his head, surprised. "Uh, chief, he's on the grid again."

Ivan's eyes narrowed. He didn't bother to ask what else the intern had been doing on the Fednet Interconn.

"With regards, chief," said Jeremy, "news of this latest validated Loch Norim site by Chief Achelous Forushen, who has four previous validated site registries to his credit, is causing substantial debate in the Loch Norim academic circles. Using my reinstated security clearances, I can tell you that Director Hor has thirteen requests in his queue from a list of media services to interview Chief Forushen on the find."

The team members looked at each other, and Ivan summed it up for them when he said, "Shiren."

"Yes, chief, I understand."

Meridia grinned. Jeremy knew its Humans.

The AI went on, "I am following the debate in Loch Norim academic circles, and much of the message traffic is centered on the clause that intern Outish used to describe the status of the site."

Oh, oh, thought Meridia. *What did the kid say?*

"And that was?" asked Ivan.

"That the surface installation was destroyed by an airburst missile attack followed by a bomb attack, but the attack failed to penetrate the underlying structure."

Ivan's eyes grew wide.

"Oh, heaven and spirits," whistled Horalznick. "Is that true?"

The three of them pinned Meridia with accusing expressions.

"What? I can't control what he says and who he says it to!" Meridia exclaimed. "You told me my job was to protect him, and here I am in Tivor!" Meridia held his hands up.

Sendrant was shaking his head. Then he looked to Ivan. "Chief, this may be our funding authorization to re-staff Dianis in force. Once the federation wakes up to an intact and potentially functional Loch Norim site on Dianis, all shit is going to break loose. The ULUP Board of Governance will demand we come back and come back now."

"If Outish is right." Ivan glared at Meridia.

"Chief!" Again, Meridia held up his hands.

Opening the Fednet Interconn news posts on his multi-func, Horalznick said, "Even if it is not intact, the assertion that the site was destroyed by an attack is probably sending shock waves through academia." A posting caught his eye, and he read the headline, "Implication of Dianis findings are the Loch Norim were at war and that they lost." He said, separate from the article, "This will add fresh support to those who say there is a greater evil in the galaxy, greater than the Turboii."

Ivan just shook his head and kept shaking it.

Jeremy picked up on the chief's consternation. "Chief, may I be of assistance?"

At a loss for what to say, Ivan sat on his eenu and looked to the looming peak of Mount Epratis. Unlike Mount Mars, the peak of Mount Epratis was bare of snow; it was an active volcano. *No hidden Loch Norim sites there.* "Yes, Jeremy. Let me know if you detect any Matrincy activity on the subject. I expect the director and maybe even the matriarch to be calling me on this."

"Hey, chief?" it was a new voice on the CivMon net.

"Yes, sir, go ahead," Ivan replied to Lieutenant Hearter.

"The recon bots have completed their survey of New Ungern, the new foundry, Marinda hall, and the Marinda gunpowder works. Mears is directing them into the city itself to do the facial recognition scans."

"Yes, sir. Any hits so far?"

The team picked up on the hesitation in the lieutenant's voice.

"No hits on either Marisa or Achelous. One of the recon bots, pinned to Boyd and his nanny, recorded this," and Hearter played the recorded audio over the team net.

<child's voice> "When Mama come back?" <silence> "Nanna? Papa? Papa come back today?"

<female voice> "Mama went to get Daddy. She'll bring him back."

<child's voice> "When? When Mama and Papa come home?"

<female voice exasperated but patient> "I don't know Boyd, but you know Mama. She will find Daddy and bring him home."

There was silence on the team net.

Meridia asked, "So neither Achelous nor Marisa is at Marinda Hall or New Ungern?"

"Negative," replied Hearter. "But I have some disturbing intel."

"What?" asked Ivan.

"The aural scan picked up a ghost resonance of Agent Maxmun's aural signature."

An eenu shuffled, and a bird called from a tree.

They all knew the common cause of a ghost resonance. A deceased Human body gave off a shadow aural signature that diminished as the body's mass decayed.

"How can that be?" Ivan asked. "Baryy has an aural dampener attached to his stomach lining. We know that from Outish."

The voice over the CivMon net said, "I'm sorry, chief. The dampeners become inactive when either expelled or the host is deceased. As designed. So the body can be found. We did a thorough recon with the bots of the area with the ghost resonance. I'm Sending the vid of their findings."

Ivan saw the image projected to his optical implant. He read the inscription and read it again and then again.

Ivan bent his head. "Atch. Atch. What have you done?"

Meridia watched the stark reaction of the three Ready Reaction agents to the image. He knew he should feel something but didn't. He'd lost so many friends his emotional armor, or maybe scaring, was thick and impenetrable. Although, he could sympathize. The pain *they* felt caused his stomach to knot. He read the inscription on the image and willed himself to feel something.

The bot vid showed the House Marinda cemetery behind Marinda Hall, and the image centered on a newly cut tombstone. The inscription read:

> Baryy Maxmun
> 293 – 332 Epis Exodi
> Agent, IDB Dianis
> Died In the Line of Service
> Friend to all who knew him

Ivan willed himself to think, to plan objectively, without emotion. In the eighteen years he'd run Ready Reaction Dianis, he'd only lost two CivMon agents. Neither of them to hostile action. Again, he looked up at the lonely, barren peak of Mount Epratis, a huge cinder cone. He thought about life, love, and his friends. His struggles and successes marched across his mind's eye in no real order. It was a long parade, the weight of it drawing him down. Amid the depression, he sought an anchor, a light. The barren peak was no help, so he turned to his three team members. The three he had alive. "Lieutenant, we will proceed to the site and confirm." It was all he could think to say.

The team rode in silence to the main gate of Tivor. Horalznick eventually said, "You know, chief, it could be j a ruse. A trick to convince us Baryy is dead, to quit searching for him."

Ivan saw the dim hope in the sergeant's eyes. He looked away and focused on the long line at the gate, at the people seeking entrance to the city and the City Watch working the line. On the ramparts, instead of the usual City Watch, there were instead Tivor-liveried archers. Not militia, but regular army. "*Shields*, you there?"

"Aye," came Mears' immediate response.

"You seeing this?"

"I am."

"Jeremy," Ivan called to central station. "Inspect video feed. Analyze. I don't remember this from before. I've been to these gates and rode right through."

"Heightened state of security," Jeremy immediately replied. "Personnel identified as City Watch are inquiring as to Nakish or Diunesis Antiquarian affiliations."

Ivan frowned. "How can you tell?"

"Analysis of their lip movements and facial expressions. I suggest you reference your connections to Wedgewood to increase your prospects for entering the city."

As they approached Marinda Hall with the ten Tivor cavalrymen as escorts or perhaps guards, Meridia saw work crews digging a trench outside the hall. The cavalry escort led them to the stables, where no less than twenty soldiers stood ready. They handed over their mounts, and Meridia casually asked one soldier who looked friendly enough, "They digging a moat?"

"Nah. Those are the foundations. They're putting up a wall. A tall one."

Ivan saw a badge he didn't recognize and whispered over the IDB CivMon net, "Jeremy, analyze that heraldic. Provide running commentary, please. Something is wrong."

"The badge is new to IDB files, chief. I've decoded its meaning. It appears to represent a House Marinda military unit."

Shiren, thought Ivan, *Marisa is arming up, but for what?*

Meridia led the way up onto the veranda. Jeremy told him the man he faced was an ensign. The way the former Marine senior corporal sized up the ensign made the man squirm. Ivan caught the interaction, but the large double doors swung open, and a man came out. His weathered face bore deep crags along both cheeks. A small, snow-white goatee made the prominent chin more prominent; his grey eyes reflected decades in the wilderness.

Before Ivan could take the lead, Meridia said, "I've come from Wedgewood. Lettern and Outish are my friends, and I need to know what happened to Baryy."

Eliot looked at the four mercs. The hall commander of the newly formed Marinda militia stood just to the side, ready to call his troops.

Ivan shouldered his way to the front and said, "I'm Ivan. A friend of Achelous. I run his mercenary guard when we are on caravan. Is he here? I need to speak with him?"

Eliot looked at each of the four mercs in turn, specifically at the handbolts on their hips. "A friend?" he stared at Ivan. "Are you certain?"

The ensign picked up on Eliot's tone and stepped away. The ten or so guards arrayed around the veranda put their hands to their weapons. Lieutenant Hearter called over the IDB Dianis net, "Particle cannon charged, but I can't get all of them."

"I'm certain," said Ivan. "I've fought with Atch, and Sedge, and Odgen. Atch is my friend, and he owes me his life multiple times over."

The two men faced off. Two seasoned vets. Then Eliot said, "The mistress told me you might be coming."

Ivan studied Eliot's pupils. The man meant business.

"She has a message for you."

Meridia, Horalznick, and Sendrant braced themselves. Mears held his finger over the firing key for the particle cannon.

"We will fight. Fight to the death. Neither she, Boyd, nor Achelous is leaving this planet. Nor will they be mind-wiped. Tivor is allied with the Doroman Timberkeeps. All the Timberkeep clans. Marisa, as special counsel to the aorolmin of Tivor, is under his protection, and that extends to the Timberkeep clans. You fight her, you fight me," and Eliot pointed to the men around him, "and you fight them, Tivor, and all Timberkeeps."

Eliot's stare matched Ivan's.

Neither man backed down.

Jeremy interjected into the tension, "Chief, he has more to say and is waiting for a specific reaction."

"Eliot," Meridia said, "We're not mind-wiping, or arresting, or whatever. I already gave my word to Outy. I promised Lettern. I was with her when she stuck Quorat with the arrow. Outish is fine in Wedgewood, picking his mushrooms and gawking over some silly woodpecker. I need to know what happened to Baryy, Eliot. I know he is dead. If someone killed him, it is time for payback. I owe that to Outy and Lettern."

The ensign stepped further away from Meridia.

Eliot took in Meridia's measure.

Then Ivan said, nodding at Meridia, "He's a cold-blooded killer. He's faced the worst there is in the galaxy, and you can see who is standing here; it's not them. Tell us what happened."

Eliot gave a slight nod.

Eliot sat at the dining table. The Ready Reaction team sat in front and beside him. He'd recounted the bulk of the story when he said, "Baryy died there," he pointed to the foyer, "hacked to death by Scarlet Saviors."

Meridia listened. Ivan nodded to Sendrant, who stood.

"The maids have cleaned up," offered Eliot, "the blood is gone."

Ivan asked, "You know who we are?"

Eliot answered, "Aye, you're Ancients."

Ivan nodded. "Then it will be no surprise to you if we can do something you can't?"

"Depends on what it is," answered Eliot.

They waited for Sendrant to finish his work. When he came back, "Blood spatter tests are positive. There's a lot of it, chief." Sendrant sat heavily. He looked away. "DNA matches Baryy. Bastards."

"I was in the kitchen," Eliot indicated the door at the end of the hall, "me and the mistress. They had us barricaded. We bashed the door down," and Eliot looked down at the finely finished table. "By then, it was too late."

Meridia asked, "Sendrant, did you get other DNA?"

He nodded.

Meridia called, in the clear, on the CivMon net, "Jeremy, isolate DNA profiles and offer postulates."

Eliot had no idea who Meridia was talking to or about what, but the rest of the team did.

When Meridia had his answer, he sat there calm, a flat gaze at Ivan.

"Where is Marisa now?" asked Horalznick.

Eliot explained the lady's plans.

Finally, Ivan rose. "Can you take us to Baryy's grave?"

Ivan knelt in front of the stone slab. The team members knelt beside him. He studied the stone from which the monument was cut, the grain, the color, and wished he were anywhere but there, then, and how. *Atch, Atch,* again, he struggled. *What have you done?* He leaned forward and rested his forehead against the cold stone. It chilled his skin. He pounded his head against the stone. *Atch, Atch, why? Why Baryy?*

He dug his hand into the fresh dirt. Closing the hand into a fist, he brought it to his chest. *I'm sorry, Baryy. I'm so sorry. It was my job to be here, and I wasn't.* He shoved the handful of dirt into his pocket.

Walking back to the hall, Ivan called over the system net, "*Shields*, you there? This is Ivan."

"*Shields* here, chief."

"I need you to reposition the recon package here in Tivor to the *Far Shore*. We need to know what is going on out there."

"We've been working on that problem, chief. Do you have a description of the ship? There are some two hundred ships with two or more masts in the possible sailing radius of where we think the *Far Shore* could be. This includes ships at dock or anchor."

Ivan thought about it. He could get the ship description from Eliot. "Eliot said that Ogden Snowbirch is with Marisa. Do you have his—no, you probably don't. Connect Jeremy to the net, please."

"Jeremy online, chief. What can I do for you?"

"Do you have Ogden Snowbirch's aural signature in the CivMon database?"

"We do."

Ivan thought, *for once, the Spirits grant a small favor.* "Excellent. Pass it to the *Shields*. They will scan for him on the sea off of Isuelt. *Shields*, when you get a hit, deploy the bots to that ship. I need to know what Marisa is doing and what she knows. Right now, she is our best chance to find Achelous."

Chapter 32
Field Trip

Corsair Mining Site, Dianis

"What is all that?" Krch twisted around in the co-pilot's seat of the shuttle.

"Weapons," grunted Gof.

Krch watched the mutated Human man-handle the object in through the side hatch of the cargo shuttle. "Is that--," she slurred, her sucking tubes wagging, a battle-drone?!"

"Yes," answered Geezer, following in behind Gof. "I stacked the six-pack of anti-air missiles outside the hatch. Gof, get them next. I'll go prep the other battle-drone. Maybe that one will start. Damn Junko for buying crap; half this stuff doesn't work. We rifled through fifty plasma rifle energy packs, and half of them were shorted out."

Gof snorted through his huge nostrils that compared favorably to the corded muscles that writhed like snakes across his body. "The auto-cannon is new."

Geezer stopped what he was doing and looked at Krch. "It's true, Junko sprung for a brand-new auto-cannon. What the hell did he bring that for?"

Sysreq answered as she ran through a hurried preflight check of the shuttle they were about to abscond with, "I heard he stole it. The jacks in the good crew were bragging about it." It was a point of conflict between the two factions of Junko's crew: the good and the bad. Krch, Geezer, Gof, Sysreq, and the recently deceased Turk were on the bad.

Geezer and Gof left for another trip to the weapons locker. Krch asked, "We've two tons of ore. How much weight do we have for weapons?"

Sysreq punched the preheater for the starboard nacelle. "Plenty. Junko's plan was to boost this shit out low and fast. We've got lots of gas."

Krch grabbed Sysreq's multi-func. "I'll prep the port nacelle."

Sysreq eyed her. "You qualified?"

"Ya," she slurred, "I was dropship pilot on Tweeunar."

Sysreq said, "Oh." The Human female looked at her Tweeunar co-pilot. "I'm sorry."

Krch scanned the engine preflight checklist and then handed the multi-func back. She didn't say anything. It was quiet in the shuttle cabin.

Sysreq said, "I didn't know. I thought—"

"Yass," she slurred. "I was a geologist before the Turboii, and their sizar cretins showed up. We killed by the thousands." She paused as she punched the fuel-vaporizer button, "but it wassssn't enough."

A thump sounded from the side hatch. "I got the second battle drone started," Geezer bragged. He backed away from the hatch and watched as the battle-drone, articulating on its six legs, climbed in the shuttle after him.

Sysreq peered aft. "Creepy. Those things always give me the spooks. Why are the optics always red? They look like two beady red eyes."

Geezer beamed with pride. "Hey, it works."

The battle drone took notice of Krch and raised its twin flechette machine guns.

Krch's eyes grew as wide as Lonely Soul. "Geeeeeez!"

Geezer slapped the disable command on his multi-func. "Oh, sorry about that. Uh, uh, oh. I see. Damn Junk. He never programmed it. The default setting is to attack anything non-Human. I will fix that."

Krch slumped in her seat, and Sysreq laughed.

"Is that thing loaded?" Krch groaned as she slumped way down in the co-pilot's chair.

"Oh yea," said Geezer happily. "Seven thousand rounds in each magazine."

Sysreq saw Krch's limp sucking tubes and laughed again.

Gof climbed in the hatch with two bulging sacks under each arm. He dropped them on the deck and hit the hatch *close* control. "All done. Weapons locker is empty."

Krch sat up enough to look back at Gof. "Everything?"

"Yep."

Then she looked at Geezer. "Everything?"

"Yea? Why?"

"What if—"

Geezer looked at her. "What if what? What if the indigins get mad and rush Junko and the *Good* crew?" he sneered.

"He's sick," said Sysreq. "Whatever you did to Junko, it laid him out good. His plasma pistol should be able to hold off the locals. If he's awake and can find it."

"What about—" Krch was about to ask when Sysreq interrupted. "Lackey, the foreman? I got his number. He'll bail to the field gen at the first whiff of trouble."

"Good," hissed Krch. "Take seats. We boost for the coordinates I gave you."

The agent on watch punched the *All Hands* comm channel. "Shuttle is leaving the mining site," he broadcast ship-wide on the *Shields*. "I repeat, the shuttle is leaving the site."

Both fore and aft hatches to the command deck opened, and soon, all of the *Shields'* crew were watching the video feed of the orbital drone above the site.

"Shit," cursed one of the agents.

"Yep," said another.

Lieutenant Hearter, commander of the *Shields,* considered the problem. "They picked the perfect day."

"We knew they would," answered Mears.

"AI," Hearter called, "given the twenty-minute video delay, superimpose their furthest distance of travel under all that cloud cover."

A red circle appeared on the display that roughly corresponded to an aircraft traveling at seven hundred miles per hour for twenty minutes.

"They could be going supersonic," said an agent.

"Probabilities are twenty-three percent that Krch would instruct Sysreq to violate sonic-barrier protocols," responded the AI.

The agents shared glances. Their AI was good; it had been paying attention to Krch.

Hearter leaned on the holodesk. The display was reduced to a plain 2-d representation due to the lack of active sensors. "Where is she going?" he asked.

"If she is boosting to Junko's ship, she'll pop out to the west here," the agent on watch pointed at the edge of the huge storm system squatting over the mining site, "in a minute or so."

"Yeah, but," added Mears, "we strongly suspect someone, using a one-time code, is rendezvousing with her. She's got two tons of filtered dash-5 ore on board." At the value of that cargo, *anyone* would come out to meet her.

"AI," asked Hearter, "do we really have no infrared or other emissions from that shuttle?"

"Negative. The storm column extends from ten to twenty-five thousand feet. The shuttle is running on a chemical propellant. There are no neutrino emissions." The *Shields* could go active with radar, but that would break their emcon protocol and alert the corsairs.

"Roger. Give me the countdown for when you predict the shuttle to emerge from the storm."

The crew made small talk while Hearter remained stooped over the hologrid, waiting for the seconds to tick by. The storm system was shaped in a long oval. The optimum path for the shuttle to boost off the planet lay on one of the shorter sides of the storm.

When the time came and went for the shuttle to exit from the storm for an off-planet boost, Hearter began having other thoughts. As the time ticked on and the shuttle still did not exit, the lieutenant began looking along the longest axis of the storm front.

"Could they have gone to ground?" Mears asked the AI.

"Unknown probability," the AI responded.

More seconds ticked by.

Hearter kept focusing on the longest axis of the storm. "No," he said. His crew looked at him. More seconds ticked by. "No," he said again.

"What?" asked Mears.

"Shit," Hearter cursed. "Get Agent Meridia on the channel now. Live. Hurry."

Mears glanced down at the hologrid. "AI, plot shuttle course and speed to Wedgwood using the storm as cover."

A red line appeared on the holodeck. Mears and Hearter looked at each other. "Did you see the weapons they loaded on that shuttle?" asked Mears.

Hearter's glare said yes. "AI, sound Battle Stations. Boost us the hell out of here. All hands," he yelled, "thirty seconds. Get to your crash couches. The AI is taking us out of here!"

"Destination?" asked the *Shields* AI.

Hearter dove into his crash couch, slapping the inertial dampener actuator. As the hermetically-sealed lid of his crash couch lowered, he said, "Wedgewood, low-planet orbit. We'll be taking the assault shuttle down. Alert Clienen. Tell him we're executing an emergency planet-side intervention and would appreciate backup."

Chapter 33
Battle Drones

Wedgewood

Meridia's embed in his thigh buzzed. He watched Outish pound another shot of rakia. He was tempted to stop him, but both the intern and Lettern were mourning Baryy's death.

The embed buzzed three more times, each in increasing intensity. "Shiren!" He dropped his feet off the tiny table in Baryy and Outish's cabin and displayed the emergency message on his vambrace multi-func.

"Hey!" said Lettern, holding the jug over his cup, "how can I pour?"

Through his alcoholic haze, Outish realized something was wrong.

Meridia stood and staggered against the doorframe. He was drunker than he thought. Focusing on the message, he read it three times. "Bloody hell. Outy, where's your atafluorazene?"

"Huh?"

"Your atafluor! You know, alcohol antidote. You're an Astro-b. You gotta have some! Mine's up in Lettern's tree house."

Outish grumbled that he didn't want to get sober. He wanted to get drunker.

Meridia shoved Lettern out of the way.

"Hey!" she squawked.

He grabbed Outish by the collar and hoisted him up, the two of them weaving and staggering like two trees in a gale. "Get it! Nowss," he slurred. "Corsairs are coming, and we need to get sober."

"Corsairssss? Where'sss?"

"Here'sss, you idiot. Now."

Meridia's multi-func buzzed with another emergency message, this one from Ivan. "Shiren, no way am I talking to him drunkss." He tossed the multi-func on the table and followed Outish out of the kitchen.

"Message delivered to Agent Meridia, no response yet."

From inside his crash couch, Lieutenant Hearter looked at Ivan's image on the interior display. They both heard the AI's response.

"I'll keep trying to raise Meridia," said Ivan. "But the best you can do is go into orbit over Wedgewood and *prepare* for insertion. Do not execute unless Clienen approves."

"I understand. If you can get Meridia and Outish to evac from the town, that's good, but what about the civilian population?"

Ivan shook his head. "Clienen says the Matrincy won't budge. They don't know who Krch is working for. We don't know who Junko is working for. One or both could be Nordarken Mining or neither. We need to follow this through. If the contractors get wind of an interdiction cutter in the solar system, they'll scatter, and it will set the investigation back months."

"Shit, chief. How many people are we going to let these assholes kill? You saw what the orange birds recorded being loaded on that shuttle. A new, fully charged auto-cannon! Come on, this can't sit right with you. We need to do something."

Ivan's face was stony. "You talked to the director."

Hearter took a small array of hope. "Yea. He said if they start killing more people, I'm authorized to use my best judgment, but that means people have to die first."

When Ivan refused further comment, Hearter said, "Get your people out of that town, and I will have my particle cannon charged up. From orbit, it will take thirteen minutes to get down in the assault lander."

Ivan looked impressed. "I know you said you had a particle cannon, but the *Shields* is an interdiction cutter?"

"Yes, this boat is new. It's only a twenty-millimeter cannon, and the cycle rate is slow, but it can reach out and let you know we are here."

"Chief, it's Meridia," Meridia was on an eenu and had just cantered through the Main gate on his way to the Twistynook mill.

"You have Outish with you?" That was chief, direct, no preamble.

"Yes." Outish, proving to be an accomplished rider, having lived on Dianis, was leading the way to the mill while Meridia was just trying to stay in the saddle.

"You getting your asses out of town?"

Meridia thought about the orders Ivan had sent to his multi-func. "Yes." Meridia had his multi-func camera hidden by the sleeve of his coat so Ivan couldn't see his face.

"You better be. I want you clear of town."

When Meridia didn't respond, Ivan followed up. "Look, Agent Meridia, you have the weapons list that shuttle is carrying. I don't want any of your Marine heroics. And nothing, absolutely nothing, is to happen to Outish, or I will boost you all the way to Avaria cleaning latrines."

Meridia swallowed, Outish had broken into a gallop, and Meridia's mount did the same. He'd never galloped on anything, let alone an eenu. Uh, sorry, chief, I'm gonna fall off this eenu. Gotta let you go." He closed the connection.

At the mill, they hustled across the footbridge, and Meridia actuated the casket lift doors.

They began to don their armor. Outish asked, "What did chief have to say?"

"The same thing as the orders. He wants us the hell out of here."

"I ain't leaving." The intern stopped his struggle with the armor's torso.

"Yeah, I know," Meridia said, not pausing. He already had most of the armor's components on and linked. "Get that armor on. Sign in to the suit's AI. And when Ivan sees you login, tell him that I ordered you to suit up for your own protection."

Meridia finished suiting up and powered on his rifle when Lettern came running through the door. He started to leave the mill.

"You done?" she asked.

"I am. Outish will be here awhile. He can help you. Did you warn the town?"

"I did. Sedge is mustering the wards. You sure those corsairs will only go to the mine?"

"No. But that's where the clan moved that huge pegmatite. To the bottom of Deep and Dark, right?"

"Yep, all the way to the bottom."

"Well, when the corsairs get here, they won't get any hot pings other than at the mine. Right?"

She looked uncertain. "What's a hot ping?"

He smiled. He reached out, seized her elbow, and pulled her to him. She was a feather to his powered armor. He kissed her long and hard.

"Woa," guffawed Outish, "you guys got to smooch now?"

Meridia released her and bolted out the door, his powered armor silent on its stealth actuators.

Lettern took a breath, trying to focus, then saw Outish attempting to link an armored arm to the suit's torso. It was all so complicated. Boots, gloves, helmet, ammo belt. She shook her head. "No way, Outy. You can have all that stuff. I'm taking my rifle and going." She reached into the crypt and retrieved her plasma. "Lettern Stouttree, owner, power on and enable," she said, just like Illian taught her. The weapon came alive in her arms. "Okay, Outy, I'm going. I'll see you at the mine."

"Wait! Wait! You're not coming with me?"

She shook her head slowly. "Sorry, Outy, Illy is going there by himself, and I need to hurry."

"Okay," he looked dejected but then added, "At least take a spare ammo belt. The replacement energy packs and cartridge clips are in it."

"Chief," called Lieutenant Hearter.

Ivan was riding his own eenu. Sendrant was with him. They'd just cleared the shift zone nearest Wedgewood but still had six hours of riding ahead of them. Breia had demanded to come along, but Ivan had forced him to stay at Central Station. He had no idea what they were heading into. If Central Station had been fully staffed, they could have done an unanchored shift directly into Wedgewood, but there were no experienced field gen operators on the planet.

"Chief, I have a powered armor signature on the move in Wedgewood. It's Meridia's."

Ivan pulled to a stop. "Where's he going, sir?"

"He's headed in the direction of the mine."

"Have you contacted him?"

"Negative. Do you want me to?"

Ivan thought about it. He knew it would come to this. "Where's intern Outish?" At least Meridia had connected the intern back onto the grid, enabling the aural emitter in Outish's embed.

"His transponder says he's at a place called the Twistynook mill."

"Yeah, that's our Wedgewood in-country weapons stash. Has he powered up one of the armor suits there?"

"Nothing yet."

"Good. If he does, I want you to override and power it down. That kid is not going into a fight against an armed shuttle with laser cannons, battle drones, an auto-cannon, and who knows what else."

"What about Meridia? I've got a lot of activity in the town. Someone has alerted them. I count at least twelve formations of militia gathering."

"Yeah, that would have been Meridia's girlfriend."

"Who?" The lieutenant's voice rose.

"Lettern Stouttree. She's in command of one of their wards."

"Okaaaay." The lieutenant's tone said it all. "What are you going to do about Meridia? I thought you gave him orders to leave Wedgewood?"

"Well, sir, Agent Meridia has his orders. However, I am not on-site, and IDB protocol allows in-country agents who are on-site a level of discretion in how they execute orders." He let a pause accentuate the point. "You want to save lives? What is the mission of the IDB?"

Hearter said, "Finally."

Meridia was in the game.

Lettern headed straight for the Main gate. The guards saw her coming and opened the doors, and her eenu raced through. Her plasma rifle slung and bouncing across her back, clear for all to see. Pine needles and dirt clods flew from the hooves as she sped past one, two, three wards double timing to the Tolkroft mine camp. They were her friends. Somewhere in the ordered columns was the Second, looking for their warden to prepare them for the coming battle.

"Where is it?" Sysreq skirted the shuttle low around a shoulder of Mount Mars.

"The A-wave scan says they moved it. It's not on the surface anymore." Krch was manipulating the scan controls from the co-pilot's seat.

"Target acquired," called Sergeant Mears. "We're tracking the shuttle, but if they get into those trees, I can't say we'll get a shot."

"Target inbound, thirty seconds." Meridia listened to his suit's AI connected to the AI on board the *Shields*. In his IDB stealth armor, he moved from Ungerngerist to Ungerngerist, seeking the best firing position at the mine entrance.

Suddenly, the target, an armed cargo shuttle, flared into the clearing in front of the entrance to the Deep and Dark mine shaft.

Meridia aimed for the starboard nacelle and triggered the plasma.

Cockpit alarms began blaring. Sysreq, seeing yellow going-to-red damage indicators on her starboard side, swung the shuttle to face the threat, whatever it was. She toggled the *arm* button on her twin laser cannons and let rip. "Contact, contact," she yelled. What the hell's out there? I thought you said it would be clear!"

"Drop the battle drones," Krch yelled. "Geeze, open the door!"

Sysreq squatted the shuttle in the clearing so Geezer could deploy the battle drones. She kept hammering the joystick fire button. Anything that looked suspicious got a twin dose of heavy laser fire.

Lettern heard the distinctive *fzzzzt-pock* she remembered from chasing Quorat. Now she knew what Illian had been talking about. She saw red beams blasting from an alien craft that was smaller but similar to the Marine assault lander she had ridden in. It was firing into the forest to her right, causing flashing explosions and bursting Ungerngerist bark.

Meridia rolled and rolled some more. Laser beams scoured his former fighting position. He looked into the clearing just in time to see a pair of crab-walking battle drones hop out an open side hatch. He fired. His targeting pip picking targets. The rifle's threat analyzer, linked to the suit's AI, prioritized the pip. Meridia overrode the AI.

Just as Gof energized the auto-cannon and was about to shove it out the door, a plasma burst hit his left arm. Another smacked him in the chest, and a third slagged against the encased aquamarine ore behind. Geezer scrambled back, away from the door. Gof lay dead at his feet.

Sysreq pivoted the shuttle left, and twin lasers burned pine needles, turf, understory, and whatever irritated her.

"They've deployed the battle drones," Hearter reported to Ivan. "Meridia has taken them under fire. They've engaged him with their lasers." Then, a new signal appeared on his sensor panel. "What? Ivan, a second IDB plasma rifle, has just been *combat-enabled*. At the mine."

Ivan pulled his mount to a frothing stop. "I thought you were going to disable Outish's armor?"

"He never powered up. This rifle belongs to a Lettern Stouttree."

"Meridia gave Lettern a plasma rifle?"

Lettern's instinct and anger drove her to run across the mining camp in the clear. They were trying to kill Illy, and she wasn't going to let that happen. She settled to a crouch, let the targeting pip -- as Illy had shown her -- acquire the priority target in the scope view, and fired her first plasma burst. The white-hot energy frames splashed and exploded against the cockpit window and hull outside the co-pilot's seat.

Krch unsnapped her safety harness and dove for the deck.

Sysreq cocked the shuttle on a left angle that caused the auto-cannon to slide out the cargo door, and spun the shuttle hard right to the new threat. "Krch! Krch! Get up! How many are there?"

Lettern, extremely pleased, saw the shuttle turning to point in her direction. "Oh, oh!" She bolted in a hard, flight-for-life run toward the mine.

Ivan heard Mears laughing on the open circuit.

"What?"

"Score one for Lettern Stouttree, Dianis provincial. She's kicking ass." Mears watched the action. Finally, the frustrations of the past month were being assuaged. Now, the provincials had the tools to fight back, and they were.

Meridia saw the auto-cannon drop out of the shuttle and the craft pivot away from him. His suit AI told him Lettern, not wearing armor, was in action against the shuttle on the other side. Unfortunately, he couldn't come to her aid, at least not yet. The two flechette battle drones were advancing on his position, and that damned auto-cannon was self-erecting and powering up its weapon. Tungsten shards from four machine guns shredded everything around him. He clawed into the lowest depression he could find and unlatched a grenade from his armor. Snapping the pin, he heaved it into the target zone.

A battle drone tracked the grenade, shot it out of the air, and resumed advancing on its target's position.

"Damn," Meridia cursed. *They're on default programming. The corsairs didn't set the drone's rules of engagement.* He hadn't thought of that. He had expected the drones to stand their ground and defend the site while the miners went down to the bottom of Deep and Dark. Instead, the drones were adhering to their default rule set, and that was engage and pursue the primary risk to *them,* which was *him.* Slithering on his belly, he expected the auto-cannon to behave the same.

"Permission to open fire?" asked Mears.

Hearter was worried. Meridia was pinned down by the two advancing battle drones, and soon, the auto-cannon would be powered up. Lettern, on the other hand...

"Krch! Who is that? They took out our left laser!"

"Geezer!" Krch commanded. "You got your armor on. Get out there and kill her. AI says it's just an unarmored female provincial."

Geezer stumbled toward the open hatch as Sysreq trained her remaining laser on the furtive target.

Lettern broke cover and ran pell-mell to the next tailings pile. She dove onto the hard gravel, gouging bare skin. The shuttle spun round to the pile and over-corrected.

Sprawled flat on her belly. Lettern saw her chance. The targeting pip centered on the pilot's window. She fired, pulsing the trigger as fast as the charge indicator turned green.

The shuttle plexi-windows blew in, and the craft yawed and skittered across the clearing until the autopilot kicked in and stabilized the craft. Krch, stunned, looked over to the pilot's chair. Sysreq was dead. Half of her face gone.

Krch took over the controls, tilted the shuttle upwards, and mashed the throttles.

Geezer, having just recovered from the violent spin across the clearing, was about to jump clear of the shuttle when Krch rocketed it upwards. He tumbled from the craft, but the fall was within the height-drop tolerance of his armor. The suit's AI gyro-oriented the fall, and Geezer landed on his feet. Immediately, three plasma bursts from a tailings pile hit him. The armor absorbed the energy, and the nano-repair circuits patched the divots. He spun the armored suit towards the target. His infrared sensors identified the female provincial laying concealed behind the pile. He stalked left to get a better firing solution, waiting for his targeting pip to go green.

"Okay," Lettern said to herself. "Let's try this." The kick of the rifle surprised her. The projectile bullet was different from a plasma shot. But when she saw what it did to her target, she didn't care about the kick. She fired once, twice, thrice. The powered armor suit toppled like a felled tree.

Meridia crawled through the undergrowth, following the track on his heads-up display mapped by the *Shields*. So far, the armor's chameleon camouflage and emissions shielding of his rifle and suit had stymied the targeting of the two battle drones, but they were able to follow his general progress by the disturbed vegetation. They were spider-walking on their six legs faster than he was crawling. The auto-cannon rolled along on a pair of treads. The tractor treads weren't as articulate as the spider legs, but they weren't in terrain that hampered it, yet. "Find me a log, a big one," he called to the *Shields*.

Krch knew she was screwed, but at least she was alive. *Who armed the indigins with plasmas!* she fumed. *That's why the IDB left! They didn't care. They gave plasmas to the locals!* She stewed over why the indigins at Junko's camp didn't have plasmas, but her mind turned to her plight. She could still make the rendezvous with Bleep Nuts, but with the windshield shot out, she'd have to don a space suit, and she'd have to do it soon as the wind howling through the cabin was enough to rip her eyelids off. She throttled back and set the autopilot. Sysreq slumped in the pilot's chair like a failed crash-test dummy. The sight so gruesome Krch's stomach started to heave. Turning from the sight, she headed aft in search of a space suit.

"Whaaaat?" Outish had just managed to link the suit's final component, the helmet, and had engaged the AI.

Locked Out appeared on his head's up display. "Locked out? Locked out," he repeated. "What does *locked out* mean?"

He was still staring, confounded, at the flashing banner, exhausted from fighting with the suit, when a voice sounded in his helmet.

"Agent Outish."

"Yea?" he answered.

"You are ordered to exit the suit."

"Whaaaat?"

"This is Sargent Mears of the *IDB Shields*. You are ordered to exit the suit."

"I am?"

"Yes, you are."

"Why?"

"If you do not exit the suit in sixty seconds, you will be locked in the suit."

"Nooo, no, no, no. I just put it on! I need to go help my friends."

"Your friends are fine." This was not exactly true, but Mears wasn't going to tell the intern that.

"Nooo. I just put it on. I got it to work. I plugged in all the right stuff, and the AI said it was ready to go."

"Sixty seconds and counting. Fifty-nine—"

"Nooooo!"

Lettern drifted in and out of the foliage. She knew they were stalking Illian, but the thing on the roller belt contraption had a really big gun. Way bigger than hers. She was impressed. Once it had turned on her, swiveled right around while the roller belts kept going and blasted the Ungerngerist she ducked behind. It had left a huge black crater on the side of the tree.

The two spider things seemed to be a matched pair and kept trying to flank Illian. She'd seen his plasma burst whenever they got too close. It worried her that they were nearing the first of the Wedgewood treeforts, and she knew the archers would fight the spiders with their bows. A ballista bolt might hurt a spider, but the crew, her friends, would have to live long enough to shoot.

"Well?" asked Lieutenant Hearter.

Mears shook his head, thinking about their particle cannon. "No shot. They're in amongst those huge trees now.

Meridia scrambled up and dove down the other side of the huge log just as a stream of flechettes ripped the dead bark off the log. He had his chance. *It's time to end this game,* he thought. Ducking down, he ran the length of the moss-covered Ungerngerist until he reached the massive root structure ripped from the earth when the tree had fallen. He followed a game track through the brush, taking care not to disturb any branches and trusting his chameleon armor. The AI connection from the *Shields* showed the position of the drones, the auto-cannon, and Lettern. He worried about her. "Has that auto-cannon fired at the female provincial?" he asked his AI.

"Affirmative. Three times. No hits."

He gritted, "Damn."

Retrieving three grenades from his kit, he set all three for auto-arming. He clicked one on the end of the bullet barrel. The track on his display showed the drones nearing the log.

Swiftly, he fired the first grenade, then the second, then the third, and then charged the auto-cannon.

Lettern badly wanted a shot at the roller belt thing, but it swiveled fearfully fast. Then she heard three shots and three explosions. Instinct said the roller belt would swivel its attention away from her tree. Sure enough. She brought her rifle up and fired. *Bang!*

She'd forgotten that the weapon was still toggled to the bullet barrel. *Too late,* she thought.

Bang, bang, bang, bang, bang, snick. She blinked.

An indicator flashed in her scope, *Projectile clip empty, engaging primary weapon.*

Okay, she thought, *that's fine with me.* She triggered the plasma and resumed firing.

A massive explosion activated the flash dampeners in Meridia's armor, and conditioned from years on the battlefield, he dove for the dirt. The shock wave caught him halfway to the ground.

Mears whooped, and the crew of the *Shields* cheered.

"What?" asked Ivan, not bothering to halt. They still had a long way to go.

"Meridia's girlfriend just blew up the auto-cannon, and the battle drones are down."

"She's not supposed to be his girlfriend," Ivan said dryly.

"Right," answered Mears. "Let the log reflect that provincial Lettern Stouttree has no unauthorized relationship with Agent Meridia." Mears smiled at Hearter, who nodded his assent.

When Meridia saw Lettern, she was dragging her rifle by the strap. Her face and clothing were dusted grey, her hair full of debris. She had a wild, dazed look about her. When she finally noticed him, she blinked, "Illy?"

"Lettern?" He unsealed and removed his helmet. "You okay?"

"What?" she yelled. "Argug." She sank to her knees. Then she looked up at him. His lips were moving, but she couldn't hear him. However, the ringing in her ears was loud and clear.

He laughed and knelt in front of her and pulled her tight to him. Nuzzling her head against his chin, her hair smelled of ozone.

He leaned back to look at her. She smiled vaguely, then rolled her head as if she were drunk. "Did I get it?"

He laughed and realized a tear was running down his cheek. At last, finally, at last, he was feeling something. "Yes. You got it."

Chapter 34
Far Shore

At sea, west of Tivor

The seas were huge, steep, and cresting. Sailing south, the *Far Shore* took them off her stern quarter.

Clearing skies heralded the storm had moved on, leaving scudding clouds and a tortured ocean slowly healing. Marisa stood at the foremast, her customary place. The wind had whipped the hood of her sea cape back and buffeted her trademark bun mercilessly, but the bun was tightly bound and pinned by a stiletto. The deck rose and rose, and then their feet became light as the ship plowed the crest and descended into the trough. She looked over her shoulder at Ogden, who caught her studying him. He braced for the bottom, and their bodies tensed with new weight as the *Far Shore* heaved itself up, climbing yet another wave. "I never asked. Is this your first time at sea?" she called over the wind.

"Oi!" he nodded fervently, and she laughed, a light-hearted, joyful sound, considering the circumstances.

"Are you afraid?"

"Noi," he said resolutely, "not with you, lady."

She studied him, a deep caring in her eyes. "Are you feeling ill?"

"Uh, oi, I might be that, though I don't really know. There's a lot of ups and downs."

She let go of the stay and moved to him, where he grasped a forestay with a grip forged from years wielding a hammer in the foundry. She hugged him. "Thank you for coming, Og."

He braced for the both of them at another crest. "Oi. I'd be nowhere else, lady, even though the ocean is not my place."

She let him go and resumed her place at the foremast. "Don't worry, Og. This is my place. I like Wedgewood and Mount Mars, but that is your world, and this is mine. We'll get them."

Perhaps that's why he wasn't sick, even though he'd been warned by the stevedores when he loaded the ten-pounder on the ship that the seas would be rough. He could have delivered the cannon and returned to New Ungern as Marisa had assumed, but he refused. He came aboard because Marisa would need his help.

When he'd showed up on the pier with both cannons, she'd been surprised. He'd tried explaining the three-pounder to her, that it had been thoroughly tested and where it should be mounted on the foredeck.

However, she paid it no attention.

There on the pier sat the object of her imagination. She had climbed on the second wagon and put her hand on the gleaming brass barrel of the ten-pounder. "Have you fired it?" she asked.

"No, ma'am."

"Bought you brought it anyway," she breathed.

He remembered his emotions. He remembered Wedgewood. He could see the foundry, a wasteland of charred timbers, dead forges, and three lonely chimneys burnt and hollow. "Because I knew you would want it."

That gleaming brass barrel now rode just aft of the foremast. At first, they had tried it in its proper place as what Achelous had called a bow-chaser, but the captain had complained that he could feel the ship was heavy at the bow. Then they had rolled it -- no small thing in the mountainous waves -- on its newly designed gun carriage - aft of the mast where the captain had beamed, "It rides well there!"

"The wind is settling," Marisa called. "The seas will too. The sun will burn off the last of these squalls, and then we shall have them."

"Sail ho!"

Marisa jerked around and scanned the maintop. The lookout was pointing to the southwest. She ran to the quarterdeck ladder and took it two steps at a time.

The captain was ready for her, holding out his glass.

She took the proffered monocular and scanned the sea. "Both," she breathed. The ships matched the harbormaster's description of the two Taldamiran ketches: stout, two-masted merchantmen.

"Sails ho!" came the second call.

Everyone on the quarterdeck turned to look in the new direction.

There, on the *Far Shore's* port beam, was the top of another sail.

The *Far Shore,* south of Tivor, was driving on a southwesterly course where the coast jutted out to meet them. Around that point lay Vaal, the second largest city of the Warkenvaal. While Tivor was currently at peace with the Warkenvaal, the tiny coves and inlets north of Vaal were the dens of Vaal pirates with whom Marinda Merchants was at constant war and with whom the Paleowrights were known to conspire.

"Three, three ships," said the first mate, Mr. Lewisto, pointing to two more top sails off their port beam.

Indeed, the lookout pumped his arm three times.

"Signal the *Intrepid*," called the captain. "Likely, we have three pirates off the port side, on an intercept course."

"Could be a convoy," the mate offered.

"Aye, could be," answered the captain, aiming his glass in that direction. "But I find it more than a coincidence that they should be heading out in apparent timing with those Taldamir merchant ketches. Since when do Vaal coasters convoy with Taldamirans?" The implication being Taldamiran trade vessels usually traveled well out of sight of land to avoid Vaal pirates, whereas these two ships were purposely moving closer to land, intersecting the three coasters.

Marisa stood beside her captain. Ogden, who had followed her onto the quarterdeck but not knowing what

301

else to do, watched her for clues. Rayamars noticed the weaponsmith's nervousness and gave him a calming expression. "I've been out here with her before," he whispered in Ogden's ear. "She's a master."

Ogden braced himself against the stern railing and nodded tentatively.

Marisa waited calmly. The wind continued to abate. The seas were calming. The sun was shining. It would be a beautiful day. A beautiful day for action. A beautiful day to rescue her love. Her crew was ready. The Marines were ready. The riflemen were ready. She waited for her captain to call it. The bronze cannon squatted on the deck of the *Far Shore* like so much gold metal, but she knew what it could do. She took a deep breath. If only Achelous were here with her. He would say something about fate, about the future, about defending Dianis against corsairs, but all she wanted was to win this day and win him back.

"Beat to Quarters, Mr. Lewisto," the captain called it. "Signal the *Intrepid* that we are going into action." The captain wanted to avoid the three ships he was certain were pirates and just pursue the Taldamirans, but the coaster ships had the lead on him and were angling for an intercept. "Inform the *Intrepid* it is our intent to smash our way through these pirates and engage the two Taldamiran ketches running south."

The boatswain beat the brass deck gong, and the deep, hollow sound reverberated across the ship.

Marisa turned to Ogden. "That would be your signal. Ready the gun."

Without saying a word, he made his way to the quarterdeck ladder and went down one step at a time.

The pirates, three sleek, low-decked sloops, lateen-rigged, kept coming. Shorter and lower in the water than the *Far Shore*, driven by a full set of canvas, were pounding in the heavy seas. Their goal was clear: to cross in front of the *Far Shore* in a nautical tactic termed *crossing the T.*

Any doubt as to the nature of the ships was dispelled when the pirate crews could be seen manning the rails holding swords, axes, shields, and grappling hooks.

"Your intentions, captain? I expect we are nearing the range of my new toy."

He gave Marisa a surprised look. "From out here?"

She smiled. "I shouldn't call it a toy."

"Very well. Helm, thirty degrees to starboard. Lady, you may have your gun commence firing."

Marisa took three steps to the ladder and slid down without touching a rung. She ran the length of the deck, weaving past winches, ballistae, and sailors as the deck rose and fell. "Ogden! Are you ready?"

"Oi," he answered as she came to stand beside him. He had three of his foundry assistants with him. Rayamars stood off to the side with the Tivor Marine Adjutant Enderma.

"You seeing this, chief?" asked Mears, watching the video feed from a recon bot perched in the rigging of the *Far Shore*.

"I am," answered Ivan, sitting in the Ready Reaction command room in Central Station. At that station's peak staffing, the room would have had another seven agents at the various control stations. Today, he was the only one; the other hologrid displays were dark.

"What do you think are the odds that cannon will blow up?"

"Spirits, sergeant, I hope none. If that cannon kills Marisa..."

The gun crew winched the brass behemoth to the railing, and they immediately saw the problem. Ogden stared dumbfounded. The barrel was too low to shoot over the gunwale.

"Axes, quick. Clear this railing," Marisa ordered. The second mate grabbed a boarding axe and began hacking at the railing.

Recovering, Ogden said, "Ula, lad. Move out of me way with the wee cleaver of yours. I have the right proper tool for that." Reaching into the equipment chest, he pulled out his double-bladed battle-axe, removed the leather cover, and took aim at the railing.

The second mate saw the weaponsmith heave the blade high and scuttled out of the way. Four strokes on either side and a swift kick, and Ogden had cut a wide gap in the solid wood balustrade. The cannon was heaved into the opening with the block-and-tackle one on each side of the gun carriage. Mindful of Marisa hovering at his elbow, Ogden called, "Slow match!"

One of his gun crew handed him the long rod with the slow match attached to the end. He took a cursory look along the barrel. Sure enough, the captain, seeing the cannon was essentially a fixed mount, unlike the ballistae, had turned the ship to point the gun at the leading pirate.

"Oi! Everyone stand back!" Ogden aimed the slow match at the cannon's touchhole, turned his head, gritted his teeth, and closed his eyes.

Kaboom!

The explosion kicked the gun back on its wheeled carriage and bucked hard at the knot-stops of the block-and-tackle.

Waiting for the splash, Mears called out on the comm channel, "Long."

Ivan breathed a sigh of relief.

"Nine hundred meters beyond the target," acknowledged Jeremy.

"Where? Where did it go?" demanded Marisa.

"Long. Way, way long," said the midships ballista captain running over. "You need to lower the barrel. That sloop is riding too low. We sit too high. You need to wait for the roll. I'd say wait for us to rise halfway up the next wave."

"Reload, reload!" demanded Marisa.

"Oi!" The gun crew swabbed the barrel to douse any sparks and began ramming sacks of gunpowder down the muzzle. "

"Og," she asked, "do we need all those sacks? If we went that far?"

"What's this?" the ballista captain asked, pointing at a capstan-like wheel sitting under the back end of the barrel. It turned a heavy steel screw that was embedded in the carriage.

"That's the elevation screw," answered Ogden. "Atch thought it might come in handy."

Ivan looked over at a second hologrid that showed the bridge of the *Shields* where Mears sat monitoring the action. They looked at each other, passing the unspoken message that such a suggestion by Achelous to Ogden was probably a ULUP violation. As if it mattered.

"Uh, Og," Marisa said carefully, "Bekakic here is one of the best ballista captains in Merinda Merchants."

Ogden looked up from supervising the priming of the touchhole. A crewman was rolling a ten-pound iron ball down the throat. The weaponsmith gave her a blank look.

She said delicately, "You've had the honor of firing this cannon for the first time and on my ship and against the pirates."

Ogden's face stayed blank, but the lead sloop was closing.

"Do you mind," she hurried on, "if Bekakic set the elevation and called when to fire?"

"Oi!" Ogden said, relieved, and grabbed the slow match from the second mate and handed it to Bekakic. "Roll the gun forward!"

They heaved the gun into place, and Ogden made room for Bekakic. After giving the sailor instructions on how to fire and not get maimed when the gun recoiled, Ogden stepped back to Marisa. "Oi, I build them, you shoot them." He grinned.

The distance to the lead pirate had closed by half. The wind had settled to a steady breeze; the seas were roiled, but their heights were down. Bekakic turned to get a view of the quarterdeck. He made a series of hand signals, and Mr. Lewisto relayed them to the captain. The ship altered course five degrees to starboard. Bekakic leaned low over the gun barrel, sighting on the sloop. He told a crewman to turn the adjusting screw. "Keep going. Turn it all the way down. I need the barrel level with the deck. Stop. That's good." Waiting, waiting, suddenly Bekakic stepped back from the gun, concentrated on the rise of the deck in relation to the far horizon. He lit the touchhole as the ship started to roll.

Kaboom! A black blur streaked outward and impacted the pirate.

"Wahooo!" Marisa jumped, jamming a fist in the air. Then she threw both arms around Ogden's neck and kissed him on his helmet.

"Oh shit," said Mears. A three-foot hole shown in the side of the lead sloop, two feet above the water line.

Ivan whispered, "Perfect shot."

The captain of the Far Shore had hoped the pirates would turn and run when hit by the new weapon, but instead, they continued to plow on, oblivious to the danger. His true quarry was fleeing south, and he needed to turn hard to port, straight through the opposing sloops to keep up. "Signal the *Intrepid*. We are resuming original course."

Jeremy calculated the optimum tactical plan for the *Far Shore* and alerted Ivan. "Chief, the *Far Shore* is changing heading. It is no longer attempting to engage the enemy at the best range for its cannon. It is unclear why they would do that."

Ivan was uncertain as well. When the *Shields* had managed to drop the recon bots in the path of the *Far Shore* a little over twenty minutes ago, he'd half hoped Achelous to be aboard, perhaps wounded and hidden below decks. Unable to complete their search of the ship yet, it was clear that Marisa was still searching. His hope vanished. *Is Atch held captive on one of those pirate sloops?*

Marisa saw what the captain intended. She issued quick instructions to Bekakic who nodded. On the new course, he was able to angle the gun just far enough left in the makeshift gun port.

Kaboom!

A white smoke ring billowed away from the cannon, and a vapor trail streaked into the stern quarter of the middle sloop. Wood splinters exploded, and shards skewered the quarterdeck crew. Immediately -- its helm turning freely -- the sloop yawed hard to port.

"So much for those soft hulls," Marisa remarked to the second mate. The shipwrights of the Warkenvaal had taken to building the topsides of their ships with a soft and spongy but resilient timber that captured impacting ballistae bolts that otherwise would puncture harder, denser timber. It appeared no construction material was immune to a ten-pound cannonball.

The lead pirate had cut hard to starboard and was now crossing the bow of the *Far Shore*. The ships were in range of their ballistae mounts, and the hard thumping of the massive bow-arms could be heard.

An incoming bolt whizzed through the rigging, and Ogden belatedly flinched. "Ula. Never had one of those shot at me."

"There'll be more," said Bekakic, helping the gun crew hoist the gun back in place. "Stay low, below the gunwale."

Ogden assumed the gunwale was the solid ship's rail he had made a mess of.

"We have six ballistae, and those pirate sloops have two each," Bekakic said.

"Uh, that one has three," Ogden said, counting the large, pivoting crossbow mounts on the pirate about to run down their starboard side.

"That's new."

Kaboom!

Bekakic was getting the feel of the new gun, as were the gun crew. Load, haul, stand clear, fire, swab, and load again. The six crewmen were getting in a rhythm when the aft mast of the middle sloop shuddered, a huge chunk of wood blasted from its stem. Slowly, at first, cable stays and lines started parting, and then the whole works, sails, and mast fell by the board, hanging over the side of the ship.

A cheer went up. Marisa was amazed. Never in all her days at sea had she seen a mast come down during a fight, except in a ramming.

"Riflemen! To the tops!"

Marisa whirled around. Rayamar's riflemen were scrambling up the ratlines heading to the fighting tops. She ran to the starboard rail. "Damn!" she smacked the hard plank with her palm. The lead pirate, having crossed their bow, was closing fast on their starboard side though it was down at the bow, having taken on water from the first cannon shot. The Warkenvaal archers were lining the rail and readying an arrow barrage. She expected that once past the *Far Shore's* midships, the Warkenvaal would loop around and grapple her by the stern. Then, attempt to board. Marisa had fought that tactic before.

She ran across to the port side, and sure enough, the captains of the three sloops were attempting to coordinate a combined boarding. Even though the middle sloop was wallowing, it wasn't out of the fight, not if the other two sloops could slow the *'Shore* down. Something didn't make sense. If the *Far Shore* had been by itself, Marisa could understand the motive for the three pirates to gang up on a rich merchantman, but the *Intrepid,* a Tivor-flagged warship, was only two miles astern. *Why are they so bold?* Each sloop had maybe seventy sailors. Between the *Far Shore* and the *Intrepid,* they had at least three hundred. In just raw numbers, it would be a tough brawl for the pirates, and as Achelous was quick to point out, the pirates rarely engaged in stiff fights. There was no margin in it. Any ship that could put up good resistance was avoided; there was easier prey elsewhere. The pirates, as he often said, were economists at heart. *Economist,* that was another term she'd learned from him. *Oh, Atch, where are you?*

"Trisha!" Marisa scanned the deck and then to the tops. She grabbed the second mate, "Find Trishna, the Silver Cup pathic, hurry!"

As she scrambled up the quarterdeck ladder, the deck tilted, and Marisa heard the lower course sails flutter and then snap tight: the captain had changed direction. Leaning on the aft-starboard rail, her eyes grew wide. "Sweet Mother— Rayamars! Rayamars!" she called to the fighting tops, "Shoot the torchmen! Don't let them near those braziers." It was a tall order, an impossible request, but something had to be done. She whirled, and the captain was standing right there. He saw the threat.

"If they can't board us, they mean to burn us," she said.

"Aye, and they don't have enough men to board us. Not board and win," he answered.

Trishna came unsteadily up the ladder. "Yes, lady?"

"Do pirates have pathics? The Paleowrights don't do they?"

Trishna appeared confused. "Telepaths? I've never heard that they do."

"Well, they're acting like it," said the captain. "I've been watching for their signal flags, and they've been few."

The crack of the first rifle shot carried down to the deck. At first, the crew wondered at the new sound; they looked up. Rayamars finished reloading and raised his gun. The crack came again, and the sailors looked to where the muzzle pointed. A pirate archer dropped his bow, staggering backward, blood staining his dirty shirt. Gunfire erupted from the fighting tops as Rayamar's riflemen went into action. Soon, the opposing archers would be close enough to shoot back.

A cheer came from the foredeck. Marisa couldn't see what was happening, but something untimely had befallen the third sloop.

"Oh, I didn't expect that." The captain pointed to the lead sloop, starting its run down the starboard side.

Marisa took in a breath. Pirates, many more, were climbing up through the hatches. "Trap. It's a trap."

"Aye, looks like they planned for this. Like they knew we would be coming."

The pirate crew on deck swelled to more than double as men came up from below. "How did they fit all those men onboard?" For the first time, Marisa was worried. If all the pirates had doubled up on their crews-- Fear struck her, a deep, corrosive, gut-wrenching fear that turned her legs to lead and sapped her soul. They were doomed. The *Far Shore,* after all these years, would meet its end here today. She turned away so the captain would not see her face. She laid her hands on the aft rail, feeling the fear turn her bowels to water, the despair deep and quavering. Then she looked up and saw the majestic sails, the bow froth, and the men at the rail of the *Intrepid.* It was bearing down on the trailing pirate.

If they are willing to fight... If those men are willing to fight for my cause.... She waded through the fatigue, uncertainty, and despair. *Who am I? Am I a woman? Or am I a mouse?*

Unsteadily, Marisa turned around and found the entire quarterdeck crew watching her. *Who am I? A woman? Or a mouse?* She gathered her shredding resolve, summoned her legs to respond, and strode to the captain.

"Captain," she said, fighting to keep her voice even. "The *Far Shore* is yours to fight. Command us and be not timid. Strike a bold stroke." Feeling the stirrings of her confidence return, "I will be on the foredeck and will lead the crew there. Today is our day, Captain. It is time to make these foul cretins pay."

A Warkenvaal arrow barrage arced across the churning sea. Marines, sailors, and riflemen took cover the best they could. Those in the fighting tops, the platforms near the tops of the three masts, were exposed to rain of death; the fighting tops were not Wedgewood treehouses. Sailors and Marines fell; A rifleman screamed, clutching an arrow to his chest as he dropped the great height and landed with a splash on the dark sea.

The blast of rifles was a new sound in the sea battle, but the Warkenvaal took the notion in stride and acted as if nothing was amiss. Rayamars braced against the mizzenmast, rammed the bullet down the barrel, seated it, and then pulled the rod. *It be no good to drop the ramrod here,* he reflected as his body went through the practiced motions. He brought the rifle up, primed the pan, dropped the powder horn uncapped on its lanyard and aimed. Another brigand was trying to retrieve the discarded torches. Having been to sea before as an archer, Rayamars waited for the deck to roll, and as it did, the muzzle rose.

Bang!

The brigand dropped flat on the deck, motionless.

The Warkenvaal lined up for another arrow barrage, this time closer. The riflemen reloaded and fired fiercely, but a trained archer could shoot three times faster than a muzzleloader. Rayamars ducked behind the mast as the volley thudded into the wood around him. He grimaced; Private Arot fell to the deck below.

Aware of the risk to his own ship, the captain of the *Intrepid* would not abandon his countrymen; the desperate plight of the *Far Shore* drove him to spin the wheel, and the brig turned hard to starboard, aiming its reinforced bows at the sloop's waist.

Caught between the Tivorian warship and the merchantman, the trailing sloop belatedly broke off its boarding attempt, but too late, its sails were drafted by the lee of the massive merchant, and it could not gain headway. A huge crash sounded across the sea. The sloop was driven into the side of the *Far Shore,* and the merchantman shuddered with the grinding impact.

"Ula, lady, is it always like this?"

Marisa flinched when an arrow thwacked into the foremast. It quivered between her and Ogden. She felt alive, scared, and determined. "It can be worse," she answered but wondered how and went to help a bow ballista reload; half of its crew were dead or wounded.

Pinioned between the bows of the *Intrepid* and the side of the *Far Shore,* the Warkenvaal's crew scrambled, like hundreds of rats, off the doomed ship, half attacking the *Intrepid* and the other half seeking desperate refuge on the merchantman.

"Shield wall!" called Adjutant Enderma of the Tivor Marines. "Form up! Attack!" Forty Marines, two ranks deep, advanced on the pirates clambering over the rail. "Now! Push! Shove them back into the sea!"

A grappling hook snagged the belaying pin rack in front of Ogden. He didn't need to ask as to what to do about it. Swinging his axe, he went about chopping every grappling line in reach.

"Og!" Marisa called, too late. An arrow hit the weaponsmith in the shoulder. He looked at the errant thing as if it were a flea. It had barely punctured his chainmail, hammered and welded by himself. The arrowhead snagged in the heavy leather jerkin beneath. He ripped it free and resumed his business.

For every line he cut, two more landed. One grappling hook, pulled by a mass of pirates, skittered across the deck and caught him by the foot. Swept off his feet, the hook dragged him to the gunwale. A sailor, sporting an arrow in his thigh, swung his cutlass and cleaved the line just as the grappling hook threatened to crush the mastersmith's foot against the balustrade.

Having cleared its wrecked mast, the second sloop made to board the *Far Shore* at the port bow. The ballista there was out of action, its crew swept clear by an arrow barrage.

"Ogden!" Marisa yelled, "Help me with the cannon!" She and Bekakic, and the two remaining gun crew were attempting to load the weapon.

Seeing the ship's plight, Ogden rummaged in the crates of powder bags and cannon balls. He came up with two lumpy burlap sacks. "Oi, we'll try these."

They rammed the sacks down the barrel after half the normal number of powder bags. "What are they?" Marisa huffed as they heaved the cannon to the port. Sweat streaked the soot on her face.

Ogden gave a mighty heave on the block and tackle, jacked the gun's muzzle as low as it would point, and told Bekakic, "Fire it!" He pulled Marisa out of the way, and the gun captain lit the touchhole.

Kabooosh!

Death and mayhem spewed across the pirate ship. All the brigands on its foredeck were swept back and knocked down. Blood, red and smeary, splashed across the bulwarks.

"Mother's breath," Marisa gasped, "what was that?"

Bekakic didn't care. "Reload! Get more of those!" Archery action from the pirate had ceased.

As the ships drifted closer, the groans of the wounded pirates from across the water could be heard. Slowly, more brigands recovered, and they began beating their shields and resuming their chant for the attack.

As Ogden jammed a sack into the gun's throat and rammed it down, he said, "It was Achelous' idea. I wondered if we would ever use them."

"What is it?" she asked.

"He called it canister. It's just a bag full of bullets, nails, whatever."

Bekakic demanded, "Hurry, they are almost too close."

They heaved the gun in place, and the five of them stood back. Arrows began to fly again. The Bekakic hesitated, gauging when more pirates were lined along the rail and yet not so close as the gun couldn't depress. *Kaboom!*

Rayamars waited for the corsair to pick up the torch and run to the brazier. The sea had calmed so that the larger 'Shore was steady, but the sloop still rocked. Reaching the brazier, the corsair lit the tar-soaked torch, *Bang!* When the smoke cleared from the shot, Rayamars saw the pirate lying flat on his back, a red smear on his side, and the torch lay burning in a careless pile of hemp line. He watched with satisfaction as the hemp began to smolder, and he resumed counterfire, sniping archers.

A guttural cry arose from the starboard side; Marisa ran to the railing and peered over. Corsairs from the lead sloop had managed to grapple with the side of her ship, heave in close, and were starting to climb the tall side. Then she saw him: the pirate captain. He was giving her the same monkey-faced smile he'd taunted her with when he tried to capture the *Far Shore* two months earlier. That was then she'd come to the rescue of the *Far Shore* on board its sister ship, the *Wind March*. In that battle, there had been only one pirate ship, not three, with treble crews. She ran forward to see the aft of the sloop. There on the transom was the name *Uktik Baktar*.

The pirate captain was making a hand gesture at her. One hand made a circle, and the other hand a prong that went in and out of the circle. He pointed first to him and then to her, all with his monkey-face smile.

She started running to midships, but already the first corsair was over the railing. Two more followed. "Enderma!" she called and drew her cutlass. "Enderma!" She took a slice at the first corsair, and like all pirates and most Tivorian sailors, he was not wearing chainmail and came without a shield. Marisa's cutlass drew a deep cut from shoulder to ribs, and the pirate's intimidating war yell turned to a screech of horror. Before she could twist her blade for a back cut at the next pirate charging her, the brigand spasmed backward. Another rifle shot sounded from above, and a third corsair fell at her feet.

Adjutant Enderma, having successfully held the port quarter against the crew of the rammed and now sinking sloop, was forced to retreat from the rail and draw his Marine contingent across the waist of the ship, protecting the quarterdeck.

Amidst the screams, curses, and clangor of battle, Marisa was aware of sailors lining up on her right and left, helping to defend the forecastle. Ogden grabbed his axe and made to attack, but Bekakic caught him by the arm. "Ere! Help me with this."

Cut, parry, thrust, Marisa wanted to move to where her shield hung on a belaying pin, but the corsairs were relentless. She saw the captain of the *Uktik Baktar* at the back of the crowd, urging his crew on.

Her parry missed a blade, and the pirate cut a grim line across her thigh, exposing the barely healed Troglodyte wound. Gasping at the flaming heat, she dropped her guard, and the corsair bull-rushed her, knocking her flat, sending her cutlass skittering across the deck.

Straddling her, the corsair made to bash her face with the hilt of his sword. She jerked her head left, and the brass guard thudded into the deck. Yanking the stiletto from her bun, she jammed it into his thigh. The brigand's eyes grew wide, and he roared with indignation. Raising his arm for another blow, Marisa pulled the stiletto free and jabbed it into his throat as he lunged down. The man gurgled, choking; his fist and sword hung bare inches from her face.

"Ula! We're out of canister," Ogden growled. "Anything, anything," he called to the gun crew, "nails, splinters, and--" he saw a length of chain.

Grabbing his axe, Ogden aimed at the bulkhead mount and counted on the chain to be soft steel forged to resist rusting. Sure enough, his battle blade cleaved it cleanly. He started hacking the links to pieces, one, two, and then stopped. An even better idea came to him. Hoisting the length of chain, he ran to the muzzle of the cannon.

Rayamars brought the rifle up, rotated his aim across the deck, and an arrow hit the stock of his rifle, gouging a splinter that stuck in his cheek.

Bang! His target fell at Marisa's feet. He edged back around the mast for its scant protection and began reloading; the pain in his hip from an arrow was a dull throb held at bay by adrenalin. Fortunately, the arrow's force had been stunted by his thick uniform coat, and it struck his hipbone. It did not reach his guts. Feeling in his bullet pouch, he had four bullets left.

Marisa scrambled on the deck for her sword. In the press of feet and bodies, she came up with it, her hair a wild tangle of black that covered her face. She whipped it clear just in time to see a Warkenvaal come at her with an up-raised cutlass. His was the heavy, brutish weapon preferred by boarders who bludgeoned and hacked rather than stabbed and parried. She hobbled on her wounded leg and raised her own cutlass: the lighter, faster Marine officer's weapon. Arm speed won over brawn. His blow, with the quillion, landed on her left shoulder, driving her down, but not before her stroke cracked his skull.

Staggering up, weaving left and right, her left shoulder numb, she made towards the melee when familiar voices, seemingly from afar, yelled, and she was shoved aside as the bronze barrel of her ten-pound monster was rolled across the deck.

Kaboom!

Being even with the muzzle, she saw the huge yellow jet flare out; the cannon's report, upfront and not from behind, was massive, the concussion a physical wall that buffeted her whole body. Out of the barrel whipped a black snake the likes she had never seen. A swath of pirates ten feet wide and more deep was scythed like so much rotten sawgrass. Those facing the thunderous explosion succumbed to shock.

"Charge!" Ogden led the remaining members of the gun and ballistae crews into the fight. The corsairs broke.

The captain of the *Uktik Baktar,* seeing his ship aflame at a brazier, hesitated. He wanted to rally his men; they still had the numbers, but that treacherous bronze beast with its black maw stared at him. His monkey-face smile gone, he heaved a spear at Marisa, who glared at him through a mass of sweat-soaked hair. Vaulting the railing, the captain swung on a grappling line and made to save his ship.

Chapter 35
Buzz

At sea, off the coast of the Warkenvaal

The last body consigned to the ocean was Bekakic's; he had died with a spear in his chest meant for her. The water was cold, but Bekakic was now in Mother's warm embrace. Marisa stood woodenly at the rail as the captain said the last words of Mother's Light, and the Marines, the half that were ambulatory, saluted the grave of the sea.

In the haze of the new day, yet to be burned away by the rising sun, Marisa struggled with her own fog. She was dull to the world. Even the good omen of an orange bird perched in the rigging, blown out to sea on the winds of the gale, failed to garner her attention, though it was the talk of the crew. Small things like that mattered at sea, especially after a battle where the survivors took stock of life for those who remained.

The day promised to be calm and warm with a slight breeze, which was distressing. No way would she be able to make up time on the Taldamirans last seen at the height of the battle heading south under full sail.

The ceremony over, Marisa limped, more like dragged her leg, aft to her stateroom. Grasping her elbow, the captain, without refusal from her, helped her through the companionway door. "Thank you for your services yesterday, captain," she said, exhaustion flaring with the rising heat. "You fought the ship well. Two pirates sunk, one captured."

He held her elbow, steadying her. "You are most gracious, my lady," he gave her a short bow. "It is, and will forever be, my honor to serve you." The respect in his eyes embarrassed her, and she looked away. "Rest," he said. "I will send word if we raise sight of them."

She nodded once, and he helped her to her stateroom, where she closed the door and collapsed on her bunk. Finally, with respect paid to their lost comrades, she could sleep.

She floated in and out of consciousness in that quasi-realm between awareness and slumber. The cabin had grown dark, the heat of the southern ocean giving way to a cooler humidity. Laying there, she took stock of the sounds of the ship at sea, the course of water along the hull, the creak of the deck, the flutter of sail, the break of a wave at the sternpost. Though her eyes were closed, the sound of the insect buzzing, flying in through the open stateroom windows, caused them to twitch. *Why did the captain bring us close enough to shore to pick up flies?* It didn't make sense. Her mental image of the charts south and west of the Warkenvaal would have the captain following the trade winds and the Padmarjar current well out to sea, as would the Taldamirans.

The buzzing, a large fly by the sound, circled the cabin, coming to roost on a beam overhead. Her eyes shot open.

"Ugh," she groaned, trying to sit up on the bunk. Her body, especially her shoulder and leg, was stiff, everything a dull ache. Blood from her thigh wound leaked through the bandage; she could feel it in the darkness, soggy, sticky.

"Morook, Morook," she called to her steward.

There was a knock at the door, and it creaked open. "Yes, my lady?" he said into the dark.

"Light the lanterns. All of them, please. And shut the cabin windows."

"Do you feel a chill, my lady," he asked, concerned, for the night was warm.

"No. No, I'm fine."

She lay back as Morook went about his business, and after he had left, she swung her feet off her bunk and went to stand by her desk that faced the door. Studying the chart laid out on the table, she pulled out her protractors. "Morook?"

"Yes, ma'am?" he said, looking in the door.

"Get me our current position, please, and the ship's log of wind speeds and direction since the time we last saw the Taldamirans."

After Morook returned with the readings, she plotted the minimum and maximum travel distance of their quarry. The result was depressing. Then she heard the buzzing and the slightest sound of scratching. *Or am I imagining it?* Rolling up the chart, she tossed it on her bunk and figured out how she was going to pull off the next move with her bad leg. The overhead on all ships was low, low enough for her to almost touch the top of the cross-support from which the scratching came. Sitting on the desk, she twisted around until she was kneeling on it and then stood to grasp the beam, keeping the weight off her bad leg. Looking along the length of the cross-support, she said, "There you are."

Sure enough, what Achelous called a Mark II Bumblebee recon bot sat there staring at her. She reached out her hand, and the nanobot scuttled out of reach. "Oh no, you don't. Don't you dare disassemble, or destruct, or melt, or whatever it is you do. I need to know who is in there. Who's behind those big beady eyes of yours?"

"Did you call for me, ma'am?" Morook stuck his head in the door. Seeing his mistress standing on the desk and clinging to the beam, he made to intervene.

"No. Don't," she told him. "It's just an annoying bug, and I want to see what kind it is."

"Kind? Ma'am? You get down off that desk, and I'll squash it for you."

At that, the recon bot scuttled to the far end of the beam.

"Nooo, you come back here."

When Morook made to fetch a belaying pin and join her on the desktop, she begged him off. "Honestly, Morook. I've got nothing better to do, and I can't sleep. I want to catch the little bugger and study it."

She glimpsed her steward's bewildered look and thought how strange it must be for him to hear that. *He must think I've gone nuts.* She swallowed, *nuts at losing Achelous, or all the dead, and everything else.* "It's okay. It has to be getting on to the mid-watch. Get some sleep. I'll be okay."

After Morook reluctantly departed, she peered at the fake bumblebee huddled in the corner. "See that? I just saved you from being squashed. Now come here. I promise I won't harm you. I just need to know who you are working for: Breia, Clienen, Ivan, the matriarch, who? It makes a difference." When the bumblebee was unmoved, she tried a different tact. "If you don't come here, I will have Morook not only catch you but rip your tiny wings off. Then where will your owner be? Now come here!" She leveled a hand at it and flexed *come hither* with her finger.

Slowly, at first, the bot emerged from its corner and then scuttled over to her outstretched finger.

"Eeeek," she squeaked. "No, no, no, don't go back. You just scared me a little." Waggling the finger, "Come on, get on."

With it perched on her finger, Marisa climbed down and sat at her desk. The bot was clinging fiercely to the finger. At first, she had a tremendous urge to shake it off; after all, it was a bee, and a big one at that. "Off. Get off my finger."

The bot hopped onto the desk and sat there looking at her.

For the first time, she had a good look at a recon nanobot. Resting her chin on the desk to get eye-level with the creature, she reflected on just how ludicrous this would look to Morook should he venture in. *He'd certainly think I've gone nuts.*

The bot was a fair rendition of a bumblebee, she had to admit, but at a hand's breadth away, the differences were obvious: the wings were made of some sort of shiny metal, the feet – all six of them – were metal, and the eyes were too large by far. But seen flying by or hanging out in a bush, no one would be any wiser.

She gave a sigh. "First, it was the Paleowrights, then the Troglodytes, then the Drakans, then pirates, and now you. Why can't you just leave me alone? Leave Atch alone? Leave us all alone?" Watching the little creature, she reflected, *figures they wouldn't let you talk, probably afraid someone would capture you and try to interrogate you before you could go poof.* Giving up trying to ferret a meaning from the bug, she retrieved her chart and rolled it out on the table. When bot had to spring into the air and fly away, she said, "Oops! Sorry. I didn't mean that. No squashing intended."

Sitting at her desk, she pondered what to do. The *Intrepid* had returned to Tivor, though its captain had requested to continue the search with them, but the damage on the *Intrepid's* bow was clear to see. The bowsprit was gone, the foremast sprung, and while the hull was reinforced, they had ruptured a number of planks and needed the crew to work the forward pump to keep her dry. The *Far Shore,* while in better shape, its crew was not. The Marines, riflemen, and sailors had all suffered horribly. The *Intrepid* had been able to take the wounded back to Tivor, including Rayamars. Ogden informed her they were down to four rounds of round shot for the ten-pounder. He'd also mentioned, almost in passing, that they'd have to arrange a better way to store the gunpowder during a battle. If the pirates had thrown just one torch up on the gun, the powder bags sitting in the ammo crate would have gone up in a huge flare that no firefighting effort could have put out.

Staring at the chart, she figured the best they could hope for was to spot the Taldamirans and shadow them until Trishna could send a message back to the aorolmin. *And then what?* she asked herself. It was part of her bargain with the *Intrepid's* skipper that he would return to Tivor only if she promised to avoid further action. Which she would have to do. If any pirates came out to intercept them, she'd have to turn tail and run, as appalling a notion as that was.

The buzzing resumed, and the bot landed on the chart. It tic-tacked across the map and stopped and tapped a leg.

Marisa wanted to shoo the bug away, but the bee tapped its foot again, looking up at her. *It is kind of cute,* she thought idly.

It tapped its foot faster.

Frowning, "What? Are you trying to tell me something?"

The wings buzzed twice. It tapped its foot.

She looked closer. "Vaal?"

The wings buzzed twice, and the foot quit tapping. "What about Vaal? Are you trying to tell me something about Vaal?"

Again, two buzzes.

"Atch? Atch is in Vaal?"

No reaction.

Her concentration grew steeper. Then recognition. Vaal lay in the cruising radius she had plotted for the Taldamirans. "Are the ketches in Vaal?"

Two buzzes.

She had to be certain. "How would you tell me no? Give me the sign for no."

One buzz.

"Yes!" *That helps. Or does it? Why would they know the ships had made it to Vaal but not Atch?* A deep fear settled on her. *Was Atch ever on one of those ships?* The fact the little bot was sitting on her desk trying to communicate with her gave her hope. "Where's Atch?" she asked, and of course, no response, which to her meant that it either didn't know or she didn't ask the right question. "Did you see Achelous get off the ships in Vaal?"

One buzz.

Consternation. "Why not?"

No reaction.

"Ugh." Marisa rested her forehead on the chart. "I'm trying to have an intelligent conversation with a recon bot."

There was a scratching on her finger, and she jerked up. The bot tic-tacked across the chart and tapped its foot, what she now considered its pointer foot. *There's nothing but ocean there? It must be some mistake*—except the spot on the map lay dead ahead of the *Far Shore*. They'd be there in three hours.

A knock sounded on her stateroom door. Then again. She lifted her head off the desk; she must have dozed off. She checked the hourglass; it was well into the mid-watch. "Come in."

A man entered and closed the door behind him, rubbing a red mark across his forehead. He stuck out his hand, Timberkeep fashion, to shake, "I'm Ivan Darinarishcan, a friend of Atch's."

Any cobwebs she may have had were cleared away by a sudden boiling anger. Holding it in check, she sat still as stone. The man approached her desk and kept his arm outstretched. He was older than she imagined. Half-bald, his face sunburned a permanent shade of purple, deep care lines crossed his brow, and his cheeks were gaunt.

"I've come in the interest of our friend. I think we can help each other."

Slowly, Marisa rose and reached out her own hand. Loath she was to grip the palm of the person who had been the source, the icon, of so many of her fears these past months. His hand was warm but soft, no callouses like a sailor's. "Did you hit your head on a beam?"

"Yes, the ceiling's kind of low. "May I?" He pointed to one of two empty chairs

Marisa eased back down, "I suppose, though I was hoping it was someone else on the other side of Buzz."

"Buzz?"

"Yea. The bumblebee."

"You named the recon bot?"

"Of course. It's actually trying to help. Unlike others who are trying to kill me, burn my ship, mind-wipe me, steal my son, abduct Achelous, and take us off-world." She let the point sink in. "How did you get on board?"

323

He shrugged, "I shifted in."

"How is that possible? We are nowhere near a shift station."

"We can do unanchored shifts. I would have been here sooner, but we've lost that capacity at Central Station, so I had to wait for a federation ship to respond to our request for assistance." He reached into his tunic pocket, and Marisa tensed.

"Don't worry, it's safe," he said. "May I?"

She gave the slightest nod.

Withdrawing a package, a very galactic-looking package, he placed it on her desk. "That's a military-grade field dressing. For your leg. You open the package, pull off the white backing, place it over your wound, and tap the green button. The dressing stretches so you can shape it to cover that nasty sword cut. Your surgeon did his best to stitch you up, but it's probably infected." He waited, and when she was non-committal, he added, "You'll want to cover it up with the wrappings you have now. It wouldn't be good to walk around for everyone to see it."

She picked the dressing up and inspected it through the clear packaging as if it might be some sort of alien instrument, which it was. Opening a desk drawer, she put it away. "Thank you," she said without her usual warmth. "How long have you been following us?"

"Since this morning."

"Ah," Marisa nodded, "the orange bird."

Ivan didn't actually smile; his jaw just softened a bit.

"By the way. A hint," she said, "there are no orange birds at sea. They are rare this far south, and I think the closest place you'd find a bumblebee is the prairie east of Tivor."

He wagged his head. "We do what we can. We're on a tight budget. Which brings me to my request." When she didn't respond, he continued. "When we finally deduced you were chasing the two Taldamiran ships, and we were able to locate them, they, unfortunately, had already docked in Vaal. By the time we could get bots onboard

324

them, we found no cargo, which tells us something. There were no signs of Helprig or Achelous."

Marisa's eye twitched; otherwise, she was still as stone. She noticed the recon bot, clinging to the lantern pedestal, watched her like a hawk. "If you are sitting here," she asked, "then who is minding Buzz?"

"That would be Jeremy, our Central Station AI, or do you know what an AI is? It is hard to tell what you know. Technically, you shouldn't know anything, and I shouldn't be having this conversation with you."

She looked at the bot. *So Jeremy is in there. You are the one who helped Atch with the alert triggers.* "Hello, Jeremy."

The wings buzzed twice.

Looking to Ivan with a ghost of a smile, "You said you had a request?"

After Ivan outlined the problem and then the request, Marisa said, "You want me, Marisa Pontifract, to sail the *Far Shore,* with that bronze cannon on the foredeck into Vaal? And then go ashore?" her voice cracked with incredulity.

"Well, maybe not you, but someone who knows Vaal. All my former Warkenvaal agents are on Dominicus, and you can see that time is of the essence. The longer we wait, the colder the trail."

"And what do you plan to do with Achelous once we," and she emphasized the word *we,* "find him?"

"Bring him back safe."

"To where?"

For the first time, Ivan's self-assurance wavered. "Central Station."

She couldn't help it. As a trade-negotiator, Marisa practiced eliminating any personal *tells,* but her eyes narrowed against her will. Her head moved first right, then left. "No."

"Well, I'm afraid you don't have—"

Her fist hit the desk, and the thud startled even the mid-watch on the quarterdeck above her. The stern-gallery windows were open, and the seas were calm. She was up and leaning over the desk. "You!" She jabbed a finger at Ivan, "are in no position to dictate terms. It's because the IDB left Dianis that we are in this situation at all." She rose to her full height. "I have a telepath on board. I heard what happened at Wedgewood again!" She took a breath to steady herself. "Plasma rifles! Battle drones! Lettern!" She threw her arms up, "Mother bless her soul. Lettern fought an armed shuttle with a plasma rifle?" her voice spewed shock.

A pounding sounded on the door, and a ship's officer came in, followed closely by a watch-stander. "Your lady?" The officer stopped cold, peering at Ivan. "Who are you?"

Ivan looked up at the man while Buzz pivoted on the pedestal to get a better view of the action. It was a recon bot, after all.

Enjoying Ivan's discomfort at not being able to provide a rational answer, Marisa finally relented. "It's okay, Mister Eller. I can assure you I am as surprised as you at finding Mr. Darinarishcan onboard our ship and the incredible means by which he came here. But here he is nonetheless."

"Shall I throw him in the brig, ma'am?"

Now, Marisa smiled, and Ivan seemed to sink into his chair. "No, Mister Eller, as much as that would please me, it probably wouldn't hold him."

"We've lots of chains, ma'am. I've not known any man to escape when properly bound and shackled. I'd mount a round-the-clock guard on him as well."

Marisa sat back down.

While Ivan didn't look afraid, he also didn't look like he relished the idea of being bound in chains.

The image of Ivan in chains calmed her bubbling blood. "No. No." Buzz skittered around to get a better look at her. She gave it a charming smile. "Mr. Darinarishcan is a reluctant guest of mine, for now. But please send for Og."

The first officer caught the subtle hint and stepped briefly outside, whispering to the watchstander, and then came back into the cabin.

Ivan shifted in his chair, trying to get comfortable, but failed. "Achelous needs to talk to the matriarch. She sent me to find him."

Marisa studied him from across the desk. *Well, that's probably true.* "And then what?"

Ivan shook his head. "I don't know, but I can tell you," and he jutted out his chin and then relaxed, "that I told her that Achelous should be arrested, but she wasn't interested. She said he wasn't guilty of anything, at least not yet. That staying behind on Dianis after Lights Out was, technically, allowed by his IDB charter, which was never revoked because ULUP never rescinded its IDB sponsorship of the planet."

"And you don't like that?" she asked.

If it bothered Ivan that Mr. Eller heard the conversation, he didn't show it. "No. He consorted with you, and that is strictly against both IDB regulations and ULUP."

In a professional way, Marisa admired Ivan's rational, resolute duty in enforcing ULUP and his simple black-and-white view of the world, but it also infuriated her. Life was not black and white. It was grey, full of irrational Human emotions like love, hate, and vengeance.

The cabin door shoved open, and Ogden stomped in. In one hand was a rifle, barrel pointed up. Taking in the scene, his gaze settled on Ivan. "Oi. You get around."

"You know this man?" asked Eller.

"Oi. Split loglard skulls with him at Battle Park. Last time I'd seen you, you were guard captain for the high priestess. That was before that Ancient came to Murali's..."

Ivan gave a subtle nod. "A sad day."

"Ula. For us all." Ogden sat heavily on the edge of Marisa's bunk.

"Mr. Eller," Marisa said, "you may return to your duties. Thank you for your attention. Should we need your help, I'll call through the window."

After the officer bowed and left, Ogden lowered the rifle and pointed it at Ivan. He had Buzz's full attention. "I know what you can do," said Ogden. "I saw Atch's handiwork with that Scarlet Britcher in the study, and good riddance too. But, you should also know," and he pulled back the hammer of the rifle," that you can't move fast enough to beat this bullet."

"No, not yet. Hold on that." When Ivan saw their confusion, he said, "Sorry, I'm talking to the *Alexis*. They are a bit alarmed up there and want to shift me out. Now."

"That would be one way of getting rid of you." Marisa gave him a sweet, nearly genuine smile.

"Hmm, can I assure the *Alexis* that you won't have Ogden shoot me unless I do something stupid?"

Marisa answered, "Og?"

The weaponsmith wagged his head, "Depends on what stupid is."

Marisa leaned forward; her gloss-black hair reflected the yellow lantern light, but her coal-black eyes reflected nothing. "I have my own proposal." She glanced at Buzz, held out a finger, and the bot obligingly climbed on. She put her finger on her shoulder, and the bot, taking the hint, hopped off.

"Oi, I've seen those. You've a new pet?"

"I do," she said, brightening. "If I had another, I could use them as earrings. Ivan, if you can shift onto the '*Shore,* you can shift me off?"

He cleared his throat. "We can, but it would be highly unusual."

"Good. I like unusual. Here's my proposal. I will help you find Achelous, and you can facilitate a meeting between him and the matriarch at a time and place of my choosing if and only if she grants him a pardon for any and all federation or ULUP transgressions that he may have incurred in, how did you say it, consorting with me. And, Clienen, his former boss, signs some sort of suitable warrant or attestment that Achelous' behaviors on Dianis post-Lights Out were in the spirit of keeping Dianis safe from extrasolar incursions and he was acting on behalf of the IDB. And finally, ULUP, or whoever is in charge of it, signs a guarantee of surety that the federation will in no way attempt to abduct or otherwise remove Achelous, me, or my son from this planet." She kept her leveled gaze on him. At that moment, those eyes were more intimidating than Ogden's rifle.

"Well," he hedged, attempting to parse her terms, "the federation can't be—"

She began to rise from her desk. Placing both hands palms down on the chart, "You don't get to negotiate. Those are my terms. Take them or leave them. Moreover, consider this: I know what the Matrincy wants. I know what Dianis has, and I know where it is. And you can't have it." She let the creak of the floorboards overhead fill the silence. "We can trade with the federation; we can barter in the future. There is aquamarine at stake; we know that. There is the cooperation of Timberkeep adepts at stake; we know that. And there is the cause of the Timber's Curse and where that came from and why there are so many adepts on Isuelt, that part you don't know. And for all those things, you will need our help, and you won't be getting it until I get Achelous back." She lifted her hands carefully off the chart so as not to smudge it and sat back down in her chair. "Og, please tell Ivan who you represent."

"Ula, represent?"

"Your role in the Clan at New Ungern."

He cheered, his ruddy complexion even redder in the lamplight. "I am the duly elected senior elder for New Ungern for Clan Mearsbirch."

"And is Tivor allied with the Timberkeep clans?" she asked.

"Oi, mutual defense it is."

"And if I were to ask you to ask Woodwern to block all access to Mount Mars to anyone other than the clan?"

He chuckled. "We may already have."

"And if I asked you, as part of a potential strategic alliance with the Avarian Federation, to allow a select few people to speak with your adepts?"

He scratched his beard with his free hand, the other hovering on the trigger. "Hmm, we'd talk about it."

She smiled at Ivan. "When I get Atch back, with my attestments rightfully authorized, then the Matrincy can negotiate with us."

"And why would you want us to shift you off the ship?"

"I need to talk to someone. She's in Wedgewood."

Chapter 36
The Mill

Wedgewood

"What?" asked Marisa.

Outish gawked at Marisa's new surveillance bot. The Seasheel parrot perched on her shoulder, watching the intern as he squinted to get a better look. "I've never seen a Seasheel parrot; I've heard of them."

The mother in her tempered Marisa's tone, "Outish, it's a bot."

"I know, but it looks so real. Field Outfitting did a really good job on this one."

"Jeremy located it in the Central Station inventory. It was a prototype slated for testing in the Warkenvaal before Lights Out. As cute as Buzz was, I was tired of flap, flap, scratch, scratch. I needed a bot that could talk." It had been a day since the *Alexis* shifted her off the *Far Shore* to Wedgewood. Jeremy was, somehow, uniquely tuned to her moods and had immediately responded with a substantially more capable bot when she made the smallest complaint.

"Awk," squawked the parrot, "Outy is a goof nut, Outy is a goof nut."

"Whaaaat?" Outish said.

"He squawks like a parrot, too," the parrot added.

Outish looked at Marisa.

She covered her mouth, concealing a laugh. "I'm sorry, Outish. It's just that life is so sad without Atch," her humor faded. "I'm always worried about where he is and what is happening to him. I told Jeremy I needed Buzz Too to have a sense of humor. The more irreverent, the better."

Buzz Too chimed at Outish, "That's right, my IQ makes yours look like a pine nut."

Marisa started snickering.

Lettern shook her head when Buzz Too turned its beak at her, "Oh, no, you don't bird brain. You give me any lip, there won't be enough feathers left to dust an ant."

The four of them, including Meridia, were at the rendezvous point near the Twistynook mill.

Serene and reticent, the Ungerngerists stood like pillars of a god's cathedral. The sun had sunk behind Mount Mars; it was the glorious time of long summer days where dusk stretched on and on.

Meridia, sitting on a mill wagon, had not met Marisa until today. He liked what he saw.

Lettern caught him appraising Marisa and gave him the evil eye. Unabashed, he shrugged. A beeping signaled the proximity alarm on his multi-func. Activating the display, he saw the two opposing teams – one of them theirs -- of nanobots and recon drones engage and inspect each other. Passing clearance codes, the two swarms melded into one larger, multi-tiered surveillance system. "Hmm." He stood up. "Our guests are here. A platoon of them."

Ivan came down the trail from behind the mill, crossed the footbridge, and approached.

Meridia tracked the movements of the troopers. He sighed at their designators, *bloody Special Forces*. He caught the brush moving upslope to his left. The Special Forces were wearing chameleon armor, so they were effectively invisible to the naked eye. Checking the emanations read out, he grunted. Sure enough, they were all packing fully charged plasma rifles.

"Buzz," Marisa said, watching Ivan approach, "Go find a branch."

"Good evening, lady," Ivan said, holding out his hand. She looked refreshed. Her hair was done up; he noticed it was pinned in place with a stiletto. *Are those care-lines at the corner of her eyes?* He'd not seen them in the light of the cabin.

"Evening, Ivan." She shook his hand, Timberkeep fashion.

"I wouldn't get too attached to that parrot. That's IDB property and expensive, too."

Her countenance softened. "Oh, I'm sure it's paying for itself with all the intel it is collecting."

"Yes, well, I've brought a special visitor. She has the documents that you requested." He inclined his head and moved to stand with Meridia.

"How you doing, chief?" Meridia asked quietly.

"Tired. I was on Dominicus this morning. Running Ready Reaction for two systems is a grind."

The black-robed figure crossed the footbridge; Meridia saw another half-dozen Special Forces appear on the surveillance grid, plus— "Nice, a Phantom aerial battle drone. No in-country camo. You can tell Ready Reaction is not running this little soiree."

Ivan said, "No."

The Phantom swooped silently into the clearing, scanned each of the members of Marisa's party, and then took station above Marisa.

Unfazed, Marisa watched the Auro Na high priestess approach.

Pulling the hood of her Auro Na cloak back, the matriarch exposed her black hair.

Outish started, "Black dreadlocks? I thought her hair was blonde?"

Lettern elbowed Outish. "Shush. Never comment on a woman's hair unless it's a compliment."

"Lettern Stouttree," the matriarch removed her glove and held out her bare right hand. "It is good to see you again." Lettern shook her hand but looked to Ivan, "The high priestess of the Auro Na?"

A corner of the matriarch's mouth curled up, and Ivan cleared his throat. "My apologies, your Matrincy, I should make your introduction. Lettern, Marisa, Outish, this is the matriarch, Grand Counselor of the Matrincy, Senator li Ianata of the Avarian Federation Senate, Judge Jurisdictia of the Federation Executive, and Rights and Honors Representative for non-aligned worlds."

"Oh," said Lettern.

Ignoring the accolades, the matriarch said, "I read the after-action report of the battle with the shuttle, as did my staff. The experts tell me it was extreme folly for an unarmored provincial to attack, in the open, an armed shuttle and that you were amazingly lucky." She held the gaze of the branch warden while holding her hand. "Personally, I think it is typical of us galactics to underestimate the skill, cunning, and courage of provincials when they are defending their home."

She let go of Lettern's hand and reached out to Outish. "And the famous Outish Byrear, Loch Norim discoverer extraordinaire." At which Outish turned a deep shade of red, deeper than Human because of his metamorphosis. "You know, of course, you have caused a substantial stir with your filing of a Loch Norim Historical Registry claim."

Tongue-tied, he finally said, "I just wanted to get the word out."

She laughed. "Well, you certainly did that. And, by the way, this is my natural hair color." She glanced to Marisa, whose own hair was close to the same shade. "The blonde was more to challenge Ivan's skills at managing his *special* package."

Marisa glanced to Ivan, who stood stony-faced.

"And Agent Illian Meridia, former Assault Brigade Marine. Now of IDB Ready Reaction, Dianis." She held out her hand. When Meridia grasped it, the matriarch held his hand firm, not letting go. "I am so pleased you are here, agent." She felt his pulse, life force, and aura. "Dianis will have great need of you before this is all over." Appreciating Lettern, while holding Meridia's grasp, "Two kindred souls who, across the wide timeless gulf of the galaxy, have found each other in mind, body, and spirit. The randomness of the universe is but a cosmic illusion. You were drawn together by forces, by the threads of fate that can be followed like yarn through the forest. It is not by random chance that Humanity faces the Turboii. Nor is it random chance that you two have met."

"I cannot condone one of my agents consorting with a provincial," said Ivan.

Before Marisa could react, the matriarch let Meridia's hand go and said, "Then make it legal, Ivan. Recruit Lettern into Ready Reaction. Spirits know you are woefully understaffed here. I know of provincials serving as undercover IDB Civilization Monitoring agents. Clienen has said that he may need to go that route here on Dianis. Clienen is willing to do the same with Ready Reaction." She anticipated Ivan's rebuttal and added just as he was about to deliver it, "It's too late, Ivan. For better or worse, Lettern is being credited for thwarting the extrasolar incursion here in Wedgewood. Word is spreading through the mining contractors that the federation armed the provincials on Dianis. The ULUP board of control has been informed of the true events, and the IDB lawyers have successfully presented Meridia's defense to the board, and through the preponderance of the evidence, the board has decided to exonerate Meridia."

Ivan, surprised, said, "I didn't know Meridia's assignment of an IDB plasma rifle to Lettern would need to go to ULUP. I thought we could handle that internally."

To Meridia, this was all news.

"The Matrincy decided it was best to preempt any possible legal actions and proactively explain the entire situation to the board. While the viability of the sting operation has indeed been placed into question, as long as the contractor community believes we purposely armed the provincials here on Mount Mars out of desperation to thwart further attacks, then we might still be able to obtain some success through the operation." She let Ivan chew through the implications.

Ivan remembered Lieutenant Hearter pleading with him to intercede with Clienen to allow the *Shields* to launch its assault lander. There would be factions in the IDB that would support Meridia's apparent foresight, and when Meridia had refused to leave Wedgewood and had instead decided to engage the corsair shuttle, Ivan himself had cited the IDB rule of *the agent on the ground has the*

335

discretion to interpret orders. Giving a plasma rifle to a provincial was an extreme interpretation.

The matriarch saw him struggle with the notion. "Yes, I know, Ivan. It's messy. And will continue to be messy until we find who is contracting with these miners. Whoever that is, it is most likely the same entity that conspired to have the IDB pulled in the first place." The matriarch hoped her reasoning would sway the recalcitrant chief. She needed him on their side, at least on the side of Wedgewood.

Ivan stared at her flatly and said, "You know that Achelous thinks it was the Matrincy that caused the IDB to be withdrawn."

She nodded and looked to Marisa. "You and I have much to speak of." Turning fully to face the trader princess, she held out her bare hand. "I have long sought this day. I have dreamed of you."

Marisa slowly lifted her hand, not knowing what to expect other than prescients and voyants preferred skin-to-skin contact to share auras. It was a way they communicated. Marisa didn't know if she wanted to share her aura with the matriarch. As their hands came close, a spark snapped between them. They both flinched, eyes wide.

"Whoa, that's aura-connectivity-overload," gushed Outish. "You need to short out."

Marisa rubbed her hand, staring at the matriarch as if she'd been bitten by a snake. She worried what *aura-something overload* was.

The matriarch, flustered, apologized, "I'm sorry. Don't worry; I'll put my glove on." She did so, and reaching into her cloak, she removed three transparent sheets of polyacrylic laced with circuitry that shimmered depending on how the sheet was held. Each sheet could fit comfortably in Marisa's artist's satchel. "I have the documents you requested. First, an award for Ultimate Cause for Chief Inspector Achelous Forushen, in acknowledgment of his actions, whatever they may be, in defense of Planet Dianis, ULUP Class E, for a period of one year prior to yesterday. Duly approved by the Matrincy and by Director Clienen Hor, IDB Margel Damansk." She handed it to Marisa. "You should know, awards for Ultimate Cause are rare, very. Laws are not made to be broken, and we do not encourage willful behavior where a person is allowed to second guess the nature of what is intended."

Marisa gave a slight nod.

"The chief inspector did what he believed was right to defend this planet. We acknowledge that. Furthermore, there is increasing evidence that he was particularly sanguine in his interpretations of the facts and the potential future course of history here on Dianis. But, we shall let Fate expose that to us as it will." The Matriarch pointed at the polyacrylic holding the Award for Ultimate Cause. "That is the physical manifestation of the attestment, which you requested. It has, of course, been registered in the ULUP Board of Control archives. Jeremy," and the matriarch looked up to where Buzz Too perched on a branch overhead. "Please confirm that the judgment has indeed been posted by ULUP."

"Brawk, always making me work. Yes, it's there."

Surprised, the matriarch's black eyes started to harden.

Marisa wanted to laugh but offered a hurried explanation, "My apologies. The insolence was my idea. I wanted a bit of humor to make the bot feel more real."

The matriarch's mouth clicked shut. "Oh."

Just when Buzz was about to say something else, Marisa's arm shot out and pointed at him. "Not now. Go to serious mode until I tell you to go back to normal."

"Mother's feathers, all these rules to remember."

When Marisa glared at the bot, it fluffed and squatted on the branch.

"Interesting," said the matriarch.

Holding out the second attestment, the matriarch said, "This is the second document you requested. It cites the specific ULUP regulations protecting Class E provincials in general and two individuals, specifically, you and your son, from unwarranted abduction and mind-wiping. It states at the bottom that said specific individuals are under no investigation with no charges pending or planned. There is not and will not be a warrant for a sanctioned extraction and subsequent mind-wipe." She handed the attestment to Marisa. "It grants you and your son a waiver against any such action to the end of your days." After a pause, the matriarch added, "That was the easy one."

Holding it in her hands, seeing her and Boyd's names shimmer into Tivorian script transformed from the alien Avarian text, she asked, "What about Achelous?"

"Yes, Chief Forushen is entirely a different matter," and she held up the third attestment. "While the chief has been absolved of all behaviors post Lights Out, he is a member of the IDB, and as Chief Darinarishcan has been quick to point out, consorting with Class E provincials is strictly forbidden."

Marisa's eyes shifted from the matriarch to Ivan and then back. Marisa was resolute. Her jaw set.

"It has been my hope, and still is, that one day Dianis will be uplifted to Class D, and that would, to some extent, ease the restrictions of integrating its provincials with the federation. However, that is not the case today, and there is a strong chance the ULUP Board of Control may change Dianis to Class F."

Ivan stood straighter, "How can we go to highly protected, from protected, when we don't have the resources?"

"Why go to Class F?" asked Meridia.

The matriarch sighed, "Because of Outish, and how he registered their find and what he said about that mountain," and the matriarch moved to get a better view of Mount Mars, truly look at it for the first time. Its snowcapped peak just seen through the upper branches of the Ungerngerists. "ULUP does not care one credit about how much aquamarine-5 there is on this planet, at least not until the federation declares it a war emergency. What ULUP *does* care about is the protection of indigenous populations and their historical and cultural legacies. That is, after all, why the free sentient worlds came together to form ULUP." Staring at the mountain, she went on. "When the ULUP board learned there was a Loch Norim site, potentially intact, in that mountain, and Lettern and Meridia had fought corsairs at the foot of it, and that Outish was doing research into the preponderance of sixthsense in the local provincial population, which is suspiciously close to the mountain, the board's entire calculus changed." She faced Marisa. "Ivan, Achelous, Meridia, and I are Avarian Humans. Which means we come from a Human gene pool that has interbred amongst many different worlds for over two thousand years. You and Lettern, however, are Loch Norim Humans. Ultimately, we all come from the Loch Norims, even Outish, our Halorite cousin. You two, however, are different." The matriarch looked at Marisa. "Your Loch Norim genes, with the potential exception of some ITA engineer's indiscretion," and she wagged her head at Ivan, "are still pure." She looked back at Mt Mars. Then to Marisa, "Your forebears are in that mountain, and to ULUP, that merits Class F."

"What does that have to do with Atch?" Marisa asked.

"Directly? Nothing. But indirectly, everything. Your threat of blocking access to Wedgewood and Mount Mars was taken very seriously. We played the video of your meeting with Ivan on board the *Far Shore* to the board this morning." Glancing to the chief, she said, "And I can tell you, Ivan, they were uniformly impressed. Marisa's stress tones in her voice pegged the meters in both sincerity and conviction. You were threatened with being bound in chains and thrown in the brig; all the while, Ogden held a gun on you. You kept your cool. The board was very impressed by Ready Reaction and you, Ivan." She paused to let the compliment take hold. "And Ivan--"

"Yes, your Matrincy?"

"It was a good thing you didn't move; the board's psychoanalytic AI predicted a ninety-seven percent probability that Ogden would have fired had you done anything he considered untoward."

The matriarch paused, digging her hands deep into the folds of her cloak. "That left us, the Matrincy and IDB, in a legal conflict in which the ULUP board was split on what to do with Achelous."

"And?" asked Marisa.

"Your demands for Achelous's absolution were clear. Unfortunately, that would only take him to today. Demanding that he would not be extradited was a point of contention with the board. What about tomorrow or the day after? Would you not want to live with and, perhaps, wed Achelous?"

Marisa looked away and then said, "Yes."

The matriarch nodded, "As I advocated for you."

Marisa's eyes narrowed out of either pain or respect. It was not clear which.

"It is certain that Achelous cannot remain in the IDB. I'm sorry, but his long career with the Branch is done." The matriarch waited, but as she suspected, Marisa didn't care. Achelous might, but Marisa just wanted him back at home in Tivor with Boyd. "So, predicated on your implied offer of a strategic alliance with the Avarian Federation, and based on your demonstrated position of influence on this world, and Achelous' deep commitment to this world, the Matrincy is prepared to make Chief Forushen an offer," and she waved the third attestment. "The Matrincy incorporates a unique code of nepotism in its operating principles. Chief, I assume you are aware of them?"

"Yes, ma'am," Ivan answered, and then to Marisa, he said, "The Matrincy plans and arranges marriage contracts with its counselors to influential members of society, both in and outside of the federation. Counselor Margret, who was here in Wedgewood, was married under a two-year contract to General Marion. They do it to increase the bond between the Matrincy and Avarian leadership."

The matriarch smiled. "Some would say we do it to manipulate the male holders of key positions, but it goes both ways, male *and* female."

"And what is that in your hand?" Marisa asked.

The matriarch reached into her robe and withdrew a small box with a clear cover. She placed it on the attestment and handed it to Marisa. "It is a decision that Achelous must make."

Lettern, Meridia, and Outish crowded around Marisa to see what was in the box.

"Oh, those are pretty," said Lettern. "What are they?"

Meridia looked up. He met the gaze of the matriarch. Then, to Ivan, he said, "Could be our new boss, chief. I mean, am I not right that Clienen would follow this person's direction?"

"What is it?" Ivan came to squint into the box. Then he asked, "What happened to Breia?"

The matriarch waggled her head, Avarian style. "Achelous Forushen is a better choice. He knows Dianis." She let the vast understatement hang.

"What are they?" asked Lettern.

"The collar pips for the Matrincy Planetary Counselor to Dianis," said Meridia. "They even have the colors of the Life Believer Defender's coat of arms."

"They come with two conditions that are not negotiable," the matriarch told Marisa. "First, he must resign from the IDB. Second, he must marry you. Failure of those two conditions will subject Achelous Forushen to standard enforcement of Class E laws, and Ivan here will be empowered to arrest and extradite Achelous from this world."

Marisa nodded mutely. She stared down at the attestment but couldn't read it for her blurry vision. Lettern hugged her, and Meridia retrieved the card and jewelry box before Marisa dropped them.

Meridia was thinking the same thing as everyone else but not saying it: they'd have to find Achelous alive before he could make the decision that would bring happiness to the woman he loved.

The matriarch waited and then, speaking into her audio implant, "Captain, can you move this Phantom away from me? I find it annoying." A pause, and then she added, "No, I don't think they are a threat. Just move it."

When the aerial battle drone had moved off, albeit a short distance, the matriarch said, and now I would like to speak to Marisa alone. Lady?" and she held out her gloved hand.

The two women walked into the deepening gloom.

"You are limping? How is your leg?" the matriarch asked.

"It's getting better. That fancy bandage Ivan gave me is helping, though the leg is very stiff."

Slowing their pace so Marisa didn't have to labor, the matriarch asked, "When are you supposed to meet with the voyant?"

Marisa answered, "Just at full dark."

Meridia, at a discrete distance, watched the two women talk in hushed tones. On his multi-func, he tracked the shifting circle of Special Forces, bots, and battle drones. Lettern hung at his elbow, watching the icons. To the chief's chagrin, Meridia explained how the display worked and the planned tactical defense vectors. Lettern leaned close, enthralled.

Marisa stopped, considering all that the matriarch had told her.

Then the matriarch added, "Should Wedgewood fall, you must defend Mount Mars with every capacity you have."

Marisa gave a short nod.

The matriarch reached out and grasped both of Marisa's hands. "ULUP defends you, and I defend Humanity. *You* must defend the Timberkeeps. They must survive. The Turboii war is in the balance. There are members on the ULUP Board of Control who, to their folly, think they are beyond the reach of the Turboii. If the Paleowrights, with their Drakan patrons, enslave the Timberkeeps, the travesty reaped on Humanity will be eclipsed only by the loss of Dianis to the Turboii's sizar hordes." She peered into Marisa's ebon eyes, down to her soul, and Marisa did not flinch. "In there, Mount Mars, seek your refuge, for ULUP will abandon you. It is the greatest of Human ironies that a war between provincials, here on Dianis, should shape the fate of Humanity across the galaxy, but so it is, so weave our threads of Fate."

Chapter 37
Cordelei Greenleaf

Wedgewood

The walk-lanterns were lit, as were the ladder and porch lights in the tree houses and forts. Seen from afar, they looked like giant Will-O-the-Wisps hovering high in the trees. Cool air from the mountain flowed down the ravines, relieving the heat of the day. Soon, it would be cold. The four of them approached Cordelei Greenleaf's bungalow; Knot Head tagged along behind, eating anything more tempting than a rock. Buzz Too's beak pointed left and right like a wind vane, taking in everything. When Outish made to pet it, it squatted lower on Marisa's shoulder and refused to acknowledge him.

"What's wrong with Buzz?" Outish asked.

"He's pouting," answered Marisa, her trepidations mounting, staring at Cordelei's grass-roofed hut half-buried in the mountainside. At the acknowledgment of its mood, Buzz fluffed and preened its fake feathers. "Okay, fine," she said, "you may resume normal mode."

"Free! The shackles are burst! May the world be enlightened with parrot wisdom! Mere Human mortals are but flotsam and jetsam in the cosmic sea without my—*Brawk!*"

Lettern's grasp had him. She tapped a fingernail on his beak. "Bird-brain," she hissed in the night, "you feel that?"

Buzz bobbed its head.

"Then, if you want to keep it, shut that little bird trap of yours." She tossed it in the air, and Buzz flew to a tree, squawking molestation and animal rights abuse and threatening legal action.

"You worried?" Lettern asked Marisa.

Her bun and stiletto hilt nodded in the dark. "What if she can't—"

"She can," answered Meridia. "Lettern confirmed it with Brookern. Did you notice the matriarch did not question the idea?"

Marisa peered at him. "I was wondering about that."

Meridia idly scratched Knot Head behind the ears as the goat sought to rub against him. "I've been reading the message traffic on the Dianis IDB-Matrincy channel. There is definitely a spirit flux centered on her. Her aural emanations are similar to the matriarch's when unshielded."

"Oi, she gives me the swamp willies," confessed Outish.

"Which one?" asked Lettern.

"Both of them," he said.

Cordelei's walk-lamp cast a yellow, unwavering illumination into the forest. Somehow, it was not as welcoming as the other walk-lights. Two candles burned in the window of the cottage. An owl piped high in the trees above, and a large animal, judging by the tread of its four legs, moved in the inky blackness. Meridia could feel the goat's head point in that direction.

"This is where you leave us?" Marisa looked to Lettern.

"Illy and I will be up in my loft. Cordelei is friendly enough. If you need anything, send bird-brain."

Marisa's bun bobbed.

They stepped on the stoop, and the boards creaked, a huge sound in the silent night.

Before Outish could knock on the door, it was pulled open. "You're late," said a woman with close-cropped hair. "The witching has begun."

Outish swallowed audibly. "Witching?"

Cordelei stepped aside, "Come in."

The bungalow was snug; the first thing Marisa noticed, other than the incense, was the multitude of burning candles. They were everywhere as if wards against evil spirits.

"Sit, we must begin."

Outish and Marisa took their seats at a small table in front of the voyant. In the candlelight, Marisa studied the woman. She'd heard the nickname: *Sour Dour*. The corners of Cordelei's mouth were turned down in severe arcs, her lips were thin, and her jaw set in a firm clamp. Sadness veritably wept from her eyes as if all the world's sorrows bore witness through their lenses. She had a measured, deliberate manner as she took her seat, carefully arranging her long woolen skirt. In stark contrast, in an apparent, if odd, attempt to obviate her character, she wore a colorful Doroman scarf over her white linen blouse. Baryy and Achelous had been here before, but Achelous had been loath to speak of the encounter. Baryy, on the other hand, had recounted it to Outish in stark detail.

"Are you going to start the hourglass?" Marisa asked.

Cordelei pierced her with a gaze that lingered a long moment. "No. For you, this is free."

"What's the Witching?" asked Outish.

"A special time," answered the voyant. "A time when the spirits in the nether realm are willing to speak. Some will even want to speak."

Marisa leaned forward. "I didn't think you were a necromancer. We don't need one of those."

Cordelei's perpetual frown sunk lower. "We scry our visions with the skills we have."

There came the patter of rain on the windows, and thunder sounded low and indistinct. A gust of wind buffeted the cottage, and all the candles flickered as one. A fresh waft of incense drifted past Marisa, a pleasant, soothing smell, not acrid and irritating like the marshcat of the Coaster hollows.

"You seek a man, so Brookern has said." Cordelei's eyes shifted to Outish and then back to Marisa.

"Yes," said Marisa, "I'm searching for a man named Achelous," and she pulled Achelous' handbolt out of her bag and sat it on the table. "Outish said you needed something personal belonging to Achelous."

"I know this man, Achelous. I have seen him here, in Wedgewood."

"Yes, he's a trader. He comes here often. He's been—"

"Yes, I know," preempted Cordelei.

Reaching behind her, the voyant retrieved a pouch and a pipe from the shelf. From the pouch she extracted a pinch of an herb, packed it into the pipe, and lit a taper from a candle.

Marshcat thought, Marisa.

Puffing on her pipe, Cordelei picked up a wooden doll rod and used it to draw the handbolt towards her without touching it. "Has this killed people?"

Marisa swallowed. "Yes, yes, I think so." She recalled the gruesome image of the Scarlet Savoir in her study with half his head sliced away.

"And did Achelous do it? The killing?"

"Yes."

For once, the voyant looked positive. She placed a finger on the hilt of the weapon, puffed on her pipe, and closed her eyes.

Outish sat transfixed. The longer the voyant held her finger on the weapon, the lower his head dipped to the table, almost as if he were trying to look in her mouth. Marisa nudged him with her foot, and he started.

Cordelei's eyes opened. "Ask me your questions."

"Is he alive?" they both said in unison. Marisa scowled at him. "I'll ask the questions."

"Yes," Cordelei said, thoughtfully considering the woman across from her.

The next question was more painful, "Is he, is he okay?"

The voyant tilted her head. "He has been tortured."

Marisa blanched. She swallowed. "How bad?"

"He survives. He is not broken, but they have time."

Marisa shook her head, "Why do they have time?"

"Because you are here, and he is there."

"Where's there?" asked Outish

"On a ship."

"Where? What ship?" Marisa rose in her chair.

347

Cordelei shook her head. "It does not matter."

"Doesn't matter? Why not?" Marisa asked, irritated.

"Because you'll not find him at sea," Cordelei answered, an edge to her voice.

Marisa settled back down, confused. "Can you tell me where he is?"

The voyant quit puffing on her pipe and held it smoking in her hand. "He is at sea, on a ship, on an ocean. And you will not find him there."

Still struggling with the notion, Marisa asked, "Why not?"

"Because my visions say you won't."

"We won't ever find him?" blurted Outish.

Cordelei turned her gaze on him. "Hold out your hand."

His mouth clamped shut, and he looked wide-eyed.

"Your hand," she demanded.

When he raised his left hand from beneath the table, she said, "No, the other hand."

Flummoxed, he showed her his right hand.

She saw the glove. "Remove it."

Reluctantly, he pulled it off.

Cordelei puffed on her pipe, but it had gone out. She set it down. Reaching out, she stroked her fingers across the fur of his hand. "You are not of this world, either."

He shook his head.

"Is that important?" asked Marisa.

"Perhaps," Cordelei answered. She eyed the dormant pipe as if it were out of answers but then offered another one of her own, "Yes, you will find Achelous."

"When," they asked in unison.

"Before the snow."

"Where is he?" asked Outish.

Exasperated, the voyant untied her scarf. "Have you not listened? It is not important where he is, but where you will find him."

"Okay," Marisa began to understand how to ask questions of prescient. "Where will we find him?"

"In the Citadel."

The End.

A Word From Frank

I write to entertain *you*. That is my passion. The story has *shifted* you, in the hours of your choosing, from Earth to Dianis, where you can find temporary relief from your Earthly trials and follow, from the safety of your abode, your favorite characters. I sincerely hope you enjoyed the time. Please go to The Matriarch Reviews (or use the QR Code below) and post your thoughts by clicking on the *Write Customer Review* button. I'd love to hear who those favorite characters are.

A preview of the next chronicle, *The Citadel,* follows.

Preview
The Citadel

The Empire of Nak Drakas

They'd gone to the heart of their enemy, and they were undone.

Christina leaned over the rampart. The battle waged below and around her. Low scudding clouds came ashore, swirling around the grey, forbidding rock of the Citadel. A cheer went up from below: the Drakans had finally retaken the Citadel's Main Gate. Rifle fire from the Tivorians dropped off to a few scattered shots.

"They're coming," gasped Alex.

Christina whirled, her great two-handed broadsword bloody in her hand. She ran to the spiral steps that led into the depths of the keep. The jingle of harness, trod of heavy boots, and the grunts of men proceeded the Drakans. Alex sat propped against the wall near the portal. He was dying. A spear thrust had missed his shield and impaled him in the side.

She waited, braced at the head of the stairs, her shield slung across her back. Holding her sword in both hands, she'd defend the top step, and then when they forced her back around the corner, Alex would stab them from where he sat. They'd have to come at her single file.

A shadow proceeded the first Drakan. He came up the steps at a run, shield at the ready, sword pumping up and down.

Christina watched him come. She backed two paces. The black anvil embossed on the green shield stayed her swing.

The soldier landed on the top step and gave her a concerned glance as he searched for an enemy. Though he didn't know her, he knew who she was. "Need help?"

"Not here," was her grim reply.

Three more Second Warders came behind him, followed by Lettern. "Dearest Mother, Alon," she gasped, I was afraid we were too late," but then she saw Alex slumped against the wall, his life draining away on the flagstones. Amongst the carnage in the tower, she saw the bodies of Christina's five mercenaries.

"They trapped us here," Christina said.

"Illy, quick, get one of your magic bandages." Lettern bent low over Alex and lifted his chainmail and then the bloodstained leather jerkin underneath.

Christina watched the soldier, clearly not a Timberkeep but carrying a Second Ward shield. He pulled out an alien-looking package from a hip pouch.

"I've got one left after this, Lettern, and I'm saving it for you." He stripped off a wrapper, tapped a pair of buttons, and the device came to life, lights glowing. He positioned it over the wound and tapped the *Activate* button.

When the man stood, Christina saw he had brown eyes, the same as Lettern. "Who is this?"

He gave her a seasoned smile of a person wholly comfortable amidst mayhem, disaster, or victory.

"That's Illy," answered Lettern as she watched her warders check the Lamaran mercs. "He's an Avarian."

Christina frowned, "Avarian?"

"Yea, like Achelous and Outish. You know, Ancients. We've brought more of them with us." Lettern looked to Christina. "I work for them now, Alon. I'm IDB."

Titles In The Dianis Chronicles

The Foundry, Book 1
The Matriarch, Book 2
The Citadel, Book 3 (in editing)
The Loch Norim, Book 4 (in outline)
more to come

Acknowledgments

Unlike *The Foundry, The Matriarch* was a fast book to write. What took many years for *The Foundry* took six months for *The Matriarch*. The process this time around was smoother and less arduous for my reviewers – I hope.

A number of individuals deserve specific mention: Steve, Ina, Jeff, Jerry, Danya, and Tom. They each, in their own way, made unique contributions that extend way beyond what I can repay. It was both an honor and enjoyment to work with them on the endeavor. Tom, in particular, brought such careful insight that he provided a long-lasting encouragement to tell a good story.

About the Author

Living on the banks of the Mississippi River, Frank Dravis has leveraged his many life experiences to write the Dianis, A World in Turmoil chronicles. He was born and raised in Detroit, Michigan, where he and his father cruised the Great Lakes. They often chose to go out boating on the roughest days when there was no traffic. Frank spent six years in the US Navy chasing Soviet submarines. His love of the sea is reflected in the chronicles, a love he has shared with his wife and two girls.

A hunter, Frank has taken game with a variety of weapons, including the bow, rifle, shotgun, and muzzleloader, the firearm developed by Ogden on Dianis and the weapon of choice in the fight against galactic extrasolars.

Frank aids his wife in her passion for horses as stable hand and riding partner of Suzette, his paint. Equines regularly appear in the Dianis series, not as horses, but as eenus.

Frank's care for Earth and the stewardship of their land in Wisconsin are reflected in the culture and ethos of the Timberkeeps.

He has two degrees, a Bachelor of Computer Science and a Master of Business Administration. Those degrees have been integral to his other careers, from software engineer to marketing executive to chief information officer. The technical and scientific acumen he gained through those endeavors is demonstrated in the series in the effort to make the Dianis brand of science practically possible somewhere in the galaxy today.

Social Media

For current information on the Dianis a World in Turmoil series, please visit us on the Web at https://www.dianisworld.com and on Facebook at Dianis Facebook where additional maps, character info, details behind key concepts, and the status of *The Citadel* (book three), and The Drakan Loch Norim (book four) are listed.

Quorat's Intruder at Contractor Haven

Most importantly, if you like the book, please post a review on Goodreads at Books by Frank Dravis